Weapons of Ruin

The Second Book of the Talesian Narrative

C. L. Scheel

Hard Shell Word Factory

To Shannon Horn who not only writes and loves fantasy,
but has also been a loyal friend and staunch
supporter through every trial and triumph.
My heartfelt thanks.
And for S. E. R.

© 2003 C. L. Scheel
Paperback ISBN: 0-7599-4069-X
Published September 2003

eBook ISBN: 0-7599-4068-1
Published August 2003

Hard Shell Word Factory
PO Box 161
Amherst Jct. WI 54407
Books@hardshell.com
http://www.hardshell.com
Cover art © 2003 Jay Degn
Printed in the U.S.A.

Prologue

FEAR RARELY OVERCAME a Siarsi warrior, but Warrior-Guardian Amstok trembled with genuine terror. Throughout his long watch, he had faced the altar stone guarding Siarsia's Hammer, a sword held in each hand crossed over his chest. He never took his eyes from his tribe's most sacred object. The tribe's namesake Daughter, Siarsia, had bequeathed to her people the silver hammer she had carried into battle, along with her most precious gift, the secret of steel. Only the Siarsi knew how to make the weapons Talesian warriors carried into battle. Men from every tribe often gave their most valuable horses, their most beautiful women and sometimes their last talin for one Siarsi sword.

Tall and serious, young Amstok did not often join in with traditional Siarsi boisterousness and their inclination for getting into trouble. He wore the hai'stam, the crossed, black-enameled bands over the chest and the long, kilt-like hai'sten that fell nearly to his ankles, with a dignity far greater than his twenty-four sunturns.

It had only been for a moment—a chilling cold that had crept through his bones and a sickening dizziness filling his mind like a deadly smoke. He had not turned his eyes from the Stone and Hammer for an instant. He was sure of it.

Amstok's heart beat wildly within his chest. The long, slender braids at his temples, threaded with fine glass beads and gold ornaments, trembled against his lean, black-scarred cheeks. The ultimate dishonor. Disgrace and shame on his family and clan. By Verlian's blood, dishonor upon his entire tribe.

The penalty would be death—he knew that. The Master of the Forge would see him flayed alive and then have his headless corpse staked outside the great Caverns for all to see, until he was no more than bones and dust. Amstok would not be Summoned to the Goddess, to Verlian's side as one of Her favored, but remain forever scorned.

Amstok turned and hurried from the high-domed chamber to find the Master. He pulled open the heavy iron doors and was about to enter the corridor when he nearly stumbled upon the crumpled forms of the outer Guardians. He knelt down and touched the nearest warrior's neck, looking for the beat of life, but snatched his hand back in horror. The Warrior-Guardian was dead. Blood ran from a gaping slit in his throat.

The other Guardian lay dead from a similar wound.

Amstok stood, shaking with rage. Who would dare violate the Caverns? Kill the Warrior-Guardians? How had they defeated the elite E'stal Guardians protecting the entrance to the Caverns?

The Master's great bell rang an ominous warning of invasion.

Swords drawn, Amstok ran toward the sound, prepared to sacrifice himself for the Goddess and Her daughter. He turned down the main corridor leading to the chambers of the crucible and the forges. Several Warrior-Guardians ran by him, frantically trying to find the intruder and seal off the chambers and their priceless secrets.

No one shouted or panicked. Only an underlying feeling of dread permeated the dark corridors as the Warrior-Guardians sought the enemy who had violated their secluded realm.

The great bell rang again, now more of a death knell than a warning.

At the Great Cavern, Amstok stopped. The order of the Caverns had been shattered. A knot of Guardians clustered around someone or something lying on the sand. Amstok brushed by a huge ironworker, his broad face agleam with the sweat of his labors, and to Amstok's surprise, tears of unashamed grief. The big man grabbed Amstok by the arm and pulled him around to face him.

"What has happened?" Amstok shouted.

"All is lost. All is lost," he said, moaning.

Amstok broke free and hurried toward the cluster of distraught men surrounding what was lying at their feet.

"Amstok!"

He recognized the voice of his closest friend, Kamchet, another Warrior-Guardian who had taken oaths and bonds with him on the same day.

"Kamchet! What has happened?"

"The end of the Caverns," the young Warrior-Guardian said, his own eyes filling with tears.

Amstok pushed his way to the center of the gathered warriors. He stopped and stared at the figure lying in the sand.

"Death to all Qualani!" one of the Guardians shouted angrily.

All indeed, was lost. The Caverns had been violated, the Sacred Hammer had been stolen and the Master of the Forge lay dead in a widening pool of blood spilling from a hideous, gaping wound in his throat.

Chapter One

A TORRENT OF WAVES crashed against the massive seawall of
Daeamon Keep, sending its white, bitter spray nearly to the
battlements. The storm had lasted all night and throughout the long day,
battering the ancient Talesian stronghold with shrieking winds and wild
winter rain.

From her high chamber window, Princess Kitarisa, first and only
child of Prince Kazan dar Baen of Gorendt and Princess Liestra of
Riehl, stared down at the angry sea beating against the black granite
and fought the mounting storm within her own heart. She had arrived
only ten days ago. In five, she would become the bride of Prince
D'Assuriel, the High Prince and Ter-Rey of all Talesia—an honor she
both anticipated and dreaded. And this somber, ancient fortress, set
high above the sea would be her home.

It was said that the Goddess Herself had chosen this place to build
Daeamon Keep and named it for her mortal husband. When Prince
Daeamon fell in battle, Verlian never overcame her grief. She wept not
the tears of a mere mortal, but her own blood. One tear had hardened,
crystallized into the brilliant jewel worn by every successive Ter-Rey
since then—a drop of the Goddess's fiery blood, dangling from his left
ear.

Kitarisa knew well about grief and about symbols. She traced a
tentative finger over the object she held in her hands, the last remnant
of her mother's family—the Riehlian crown—a delicate chaplet of
filigreed gold, intertwining like gleaming lace around the image of a
falcon, the royal symbol of Riehl. She had never worn it, at least not in
public. Her father had forbidden her to wear it, as he had forbidden her
mother.

Kitarisa set the chaplet on her dark hair and studied her shadowy
reflection in the glass of the chamber window. Her face was too heart-
shaped for her own liking, even though her attending lady's maid had
readily complimented her delicate features. She frowned slightly. Her
chin was too sharp and her eyes too wide-set. Rhynn, her dearest
Rhynn and long dead now, had loved her eyes. He said they were as
dark and as luminous as a forest pool.

She touched the edge of the deep-red velvet sleeve of her yet unfinished bridal gown. It was the most beautiful garment she had ever worn. Cut in the Talesian style, the snug bodice fit her to perfection. The long sleeves, so warming for the winter, had been tailored to conform to her good right arm as well as covering the remaining bandages protecting her left arm—the final reminder of her terrible battle against the 'Fa.

The bell-shaped skirt flared out like the petals of a flower and swept back in a short, elegant train. Gold fringing ran from her left shoulder to the right side of her waist and continued down in alternating diagonal bands across the front of the gown, adding a regal touch to her appearance.

She studied her reflection again. Only her long, dark-brown hair pleased her. It gleamed from constant brushing—lustrous, like polished wood. Its shining mass had been plaited into one thick braid, intertwined with a gold cord and deep red and black ribbons. Prince Assur's colors. A heavy gold necklace with one black pearl suspended from it hung almost to her waist—the honor gift he had given to her the day he paid bride-price to her furious father. She touched its smooth surface, gaining some small comfort from its cool beauty.

The chamber door opened and she heard the soft rush of skirts against the floor.

"Please, you must come away from the window, my lady, you will catch your death. It is so cold this evening," a gentle voice admonished.

"I am not cold, Davieta." Kitarisa turned anyway, obliging her. Lady Davieta's devotion had surprised Kitarisa. After the Rift Cut War, she had firmly attached herself as Kitarisa's senior attending lady. While Assur and his legions wintered in Riehl, waiting for the snows to subside, Davieta had become her first true friend and confidante. The long trek from Riehl over the Adrex Mountains to Daemon Keep had proven her loyalty. Davieta had willingly left Riehl, leaving behind only a handful of relatives, along with bitter memories. Kitarisa knew Davieta had an unhappy past but did not press her, knowing it had to do with the loss of her husband and two little sons.

Davieta approached her carrying a sewing basket, then curtsied. "This will not take long, my lady. Only the hem needs adjusting." She knelt and opened the basket. "The gown suits you. It is so lovely, his highness will be pleased."

"You think so?"

Davieta looked up and smiled mischievously. "Of course. But, I think he would be pleased even if you were dressed in rags."

"You are teasing, Davieta."

"I am, but it is plain to everyone that the Ter-Rey loves you. Everyone, that is, but yourself."

Kitarisa sighed and lifted the chaplet from her hair. "I believe the prince would have chosen me even if I were as ugly as a toad. Dearest Davieta, Prince Assur chose me because..." She raised her arms helplessly. "Because I was the obvious choice. The war is over, my father has been destroyed. My half-sister and brother have been banished and what remains of the Reverend 'Fa, Malgora, lies at the base of the Rift Cut. Prince Assur chose me because I was the only sensible choice."

"My lady, that is not true. His highness loves you, I have seen it with my own eyes. Surely, you *must* have some feelings for him?"

Lady Davieta's anxious gaze made Kitarisa smile. She reached down to touch her maid's cheek, consoling her. "Perhaps you are right. I *do* have feelings for him. He has been kind and good. He freed me from my father and he has honored me..." She caught the gleaming pearl in her fingers. "And yet, I cannot quiet the unease in my heart."

Davieta tugged at the hem and pressed several pins into the soft velvet. "You have nothing to fear. It is not just Prince Assur, but all Talesia honors you. You killed Malgora, that dreadful witch." She coiled a length of wine-red thread tightly about her fingers until it snapped away from the spool, then threaded it into a needle. "The Eastern Lands are safe now."

Kitarisa said nothing. She could not contradict her maid. She had done as Davieta proclaimed, yet it caused her no happiness in recalling it. She had killed the 'Fa for all of Talesia, but at what price?

A dreadful, frightening secret pressed heavily on her mind.

She looked at her left arm. Beneath the rich velvet of the sleeve, a tight layer of bandages still encased her arm, binding the healing work of the Daughters. Malgora had caused that—had burned her arm and brought her so close to death that she had almost been Summoned by the Goddess Herself. The Daughters had restored her by their empathic powers. They had called the affliction from her, binding up the hideously burned arm and bringing her back from death.

Kitarisa shuddered at the memory. As Assur's legions defeated her father's armies on the ground, she had fought Malgora in the skies. Both she and the 'Fa had become fiercsome winged beasts, brought to life by an ancient, monstrous conjuring from a time no longer known to this world.

The creatures took form within her and Malgora, embodying their flesh, using them to fight their terrible battle. Destroying the 'Fa became a bittersweet victory. Kitarisa still felt the dark animal presence within her, a terrifying, savage force capable of death and destruction. It would not leave her—it remained a cruel, sinister power, always pressing at her, demanding to be released.

"I am finished now, my lady. My lady?"

Kitarisa started out of her daydreaming. "Forgive me. My mind wanders."

Davieta gathered up her sewing things and stood. "I believe it is time to get ready...?"

"Yes, of course."

After helping her change into a gown more suitable for the evening, Davieta carried away the magnificent bridal gown. Kitarisa felt a sudden rush of relief as she turned to replace her mother's crown into its velvet-lined box. Out of sight, the crown would no longer remind her of future obligations, or her promise to Assur.

Another knock on the door sent Davieta hurrying to answer it. Kitarisa's gloomy mood was at once forgotten as she eagerly welcomed the visitor.

Hair, red as a brilliant sunset and shot with amber-gold, crowned a face of unfeigned sweetness. Princess Sethra did not resemble her brother, Assur, but her eyes, now dancing with mischief, were the same deep blue color. She embraced Kitarisa like a sister.

"If we do not go down at once, father will force Assur to have the hunting dogs slain and served up."

"Am I that late?"

Sethra took her arm and began heading for the door. "No, but you know my father has no patience when it comes to food."

"Prince Achad would eat the dogs?"

"Father would eat anything if he were hungry enough. Come, Kitarisa, we must hurry before Assur runs out of excuses."

Half-believing her, Kitarisa hurried to keep up with Sethra.

Eat the dogs? Surely, she was jesting.

From the heights of the balcony above the great hall, Kitarisa looked down upon the gathered warriors, the grave-looking officials, council members, she presumed, and a few women.

In spite of the luxurious amenities in the private, upper chambers, parts of Daeamon Keep still clung stubbornly to its barbaric past including the massive court hall. Even though tables had been laid out with new silver plates and goblets, the hall itself was still lit by torches, each held in place by an ancient iron bracket hammered into the shape of a beast or some long-forgotten demon.

The vaulted ceiling, supported by great pillars, had been carved in intricate patterns, beaten over with silver and inlaid with rare corals from the sea. Unlike the floor in Riehl's Falcon Hall that boasted richly hued tiles, the floor in the hall of Daemon Keep was still made of wood, polished to a high gleam and covered with a scattering of patterned carpets brought back from long-ago conquests.

The center floor had been left bare to allow for dancing or amusements, but Kitarisa knew there had been a time when the hall rang with the shouts of Talesian warriors as they grappled and fought one another in mortal combat. Dark stains still marred the wood where the blood of the long-dead warriors had been spilled.

From the highest beams hung the tribal war banners, tattered and blood-stained—some so faded it was impossible to make out their original designs in the darkness. The banners were the relics of a proud people, symbolizing their savage past as well as their victories in battle.

At the head of the great room she noticed a large table placed on a raised dais, set for only six people. A massive silver candlestick had been placed at each end. She hoped Sethra would sit next to her and help her through the intricacies of a Talesian feast.

In front of the table stood the Ter-Rey. His armor and swords had been replaced with the formal black and gold, web-like harness encasing his chest and shoulders. Like all Talesian men, his long, almost black hair had been bound tightly at the crown, the shank falling past his shoulders. The only identifying mark separating Assur from his men was the plain gold band across his brow signifying his rank. A molten-red jewel, Verlian's Tear, dangled from his left ear; a neck collar of gold linked-plates encircled his throat, each plate enameled in the design of a black rose and sword ringed by a crown.

He appeared deep in conversation with an older man whose long, silvery hair was not bound by the traditional ring, but tied back with a braided rope, an orange cording. He wore a long, dark-colored tunic and an over-robe decorated in bands of orange and deep red. The wide sleeves were edged in more of the orange and embroidered with strange symbols and markings. Around his neck he wore a heavy chain and hanging from it, a glass disk edged in silver.

Assur did not hear her or Sethra approach, until everyone around him bowed. Kitarisa looked down, even now afraid to look at him for fear he would disapprove. He turned and stared at her, ignoring the older man at his side as well as his sister and Prince Achad. The fingers of her right hand toyed nervously with the pearl at her waist.

"Kita," he said softly, bowing to her.

It still unnerved her to look directly into his eyes. Their deep blue color only emphasized the markings, the distinctive patterns embellishing them—a bold black stroke just underneath each eye, sweeping from the inner corner to the outer edge, and another, from the outside of the upper lid, flaring back, almost touching the end of the brow. Neither tattooed nor painted into the skin, the marks were a natural feature seen only on Talesian males.

"If you do not arrange for the joining ceremony this instant, Assur, I will have her for myself," Achad exclaimed, smiling wickedly at her.

"Father," Sethra said sharply. "Where are your manners?"

"I am an old Talesian dog, used to taking what I want. In the old days, I would have fought your brother for her, now I must be civilized." He winked at Sethra.

Assur scowled. "Enough, or I will have you sent from the hall," he warned, but regained his good graces by taking Kitarisa's hand and turned to the tall, silver-haired man by his side.

"This is the Adar, Tethket. He is the Wordkeeper."

The Adar bowed deeply to her. "I am honored, great lady, to meet the destroyer of the hated 'Fa. An extraordinary accomplishment and one, I am told, not achieved without great sacrifice." He nodded at her arm. "My Lord Assur tells me you were restored to us by a Holy Daughter, one of the last healers of Verlian. Sometime, at your pleasure, I would enjoy hearing your deed so it may be written into the chronicles for all time. Such a victory must not be forgotten."

"The Adar keeps the Words, Kitarisa," Assur explained. "It is his task to record all the great events."

Kitarisa nodded. Her father, Kazan, had long ago dismissed the Gorendtian Adar and the Chanter as useless appendages to his court. No great events had ever been chronicled after her mother died and Kitarisa privately knew her father never intended for Princess Liestra's death to be recorded, or anything else that might incriminate him in any wrong-doing.

"I would be happy to assist you, Adar Tethket, if you would be good enough to give me lessons on Talesian history. I know so little. I was not allowed to learn..."

The Wordkeeper's brows arched in surprise. "It would give me great pleasure. Indeed, an honor." He bowed again, pressing his palm to his chest.

"When do we eat?" Achad demanded in a loud voice. "I pray the

Goddess we eat something better than camp swill and teki-bread."

Achad's jibe was met with raucous laughter as Assur led Kitarisa to the table. To her relief, Sethra was indeed placed to her right, with Assur at her left. Prince Achad sat on the other side of Assur with the Adar next to him, and far to the right, next to Sethra, sat a beaming Kuurus. Kuurus held the rare position of Assur's most-favored and it pleased Kitarisa to see him dine at his lord's table.

Throughout the entire feast she was treated to a bewildering array of dishes and foods she had never tasted: exotic fish in spiced sauces; a pastry laced with dark honey and sweet seeds, tasty little morsels that were the meat of a shellfish, gathered only that morning from the shores along the Keep.

Instead of the rough-cut joints of breok that had been served at her father's table, she was given only the choicest, most tender portions.

Out of the corner of her eye she watched Assur. He was at last at ease with his own people. The former lines of fatigue and stern resolve had vanished from his face. Relaxed and in a lighthearted mood, he joked with Prince Achad and occasionally called out to a familiar warrior. At times, he would drape an arm across the back of her chair and lean near her, speaking in private tones.

"The food is to your liking?" he asked.

"I have never seen such a feast, my lord. You Talesians always surprise me. I had no idea barbarian warriors dined so well."

"Not the savages you had imagined, eh? I assure you, we are *trying* to end some of our blood-thirsty ways. You will notice I have not eaten any of the dogs. Yet."

For the first time, Kitarisa saw humor light his dark blue eyes.

"But, do not let any of this civility deceive you," he went on. "Beneath it lurks a pack of ruthless animals."

Kitarisa caught the wry smile and she, too, laughed out loud. "Then, I will simply have to learn to be just as ruthless so I may enjoy more of these feasts."

When the remains of their meal had been swept away, Assur called for the musicians—a modest ensemble consisting of six, playing upon two harps, the nine-stringed dalcet, drum, tambour and flute.

Kitarisa allowed some of her earlier misgivings to slip away. At last, she felt like Assur's lady. She was, as he had promised, far from the cold misery of her former life in Gorendt and forever beyond her father's cruel torments. Her half-sister, Alea, and twin brother Prince Alor, had been banished. There was no one was left to hurt her.

A sudden loud noise from the back of the hall forced the

musicians to stop playing. The sound of angry male voices and scuffling boots rose above the polite conversations. Assur looked up, clearly annoyed. Guards, weapons drawn, rushed from their posts forming a tight circle around a handful of men who had burst into the hall.

The Ter-Rey rose from his chair, fists at his waist. Furious indignation replaced his former elated expression. "How dare you intrude like this!"

Kitarisa stood, uncertain what she should do. She heard the hiss of dozens of swords escaping their scabbards; a phalanx of cold-eyed warriors instantly surrounded her. Kuurus stepped down from the dais and moved directly in front of her using his own body as a shield from the threat of a half-dozen, exhausted Siarsi tribesmen.

Unlike their Chaliset and Ponos brothers, the Siarsi cut and stained black scars into their faces, giving them an appearance particularly effective in terrorizing their enemies. One burly man stepped forward dressed all in hides, his snow-dusted shoulders covered in long, shaggy breok hair. His face and clothes were dirty from many days of hard riding, but fatigue could not hide the passion in his eyes.

"I demand to see the Ter-Rey!"

"You may demand nothing until you show proper respect to your lord!" Kuurus barked at him, pointing to the floor in front of Assur.

"We have no time for such courtly manners," the big man answered angrily, looking first from Kuurus to Assur. "We have come to demand retribution."

An ominous tension surrounded her as Assur's warriors reacted to the intruder's impudent outburst. Both Kuurus and Assur bristled at the insult.

"On your knees," Kuurus ordered, snatching a sword from the nearest warrior and pointed it directly at the Siarsi's throat. Reluctantly, the man dropped to one knee, as did the others behind him.

Assur folded his arms across this chest and scowled down at the men. "Who are you? You are a long way from Kronos Keep, Siarsi."

"I am Wobran. We have come directly from the high seat of Prince Exbrel. We bring bad news, my lord. An outrage has been committed against the Siarsi. The Caverns have been violated; the Warrior-Guardians killed. And that is not the worst of it!" The big Siarsi's voice shook with anger. "The Sacred Hammer of the Daughter Siarsia has been stolen and the Master of the Forge has been murdered!"

A stunned silence filtered through the great hall. Many of the attending warriors were Siarsi. In spite of their loyalties to Assur, the news brought angry muttering and looks first of disbelief, then of rage.

She watched Assur frown. Kitarisa knew this *was* serious news. Each of the three major tribes kept one treasured relic of their own Daughter of Verlian. Only Assur wore the Tear, the Goddess's blood-red ruby that dangled from his left ear. But it was Chalisetra's Spear, the gift of her first Daughter, Chalisetra, that had become the soul of the Chaliset tribe. Assur carried the Sacred Spear at all the important functions of his court.

The Ponos kept the Sacred Bow, the weapon bestowed by Ponosel, the second Daughter of Verlian.

The Siarsi tribe possessed Siarsia's gift, a great silver hammer, together with the secret of making steel. Only the Siarsi knew how to make steel weapons—the lasting legacy of their revered Daughter, the third of Verlian.

Stealing the sacred relics was not only an outrage, but an act that undermined the very fiber of the Talesian soul.

"When did this occur?" Assur demanded, still not permitting the Siarsi to rise.

"Ten days ago, my lord. We have ridden as fast as possible. I bring a message from Prince Exbrel himself." Wobran pulled a folded and sealed paper from the inside of his jerkin and handed it to Assur.

Assur signaled the weary men to stand and for the assembled warriors to put up their swords. "Who committed this crime? Who would dare violate the Caverns?"

"It was the Qualani, Great Lord! It was they who did this deed. Warrior-Guardians have been slain. The Master lies in his own blood and the Sacred Hammer is gone. But the Qualani were fools, my lord. They left this."

Again, Wobran reached inside his jerkin and pulled out something and waved it over his head for everyone to see.

"It is the neck collar of a Qualani clansman, dropped during his foul mission. By Verlian's blood and blade, he and all of his kind will die!"

Assur took the neck collar and examined it. Kitarisa peered over his shoulder at the object in his hands—a necklace or collar of some kind—black onyx beads threaded together with the claws of a bear.

"You found only one?" Assur asked sharply.

"Yes, Great Lord. Only one collar, but there were signs of many Qualani who desecrated the Cavern."

Shouts rose from angry Siarsi warriors. "Death to the Qualani! Vengeance to the Siarsi! Verlian be with us!"

Assur held up his hand.

"Silence. You will have retribution, but only after all the factors have been examined. You, Wobran, will follow me to my private chamber. Kuurus, Achad, attend me. Adar Tethket, you will honor us with your presence."

Assur turned to stride out of the hall, then stopped next to Kitarisa. Oblivious to the stares of those about him, he took her right hand in his and pressed it to his lips. Regret mixed with anger traced his lean features.

"I am sorry Kitarisa, but this cannot wait."

She curtsied to him. "I understand, my lord."

He swept past her with the Siarsi and his favored warriors close on his heels.

An ominous presence formed within Kitarisa like a knot of cold fire—something bestial, enraged.

Find them. Kill the defilers of Siarsia!

She pressed her palm to her middle and hoped no one would notice the gesture.

As she watched Assur leave the hall, a new sense of dread rose within her. Scarcely home ten days and the High Prince was already planning for another war.

Chapter Two

THE SOFT, HOT wind blew gently across the wide expanse of pink-hued tiles, fluttering the silk draping dividing the inner chamber from the balcony—a balcony built high above a sapphire-blue sea.

The Dolmina Shakiris watched as four silk-clad slaves knelt expectantly alongside a cushioned couch, upon which lay their mistress. Eyes downcast and hands folded across their knees, the slaves awaited her slightest wish. Two other girls stood at the head and foot of the couch waving enormous feather fans in gentle, rhythmic strokes. Abruptly, their mistress stood and angrily cast her own fan across the tiled floor.

"Where is he?" she demanded, pacing around the room, the tiny gold bells around her ankles making harsh jangling noises with each angry step.

Shakiris watched the servant girls cast secret, worried glances at each other. No one dared to say anything for fear of angering their mistress any further.

The young Lady Ghalmara was not one to trifle with in spite of her youth and beauty. She clenched her hands in small, hard fists and with each step, the diaphanous material of her gown lashed around slim, shapely legs. Her golden hair, like honeyed silk, hung straight to her slender hips. A gold band with tiny pendants dangling along the lower edge held the shining hair in place—each droplet quivering and shimmering as she paced about the room.

"I demand to know where he is," she continued. She fastened her blue gaze on him as Shakiris passed a hand over his own black, oiled hair, drawn tightly back and fastened at the base of his neck by a fine, green-braided cord.

He was clean-shaven, save for a trim moustache and a meticulously groomed patch of beard on his narrow chin. He placed his long hands together, fingertips to fingertips, and bowed slightly over them.

"I am sure I do not know, mistress" he said in a silky voice. "Perhaps the courier was delayed—roadwilds or maybe marglims...?"

"There are no marglims near Volt," she snapped. "He was sent under heavy escort. No roadwild would dare attack an escort riding under the Zoras banner!"

Shakiris shrugged slightly. "Then we must be patient, my lady. All has been set in train. We have only to wait."

"I hate waiting," she said sulkily, flinging herself again onto the couch. She tossed back a gleaming strand of hair from one cheek.

With great care, Shakiris averted his gaze from the bare expanse of supple thighs and a partially exposed hip—skin like rich cream, covered by a mere whisper of peach-hued silk. It was enough to drive a man mad. If this were the old days, he mused briefly, the girl's impudence would have been ravished long ago.

"My lady, if I may withdraw, I will make some inquiries...?"

He paused, hesitant. There was no use in further angering her. Spoiled and willful, the Lady Ghalmara was powerful enough and just spiteful enough to have his skinned, fly-eaten carcass hanging in the bazaar—and for the slightest offence. But once the great sacrifice had taken place she would no longer be so arrogant.

Lady Ghalmara reached for a small fruit on a nearby brass tray and began nibbling at it. A tiny thread of juice glistened from her full lower lip. She ran a moist, pink tongue over it, catching up the last drops.

His eyes narrowed ever so slightly. So sweet....

"Shakiris, I need your advice," she said, as she finished the fruit, then casually dropped the black pit to the floor.

"Of course, mistress," he said calmly, regaining his composure.

"I would know more about this man...this contact. Is he not your spy?"

Shakiris pressed his mouth into a thin smile. "'Spy' is too harsh a word, my lady. Rather "informant" is better suited to his talents. He has been extremely useful in the past, obtaining valuable information."

"I see. Valuable information that could make one extremely powerful?" She arched an eyebrow at him. "Be careful how much information you acquire. Too much information, particularly concerning those who you serve, might be considered dangerous."

Shakiris felt a low chill shoot through the base of his spine. He was treading on perilous ground. Only his rigid training prevented any reaction to show on his face as he evaluated Ghalmara's veiled threat.

"Information used only to further the purposes of House Zoras," he said carefully, lowering his gaze just a fraction.

"And yours," she finished for him. "My lord husband has benefited greatly from your informants and your loyalties to House Zoras."

Shakiris's breathing eased imperceptibly. "My lady is gracious as always." He bowed.

A polite cough from the back of the great chamber interrupted their conversation. A house guard, resplendent in crimson and yellow, signifying House Zoras, stepped forward and bowed before Shakiris and Ghalmara.

"The courier has just arrived, my lady...my lord."

Shakiris signaled the guard to allow the visitor into the room.

Lady Ghalmara observed the approach of the little man, unable to conceal her annoyance. He was filthy from many hard days in the saddle. His own dirty brown hair had escaped the confines of its binding cord and hung in a tangled mass about his shoulders. It appeared he had not shaved in several days and he reeked of horses and sweat.

Ghalmara wrinkled her nose and turned away. "How dare you come into my presence, unwashed and unshaven? Have you no manners, soldier?" she demanded coldly.

"With all respect, my lady," Shakiris interjected, "you did request to see the courier the moment he arrived. He was not to be delayed an instant."

She sniffed, clearly not at all pleased with having to be reminded of her instructions. "So I did," she said coolly. "Very well, proceed." Ghalmara motioned for her slaves to begin fanning her again, dispelling some of the odor.

The courier ignored such niceties and dropped to one knee. From inside his stained leathern jerkin, he pulled out a dirty, much-creased paper. Holding it up in one grimy hand, he offered it to her.

Lady Ghalmara recoiled delicately and gestured for Shakiris to take the soiled document. "Read it to me."

He offered another slight bow then cleared his throat: "*We have taken the first prize and it is now in safe-keeping. The great eagle has flown to his nest. Await your will.*"

Lady Ghalmara shot him a questioning glance then fastened her cool gaze on the kneeling courier. "Did you receive the note directly from the hands of the contact?"

"I did, mistress," the courier responded promptly.

"And, who but yourself knows of this note?"

"No one but myself, mistress. I kept it with me at all times. No one has touched it."

"I dare say," she commented dryly, noting its soiled and stained appearance.

Lady Ghalmara nodded and stood. "You may go, soldier. You have done your job well."

The courier rose and bowed before retreating from the chamber.

With a wave of her hand, Ghalmara dismissed the rest of her slaves including the fan bearers until she stood alone with Shakiris.

"How can we be sure no one else has seen this note or how many know of its contents? I am surprised the contact sent a note instead of having the courier commit the message to memory."

"I agree, my lady. It does seem odd; very unsettling."

She began pacing again.

"Too much has been set into motion to risk discovery now. Something may have gone amiss. I did not like the message "the eagle has flown to his nest..." I thought *he* was to have remained with his legions in Riehl Keep to wait out the winter."

"Evidently not, my lady."

"Then it must mean he has returned to Daeamon Keep and may have learned what has happened."

"Perhaps." Shakiris nodded. "But, from what my sources tell me, he is to marry quite soon."

A sneer formed on Ghalmara's pretty mouth. "Marry indeed! That arrogant painted-up savage wedded to a stupid fool! They deserve each other," she said sourly. "There remains only one question: how long will this "wedding" distract him from the events at hand?"

"Remember my lady, it is winter in Talesia. The snow can be quite confining. I would safely assume he will wait until the snow melts before taking any serious action. There would be time..." Shakiris paused.

Ghalmara nodded in agreement. "We need to know what has happened. It is too dangerous to send another courier, or a message bird." She stopped suddenly and looked up at him. "Unless, we find out first hand." Her eyes widened. "Of course, Shakiris, it is quite simple. The barbarian will marry soon. There will be a grand celebration—days and days of festivities. And, we *must* pay our respects and show homage to our new High Princess, the Ter-Reya. But," she held up a warning finger, "we are ill. No, my Lord *Jadoor* is ill, so ill he cannot travel and I cannot possibly leave him for a moment. Shakiris, listen. You must go in our stead. You must represent House Zoras with our humblest apologies. You will take gifts and offer regrets. Then, you will be able to seek out our contact and discover what has happened."

Shakiris stroked the small patch of beard and nodded. "Excellent, my lady. And amidst all the confusion, one humble Volten shall not be noticed." He bowed, acknowledging her cleverness.

"Good." For the first time, Ghalmara smiled, a sweet seductive smile. "Now, get rid of the courier but do it discreetly. And burn the note. We do not want anything to fall into the wrong hands."

He bowed once more and backed away with practiced ease until he reached the door. Once outside the chamber, he tucked the grimy note up one sleeve then turned, heading for the back of the palace, toward the servants' quarters where he knew the courier would be waiting for further instructions.

No, my scheming little spider, the courier shall not die.

Deep within the folds of his long robe was a leather sack containing five hundred gold talins—a goodly fee for the services of a mere courier, but more than enough to buy his silence. Shakiris smiled to himself. The courier had other uses.

And then, my beautiful serpent, I shall indeed go to Daeamon Keep and take...everything the Master wants.

SNOW FELL CONTINUOUSLY for three days, confining the Siarsi visitors inside the keep and thwarting any plans both they and Assur had begun.

There was little else for Kitarisa to do but wait in her chambers along with a fidgeting, restless Sethra. Assur's sister did not take well to the confinement and paced around Kitarisa, snapping the heavy skirt of her riding dress behind her.

"I am going mad with boredom," Sethra complained. "I detest the winter. There is nothing to do but wait and eat, and then wait some more. I cannot even ride. Assur allows no one outside the keep when it snows."

"I am sure that is for your protection, Sethra," Kitarisa murmured.

One of the junior waiting ladies had found an embroidery hoop and Kitarisa contentedly plied the needle through the bit of fabric. She had no idea what she was trying to create, but the simple task was calming and restful. She watched Sethra pace, amused at the girl's impatience. She had offered to teach her how to stitch, but the young princess refused with a wave of her hand. Too dull.

"Would you care to take a walk? I still have not seen much of the keep."

Sethra stopped her pacing. Her eyes lit up. "We can go to the stables, or go watch the warriors practice."

The princess tugged the embroidery hoop from Kitarisa's hands, forcing her to her feet. Both she and an obedient Davieta followed

Sethra down corridors and stairways to the practice arenas below.

"They never stop," Sethra advised. "They practice every day. The Swordmaster is very harsh. No one rests, even for a day."

Beneath the living quarters and stables of the keep, the ancients had built massive practice arenas, filled with deep sand and surrounded by tiers of spectator seats. Across from the arena, a darkened opening led to the baths and the equipment rooms.

Kitarisa watched in amazement at the scene before her. In Gorendt, the warriors always practiced within the outer courtyard on the hard cobbles. Here, sweating, grunting Talesians, stripped to the waist, fought each other on pure white sand. Various obstacles littered the arena floor—an overturned cart, stacked crates, and in the center, a high wall had been erected where the warriors practiced scaling it with stout ropes stretched over the top edge. At the far end a low bonfire, tended by a youth, blazed on the sand. The fire served as another, rather ominous obstacle for the practicing warriors.

In the center of the melee stood one man overseeing the practice session, dressed all in dark leather—a plain jerkin, open at his throat and snug-fitting trousers tucked into knee-high boots. He did not wear his hair bound up at the crown by a silver ring, but loose and heavy about his collar. Even more astonishing was his remarkable resemblance to Assur. For a moment Kitarisa thought it was Assur himself conducting the practice session.

"Who is that?" Kitarisa whispered as she and Davieta sat down on the wooden bench next to Sethra.

"That is Swordmaster Ramelek."

"Oh." Kitarisa nodded, remembering Assur's referral to Swordmaster Rame, the same swordmaster who had instructed him to strike only when his heart was cold and without feeling. Kitarisa now understood why. This practice session was not a mere exercise in swordplay, but a rehearsal for battle that united all the elements of Talesian ruthlessness: cold evaluation of the enemy and an utterly fearless, almost disdainful regard for death.

Standing amidst them, arms across his chest, Swordmaster Rame paced and barked curt instructions, occasionally stopping to adjust an incorrect grip on a sword or an unbalanced stance. The sounds of clanging steel and labored breathing filled the arena as each warrior strove to please their hard-eyed master.

"He looks like Assur, only older," Kitarisa again whispered to Sethra.

Sethra winked and smiled. "Yes, he does."

"I think he is splendid," murmured Lady Davieta, sitting next to Kitarisa.

Startled, she turned to her. "Davieta?"

Lady Davieta smiled at her. "Even *I* am not immune to these handsome barbarians, my lady."

Kitarisa returned her gaze to the fighting warriors, who had gathered in a circle around two young men: one, a tall Chaliset wielding a sword, and the other a fierce-eyed Ponos handling a long, dangerous-looking spear. Fully a foot in length, the iron point reminded Kitarisa of the knives Talesians strapped to their saddles.

Swordmaster Rame stood close by, arms folded, a scowl darkening his stern features as he watched the two warriors.

"No!" he snapped to the Chaliset. Both warriors stopped, panting and wringing wet from their exertions. "You leave yourself open here and here," he said, gesturing to the weaker areas. He snatched the sword from the young warrior's hands and faced the Ponos.

"And now!" With lightning speed, the Swordmaster struck at the startled Ponos. Reflexively, the young man blocked the strike, barely escaping a lethal blow. Swordmaster Rame attacked a second time, driving home the lesson again and again for the watching Chaliset. The Ponos warrior fought bravely, until with another shearing blow, the Swordmaster shattered the shaft of the spear sending the metal tip spinning into the sand. Barely winded, he stopped and tossed the sword to the Chaliset. "Finish it," he ordered.

"Master Rame," the young Ponos protested. "The spear is ruined. I cannot—"

The master turned on him, eyes blazing.

"You think this would not happen in real battle? There will come a day when you may hold only a stick between you and your Summons! A Talesian fights with what he has, even his bare hands if necessary. Do not whimper to me, boy. Fight him or yield."

The two squared off again and this time the young Ponos flew at his opponent, desperate to outfight him with only a broken staff as a weapon.

Struggling to keep his balance, the Chaliset stumbled back, tripped awkwardly, then dropped to one knee. The Ponos pressed his advantage and lunged at him, driving the splintered tip past a defensive parry. The Chaliset ducked, then swung around, leaving his left side bare to his opponent's attack. The Ponos stumbled forward, lurching in the sand, and drove the ragged end of the spear into the Chaliset's side. Kitarisa heard a sickening, splitting sound as the spear shaft broke again, leaving a rough splinter imbedded in the young man's chest. The warrior dropped his sword then fell to his knees, pain and surprise riddling his face as he clasped his hands at the gushing wound.

"Send for the physick!" Swordmaster Rame barked, lunging for the young man to help break his fall to the arena floor.

Kitarisa gasped and stood along with Davieta and a horrified Sethra.

All the warriors stopped their fighting; a handful broke away and rushed out the arena doors to find the physick while the rest hurried over to try and offer some kind of help to their fallen comrade.

Kitarisa brushed past Davieta and hurried through the access opening to the arena and down the short flight of steps. Heedless of proprieties, she lifted her heavy skirts and skimmed across the sand to the fallen Chaliset where he lay surrounded by tense-faced warriors and a stricken young Ponos.

"Let me see him," she demanded, pushing against sweaty arms and backs. Many of the men recognized her and immediately bowed their heads. Those who did not, stepped back, surprised by the intrusion of this unknown woman who seemed so determined to see their fallen companion.

Both Sethra and Davieta were right behind Kitarisa as she knelt down next the Swordmaster.

"Who are you?" he demanded.

"She is the princess, Kitarisa, Swordmaster Rame. She knows about these things. She has the way; she saved Kuurus from marglim poisoning," Sethra advised.

Master Rame cast his hardened look from Sethra, then back to Kitarisa, clearly displeased and wanting no part of some meddling woman.

"Where is the physick?" he demanded, looking beyond them.

From the crowd, two red-faced warriors shoved their way through. "The physick is nowhere to be found, Master," one of them panted.

Rame made a growling noise in throat, not unlike Assur, as Kitarisa watched his harsh gaze turn on her.

"What can you do, my lady?" he asked sharply.

"Ease him down flat, Master Rame."

Low, agonized groans escaped the young warrior as he was lowered to the sand. The large splinter from the spear shaft lay wedged tightly between two ribs, beneath the skin and first layer of muscle— the raw wooden end just showing through the skin. Blood ran through his clutching fingers and down into the white sand, where it thickened into dark, gritty clots.

Kitarisa looked up at her maid.

"Quick, Davieta, find my satchel and bring it here at once."

Davieta sketched a hasty curtsey, turned, and sprinted across the sand, her skirts caught up high in one hand.

"Bring a litter. Help me get him into the surgery."

Eager hands eased the warrior from the sand onto the litter, but in spite of their care, the warrior could not refrain from crying out. Kitarisa placed her hand over the wound to try and staunch some of the blood.

"Hurry!"

The Swordmaster nodded and the warriors quickly lifted the litter to their shoulders and carried it into the surgery.

Kitarisa skidded to a halt when she entered the surgery. Appalled, she stared at the filth and debris littering the room. Empty, reeking jugs of ale, unwashed tools, and a hide of some animal were scattered on the wide surgery table. Sodden rags and a garment that stank of vomit had been piled in the corner. Bottles and more dirty instruments lay scattered along the counters. And everywhere, the sound of scurrying vermin.

"Who would keep a surgery like this?" she asked in a shocked whisper. "This is an outrage."

She marshaled all her courage and drew herself up. "Get rid of this mess and get him on that table!"

Jugs and filth flew as the first two warriors cleared the table.

"Sethra, find a place where you can boil water, lots of it, and get me as many clean linens as you can find."

Sethra did not hesitate, but simply ran to obey her, never once questioning the fact that she was the sister of the Ter-Rey, and under any other circumstance would not have dreamed of performing such a menial task.

Kitarisa looked up and met Master Rame's cold blue eyes—so like Assur's, but infinitely harder. She saw no apology, only suppressed anger.

"Does not your physick realize this is the surgery in Daeamon Keep—a place that must be kept clean at all times?"

"The physick has received several warnings, my lady. This will be his last. I shall personally see to it that he is punished. Of that you can be sure," he said evenly, never taking his eyes from her.

Kitarisa nodded and turned back to her patient. She touched his brow gently. "What is your name, warrior?" she asked softly.

"It is...is Cai," he said through clenched teeth.

"Hush, that is enough, Cai. You will not die, but I must cut to remove the splinter. I will give you something to help with the pain."

In moments, Sethra returned carrying an armload of towels. With her help Kitarisa eased as many as she could under Cai's body then folded one and placed it under his head. She spoke again to the Swordmaster.

"I will need a thick piece of leather, or a soft stick." She noted Rame's slightly puzzled expression. "He will need it to bite down on so he will not sever his tongue."

The master nodded and signaled one of the nearest warriors to comply with her wish.

"There are far too many men in this room. I will need only Davieta and Sethra—if she wishes to stay—and three other men to hold him down."

Rame appeared not too proud to recognize the voice of authority and only nodded again, making sure each of her wishes was carried out.

When Davieta returned, Kitarisa settled her small armament of medicines and instruments in the first basin and washed her hands in the second. She was not sure why, but the lessons driven into her by her old Nans were not to be dismissed. Nans had insisted everything must be clean and Kitarisa's own sense of fastidiousness concurred.

From her cache of bottles she selected one, opened it, and dropped several drops down Cai's throat.

"It will ease some of the pain, but not all of it." She placed the thick piece of leather between his teeth then touched his brow again, trying to comfort the warrior. "Bite down, hard. Scream if you wish."

"He will not scream, my lady," Rame said calmly from across the table. "He may groan, but he will never scream."

Kitarisa shook her head in disbelief. She would never understand their harsh indifference to pain. She returned Rame's even gaze. "We shall see Swordmaster," she said coolly.

"Yes, we shall soon see," a heavy, slurred voice cut over their heads.

Kitarisa turned to see who belonged with the voice. In the doorway stood a stocky man, thickset from too much drink and a sallow skin that could not hide the deep pitting and scarring—a face long-destroyed with dissipation and debauchery. He cast his bleary-eyed gaze about the room, taking in the wounded warrior and the woman standing over him.

"Just who do you think you are, coming into my surgery?" he demanded, swaying against the doorjamb. He grabbed for the latch just in time before stumbling into the room. "I demand you leave at once."

Kitarisa rounded on the reeking man, her own eyes blazing like the Swordmaster's.

"I assume you are the physick? You, of all people, have no business in this room. This man needs immediate attention or he will bleed to death." She looked at Master Rame, who by now was signaling the nearest warriors to grab the staggering physick.

"You have no right—" the man shouted, breaking free of the warriors' grasp and lunging at her.

Swordmaster Rame struck like a coiled viper. Grasping him by the collar with both fists, he slammed the drunken physick into the wall, rattling bottles and shattering the plaster behind the man's head.

"You are to blame for this, you worthless...excrement of dogs! I'll see your flayed skin hanging from the highest battlements!"

Rame jerked the physick away from the wall and flung him toward the nearby warriors.

"Take him below! Chain him!"

The warriors hastened to obey, dragging the dazed physick away before he could utter another complaint.

Kitarisa turned back to Cai, dismissing the ugly incident, and pressed on with the matter at hand. Master Rame assumed his place at the young warrior's head and grasped his wrists. She nodded to the other men to hold him down.

With a short quick stroke she opened the wound, exposing the jagged splinter. Cai arched his back in agony, but as Rame said, never once cried out. She was grateful the thing sat so close to the surface, that it was relatively easy to grasp it in her fingers and pull free. Once out, she hastened to cleanse the wound of any more wood fragments, then neatly, as with her embroidery, stitched the wound close.

The warrior shook and strained against the men who held him down. Kitarisa's heart cried out, hating herself for causing him so much pain. Once stitched, she washed the wound again, then applied salve of trisroot. She glanced up at Davieta. The maid was as white as the towels covering the warrior, but her eyes were calm. Sethra had prudently retreated to the back of the filthy chamber, obviously not daring to come any closer for fear of fainting at the terrible sight.

"Davieta, bring the linens. Tear them into narrow strips while I make a poultice." She nodded to the men to ease their hold on the warrior's arms and legs, then removed the leather from his mouth. Cai was remarkably clear-eyed and calm; his rapid breathing had eased some. Kitarisa could only attribute his strength to the years of unrelenting discipline in order to face down pain and fear. She remembered the night when she had saved Kuurus from the effects of marglim-blood poisoning and his fierce determination to live.

She touched a damp towel to Cai's face and smiled. "I am afraid you will live to fight another day."

The young Chaliset managed a weak smile before closing his eyes.

With Davieta's help she wrapped the warrior's chest in layers of the clean linen, tying a solid final knot over her work.

"Take him to a quiet bed. He is not to be moved for three days. His every need must be seen to and he is to have only broth and shen tea. No wine and no strong drink," she ordered firmly. "I will change the bandages myself."

With great care, Cai's comrades eased him to the litter and carried him out and away to his bed.

Kitarisa washed the blood from her hands and dried them on one of the last clean towels. Swordmaster Rame stood aside, assessing her with the same cool look Assur had done the night she had saved Kuurus. She saw both relief and grudging admiration sketch across his hard features. His eyes narrowed slightly.

"You are worthy of him, my lady. Assur has chosen well."

"I thank you for that Master Rame, but this matter must be discussed. I am not the Ter-Reya yet, and I would not trespass in an area where I am not welcome, but this," she gestured to the room, "is an abomination. That warrior would have bled to death. Was that the physick who is in charge of this hovel?"

"Yes. His name is Nadir; he is neither Chaliset nor Siarsi. In fact, he is not Talesian at all but of the Jek, a sub-clan from the south."

"Why is he permitted to attend to wounded warriors? He is no physick, but a monster, a drunken beast."

"Agreed, my lady," Rame said, not disguising the disgust his voice.

"And, Lord Assur permits this?" she asked, again aghast at the thought of such a man tending to so many warriors.

"I am certain Assur is not aware of this. Overseeing the household staff lies within the province of our esteemed dolmina, the Master Imroz." There was no missing the sneering sarcasm in Rame's voice.

"Surely you have spoken to him about this? You are the Swordmaster of the Keep. Prince Assur would certainly heed your words."

"Assur and I...do not always agree," he said carefully.

From the back of the room, Sethra approached the bloodied table and touched Kitarisa's arm.

"Kitarisa, Lord Rame and Lord Assur have not always gotten along so well," she explained, then shrugged. "Sometimes I have served as a go-between for them."

"*Lord* Rame?" Kitarisa asked incredulously.

"Yes, Kitarisa. Lord Rame is our uncle."

Chapter Three

THE NEWS OF KITARISA's surgery on the young Chaliset warrior
raced through Daeamon. From the imperious dolmina who oversaw the
entire running of the keep, to the lowliest stable boy, everyone knew
that Prince Assur's bride had saved the life of an untried warrior.
Members of the council raised their brows, a few indiscreet ladies
whispered between themselves behind closed doors, but no one dared
say anything to the Ter-Rey or to Lord Ramelek. Risking the High
Prince's wrath was too dangerous; risking the Swordmaster's temper
was often fatal.

Kitarisa had no time for gossip, but directed her attentions on
having the filthy surgery room thoroughly cleaned and swept. She did
not even care if she overstepped her authority and the house servants
who assisted her did not seem to mind, either. Eagerly they hastened to
carry out Kitarisa's exacting instructions.

While they cleaned, she took the opportunity to examine all of the
physick's store of herbs and supplies. It was worse than she expected.
Briar root liniment! A substance good only for horses and other
animals. Demesian powder—a worthless concoction commonly used
by many household physicks as a cure-all for everything from a
stomachache to broken bones. She relegated both to the trash. Most of
the herbs and medicines in the room were equally as useless.

When the shelves and cupboards were spotless, the floor washed
and the work table scrubbed till it shown, she then proceeded to have
the few jars and bottles worth keeping washed and stored away. Fresh,
clean bandages were rolled and stored in the cupboards. The surgery
was primarily a repair room, not a place for those who were sick.
Wounded men, with assorted cuts and bruises were the physick's only
patients.

As she finished straightening the towels in the cupboard, she
heard the door open and shut. Swordmaster Rame entered the room and
stood next to the work table, arms folded across his chest.

"Your work is commendable, my lady, but hardly a place for a
Ter-Reya. Lord Assur will not approve."

Kitarisa snapped open a towel and began folding it with short,
crisp movements.

"Lord Assur gave his consent for me to bring my skills to Daeamon, to try and be of some use. I have no intention of becoming the physick for the keep, but I cannot stand by and see this sort of thing continue. What will happen to this Nadir?"

"He will be severely punished for his crime. There are many more chambers that lie deep within the Keep, my lady. Rooms that are not nearly as pleasant as even this one," he said ominously.

Kitarisa swallowed, fully realizing Rame's meaning.

"I think a mere dismissal would be in order, Lord Rame, not torture."

"You think not? Cai would have died—you said it yourself. I will not let that worthless dog escape so easily. The physick *will* pay for his crime," the tall Swordmaster said passionately.

Kitarisa swallowed again and looked down. Assur was right about Talesians; beneath Rame's veneer of civility lay the heart of a barbarian. She sighed heavily, then placed the towel on the neat pile within the cupboard.

"Lord Rame, I have no wish to be your enemy or anyone else's for that matter. At this moment, my only wish is to make sure these men, *your* warriors, get proper care." She did not dare look up at him. The old terror of punishment pulsed through her. "If I have overstepped my place, I am sorry. The physick is your concern, of course."

A heavy pause hovered between them. She sensed Master Rame shifting his stance. He cleared his throat and Kitarisa forced herself to look at him. Some of the hardness had left his eyes. In fact, she thought she detected a thread of regret filter across the harsh planes of his face.

"Perhaps I, too, have overstepped my authority. If not that, at least my manners. You have already achieved great honor among these warriors and I am grateful to you, my lady. I will make certain Cai takes his Oath of Duty to you. However, you must understand that the physick has placed himself in great jeopardy. He must be punished."

Kitarisa nodded. "You said that the dolmina was to blame for bringing this Physick Nadir to the keep. If I were to speak to Lord Assur and we confronted the dolmina, perhaps we could gain some—?"

"I will speak to Assur. You need not bother yourself with this matter. It shall be handled, I assure you."

Again, Kitarisa nodded mutely having no wish to further upset this fierce, unyielding man.

The Swordmaster's sharp gaze took in the neatly arranged bottles and vials on the shelves, the stacks of clean towels and bandages and the scrubbed shininess of the work table. He nodded.

"Verlian has truly blessed us with your presence," he said shortly, then turned on his heel and left the room.

"KITARISA, COME QUICKLY!" Sethra called excitedly, bursting into her room.

Kitarisa turned from the mirror and gave her hair a final pat. Davieta had just completed helping her dress into another of the new, full-skirted gowns. Kitarisa never tired of the heavy, rustling sounds of the petticoats and the train sweeping behind her—imminently more satisfying than the plain, straight gowns of Gorendt and Riehl. Even Davieta, a Riehlian from birth, had begun adopting the Talesian style, looking regal in a gown of violet and cream.

"Kitarisa, you must come. Now!" Sethra went on breathlessly. "Assur and Rame are fighting."

"Fighting?"

Sethra caught her elbow and hurried her out of the room.

"You know...over that warrior you saved and that drunken physick. They are shouting at each other. It is very exciting."

"Sethra!" Kitarisa stopped and pulled her arm free. "You must tell me why Rame and Assur dislike each other."

"They have detested each other for many turns. It's because of that woman."

"A woman? Sethra, I will not move until you have told me everything."

Assur's impetuous sister sighed, giving in. "Very well, but come with me and I will tell you."

They hurried from Kitarisa's chamber, down darkened passageways and up shadowy stairs, while Sethra untangled the curious relationship between the High Prince and the Swordmaster.

"Uncle Rame is really our father's half-brother," Sethra continued breathlessly. "Our grandfather, Prince Taksma remarried *very* late in life. His young, third wife produced Rame, but the poor lady died having him. Later, when father, Achad, married our mother, it was she who raised Rame until Assur was born. Rame treated Assur more like a younger brother than a nephew. Even at a very young age, Rame had a special gift for weapons. So, it became natural for him to assume the duties as Swordmaster.

"When I was little, Rame fell in love with a lady. I do not recall her name. She was Siarsi, I believe. Anyway, she is gone now, but she would have nothing to do with Rame. At the same time, Assur became infatuated with her. I remember mother becoming exasperated with both of them. Well, the lady was only interested in Assur—after all he *was* to become the Ter-Rey. When Rame found out, he was furious. He offered bride-price to the lady and when Assur discovered that, he challenged Rame to a fight. They say it was terrible. I was not permitted to watch, but I was told they wounded each other quite badly. When they recovered, the lady left, insulting them both. Since then, neither one has had anything to do with the other. Particularly, Rame. He grew very jealous of what Assur would become and what he would inherit. But, he serves the Ter-Rey by training loyal warriors and Assur leaves him alone. In private they avoid one another. Before the court, they are barely civil."

"Such a waste, Sethra."

"They are hard-headed, stubborn, and too proud for their own good. If mother were here, she would whip their backsides for certain."

Kitarisa smiled. "I cannot imagine *anyone* taking a hand to either of them."

"Oh, you should have known mother, Kitarisa. She was like Assur, only worse. She was not afraid of either of them and believe me, they *obeyed* her!"

The shouting could be heard half a corridor away, even through the heavy door to Assur's private room. Two warriors stood outside the door, eyes focused straight ahead, but Kitarisa could feel their dread. They recognized her immediately and bowed their heads.

"Will you allow me to pass?" she asked softly.

"If they will not let you, they *will* let me," Sethra said firmly.

"You are the Ter-Reya, my lady," one of them said.

Kitarisa shook her head. "No warrior, not yet."

"You have killed the 'Fa, that is enough," the other said.

Kitarisa looked at Sethra. Her pretty mouth was set in a determined line. She nodded, and Kitarisa pushed open the heavy door.

Two men, so alike they could have been mistaken for twins, faced each other across a heavy, dark wood table. Except that Rame, on the right, was clearly older than Assur—his thick, dark hair fell to his shoulders and was shot through with gray at the temples and his beard. Fine lines creased the black patterns around his eyes, but could not diminish the fire within his gaze. Both men were the same height and build and both leaned over the table, heads down, glaring at each other. In fact, the scene reminded Kitarisa of two stags she had once seen, antlers locked in mortal combat, their shoulder muscles bunched and tense as they strained to defeat each other.

"How dare you allow her to be involved in such a demeaning

incident!" Assur shouted.

"She involved herself before I could stop her. She saved Cai's life by her own doing. She wanted to confront you herself concerning the physick!"

"I will not have her dragged into this sordid business..."

"Then bring the dolmina here so he can answer for the physick's actions. It was Dolmina Imroz who brought that worthless dog here in the first place," Rame said angrily.

Sethra accidentally bumped the door causing the latch to rattle. Both princes turned on the intruders like furious eagles.

"What?" Assur snapped.

The two women hastily dropped into deep curtsies.

Suddenly realizing who they were, Assur was forced to stop his raging at Rame. A light smile touched his lips.

"Kitarisa," he said awkwardly. "You catch me at a bad moment."

"I am sorry to intrude like this, but it is necessary." She glanced from one man to the next. "I want to clarify this misunderstanding." She took a deep breath and approached the two seething princes. "I am responsible for interfering and for aiding that warrior. I insisted on helping him. Please do not blame Lord Rame."

"Lord Rame should have not allowed you to become involved in an area that was clearly his responsibility. The care of warriors is his province and not that of a Ter-Reya."

Kitarisa nodded. "I know, but I *did* insist. There was no one else. My Lord Assur, it was the same as with Kuurus when he swallowed the marglim blood. I could not let him die. The physick was drunk. I could not allow him to attend to Cai; he would have killed him!"

"It is true, Assur," Sethra interjected. "I saw Cai myself."

Assur turned toward Rame, scrutinizing his uncle. His eyes never left his look-alike's face.

"Very well. I *will* have the dolmina brought to me to find out what is going on. I will not hold you responsible until I find out who is to blame."

"My lord is too kind," Rame said sarcastically. Without another word, the Swordmaster turned on his heel and strode to the door, sketching a brief nod to her and Sethra. The heavy door slammed behind him.

"I am sorry you must be part of this unpleasantness, Kitarisa," Assur said quietly. "Rame and I do not often speak to one another and unfortunately when we do, we always seem to lose our tempers."

"I am sorry, too, my lord. He seems a fine man. A bit hard—"

"As hard as a stone," Sethra interjected, smiling. "Let me go and try to calm him down. Sometimes he will listen to me."

Sethra left the room with a rustle of heavy skirts.

Kitarisa approached Assur hesitantly. "Have I really caused so much trouble? I have scarcely been here a few days and already the family is quarreling over me." She smiled ruefully at him.

"No, Kita. You are not to blame. You have done the right thing. It is Rame and I who cannot seem to see things clearly."

"He is very much like you, you know," she ventured.

"Hard-headed and stupid as pit-mules."

Kitarisa smiled up at him mischievously. "No. Just both determined to have your way. You are like two little boys, always quarreling over the same toy."

Assur nodded. "You are right, of course." He eased one long leg on the edge of the table, sitting sideways facing her. He folded his arms across his chest. "So, what do you suggest we should do with this drunken physick? Rame favors skinning him and hanging his wretched hide from the highest battlement." A smile tugged at the corner of his mouth.

Kitarisa blanched. Torture had been her father's favorite tool to keep his subjects obedient; her own Rhynn had been tortured to death.

She turned and began to pace Assur's chamber. "Well..."

The room was actually quite small, almost filled by the presence of the desk and a few straight-backed, intricately-carved chairs. At the back of the room, heavy velvet drapes half-hid a full-length mullioned window, set overlooking the sea. A cheery fire crackled from a hearth behind the desk and on the opposite wall, behind her, hung a magnificent tapestry depicting some memorable Talesian battle.

"First, I would speak to the dolmina. Sethra informed me that he is responsible for the running of the entire keep. I assume he would also have some authority over the physick—my father's dolmina had that authority."

Kitarisa remembered the dolmina at Gorendt Keep, a quiet little man, thoroughly frightened of Prince Kazan. He ran the household staff with silent efficiency, oversaw the kitchens and laundry, the carpentry shop and the ironworker. He made certain the rooms and halls were cleaned and that the maids changed the linens.

The tending to the great baths fell under his jurisdiction, too. He made sure the larders were well stocked and that plenty of ale and wine were stored in the keep's deep cellars. He saw to the hiring and dismissal of the staff; watched for stealing, cheating and other indiscretions. He made certain only the most respectful servants waited at their lord's table and that they all were neatly dressed and clean.

The only places where Kazan's dolmina had no authority were the stables and the warrior's quarters, and curiously, her own apothecary.

"He does," Assur said soberly, stroking the edge of his trim beard.

"If he does not have a satisfactory answer as to why the physick cannot keep an orderly and *safe* surgery, then I suggest the physick be dismissed and sent back to wherever he came from. Lord Rame says he is of the Jek. Perhaps he should go there. Dolmina Imroz should be warned against any further misconduct and asked to find another physick. If that one proves unsatisfactory, then both shall be dismissed."

Assur pondered her words for a moment then stood and turned to face the fire.

"You do not think a little physical punishment would be in order?" he asked, glancing back at her.

"My lord, I would not wish torture on any man. I have seen enough already." Kitarisa lowered her gaze, hoping she had not displeased him.

"Very well. It shall be as you wish. I will speak to the dolmina and you will be present. It is time you started to earn your keep around here," he said, grinning at her.

Assur turned from the fire and moved toward her, his expression swiftly changing from humor to a more serious, almost ardent one. He placed his hands gently on her shoulders and studied her for a moment.

"I would see us joined as quickly as is considered appropriate, Kitarisa. As custom dictates, it is my decision as to the appropriate time. I had hoped within the next few days, but this difficulty with the Siarsi... I have decided that as soon as the snow melts, we will select the day. It will give you time to prepare and I can attend to this other business. Will that be satisfactory?"

Kitarisa stopped herself from taking an involuntary step back from him. As always, when she was this close to Assur, she felt surrounded. He towered over her unlike the stockier Gorendtian men she had known. And those compelling, embellished eyes, usually so fierce, were now dark with ardor.

"Very well," she said softly, lifting her gaze to meet his. "I will be ready."

Assur pulled her closer to him, his arms slipping around her back. He did not hesitate, but pressed a long, possessive kiss on her mouth. Kitarisa rose up on her toes so she could reach behind his neck and return the kiss.

"Kita-lara," he breathed softly against her neck after releasing her a little. "Waiting until spring will not be easy for me." He caught one of her hands in his and brought it to his lips. "I am not made of stone."

Kitarisa blushed. Her heart beat so furiously in her chest she was afraid he would feel it holding her so close to him. It was the first time Assur had spoken to her in such an intimate manner. She was no untouched girl, having already known the love of one man, but Assur's nearness was deeply unsettling. A part of her wanted to love him and eagerly seek his touch, while the other part, the cool, distant princess in her, fought for control and the safety of seclusion.

She placed her hands flat on his chest and tried to think of some way to answer him.

"Kita," he went on quietly, still not loosening his embrace. "I know you do not love me as much as I love you. I know your heart is still with that warrior...Rhynn. All I ask is for you to find a place for me—"

"Assur," she whispered, pressing a finger to his lips. "Rhynn is dead and my heart is not with him. For a time it was, but I cannot live my life for a dead man, no matter how dear he was to me. You have given me your Oath. You have restored my life to me and paid bride-price. You have made me feel safe. You have given me all this. If that is not reason enough to love someone, than I do not know what is... But, it is so difficult for me. All my life it has been taken away. Those dearest to me have been destroyed and I have been punished for loving them."

She eased from his grasp and turned away, suddenly embarrassed by her rush of emotion and the hot tears threatening to break through her resolve.

"There is something else—something that frightens me, terribly."

"What is it that frightens you?"

"I am not sure. Something that has stayed with me since that dreadful day when the Holy Daughter changed me into..."

"That creature, like Malgora?" Assur asked.

"Yes."

"But that is over. You killed the 'Fa and the Daughters restored you to me."

"I know," she whispered, "but there is still something that grows within me. I cannot explain it. Something terrible that I am unable to stop."

Assur said nothing for a moment. "Kita, whatever it is, I know there must be a way to control it. Perhaps the Holy Daughter Thespa—"

Kitarisa swiftly reached up and again pressed her fingers to his lips, silencing him. "Promise me, Assur, that if anything should happen...if anyone's life is in danger because of me, you will do what is right, even if it means *my* life."

"Kita—"

"Promise me!" she said fiercely. "If you truly love me, then you will do this."

Assur nodded as his hands reached for her shoulders. "Very well, I promise, but on the condition that you will learn to trust me."

She turned from him again, her head bowed wearily. "It will not be easy. I have built so many walls to protect myself, I do not know how to break them down. I *want* to trust you...love you Assur, but I am so afraid I will be punished for it."

He did not move as he absorbed her heartbreaking confession.

"What would make you less afraid?" he asked softly.

Startled by the question, Kitarisa turned back to face him; she could not answer him.

"Perhaps, if you stopped running from me, Kita, you would see that your fears are groundless. How can I punish you for something I want so much?"

Tears caught in her throat. The back of her hand went to her mouth as she tried to suppress a sob.

Assur opened his arms to her and waited and this time she did not hesitate. She ran to his embrace, unafraid, and at long last, surrendered her heart to him.

THE DOLMINA IMROZ flicked an imperceptible speck of dust from his immaculate dark green robes and readjusted the collar more smoothly about his neck. It would never do to appear untidy or shabby before the Ter-Rey. It was a rare thing indeed to be summoned by the prince himself for a private interview. He did not necessarily relish the prospect of facing Assur, particularly over such a trivial matter as the physick's housekeeping practices. Was not that the jurisdiction of that ill-tempered boar of a Swordmaster?

Imroz studied his reflection in the long glass—a fine piece he had brought personally from glorious Volt. He smoothed his long, oiled hair tied back at the base of his neck by a green braided cord. Green for the rank of dolmina, orange for the Wordkeeper and white of course, for the Chanter. He admitted his complexion looked too pasty, but that was due to the long, dreary winters spent in the confines of the keep.

He squinted sharp eyes at his reflection and ran a nervous tongue over his teeth. How he longed for the sunny, warm days in Volt—languid afternoons spent in quiet repose on a high-terraced veranda overlooking a radiant blue sea. A long way from this cold, miserable keep. Whatever possessed him to be lured away from the beauty and warmth of Volt to live within this dark, stone hulk set by a dismal, gray ocean?

Perhaps it had been the lure of adventure, or more likely the prospect of a handsome remuneration for serving as the dolmina to the Ter-Rey. It was quite an honor—not that Imroz had any real admiration for the Ter-Rey... Still, it was a position of great authority and responsibility. While he enjoyed his superior position in the High Prince's household, he neither respected nor liked Assur. And why should he? The prince was a painted-up savage, descended from a line of bloodthirsty animals whose only purpose in life was to wreak destruction and glorify death.

He sniffed and made one last adjustment to his robe. In four sunturns he could petition the Ter-Rey to be released from his bond and return to the warmth of Volt and all of its pleasures.

It was a pity the Talesians had no such pleasurable inclinations. Such a rude, serious lot—always warring over one trivial thing after the other. And then there had been that unpleasant business with Gorendt and how Princess Kitarisa had killed the 'Fa. He readily gave thanks to Verlian for that. Everyone had hated Malgora and her White Sisters.

Imroz had observed the new princess at the great feast from a respectful distance. He had been only moderately impressed. A modest little mouse of a thing, but pretty enough. It would be easy to flatter such a meek creature. A well-placed word and tactful praise did wonders for one's position among the high-born.

It had surprised Imroz to learn that the princess possessed such superior healing skills and it was an even greater surprise that she bothered to waste them on some noisy, bloodthirsty youth. That was the physick's job. Well, there was no accounting for taste, or inclination for that matter. What the princess did was her concern.

Imroz made another minor adjustment to his robes then turned to leave. How did one approach the Ter-Rey? With caution or with confidence? There was no telling what temper the Ter-Rey would be in today and Imroz finally decided upon the first course of action. Caution, coupled with a mild, non-abrasive manner seemed the best tactic. There was no sense in antagonizing the High Prince.

He left the room and walked quickly down the corridors, passing some of his own staff attending to their duties. Imroz had a sharp eye and missed nothing, particularly slip-shod work or laziness. Two young linen-maids were huddled together in a dark corner of the hallway, giggling over something. They were Talesian girls, brought up from the south—girls of good, if not high-born families. Imroz was particularly careful about disciplining Talesian girls. The barbarians took great exception to any sort of punishment to their women—probably due to the fact there were so few of them, Imroz surmised. With servants from the sub-clans, or those brought in from distant areas, he had a much freer rein with his punishments. Or desires.

In Volt, Imroz had enjoyed the leisurely, almost casual attitude toward servants. Delectable housemaids and willing laundresses were his for the asking. Even the occasional ladies maid had fallen to his cravings. But here, one had to be exceptionally discreet. He learned quickly to avoid any Talesian woman, no matter how lowly. He had nearly been caught trying to seduce the wife of a mere guard—escaping a grisly death by sheer luck and some fast talking.

No, Talesian women were off-limits, but there were others if one were careful. He had spotted that new lady's maid, Davieta. She was Riehlian and lovely. She was also somewhat similar to the Ter-Reya with dark hair, touched with red, and warm, dark-brown eyes to match her affectionate personality. Davieta was a lady of polish and great refinement and Imroz was determined to have her.

"What seems to be going on?" he asked the girls sharply.

The linen-maids jumped apart, embarrassed at having been caught. Both dropped hasty curtsies.

"We were only sharing a little joke, Master," the first girl explained.

"A little joke, indeed," Imroz said severely. "Perhaps you would care to share such a joke with me?"

"It was nothing, Master, truly nothing," the second girl protested.

"Then, I suggest you return to your work. There is much to be done, especially with a new Ter-Reya."

The girls resumed their duties, eyes downcast to avoid his sharp reproving looks.

Imroz turned on his heel and proceeded to the audience chamber. In Volt, he would have had the girls thrashed for such impudence.

At the entrance to the chamber, two tall Chalisets stood guard. They eyed him with a touch of distaste marring their proud features. Imroz felt uncomfortable under their penetrating stares and nervously readjusted the collar of his robe.

"I am here to see the Ter-Rey," he said firmly, trying to cover his growing apprehension.

The guards made no sound but merely opened the heavy doors that led into Assur's private audience chamber.

As with most of Assur's rooms, it was simply but elegantly furnished. A curious incongruity, Imroz thought as he approached the two figures waiting for him. Assur sat on a finely-carved chair of blackoak wood; the ingeniously crossed slats of wood were bent and curved to accommodate the occupant, but the entire chair could be folded together and stored away when not in use. It reminded Imroz of a pair of opened shears. The High Prince sat casually, legs outstretched, one hand tugging aimlessly along the trim beard edging his jaw.

To Imroz's dismay, Princess Kitarisa sat next to Assur on a similar chair. He frankly had to admit to himself that she was a pretty woman, dressed in deep blue with her dark hair bound by a matching headdress. Behind her stood the lovely Davieta. Both she and the princess appeared calm and serene—a sharp contrast to the man standing at the far end of the room. There was no mistaking the seething form of the Swordmaster, Prince Ramelek.

Dolmina Imroz bowed low to the Ter-Rey and waited expectantly for him to speak.

"Punctual as always, Dolmina," Assur said, pulling himself into a more upright position.

"As you command, Great Lord."

"I shall come to the point, as I wish to resolve this matter quickly. I must assume you know why you are here?"

"Indeed, lord, I can guess. It concerns the physick and his "untidy" housekeeping?" He paused delicately.

"Untidy is hardly the word, Dolmina," Kitarisa said, stepping into the conversation. "The warrior could have died because of the physick. It is not only that the surgery was filthy beyond recognition, but that the physick himself was nowhere to be found, and when he did appear, he was drunk."

Imroz carefully evaluated his next words, avoiding Kitarisa's penetrating look. Damn the barbarian! And damn her!

"Is he, or is he not under your supervision?" the Ter-Rey asked bluntly.

"Great Lord, am I being accused—?"

"You are being accused of nothing," Assur's voice cracked sharply. "We are only trying to discover who holds authority over the physick."

Imroz cast a nervous glance at Prince Ramelek. It was unnerving looking at two men who so closely resembled one another both in looks and in temperament, although he fervently wished never to cross the Swordmaster.

"It is my understanding," Imroz began cautiously, "that while I am responsible for the physick himself, the arenas, baths, training rooms and warriors' quarters all come under Lord Ramelek's authority, including the surgery."

"The surgery and the physick are of one and the same purpose," Rame said heatedly. "I have warned Physick Nadir several times. I will not risk losing another warrior."

Imroz felt the blood leave his face.

Assur held up one hand to silence the furious Swordmaster.

"It seems we have a simple misunderstanding," Assur said. "This should resolve it once and for all, for both parties. Dolmina Imroz, the responsibility of the physick and his quarters shall be under your jurisdiction. As Physick Nadir has not proven worthy of his station, he is to be dismissed, but not until he has served a time in the cells. There must be some kind of punishment for his irresponsible behavior. Do you agree, Dolmina?" Assur asked while glancing at Rame.

"And, it shall be your duty to find another to replace him," Assur continued. "You shall see that the next physick is responsible, orderly, *and* sober. Am I clear?"

Imroz bowed slightly at the waist. "Perfectly, Great Lord."

"If the next physick proves unworthy, then I shall deal with both of you. Next time, I shall not be so lenient."

Imroz nodded.

"My Lord Rame shall report to me personally on this matter, as it progresses." Assur paused a moment to study him. "You may go now," he said more kindly.

Again, Imroz bowed and backed out of the chamber as swiftly as he could manage. Once out, he sighed, almost sagging against one of the guards.

Immediately, he pulled himself together and straightened up. The guards must not know how frightened he was. He smoothed the edge of one sleeve, then passed a hand over his tidy hair and the green cord. Once the initial fear had subsided, Imroz assessed his situation.

Very well, you savage animal, you have won this round, he thought bitterly, as he strode down the long corridors to his quarters.

The physick would be dismissed, cast out, thrown away just as the

Ter-Rey commanded. A replacement *would* be found. But Imroz would find a way to even things. No one, not even a Ter-Rey could humiliate him and dismiss him like a disorderly schoolboy without paying a price.

He would have to think of something quickly. He must think of a way to strike back in such a manner as to inflict equal humiliation, if not more. He must think of a weak place, someplace where Assur was most vulnerable. Princess Kitarisa? The Ter-Rey was hopelessly, foolishly in love with her.

No. He promptly dismissed that idea. If Assur suspected anything or sensed the slightest harm toward Kitarisa, Imroz knew for certain the Ter-Rey himself would personally carry out his sudden and hideous death. If not the Ter-Rey, then that madman, Rame.

But there *was* someone else. He smiled as he thought of Lady Davieta—gracious, serene and charming, like the princess. He thought of her soft, creamy body yielding to his embrace and completely helpless in escaping him. Imroz licked his lips in eager anticipation.

Take care, barbarian. I will have the last word in this matter.

Imroz strode down the corridor to the stairway that led to the dungeons and cells below the great keep. The physick was being held in a special chamber, not quite a cell, but a severe- enough confinement for him to know he was a prisoner of Daeamon Keep. Imroz would dismiss Nadir, but not until he had given him a harsh reprimand.

The guard stood aside when Imroz approached and allowed him to enter the tiny room where the physick awaited his sentence and punishment.

Physick Nadir lay stretched out on a bare pallet fastened to the far wall, his arm over his eyes.

"Get up," Imroz snapped.

The startled physick sat up, blinking and rubbing his eyes. Mercifully, he was sober, Imroz noted.

"Dolmina?"

"Sleeping off another drunken night, I see," he said sharply, seeing the physick's disheveled state and wine-stained tunic. "You should be thanking the Goddess you are alive and have not been boiled down to your bones. By some remarkable stroke of fate, the Ter-Rey has spared you."

"Spared me from what?" the physick snarled, coming to his senses and rallying to Imroz's verbal attack. "I have done nothing!"

"That is exactly the point; you did nothing. Have you thought what would have happened to you if that warrior had died, had the princess not intervened?"

"The Goddess would have Summoned him—"

"He would have been dead! And so would you, you gibbering imbecile," Imroz retorted.

The physick jumped up from the pallet, fists clenched at his sides. "The princess was not where she should have been; she should have not interfered. I would have treated the warrior and he would have lived."

"That is not what I understand to have happened, physick. But, we debate a pointless issue. What is done is done." Imroz met the physick's bleary red gaze and shook his head. "The Ter-Rey has decreed you are to spend time in a cell as punishment. For how long, he did not say. When you have served your time, you are to be dismissed. You will leave Daeamon Keep and return to that hole of a place where you crawled out of."

"He cannot do that. I have served faithfully for many turns of the sun."

"Evidently, not well enough. Now you listen to me, physick. You thank the blessed Goddess you still live. By Her blood and blade, if the Ter-Rey had not decided your fate, you would have been left in the hands of that lunatic Swordmaster!"

Physick Nadir clamped his jaw shut, still visibly maddened by Imroz's tirade. He turned away from him and ran a shaky hand through dirty, thinning hair. "Well, now what? Where am I to go, especially in the dead of winter? I cannot leave."

"I do not care what happens to you. My only concern is how I shall replace you. His Highness has demanded I find a new physick, and quickly."

The physick glanced back at Imroz. "A new physick? Who will come to this keep in winter?"

The dolmina shrugged. "I have no idea, but it must be done. If I do not succeed, I will have to answer to the Ter-Rey and Lord Rame—a prospect I do not relish."

The physick sat back down on the narrow pallet and placed his hands on his knees. He watched as Imroz began to pace, then spoke cautiously. "I might be able to help you, dolmina, *if* we can make an arrangement...?"

"An arrangement? I do not like the sound of it," Imroz said.

"Do you want this new physick?"

"I must find a new physick or face the consequences," he added sourly, noting that Nadir was smiling now.

"I can arrange for a new physick, *if* you can manage to have me released for a short time."

"It might be possible," the dolmina said reluctantly.

"And I will need a message bird—a bird that will return to Port Eeas."

"Port Eeas?" Imroz asked, surprised.

The physick leaned forward, until he could clearly see the red-veined eyes and smell the stench of sour wine.

Nadir lowered his voice so the nearby guard would not hear him. "I will have your new physick, one that will please the princess and the wrathful Swordmaster."

Imroz took a hesitant backward step, uncertain of the look in Physick Nadir's eyes. The physick smiled slightly, a thin terrifying smile.

"He will be a physick that will change the very foundations of this Keep."

Chapter Four

ONLY THE GULLS heard the whispered hiss of the ships' hulls sliding against the sandy shore—dark ships and lean as the men who sailed them. No moon shone to light their silent landing. A cold winter's night welcomed the marauders to the windswept shores of the Ponos.

Through silent signals, the intruders crept up the crags and onto the rising shoreline to spot their quarry. Only the flickering light from the torches outlined the graceful lines of the Sacred Lodge.

It stood, facing west, toward the setting sun and the horizon where, as tradition said, the tribes' revered Daughter Ponosel had sailed away to find her resting place. The Sacred Lodge awaited her return, a place for Verlian's second daughter to receive her people. The Guardians of the Lodge maintained their solemn duties as protectors and of its most holy relic, Ponosel's Bow.

The lone night Guardian did not hear their approach as he had been too absorbed by his final duties. He made certain the long altar tapers had been lit and that the offertory vessels, set at the corners of the altar surrounding the Bow itself, were filled with the sacred four elements: grain, salt, water, and the blood of a white breok.

Again, he bowed solemnly to the altar and backed slowly to the door. Once outside, he would continue his night vigil until the dawn broke and his relief resumed the post.

The Warrior-Guardian carefully shut the great doors and turned around to face west toward the sea. As the ancient ritual demanded, he, like his brother Guardians in the Caverns, drew his two swords and crossed them over his chest to await the dawn.

At first, he thought it was only the cold air from the sea affecting him. He shook his head, clearing the heavy, smothering sensation threatening his ability to think. Bitter cold seeped into every part of him like icy tendrils threading their way through the very fabric of his being.

It was then he saw them, or thought he saw them: dark sinister shapes in the flickering light of the torches. He wanted to cry out loud, to warn anyone who might be near, but in that instant he knew his efforts would be futile. No one would hear him. Alone, he struggled to raise his swords against the encroaching enemy and the coldness threatening to steal his sanity.

In silence they surrounded him, menacing as death. Helpless, he watched as his swords were wrenched from his grasp, his knees knocked from beneath him. He fell to the ground and struggled to find his swords, reaching for them with useless arms and frozen fingers. Both swords lay just out of his reach—the faint gleam from the hilts seemed to mock him, taunting his efforts.

He heard footsteps behind him and the crash of offertory vessels and the tall tapers being flung to the floor of the temple.

They are stealing the Bow! Get up! Stop them!

More footsteps and a pair of boots stopping within inches of his face. A rough hand yanked him up until he saw the black eyes, fathomless and horrible—no whites, no pupils within their sinister depths.

"The Bow is ours, Talesian dog. Your usefulness as Guardian is over!"

Another pair of hands from behind reached for his neck and jaw. Pain seared across his throat and he felt the warm wetness of his own blood run down his chest, over the blue enameled hai'sten.

He had no strength and almost no will to live. What remained was only his hate. With the last of his determination, he looked at the enemy, burned the sight of those terrible eyes and the mark—the diamond tattoo with the knife thrust through it—deep into his memory.

They dropped him to the ground like a discarded garment. From the tortured angle where he lay, he watched them leave for the ships awaiting at the shore below.

Struggling for his last breaths, the Guardian held hard to the remainder of his life, praying for the Goddess to let him live long enough to tell his brother Ponos of this outrage to their tribe.

He choked on the hot blood running from the wound in his throat.

"Verlian, summon me!" he managed to gasp. "Permit me to tell them!"

THE SWORDMASTER, PRINCE Ramelek dar sa Sabiann, disliked formal functions—he disliked them even more than Assur, but he knew they were an undeniable part of being a prince. He made it his policy to avoid as many court functions as possible, but this one he could not escape.

His personal servant helped him into the webbed, harness-like garment that bound him around his chest and over the shoulders—the traditional Talesian garment for important occasions. Rame studied himself in the glass, reasonably satisfied. At least he wouldn't have to wear his swords.

"The arm guards, Trejik." He nodded to the attentive young man standing nearby who swiftly began buckling the guards from his wrists to the elbows, hiding the black firemarks burned into the inside of Rame's lower arms.

How ironic, he thought, that these marks, earned with such pride and endured in such pain, were covered up as if in shame. His own marks were different from Assur's. Only those in the direct line of the Ter-Rey were entitled to wear the rose and sword encircled by the crown. If Assur died without a son, then he would take the marks, but until that unwanted day, Rame bore the marks of House Sabiann, his mother's house: a great winged owl clutching a scythe—wisdom, diligence, and silent ferocity. Sometimes he wondered about the *silent* part.

He knew he was irascible. He angered too easily and sometimes that troubled him. Simple, unimportant things made him angry and the truly serious matters always sent him into a rage. Fortunately, he had enough sense not to use his temper in an uncontrollable manner. His hard-edged, hard-won discipline held him in rigid check.

Except for that damned physick. He had nearly smashed the man's head open against the wall, not caring if he had killed him.

He remembered how Princess Kitarisa had stood up to him and demanded certain action be taken in order to save Cai's life. And then, there was Lady Davieta. She had hung onto that bleeding, thrashing youth, her face turning paler and paler by the moment, until he noticed her huge dark eyes looking up at him for encouragement, making him realize how close she had come to passing out herself. It was the thought of those two frightened women that had made him so angry. Killing the physick would have been gratifying.

The servant finished buckling the guards and made one last adjustment to Rame's long cloak, fastened at his right shoulder and across his back to the left hip. It was nearly identical to Assur's attire, except for the fact that Rame wore his mother's colors, deepest blue and black, with touches of silver. A silver-linked neck collar encircled his throat and silver threads had been woven in and through the body harness.

The only other difference was his hair. He refused to wear his hair in the traditional Talesian style, bound up by a ring at the crown. Instead, his hair had been clipped shorter, and the heavy, black waves about his shoulders were held off his face by a silver band around his head and across his brow.

As a boy he had laughed out loud when the Holy Chanter explained to him that a warrior's long, tied-up hair was done this way so that Verlian would recognize her Summoned warriors and catch them up when they died in battle, to take them to Her Hall.

The other boys had stared at him, not amused by his irreverence. Rame did not care. He did not believe in such nonsense. In his own heart he had made a kind of truce with the Goddess: he would give Her strong, brave warriors to fight for Her, if She would give him the ability and wisdom to teach them. So far, the arrangement worked. He would not bind up his hair for Her or anyone else. Particularly Assur.

Rame turned to go, waving the servant away. He strode out of his austere rooms and down the corridor toward the great hall. Tonight, Assur would welcome another delegation from Kronos Keep, more Siarsi demanding retribution for the loss of their Sacred Hammer.

He passed several guards who snapped to attention. He turned another corner and was about the descend the stairs, when he heard a strange sound coming from the opposite end of the corridor.

Rame stared in astonishment. It was Lady Davieta kneeling on the floor, her pretty skirts spread out about her like the petals of a great blossom. Her arms were outstretched in front of her, while her fingers patted and touched the floor. She appeared to be looking under a heavy hall table, searching for something.

"Are you unwell, my lady?" he asked politely.

Lady Davieta looked up at him. An embarrassed smile touched her lips. "Oh, Lord Ramelek. No, I have lost one of my ear jewels. I was in a hurry you see, trying to fasten it while running down the corridor, when I dropped it. I think it is under here." She resumed touching the floor and peering under the table.

Rame squatted down beside her. Without thinking, he too, began examining the floor. "Perhaps, if I looked under here—my arms are a bit longer." Rame bent down and reached under the table and felt around until his fingers brushed something small and hard.

"Is this it?" he said, producing the ear jewel in front of Davieta's delighted face.

"Oh, my lord, thank you!" She took the jewel from his fingers and replaced it into her ear. She grasped his still outstretched hands. Rame helped her to her feet; she stood quite close to him and for a moment, Rame found himself staring into her dark brown, luminous eyes, completely captivated. She smiled up at him mischievously.

"Not only are you skilled with the sword, but also at saving ladies from desperate predicaments. I would have never found that jewel if you had not come along and then I would have gone downstairs..." She tilted her head to one side and laughed. "Unbalanced?" Her eyes danced at her own little joke.

Rame smiled, now utterly enchanted. "It is not often I have the honor of saving ladies. Most ladies dislike me."

She smiled at him and let go of his hands. "You must try not to look so angry, my lord. You frighten everyone."

"It is my gravest fault," he admitted.

"Well," she said warmly, taking his arm, "you must promise not to frighten anyone tonight, or I will make you pay the price."

"And what price is that?" he asked, becoming amused by her gentle teasing.

"I shall hide every one of my ear jewels throughout the keep and make you find them!"

It was a ridiculous threat, a shameless bit of flirtation, but it charmed him. Women never teased him. They always avoided him and his chilling manner, but he never really did encourage anyone.

"I promise I will behave," he said with equal warmth.

It pleased him that Lady Davieta chose to stay by his side and that she also chose to sit next to him during the great feast. He forgot about Wobran and the hotheaded young Siarsi lord making demands on Assur. He also forgot how much he detested public functions. Instead he found himself basking in the warmth of Davieta's presence. He even surprised himself by sharing a joke with her and laughing a little. The only thing he had not counted on was the unpleasantness of jealousy.

From his place at the high table, Rame studied this Lord Teel, one of the lesser Siarsi lords Prince Exbrel had sent to appeal to Assur. The young lord had ridden for nearly four days, across the frozen River Siar and the deep snows of the northern plains to Daeamon Keep, determined to have Assur grant Exbrel permission to ride against the Qualani and destroy them for their defilement of the Caverns.

The feast was in true Talesian form: plenty of food and of great variety. Even in the Siarsi hall of Kronos Keep, honor-feasts were always sumptuous, but as to be expected, the fare at Daeamon Keep was indeed a rich one. The young lord ate hungrily, downing many goblets of the good wine and sampling all the succulent dishes offered to him. Even as a lesser lord, proper respect kept him from joining in much of the joking and revelry, but occasionally he would cast an amused glance about the hall.

Like many Siarsi, he was dark to the point of being swarthy; his black hair and black eyes only served to heighten the severity of the black scars on his cheeks.

Teel's hand-picked warriors did not eat with the rest of the those in the hall, but chose to stand off to one side, arms across their chests, unamused and unaffected by the proceedings.

Rame held great respect for the Siarsi, even though they were usually too boisterous and occasionally too quick with their knives. He admitted to his own bristly temperament, but he also knew *when* to pull a knife. However, the theft of the holy relic had made everyone tense and short-tempered.

As he had promised Lady Davieta, Rame kept his good humor. He was even civil to Assur. The ugly matter with the physick had been resolved, at least for the moment, and harmony had been restored to the practice arenas.

Lady Davieta sat next to him, lovely and serene in her deep violet-hued gown and dancing little ear jewels. He was having a difficult time not staring at her. When the dining was over, the great tables were removed to make more room for some rather constrained entertainments.

Their high-ranking Siarsi guest moved about the hall, recognizing familiar faces and greeting old friends. When Lord Teel came up to Rame and Lady Davieta, he bowed politely to his former swordmaster.

"Swordmaster Lord Ramelek, I am honored to see you again," he said formally.

"It is good to see you again, young Teel. Your sword is still sharp?"

"Yes, my lord, and eager to cut Qualani flesh from their bones."

Lady Davieta looked down and paled. Rame did not miss the look and hastily redirected the conversation to something more pleasant.

"Lord Exbrel is well?"

"Yes, and as eager as I to decimate the Qualani. We will cut open each one of those defilers and place their entrails upon the altar of our sacred Daughter Siarsia. She shall have her revenge!"

Davieta's hand went to her throat. Rame scowled at the young, ardent Siarsi. Teel immediately recognized the warning look and tried to cover his blunder.

"Your pardon, my lady. I speak in such a manner because of the great wrong done to my people."

Davieta nodded and took a small step even closer to Rame, a gesture that pleased and surprised the surly swordmaster.

"Perhaps I can make up for my rude manners by offering a dance? Lady...?" Teel looked questioningly at Rame, who quickly remembered his own manners.

"This is Lady Davieta, the senior lady to Princess Kitarisa. She is Riehlian."

"Ah. Will you—?" Teel held out one hand for her to take, and gestured to the floor with the other.

Davieta hesitated, then accepted the young lord's offer, leaving Rame to watch. He had no personal animosity toward Teel, but the long-dead feelings of jealously surged through him. He had no claim to Davieta and Lord Teel was far too young for her. Still, he did not like it. He watched closely to see if the smiles and glances she bestowed on Teel were any warmer or more ardent than those she had paid him. He decided they were not and that eased his mind somewhat. She danced the circle dance around the young Siarsi lord with practiced ease. Riehlians were known for their courtly graces and Davieta fitted all those characteristics.

When the dance ended, Davieta dropped a hasty curtsey to Lord Teel, her face flushed, then moved quickly to resume her place next to Rame. He swallowed back the deep pleasure it gave him, knowing she clearly preferred his company over the visiting Siarsi lord.

"You did not enjoy your dance with Lord Teel?" he asked, noting her flustered appearance.

"No," she said firmly. "He is a thoughtless young man, too full of himself. It is not my custom to encourage bragging little boys."

With that, Rame threw back his head and laughed heartily. Davieta looked up at him, startled, and smiled.

"So, the Swordmaster does have a sense of humor."

"I find your opinion of Teel extremely amusing. It is an accurate description of him, one I wish I had thought of myself."

"I only hope the Ter-Rey recognizes it himself. Lord Teel is too...bold...too..." She struggled for the right word.

"Reckless?" Rame offered.

Davieta nodded.

"You are correct. I spent many hours trying to beat some sense into him. He is impatient and headstrong. He fights like a Siarsi, with a rage in his belly instead of using his head."

"Do you think Prince Assur will see this in him?" she asked.

Rame nodded. "He knows Teel and Prince Exbrel. Assur will know how to deal with them. The desecration of the Caverns is not to be dismissed, but he will not act until he knows all the facts. I may not get along with my esteemed nephew, but he is no fool."

Davieta studied him for a moment. In the course of their conversation, they had slowly made their way under one of the alcoves to the side of the hall, shadowed and partially hidden from onlookers.

"Why do you not get along with him, my lord?" she asked softly.

Rame sighed and shrugged his shoulders. For once he did not bristle at such a personal question. He looked down at her gentle face and questioning, soft eyes and felt himself give up some of the long-buried resentments. Without quite realizing it, her mere presence eased the ache in his heart.

"I suppose it is because I cannot quite forgive him for something that happened a long time ago," he confessed.

"I can understand why forgiveness would be such a difficult thing for you—for all Talesians. You are a very proud race. I know it is hard to forgive, especially when you feel some great wrong has been done to you," she said sadly.

"Has a great wrong been done to you?"

Davieta looked down. The pleasant mood suddenly shifted to an uncomfortable tension between them.

"Yes," she said quietly, so quietly, he almost did not hear her. She looked up at him again, her dark eyes liquid-soft with tears. "Forgive me, I must go. I have enjoyed our evening together, but we are talking of things that are too unbearable." She pressed her lips together, struggling to contain the flood of emotions he sensed she was trying to hide. She sketched him a curtsey then slipped around him and down the long corridor to the stairs. Bewildered, he watched her go. Her last words both surprised and thrilled him.

"Goodnight, dear Rame."

ONCE AGAIN, PRINCE D'Assuriel found himself saddling his warhorse Adzra, for battle. Young Lostic, who usually attended him, made certain his two swords and the five saddle knives were honed to razor-edged sharpness. Fresh clothing had been packed into the saddlebags and wrapped deep in a piece of thick fur was his gold circlet, the only indication of his high rank. It would be necessary for him to wear it once he faced the Qualani.

Assur sighed deeply as he shrugged on the heavy fur cloak. A mantle of long breok hair had been placed across his shoulders for added warmth and long fur-lined gauntlets ran up his arm, under the sleeves of the cloak to his elbows. Assur did not want to leave. The burden of battle was still close in his memory and he dreaded it. But the violation of the Caverns was something not to be dismissed.

He glanced across the wide courtyard where Rame was preparing to mount his own horse. It was necessary to have his uncle come along as Rame was one of the few Talesians who spoke the Qualani tongue. How Rame came to have this unusual skill was something Assur was never knew, but it was vital that there be complete understanding between himself and the Qualani chief.

Assur did not particularly relish having to deal with Rame at such close quarters, but there was no escaping it. So far, the Swordmaster had been relatively civil to him and he hoped it would continue throughout their journey.

Unlike his travels to the Eastern Lands when he only took six of his favored warriors, Assur now traveled with an entire company who were well armed and eager for a fight.

He also made certain another item had been placed into the packs on the baggage horses: borgonwort—the powerful herb that had saved Kuurus's life when he accidentally swallowed the blood of a marglim during a brief battle with them. Kitarisa had carried borgonwort with her during their escape from Sherehn Keep, and much to Assur's astonishment, he watched her use it to cure Kuurus of the deadly poisoning, even when the fierce Siarsi had resigned himself to die.

Borgonwort was now a mandatory addition in every warrior's saddlepack—Assur would lose no more men to the flesheaters.

Prince Achad approached him as he began winding the black woolen shirka cloth around his head and face, tucking the ends in at his throat.

"You *will* get along with Rame," Achad ordered in a low terse voice.

"Are you threatening me, Father?" The shirka muffled his reply.

"No, but it is time you two settled your differences. The Siarsi are begging for war. If the two of you do not handle this well, there will be a bloodbath."

"I thought it was you who said a Talesian is not afraid to die," Assur said sharply, jerking the cloth away from his mouth so Achad could hear him better.

"When it is merited, boy," Achad retorted. "You have lost almost two legions in the war against Kazan."

"They are blessed and with Verlian, but I take your point. It is something I have not overlooked. I will not waste men, Father, but if the Qualani have stolen the Sacred Hammer, then they will pay for their sacrilege. If I do not see to this matter, then the Siarsi will do it themselves and there will nothing I can do to stop them."

Assur readjusted the cloth over his mouth and nose then swung onto the big gray. He studied his father's face for a moment, noting there wasn't a trace of the usual humor in his dark eyes.

"Verlian's blessings be with you, son," Achad murmured.

Assur nodded and heeled the warhorse around, signaling the rest of the company to follow him.

The journey to the rendezvous point across the high plains of Talesia would be relatively easy. By skirting west of the Serpent's Back, the great serpentine lake separating Chaliset from Siarsi lands, they could make the journey in three days. Crossing the frozen lake was shorter in distance but treacherous and Assur would not risk one man or horse to the icy depths of the lake.

Mile after mile they galloped over the snowy wastes of the high plains, stopping only long enough to rest the horses and eat a cold meal. At night, traditional Talesian tents of breok hides, lined with the woven wool from their hair, kept out most of the wind. Small charcoal braziers added a bit of warmth, at least for the brewing of strong cups of shen tea.

Only a few hours of sleep were permitted so no one would become too deeply chilled or freeze to death. Even Assur took his turn sharing the night watch with the others.

He squatted by the brazier, warming his hands and sipping the strengthening tea. He happened to look up and realized he was sharing the same watch with Rame.

By what quirk of the Goddess had She decided that the two of them should look so alike, he mused, studying the slightly older version of himself. While Rame was only five sunturns his senior, Taksma's last son by a young and beautiful third wife, he could have been Assur's twin.

He glanced at Rame again. It was the woman, that Siarsi woman, who had separated them and caused the terrible rift that had kept them at odds for so long. He couldn't even remember her name now.

"Achad has counseled me that we should be settling our differences," he said bluntly.

"I thought we were getting along rather well, considering everything," Rame retorted.

"Yes, but his concern is for the outcome of this business. He does not want us to lose any more warriors than necessary. The success of this mission rests on the two of us. We cannot afford to be bickering."

"There is nothing to "bicker" over, Assur. The Qualani will drown in their own blood if they have committed this violation against the Caverns."

Assur nodded and took another sip of his tea. "And if not?"

Rame frowned. "You mean, if they are innocent?"

"I do not see how that is possible...the signs were clear. There were the beads and—"

"Circumstantial. Anyone could have placed those beads near the Master of the Forge."

"Are you suggesting a Siarsi could have done this?" Rame looked genuinely shocked at Assur's implication.

"No, not a Siarsi, but someone else...I don't know who, but it is possible."

Rame took his words in silence and Assur knew they were deeply unsettling words. Who but the Qualani could have done the atrocity? Surely not a Chaliset? It was unthinkable.

"Rame," Assur went on, "I want you to promise me you will consider the possibility that someone else stole the Hammer and murdered the Forge Master. I cannot allow the slaughter of the Qualani based only on the evidence of a beaded necklace."

"The Qualani are animals, savages..."

"True. But they are under my protection and rule as are the Huons and the Oduns. Besides, I distinctly recall being referred to as a "savage" and a barbarian. I believe Princess Kitarisa is still convinced we drink the blood of our enemies." He smiled at the thought of her.

Again, Rame paused to absorb Assur's words. "I will take this into consideration, Assur," he said slowly.

"Be assured, I am not totally convinced myself, particularly after I heard what happened to Lady Davieta."

Rame nearly started at Assur's referral to her.

"What happened to her?" he ventured cautiously.

"Kitarisa told me. Rame, you must keep this in your confidence." He shot a warning glance at him and Rame nodded.

"Lady Davieta lost all her family to a Qualani attack. They killed her husband and two little sons."

It did not take much to anger Rame and Assur immediately felt the white-hot heat of the Swordmaster's rage.

"Were they caught?"

"No. From what I understand, she and her family were attacked by renegades, outsiders of the tribe. Roadwilds. They have not been caught, yet. This is why we must tread cautiously. If we accuse these people of violating the Caverns, then we risk more indiscriminate attacks on innocent people and we lose more men."

"If they are guilty, then they deserve to die," Rame said heatedly.

"I agree and I will be the first to call the warriors to battle."

"Lady Davieta is an extraordinary woman to have endured such a loss and remain the lady she is today," Rame said.

"Yes, particularly since she was the only one who survived the attack."

Rame stared at Assur. "Survived?"

Assur drew a deep breath, knowing his next words would probably send Rame into a tirade.

"After they killed her family, they violated her and left her for dead."

Even in the deep shadows of the tent, Assur saw Rame turn white. He clutched the steaming cup so tightly, Assur was certain he would crush it.

"I will agree to your wish, Assur, but I will make a promise to you: I will find out who they are and destroy them."

Assur nodded grimly. "I will assist you."

He watched Rame down the last of the warming hot tea, knowing full well it would do nothing to thaw the dead-cold rage in his uncle's heart. Lady Davieta's attackers were already dead.

THE DISCIPLINED ROWS of the company eagerly followed their Ter-Rey, along with Wobran and his warriors and the Swordmaster Rame. For much of the journey, Rame kept to himself, riding alongside one of the Siarsi Lead Captains. It was actually quite agreeable to be riding out again, since he had not joined with the legions when they rode to fight with Riehl against Prince Kazan. He had been needed at the Keep to maintain order and to act in Assur's and Achad's stead.

Rame's own horse, a fiery mountain breed, had been excited and nearly unmanageable at the start of the journey, but finally settled into a ground-eating gallop, easily keeping pace with the others.

"That is an unusual horse, my lord," the Siarsi Lead Captain said politely.

"He is a Mountain Trigian, known for their endurance and their hardiness. He can survive on next to nothing."

"I have heard of them, but never seen one. They are quite rare?" The man nodded at the unusual coloring of the animal: a gleaming black coat with a blazing white mane and tail. Rame had chosen silver threads to be woven into the black bridle. Heavy dark blue tassels danced and fluttered from the bit shanks and cheek pieces.

"Rare enough," Rame responded shortly, ending their brief exchange. The Lead Captain took the hint and rode on in silence.

Rame chided himself for being so abrupt with the Lead Captain, but he truly did not want to talk at the moment. Other matters absorbed his thoughts: the violation of the Caverns; the Qualani, Lord Exbrel, and Lady Davieta.

He rarely allowed himself the time for women, much less thinking about one, but the image of Davieta would not go away. He had not seen her since the night of the feast for the Siarsi guests and the memory of her was quite pleasant. Most women irritated him, even his own niece, Sethra. Her bouncing, overflowing high spirits were often tiresome, even though he did love her dearly.

The majority of the women in the Keep stayed out of his way, thoroughly frightened by his brusque manner. But Lady Davieta was neither frightened nor impressed by his temper. Her calm, sweet presence seemed to cool the fiery blaze of his anger and took away the biting edge from his sharp tongue.

And then he thought about Assur's words, what he had told him about Davieta's attack. Rame's stomach churned; his blood boiled in his veins, beat behind his eyes and at the base of his skull. He recalled Davieta's sudden tears at the feast and understood her meaning when she spoke to him of forgiveness. He was suddenly in awe of her serenity and her remarkable sense of humor. It had been a long time since he had taken a personal vow of vengeance. He was so angry over the Qualani, he did not recognize his own growing feelings for Davieta as the justification for his revenge.

Rame's warrior discipline dissolved the heat of his rage, turning it into a cold knot of hate. Kill only when your heart was cold and without feeling. For Davieta's attackers, his heart was as cold and hard as the ice under his horse's hooves.

AT THE EASTERN point of the Serpent's Back, Tribe Prince Lord Exbrel himself awaited the Ter-Rey astride a huge roan. Behind him waited a company of mounted Siarsi, milling restlessly about, trying to keep warm and to relieve their tension.

Exbrel's face was wreathed in broad smiles as he greeted Assur in his booming, deep voice.

"My Lord Assur, the Siarsi are yours!" Exbrel pounded his back in friendly greeting the moment Assur's horse sidled up next to him.

Lord Exbrel reminded Assur of his father, only bigger and noisier. A huge man, Exbrel was as tall as the High Prince, but resembled a breok bull in size. A full black beard framed his round face. Black eyes, set into the severe black eye-patterns, danced like Achad's. His thick, black hair was caught up high by the traditional silver ring and braided through with leather thongs. The braids at his temples, laced with bits of bone and glass beads, beat against the hideous black scars on his cheeks, almost hiding the flashing, generous smile.

"It has been a long time, Exbrel," Assur said, tugging down the woolen shirka cloth from his face. "We missed you at the Rift Cut, fighting against Kazan and the 'Fa."

"Ah, I am only a poor, old man, left to watch the women and children," he said, sighing with mock dismay. "Soon I shall be left in the kitchens, a toothless nuisance."

Rame made a disbelieving noise in his throat and Exbrel turned to face him, grinning.

"And I see you have brought your ill-tempered uncle, Lord Assur. How are you Lord Rame?"

"Well enough," Rame answered curtly.

"I have brought enough Siarsi to more than make up for my absence at the Rift Cut. We shall dull our swords on a few Qualani bones, eh, Rame!"

The big Siarsi laughed, reaching across the space between them and clamping a friendly hand on Rame's shoulder. The Swordmaster appeared only slightly amused and returned a trace of a smile.

Exbrel turned back to Assur and was at once sober. "The Qualani must die, my lord, just as in the old days when they harassed our northern borders. Our brother Ponos will join us if we ask—I know it."

Assur kneed Adzra closer to Exbrel's horse and leaned over toward him so the nearby officers would not near him.

"Lord Teel and Wobran have made your demands quite clear. The Qualani will be punished, but *only if* it can be proven. I have lost many men fighting Prince Kazan. I will not risk any more, especially over a beaded necklace!"

Exbrel's face darkened, causing his black scars to look even more sinister. "My lord, the Qualani are guilty, I know it. Who else hates us enough to defile the Caverns?" Exbrel's voice rose angrily.

Assur raised a warning finger. "I will make that decision. I will hear their side in this matter, Exbrel. Not a hand will be raised against them, unless by my command. Anyone who defies my authority will be punished by my own sword. Is that clear?"

Exbrel frowned, clearly not pleased his lord's terse instructions, but he jerked his head down in a curt bow indicating his acquiescence.

"It shall be as you wish, Great Lord."

Assur nodded. "Then let us get moving. It is too cold to debate this any longer," he said with a thin smile, showing a return to the earlier friendly mood between them.

Exbrel grinned, then turned in the saddle, raising his arm to signal the awaiting Siarsi. Quickly they joined ranks with Assur's company and without another word, Assur put his heels to Adzra's flanks and led his warriors northward to Qualani lands.

Chapter Five

IT TOOK TWO MORE days of slow but steady progress to reach the foothills of the mountains that marked the boundary between Talesian and Qualani lands. No one trusted the Qualani, even though there had been an uneasy peace between the Talesians and the northernmost tribe.

For generations, they had openly defied Talesian interference in their tribal matters and were unafraid to defend their way of life as well as their ancestral lands. Qualani warriors had battled endlessly against Talesia over land boundaries, the rights to certain herds of northern elk, breok, water, and ultimately their own determination for self-rule. The last war had come to a bloody end with an uneasy peace.

Still under the Ter-Rey's rule, the Qualani reluctantly accepted Assur and only because the Talesian tribes greatly outnumbered them. The Qualani would be allowed to live as they wished, as long as they acknowledged the Ter-Rey as High Prince and they did not cross the Empty Border—the specified strip of land dividing their traditional territories from those of Talesia. Since the days of Assur's grandfather Taksma, there had been peace until the incident in the Caverns.

An apprehensive Exbrel removed his sword and held it across the bow of his saddle. "I do not like this, Great Lord," he muttered, casting furtive looks into the thickening woods. "I feel their eyes upon us. They could strike at any time."

"They could, but I believe they will think twice before doing so." Assur had prudently removed the gold circlet from his saddle pack and placed it firmly over his brow. No spying Qualani would fail to recognize him.

They slowed to a silent walk—the only sounds came from the creak of leather, the soft rattle of bits and the shuffling beats of so many hooves in the snow. For the most part, even the horses remained quiet, but occasionally, one would blow out explosively, or whicker to its traveling companion.

At the edge of a clearing, Assur ordered them to stop and wait. Long moments passed, until at last, they made out the forms of five Qualani advance scouts approaching them. Arrows were nocked in their bows, held at the ready.

Their leader stepped forward. The stocky man was completely

swathed in skins and hides; a hide quiver full of arrows was slung across his back and a large knife hung at his waist. Dirty blond hair escaped a leather cap with long, fur-lined earflaps. The wind had entangled the leather string ties in his full beard—portions of it having been braided with tiny beads and bits of glass, much like the temple-braids the Siarsi wore.

He spoke in the thick guttural accents of the Qualani tongue—a demanding tone, clearing wanting to know their purpose in approaching Qualani lands.

Rame nudged his boldly-colored horse to the front and lifted his right fist. "The Ter-Rey of the western tribes brings greetings to the People. Prince D'Assuriel respectfully asks to speak to the Holy Shalman," he said in perfect Qualani.

The tribesman acknowledged Rame's complete command of their language by nodding to him, then to the Ter-Rey. He appeared to recognize the gold band and the brilliant ruby, Verlian's Tear, dangling from Assur's left ear and gestured to his companions to lower their bows.

"The Shalman rests in his winter lodge. He will have no dealings with Talesian intruders. When the snows melt, he will consent to see the Ter-Rey."

Rame swiftly translated the scout's words to Assur. Exbrel bristled and fingered the hilt of his sword.

"Lift that blade, Exbrel, and I will use it to cut out your eyes," Assur warned in a low, angry voice. He turned to Rame. "Tell the scout that this meeting cannot wait. It is of the greatest importance to the Shalman as well as to the Qualani tribes. Tell him in the firmest tones, I *must* see the Shalman."

Rame nodded and turned back to relay the message. The Qualani scout appeared uncertain. He gestured to his comrades and began to discuss the situation.

"Well, now what do we do?" Exbrel asked irritably.

"We wait," Assur said, tugging the edges of his fur cloak around him and resettling himself into the saddle.

The Qualani scout looked to have come to a conclusion and stepped forward again.

"We will take the Great Lord along with The-One-Who-Speaks-As-Us, and three of your warriors to the Shalman. The rest must stay here."

Rame relayed the instructions and Assur nodded his assent. He motioned for Kuurus, Wobran, and young Lord Teel to come forward and eyed Exbrel who was about to protest his selection.

"You will stay here and hold the companies. If we are not back by the mid of the night, you must assume something has gone wrong and consider an attack—then send for reinforcements."

Again, Assur raised a warning hand both to Exbrel and the fiery Teel. "I will remind you once more: until I have heard all the factors you will do nothing. Hold your men, Exbrel. The first man who raises his blade against my orders, will die by mine."

He didn't wait for their nods of obedience, but spun the great gray about and headed after the jogging Qualani scouts just ahead of them.

The five skin-clad men led them tirelessly through the deepening woods toward the Qualani encampment. The sun was nearly gone as they crested the last ridge before descending into the village settled deep in a hidden mountain valley. More Qualani warriors lined the outer boundaries of the village—their bows also nocked in preparation for a battle. They eyed the Talesians warily. Outsiders and strangers were rarely seen in Qualani villages, especially those who were their most hated enemy.

The entire village consisted of long wooden lodges covered in bark. An opening in the roof relieved the smoke rising from the fire pit inside. The lodges were placed in two large concentric circles, surrounding one large lodge at the very center of the village, the Shalman's lodge. The inner circle of lodges protected the women, the children, and the food stores. The outer circle housed the men and weapons.

Assur, Rame and the others were not permitted to ride through the village, but forced to dismount at the outer circle and leave the horses. Both Rame and Assur noticed there were no women to be seen and no children played within the inner circle. Suspicious Qualani warriors watched their every step until they stopped at the opening before the Shalman's lodge.

"You will wait here until the Shalman agrees to see you," the first scout informed Rame, who in turn told Assur.

The time dragged on interminably as they waited in the bitter cold, until the lead scout came out of the lodge and motioned for them to enter.

"The Shalman will see you now, but you must wait for him to speak first."

Assur nodded and ducked his head under the large hide that served as a doorway to the lodge.

Inside, the light was dim and shadowy, the air thick with smoke.

A fire snapped and flickered from the central fire pit. Simple pallets covered with furs lined the walls of the lodge. Cooking tools and other implements hung from the arching beams above their heads and a wooden rack filled with long spears stood by the entrance.

To the left of the fire pit sat the Shalman. Instead of a withered old man with stringy, gray hair and rheumy eyes, a far younger, vigorous-looking man sat before the fire, back straight, his eyes staring directly into the flames as if unaware of their presence. Unlike the other men of the village, the Shalman was completely draped in a heavy breok-hair robe and fur cap. From the edge of the cap dangled dozens of claws—bear claws—the symbol of his high position among the Qualani as their Shalman, their holy man and leader.

Assur and the others bowed politely and waited for the lead scout to indicate they could sit in the Shalman's presence.

Five cut log sections had been placed in a row near the Shalman and Assur sat down on the one closest to him. The others followed his lead, but watched nervously as several armed Qualani warriors stepped from the gloom and surrounded their Shalman.

The Shalman appeared indifferent to their presence, until after more waiting, he finally cleared his throat and spoke to Assur while still staring into the fire.

"Why have you come, High Lord of the Talesians?" he asked calmly. "What brings you to the lodges of the People?"

Once Rame had translated the request, Assur too, cleared his own throat and began speaking, choosing his words with the utmost care.

"I bring you grave news that may involve the people of your tribes, Holy Shalman. Not long ago, the great Caverns of the Siarsi were attacked by an unknown enemy. The Sacred Hammer of Siarsia was stolen and the Master of the Forges was slain. An object was found near his body. Holy Shalman, beneath my robe is that object. If you will allow it, I will reach for it and show it to you."

Rame translated his words with deliberate slowness, so the Shalman and the warriors watching them would not misinterpret his movements. The Shalman nodded, still not turning his gaze from the flames.

Assur reached within the folds of his fur cloak and pulled out the necklace. He set it before the Shalman's feet.

The Shalman never moved.

"You are here to accuse the Qualani of this crime?"

"No, Holy One, only to inquire if you were aware of it."

At last the Shalman turned his gaze to rest upon Assur. He studied him for a moment and then spoke—in flawless Talesian.

"The-One-Who-Speaks-As-Us, speaks your words truthfully, Great Lord. How is it he has your face, but not your face? Is he your womb-brother?"

"No, but he is close to me by blood. We believe it is our Goddess who has caused the similarity."

"The Qualani do not worship the goddess Verlian, but the mothersun, She-Of-The-Light. Perhaps she has given the world two warriors of the same face to carry out one purpose."

Assur nodded, careful not to debate the issue and antagonize his wary hosts.

"The Qualani did not steal the Hammer of the Scarred Ones," the Shalman said abruptly. "We have no quarrel with them; we are at peace. The neck collar is not proof. Anyone can place such a thing wherever they wish."

"Agreed, but it is our only clue. I was hoping you might have new information, or perhaps your warriors might know who has done this."

The Shalman narrowed his eyes shrewdly. "You speak carefully around your true meaning, High Lord. But again, I tell you, the Qualani know nothing of this. We are in winter sanctuary. The breok and red elk will not return to us until the snow has melted. We would not waste our strength to commit such an act. For what purpose would it serve the Qualani to steal the Hammer?" The Shalman's voice rose a little from its customary calmness, betraying his anger.

Assur could sense young Teel fighting his own rising hostility toward the Shalman and quickly responded before the hot-tempered Siarsi said anything foolish.

"It was the same question I asked myself. For what purpose would the Qualani do such a thing? I am only searching for possible answers. Perhaps there have been Outcasts of the tribe who might try to arouse new troubles between our people," Assur said cautiously.

The Shalman said nothing for a moment, as he considered Assur's words.

"It is a possibility. There is a band of Outcasts, but they are known to ride far to the east on the other side of the Adrex, near Riehl. But they are too few in number and would not have the courage to make such an attack."

Assur knew Rame was seething with curiosity over the Shalman's new information, impatient to ask questions and find out if these Outcasts were the same ones who had attacked Lady Davieta.

Assur reached down retrieving the beaded necklace and returned it to the inner folds of his cloak. "Would such Outcasts leave their neck collars behind them, if they did commit such an attack?"

"Outcasts may not wear the collar of the People once they have been turned away from the tribe. It was probably stolen," the Shalman said.

"Then perhaps, we can help you in locating these Outcasts and speak with them," Assur offered.

"They are unworthy, despised. The Qualani will have nothing to do with them. Yet, if you wish, you may seek them. They are led by One-Having-No-Name. He is an Outcast who has no name and has no a'kenns within his spirit to guide him. His band is to the east should you wish to find him. You will know him at once—the mothersun has chosen to punish him. She has blinded him in one eye." The Shalman touched the outer corner of his right eye and nodded toward Rame. "You have much interest in this man, One-Who-Speaks-As-Us," he said to Rame.

"There is someone who has suffered by the hands of these Outcasts, Holy Shalman," Rame said in a low, tense voice. "They must be punished for this."

"Then it is the wish of the mothersun that you two, of the same face, must find these Outcasts. Two, who are one, to fulfill the same purpose."

The Shalman stood up indicating the interview was at an end.

Assur rose, followed by the other four and bowed again to the Shalman. "We are grateful for your time, Holy Shalman, and will now leave you."

"You will not attack us, High Lord?"

"There is no reason to—"

"No! The Qualani must die!"

Instantly, Wobran and Kuurus turned and leaped on the man who had spoken those words, wrenching the saddleknife from his hand. Six Qualani bowmen lunged in front of their Shalman, arrows aimed directly at Assur's head and chest.

Disregarding his own life, Assur strode past the bristling arrows and stood before a sullen Lord Teel who was now on his knees. Assur drew back his right arm and backhanded the young Siarsi lord in the face.

"How dare you shame me! How dare you defy my will and jeopardize our purpose in this mission!" Assur said through clenched teeth. "You disgrace your family and your clan. You have brought dishonor to your tribe."

"I beg forgiveness Great Lord," Teel said, nearly sobbing. "I...I forgot myself..."

"There is no excuse for this!" Assur snapped.

He turned to face the Shalman, who had remained surprisingly calm throughout the entire incident.

"I will not pardon this man's act of treason. With your permission Holy Shalman, I will execute him here and now."

There was a long, tense moment as the Shalman appeared to consider Assur's words, weighing them against the outrage nearly committed against him. A new and violent war between the Qualani and Talesia hung in the balance—a war which would certainly signal the end of his people forever.

The Shalman nodded his assent and signaled his warriors to withdraw. "I have been told a Talesian warrior will not be Summoned by your Goddess if he dies in disgrace."

"This is true, Holy Shalman," Assur said grimly while motioning for Wobran and Kuurus to remove the offending Siarsi warrior and take him outside the lodge.

Once outside, an eager crowd of curious Qualani warriors gathered around the tall, strange visitors to watch the grim spectacle.

Assur watched as Rame took over the proceedings for Teel's execution. He shoved the young man to his knees, facing the Holy Shalman. Swiftly, he removed the Siarsi's swords and the heavy fur cloak then set them in the snow at Assur's feet.

"You shame me with your tears, Teel," Rame growled at him in a low voice. "You do not die well and deserve no grace from Verlian."

Teel said nothing, but lowered his head submissively and placed his palms down flat in the snow by his knees. The cold night air whipped the shank of his long hair across his face, but he made no effort to remove it.

Assur picked up the two sword scabbards from the fur cloak, and with both hands, extended them toward the Shalman, bowing slightly.

"I offer you this warrior's swords as forfeit for his life and honor."

The young Siarsi trembled, facing the ultimate humiliation to his family and clan.

The Shalman took the swords and returned the bow.

"I accept this offering and will pray to the mothersun that this warrior's death will repair the misunderstanding that has become between us."

Assur turned back to the kneeling Teel and signaled Rame to position him for the final stroke. There was a soft hiss of steel as Assur drew the sword from the scabbard on his back and held it high above Teel's head.

"I will allow you one moment to ask Verlian's forgiveness," he said coldly.

Lord Teel nodded; his lips moved rapidly as he prayed the last words any man would hear.

A soft whoosh was the only sound in the Qualani encampment as Assur's blade descended on Teel's neck. The stroke was clean and swift. Teel sank forward into the snow, dead.

As was custom, Assur wiped the blood from his blade with the ends of Teel's hair and replaced the sword on his back.

"We will not defile your ground with his body. We will take it to his family."

For the last time, Assur bowed curtly to the Shalman, turned and strode toward the awaiting horses.

Teel's body was wrapped in his cloak then strapped to the back of his horse. Without a backward glance, the four remaining Talesians rode out of the Qualani encampment, back to the awaiting Exbrel and the companies of warriors.

Rame rode quietly beside Assur, then spoke. "That was the correct thing to do."

Assur did not reply for a moment, but stared directly ahead into the dark forest.

"Yes, but I did not want to do it. Teel deserved to die, but it should not have happened. He knew the price. It is such a waste!"

Rame said nothing; Assur knew he had no words of comfort, but honor had been restored to both the Siarsi and to himself as the Ter-Rey. Honor and duty were things all Talesian warriors understood and nothing was said when Kuurus handed the reins of Teel's horse to a grim-faced Exbrel.

When the first pale streaks of dawn touched the eastern skies, the long columns of warriors broke the rough camp and resumed their cold journey back to Kronos Keep. Grim silence pervaded the ranks of both Siarsi and Chaliset warriors. Lord Teel's death had served to reinforce Assur's absolute authority and his promise to deal fairly with the Qualani. It also reminded every warrior of their own oaths and bonds to their High Prince.

No one doubted Assur's right to take Teel's life, but uneasiness rose among both Siarsi and Talesian. Loyalties were suddenly in question. Had not the Qualani been the cause of these terrible events? Or was Lord Assur right?

The discipline of silence forbade anyone to speak as they rode through the deep snow along the base of the Adrex, but Assur felt their unrest.

Even Exbrel remained quiet, although it was clear he was not pleased with the outcome of the meeting with the Shalman. Honor had been restored, but it was he who would have to tell Lord Teel's family of his death and that the young warrior's swords were now in the hands of their most hated enemy.

Lady Pryma, Teel's mother, would undoubtedly slash her own cheeks and wear bloody-red mourning for the rest of her life.

Near the mid of the day, the company was permitted to stop and rest. Hasty meals were eaten from the saddle—the flat, cracker-like teki-bread, some cheese, and a handful of dried breok meat. They were allowed low conversation and Lord Exbrel took advantage of the reprieve to speak to Assur.

"My lord, if you are convinced the Qualani did not commit the atrocity against the Caverns, then who would have done this? There are none else this side of the Adrex who would dare attack a stronghold of Talesia, much less the Caverns."

"It is a disturbing question, Exbrel. I do not know. The Qualani fight fiercely, but they do not have the strength or the means for such an attack. Besides, they are in winter sanctuary. There was no *reason* for them to attack us and risk annihilation."

"Then who else? The Oduns are too far east, the Huons are also too far away."

Assur lowered his voice. "Unless it is from within us."

Exbrel looked alarmed. "Treason? That is...unthinkable."

Assur nodded. "But even if there was an attack by one of our own tribes, it does not explain how they entered the caverns unseen and unheard. Talesian stealth is well-known, but we are not that clever."

"Then it must be something else. Perhaps an unknown force of some kind...something we do not know."

Assur nodded again. "That is what I fear. Something we do not know and cannot fight."

From the surrounding trees, two patrolling outriders suddenly burst into the clearing and galloped directly toward Assur and Exbrel. Steam rose from their sweat-stained, heaving horses as the warriors reined them to a stop.

The nearest warrior jerked the shirka cloth away from his face and nodded briskly to Assur. "My lord, there is something you must see, right away."

"What is it?" he demanded, immediately alert. Adzra picked up the other horses' excitement and began to paw the snow.

"There are marglims, my lord," the other said. "A great horde of them and they are attacking a band of warriors. We do not know who they are."

Assur wheeled the gray around and signaled to Kuurus and the others to follow. No shouts were raised, no battle cry rang through the deep woods as they galloped after the two outriders.

From the top edge of a low ravine, Assur and the entire company looked down upon a too-often repeated scene: humans battling desperately against the flesheaters—marglims. A horde of at least thirty of the creatures surrounded a mere handful of unknown warriors, bravely holding their own against the odds.

Exbrel made a face and pulled his shirka cloth up higher over his nose. "I am surprised we did not smell them."

Assur did the same, tucking the ends of the black wool around his throat. He pulled both swords from the scabbards on his back and nodded to Rame and Kuurus, who were also making their own preparations. They had no time to lose. The marglims ate anything that moved, even while it was still alive and fighting for its life.

The signal was given. Dozens of Talesian horses were urged over the edge of the ravine and down the steep slope toward the clearing below, the snow billowing and churning under their hooves. At last war cries were permitted and the piercing, bloodcurdling sound rose above the unsuspecting marglims, drawing their immediate attention away from their prey.

Marglims. The unclean ones. Flesheaters. The ones you feared in your dreams. Generations of children had been induced into obedience by the mere thought of one of the gray-skinned creatures. While stupid, they were quite strong and a considerable threat to anyone traveling through the woods.

The huge man-like creatures stank of carrion and blood using their taloned, claw-like hands to rip living flesh apart and devouring its prey while it still breathed. In spite of the intense cold, they were hairless and chalky-gray in color. Their wide, flat heads bore large scoop-like ears and long tusks grew from massive lower jaws. They hunted in large packs of twenty or thirty and if they were not stopped in time, a good sized herd of deer or even red elk were devoured in moments. An unarmed human had no chance.

Five warriors stood in the center of the clearing, the remains of their dead and dying horses around them in the blood-stained snow.

The men were still on their feet and fighting, but the arm of one warrior was drenched in blood and hung uselessly at his side.

"They are brother Ponos!" Assur heard Exbrel shout above the carnage and noise.

Surprised, the marglims turned to face their attackers and howled in pain as Talesian swords found their marks.

Warhorses were urged beyond their inbred terror of the beasts and rose on their hind legs to strike with sharp hooves and teeth.

Assur swung Adzra around and spurred him toward two marglims that had managed to single out one of his own warriors and his horse. One marglim lunged for the horse, grasping the animal by the neck with its talons. It sank its hideous teeth into the flesh just behind the ears. The horse screamed and reared, nearly flinging its rider to the ground. The creature would never let go unless its arms were chopped from its body, or it was killed.

Assur drove his right blade deep into the beast's back. The marglim roared and let go of the warrior's horse, trying to reach behind it to remove the source of the terrible pain. Kicking his foot free of the stirrup, Assur placed his heel against the marglim's back and pulled the sword free. Blood gushed from the wound and the creature sank to its knees. In brutal chopping strokes, he brought his swords down again and again, cleaving the marglim from shoulder to breastbone. It groaned and fell forward into the snow, still flailing uselessly at its prey.

The second marglim lunged for the rider and almost managed to pull him from the saddle but the warrior slashed down furiously, cutting the vile beast into dozens of bloody wounds.

This time, Assur drove both blades into the creature until it was forced to let go of the warrior's leg. He glanced at the Siarsi—his fierce black eyes just showing above the shirka. He nodded to him and the warrior plunged his own blade into the marglim's chest. The beast staggered back, choking on its own blood and fell heavily into the snow.

Assur turned again to face more of the hated beasts. Above the shouting and death screams, he saw Rame, fighting like a mindless machine, striking at marglims with ruthless accuracy. Four of the creatures lay beneath the churning hooves of his fiery mount and a fifth had been backed into a tree. Rame spurred his fearless horse toward the beast and plunged both blades into the marglim's throat.

Slowly, methodically, all the creatures fell beneath Talesian swords. Not one could be left alive—if any marglims survived, they would follow after them, relentlessly, until their horses became exhausted and too weak to fight.

When the last marglim fell, Assur looked about at the panting warriors. Even he was breathing hard from his exertions.

"Anyone killed?" he called out. "Has anyone swallowed their blood?"

The warriors coughed and struggled to regain their breath.

"None, lord," he heard Kuurus answer.

From the center of the clearing, the five Ponos slowly resheathed their swords. Their leader stepped forward and offered a tired bow to Assur.

"A lesson has been well-learned, my lord prince."

Assur blinked in surprise at the man before him. The red-patterned eyes were barely distinguishable from the blood on his face.

"We Ponos have forgotten the dangers of the marglims. We are not bothered by them, living so close to the sea, but I thank you for your timely intervention."

"How do you know who I am?" Assur asked.

The Ponos warrior tugged down the shirka, but did not smile, only nodded to him in respect.

"Do you not recognize me, Great Lord? I am Prince Saar of the Ponos."

Assur resheathed his own swords and swung down from Adzra's back. "Saar?" he asked incredulously.

"Yes, lord."

"What brings to you these woods? Certainly you can send others on the errands of a tribe prince?"

"Not this time, my lord. We were on our way to Daemon Keep to seek you out and bring you grave news."

Assur frowned and stepped closer to the Ponos lord.

"Bad news? By Verlian's blood, I need no more bad news."

Prince Saar shook his head sorrowfully.

"There is chaos in our land. My people are near to rioting. My Lord Assur, the Sacred Bow of our Daughter Ponosel has been stolen and the Warrior-Guardian of the Lodge has been slain, butchered!"

Chapter Six

THE DOMED KEEP of Kronos shone pale pink and icy blue in the faint morning light. The great Keep, set high on the knoll of a hill, was patterned after the shape of the traditional Siarsi tents—the tents of a nomadic people who, for hundreds of sunturns, had followed the breok and raised horses on the open plains. Four slim turrets—graceful, intricately carved spires—stood at the four compass points of the Keep.

Unlike the symmetrical order of Riehl, or the imposing size of Daeamon, the city surrounding Kronos Keep sprawled in a haphazard fashion—a city filled with mysterious alleyways and back lanes, countless bazaars and markets—full of secrets and hidden places. It was a colorful, noisy, wide-open city, catering to peoples of all tribes and clans.

Even in the dead of winter, Kronos managed to give the impression of an unending fair: loud street vendors hawking their wares, horse traders with strings of wild-eyed, unbroken horses, and the merchants standing behind their stalls, vying for the purses of citizens and travelers alike. Jugglers and fools played for the odd coin, and everywhere, there was the rich smell of breok meat roasting on spits over open fires.

The Sacred Hammer might be stolen, but business was business.

The somber columns of returning warriors rode silently through Prince Exbrel's city. Even the most exuberant and vocal vendor held his peace as the Ter-Rey passed by—his grim expression stilling all activities within the colorful bazaar.

Inside the massive walls of the Keep itself, they dismounted and surrendered their tired horses to Exbrel's retainers.

Without explanation or apology, Teel's horse was given to a clan member. The warrior accepted the reins and stared in stunned silence at the headless body strapped to the horse's back.

The Siarsi love for color and opulence had been carried to near extreme when Assur entered Exbrel's great hall. It recalled the sumptuous palaces of ancient Volt with its rich draperies and luxurious cushions scattered over the bright carpets.

Assur had to keep a wry smile to himself. No real tent of the ancient Siarsi would have looked like this—like a place where the women of the silk rooms practiced their skills.

Assur permitted one of the numerous servants to remove his heavy furs, the sodden shirka cloth, and his swords for cleaning and sharpening.

More servants, slim-legged girls in long silken robes, hovered expectantly over their illustrious guests, bringing trays with steaming pots of shen tea, warm breads, and plates of nourishing meats for a hearty early morning meal. They set the food on the low honeywood tables and retreated hastily from Exbrel's scowling looks. It was a rare thing for Lord Exbrel to be in such a foul temper.

A palpable, unsettling tension strained the usual conviviality of the hall. More servants brought additional food to satisfy their hungry guests, fluttering like large, unwanted insects until Exbrel's patience was exhausted. He pounded one meaty fist on the low table, rattling the platters and goblets. The servants scattered to the edge of the hall.

"Are you now convinced, my lord!" Exbrel thundered. "The Qualani have committed two crimes, so contemptible I can barely speak of it. If you do not order the immediate annihilation of the Qualani, I shall not be responsible for the actions of my own people."

"You are wrong, Exbrel," Saar interjected. "I do not believe the Qualani are responsible. There is something else."

Assur turned to face the Ponos lord.

"Why do you say this, Saar?" Assur asked.

"Because the Guardian of the Lodge lived long enough to tell us something." Saar reached inside his jerkin and pulled something out and tossed it onto the table in front of Assur. "It appears to be a Qualani neck collar, like the one found in the Caverns, except it is not a true neck collar. Look at it."

Assur picked up the collar and examined it closely.

"What makes it so different, Lord Saar?" Exbrel asked. "All the Qualani wear those."

"Yes, except this one is a contrivance, made to look like a Qualani neck collar. Look closely at those claws, my lord. You will notice that the claws are quite a bit smaller than those of a bear and the onyx beads are not onyx at all, but simple black glass."

"Telling us what, Saar?" Assur said while fingering one of the blackened claws.

"That they are not claws, my lord, but teeth; teeth cleverly fashioned to look like claws."

Assur quickly pulled the other neck collar from his own jerkin and held it next to the one Saar had handed him. They were identical.

"Teeth from what?" Exbrel asked dubiously. Assur handed him both neck collars for his own examination.

"Sharks," Saar explained. "Gray rock sharks. Their teeth are soft enough to cut or reshape with a sharp knife. A little briar root staining, and..." He shrugged.

Exbrel handed the neck collars back to Assur, who set them carefully on the gleaming surface of the table.

"And there are no gray rock sharks this far north, if I recall," Assur said.

"Yes lord," Saar agreed with him. "Gray rock sharks only inhabit the southern seas, where it is warmer."

Assur paused, thoughtfully stroking the narrow beard edging the line of his jaw. "What did your Guardian say before he died?"

"He was dying, of course, and could only manage a few words, but what he said was clear enough. He said: "narussss" and "tattoo". At least, that is what it sounded like."

Assur frowned. "It does not make much sense. What do those words mean? "Naruss" and "tattoo". Not much to go on. Anything else?"

Saar nodded and downed the last of his tea.

"We found keel marks in the sand along the beach near the Lodge. Footprints, too. There were at least fifty of them, my lord. Whoever they were, they came from the sea, not from the Qualani."

Assur absorbed Saar's information in silence.

"Then it is clear these marauders were also the ones who stole the Hammer." Assur rapped his knuckles nervously on the table. "But for what purpose? Who would want our most sacred relics?"

"Profit?" Exbrel rumbled from his end of the table. "The Hammer is silver and the sacred Bow is covered entirely in gold and breok horn."

"Any common roadwild would recognize them immediately. They could not be sold anywhere," Saar protested.

"Unless they were to be taken elsewhere...where they are not known?" Assur shot a questioning look to both Saar and Exbrel. He looked beyond Saar and his favored captain sitting next to him...to Rame. The Swordmaster held his cup in his long fingers, idly swirling the last drops of tea around in circles.

"You have nothing to offer, Rame?" Assur asked his sullen uncle. "What is your opinion?"

Rame set the cup down and looked up at him. "I am not sure, my lord. But one thing is for certain, these crimes were not done for mere profit. It is something else, far more sinister than just theft. No, the holy relics mean more to the thieves than money."

Exbrel shook his head, bewildered, stood up and bowed to Assur then to the others. "We will find no answers now, my lords. Come, we have all ridden hard, we are cold, and we have fought the vile ones. We must rest. You have all been here before and I commend you to my faithful dolmina to show you the way to your rooms."

Assur nodded in agreement, draining the last of his own tea, now gone tepid during their long conversation. He glanced across the table at his near-twin and suddenly knew Rame was right. The stolen relics had nothing to do with profit, but with war.

ASSUR WATCHED KITARISA walk toward him. The warm, summer breezes caught up her long hair and it fluttered behind her like a soft, dark banner. She was smiling at him, a loving happy smile. Grimy little fingers of a small dark-eyed boy clutched her hand. His black eye-markings seemed somehow out of place in such a mischievous face. Tucked in her other arm, Kitarisa held another child, a girl. She was fair as a little flower and her bright blue eyes—his eyes—were laughing at him.

The boy spotted him and pulled free of Kitarisa's hand. He ran to him, laughing and shouting, flinging himself at Assur, burying his face into his knees.

The girl squirmed free of her mother's grasp and also ran to him. A second small pair of hands grabbed for his knees.

Assur watched himself, laughing, as he swung the shrieking little girl over his head.

"Falla," he heard Kitarisa say. "Don't scream so."

He gathered his family close to him. At last there was peace in his heart.

And then, he looked over the top of Kitarisa's head and saw it. A chilling dread filled him.

Hideous dead-black creature; tongue slavering over razor teeth. A scaled, stinking body squatted over short legs that ended in long, yellowed talons. Cursed creature of the Catacombs; the changed form of a hated enemy. It hissed at him, spewing out its vile breath, reeking of sulphur and fire.

Assur moaned.

"Get behind me Kita," he whispered, never taking his eyes from the beast.

He saw his sword in his hands, but it was heavy. So heavy, he could scarcely lift it.

"Run, Kita," he shouted. "Take the children and run."

The beast coiled and drew back its elongated head. It reached upward, exposing its long neck to the sky. He saw the mark, a tattoo embedded in its throat—a diamond with a dagger through it.

The beast roared at him. Fire blasted from the great maw of its mouth. It looked down and cocked its head at him; baleful, yellow eyes searching and waiting.

Suddenly it lunged toward him. Its huge jaws snapped at his feet. To his horror, the creature drew back and again lifted its head to the sky with something held fast in its teeth. Barely missing flesh and bone, the beast held the terrified child by her skirts. His little girl. His Falla.

"No!" he roared back at the beast.

He looked at his hands. The sword had been replaced by a spear. The Sacred Spear of Chalisetra, the weapon of his tribe, gleamed in his hands. He raised it high over his shoulder and aimed for the vile creature's heart, just below the black tattoo.

"Falla!" he heard Kitarisa's sobbing scream.

The Spear flew from his hands, arrow-straight to its mark in the ashen scales.

The beast roared out in pain and fear; great gouts of blood gushed from the wound. It poured out in rank rivers, while the creature groped and twisted, trying to grasp at the gold-tipped spear imbedded in its body.

The ground burst into flames where the blood fell. It sprang up into white hot sheets, a wall of fire licking at the great beast, burning it, consuming it into a writhing, roaring mass of incinerated flesh.

He sank to his knees, sobbing. He could not find her—his little Falla.

Before I leave the sky, D'Assuriel!

"Assur!"

He jerked up, shaking, drenched in sweat. He drew in a shuddering breath and tried to calm his pounding heart. It took him a moment to shake off the effects of the nightmare and focus on the person before him.

"Assur, wake up. You are dreaming."

He looked into Rame's concerned face and almost sighed with relief.

"By the Goddess, I have not had a nightmare like that since... I cannot remember."

He sat up and pushed off the damp fur covering him.

"Is it dawn?" he asked Rame, who had retreated to the other side of the room to wait for him to get up.

"No, but near enough."

Assur noticed Rame was dressed for riding. He paced the room, slapping the long, fur-lined gauntlets against his thigh, eager to be off.

"We must go home, Assur," Rame said sharply. "We must return to Daeamon as quickly as possible. I know what that Guardian was trying to say. I have spoken to Exbrel's Holy Chanter. It was he who confirmed what I have feared the most."

Assur kicked off the remaining furs and stood up, reaching for his clothes and swords. "What is it? Tell me."

Rame turned to face him; there was no mistaking the serious light in his eyes.

"Narusuba, Assur. "Naruss" is Narusuba. Shadowmen, assassins. The Guardian of the Lodge was killed by Shadowmen. He tried to say it as he died."

Assur frowned, trying to recall the name.

"I thought the Narusuba died out in the Volten Wars, over three hundredturns ago."

"No, they fled to the Shygul Islands where they have been living, virtually unnoticed, until now. They most certainly killed the Master Forger and took the Hammer, too."

"What would the Narusuba want with the Bow and Hammer?" Assur asked, still not thinking quite clearly. He tugged on the heavy, leather jerkin and looped the swords over his back, the hilts rising just above his right shoulder.

"Dissension. To cause strife and conflict among us. A new war Assur, but this time against our own."

"Buy why?" He shrugged on the heavy fur robe and reached for his shirka and gauntlets. "There must be a better reason than that."

Rame shook his head. "I don't know, but the Bow and Hammer are gone. If I am right, the Spear will be next and they will strike at Daeamon Keep. They may be already landing on our shores."

Assur felt his heart chill to a knot of ice. The Sacred Spear— symbol of his rank and authority, the soul of the Chaliset people. His power and his right.

He thought of his nightmare and the beast he had slain. And the children. Those two little ones that were his but did not yet exist. His and Kitarisa's.

He felt a sickening stab of panic knife through his belly.

Kitarisa.

IT WAS NOT ONLY Dolmina Imroz's task to inspect all the rooms, corridors, and halls of Daeamon Keep, but it was also his unpleasant duty to see that the dungeons and cells were kept in good order. He detested this, as no dolmina serving any house in Volt would have had such a distasteful responsibility. But this was the Keep of the Ter-Rey and Imroz had to obey.

The lower levels, the dungeons, had retained their grim look from the days when the Keep was nothing more than an outpost on Talesia's western border, used to house warriors and to hold prisoners. Many of the chambers used specifically for torture had been closed off long ago. Prince Assur frowned on the use of torture as had Prince Achad, but there were the rare occasions when the hideous instruments were actually put to use.

Imroz shuddered as he stopped briefly in the central chamber where the worst of the tortures had taken place. How many luckless souls had died horribly in this chamber, he thought as he examined the swept floor and the instruments hanging neatly on the far wall.

They were all uncivilized barbarians who gloried in blood! How he was growing to detest them. If only he could get out and return to the warmth and serenity of Volt.

He strode from the chamber and continued down the dank corridors, passing the prison cells and up another set of stairs to the practice arenas.

Ever since that unpleasant incident with the wounded warrior, Imroz made certain the surgery was not only orderly, but immaculate. Physick Nadir had kept his promise. A new physick had been found and arrived within days after the message bird had been sent to Port Eeas. Physick Lael seemed a competent man and had a natural affinity toward neatness—a quality for which Imroz was eternally thankful.

As much as he feared the Ter-Rey, Imroz lived in constant, secret terror that the Swordmaster would find something out of order and have him carried off to one of those grisly tables in the torture chamber. Swordmaster Rame was no one to trifle with and Imroz vowed to make certain the new physick understood this, too.

There were only a handful of young warriors practicing on the white sand in the arenas, as most of the working sessions were over and nearly all of Swordmaster Rame's pupils were now resting or about other business. He scanned the arena for any possible defect, then hurried into the physick's surgery.

The room smelled of strong soap and the myriad odors of the herbs and medicines kept in the bottles and jars on the shelves. The physick was bending over the table, scanning what appeared to be some ancient volume.

"Ah, Physick Lael. Do I disturb you?" Imroz asked courteously.

The lean physick looked up and carefully closed the great book. He smiled and pressed a neatening touch to the high collar of his tunic.

"Indeed no. I was only perusing an ancient discourse on the setting of bones. Most interesting." He patted the old leather cover. "How may I assist you?"

"It is nothing, except for my weekly visit to see if all is in order. No serious injuries, I trust?"

"A few minor scrapes and cuts, nothing more. Without the leadership of the Swordmaster, I sense our brave warriors are holding back—not quite as bold in their practicing." A thin smile touched the physick's mouth. "Thus, I find myself returning to my studies while Lord Ramelek is away."

"And best to stay prepared should anything unpleasant happen."

"To be sure," the physick agreed, stroking the small patch of beard on his chin. "It was unfortunate that the previous physick so obviously failed in his duties. I wonder what happened to him?" he ventured cautiously.

"Hah!" Imroz snorted in disgust. "A fool if I ever saw one and a sodden drunk, too. He nearly cost me my own life." He jerked the edge of his long robe into place across his chest. "You must never cross the Swordmaster, Physick Lael, if you wish to return to your home in one piece."

"How so?" the new physick asked quietly.

"You know what happened. That fool, Nadir, made the mistake of threatening Princess Kitarisa right in front of the Swordmaster, while *she* was attending to a wounded warrior. I did not see it, but they tell me Lord Rame nearly killed that fool—threatened to skin him right then and there and hang him on the highest battlements!" Imroz shuddered at the thought. "I am certain he would have done it, too, if the Ter-Rey had not intervened. They are all animals, I tell you."

"How dreadful," Physick Lael said smoothly, unruffled by Imroz's story. "But whatever happened to this luckless fellow?"

Dolmina Imroz looked up startled at the serene-faced physick, then glanced about nervously.

"After he was taken into custody, he was put into one of the cells below. I was ordered to dismiss him and send him on his way, when he then assured me he would locate a new physick. I assume you knew of this?"

"Ah, yes" Physick Lael turned from Imroz to study the rows of vials and jars set on the shelves behind him. "I did receive the message and came as quickly as I could. However, it is a pity Physick Nadir can no longer be here. I would have liked to discuss some of his methods, however questionable they might have been and how he has handled some of the more serious injuries."

The dolmina watched the slim physick pick up one of the glass vials to examine it, then replace it carefully alongside the others. It was a curious thing, that a man from Port Eeas should look so remarkably like a Voltan, even down to the way he kept his long black hair tied back at the base of his neck with a fine violet-colored cord—violet being the color for physicks. Even his mannerisms did not speak of a man from a rough seaport like Eeas, but of someone with refinement and polish, with manners and restraint. Someone from Volt.

Imroz frowned.

"However, Physick Lael, you may wish to confer with our new Ter-Reya. She seems to have some knowledge of this work."

"An excellent idea. Perhaps we can discuss her methods," Lael said enthusiastically, dismissing any further discussion concerning his luckless predecessor.

Again, an uneasy sensation of familiarity flitted through Imroz. And something else...something vaguely sinister. Physick Lael's meticulous robes could not quite hide a lean, muscular body attuned to things far more deadly than simply wielding a surgeon's knife.

"But now," Lael said, moving away from the counter behind him. "I must accompany you on your rounds of the keep and see to my patients. Perhaps I will take a brief look at the poor wretches below...those in the eternal torment of imprisonment."

Imroz did not like the almost reptilian look in those cold black eyes. They were not the compassionate eyes of a physick, a healer, but expressionless. Dead. Imroz had the distinct feeling he was looking at a man who had utterly no interest in the work of healing, but strove for a darker purpose. He sensed corruption; he could almost smell it.

Dolmina Imroz hastily dismissed the notion as the two of them left the orderly chamber and headed down to the first level of cells. The dank smell was nearly unbearable for the fastidious dolmina as he pulled a handkerchief from his sleeve and pressed it to his face.

"Hideous place," he muttered to the physick.

"There are worse places, Dolmina Imroz," Lael said, unperturbed.

The first level guards let them pass with little trouble. They were Ponos—tall, cruel-looking men with the gruesome red eye-markings, rather than the usual black ones seen on members of the Chaliset and Siarsi tribes.

Of the three tribes, it was the Ponos who gave Imroz the worst frights. Unlike the rowdy, boisterous Siarsi, or the proud Chalisets, the Ponos were a silent and severe people, utterly devoid of humor or warmth. The red strokes underneath and at the outer edges of their eyes gave them the horrifying appearance of bleeding—a frightening and an effective weapon in battle.

The Ponos were usually as fair as the Siarsi were dark, and the two guarding the first level were no exception. The guard on the right eyed Imroz coldly.

"What is it you wish, Dolmina?" he said in a threatening voice.

Dolmina Imroz paused, growing panicky. Surely, the guard would see through their deceit. He passed a nervous hand across his hair and touched the green cord.

"The Physick Lael and I wish to check on the condition of the prisoners."

"It is the wish of Princess Kitarisa," Lael interjected. "She has been concerned for their welfare."

The Ponos guard was not thoroughly convinced, but let them pass with a jerk of his head.

"See the First Captain Rykal. He will show you the prisoners."

Imroz only nodded and hurried by the guards and on down to the lower tier of cells. Like the outer guard, the First Captain was also Ponos and appeared not at all pleased to see them.

"What brings you to the cells, Dolmina?" he said coldly.

"The princess, Kitarisa, has expressed some concern over the welfare of the prisoners. She has asked that Physick Lael and I look in on them and report to her," Imroz said smoothly. He glanced at Lael. The physick's face remained impassive as if he had not even heard Imroz's version of their little lie.

The captain scowled. "It should be of no concern for the Ter-Reya. A mere message would have been sufficient. However, it cannot do any harm. Come with me."

He picked up a heavy set of keys from his orderly table and a torch from the bracket in the wall.

The lower passageways were even darker and more terrifying than those above. Few torches lit the way and the captain's hand-held torch only served to cast deeper, more sinister shadows on the damp stone walls.

"How many levels are there below this one?" the physick asked.

"Five more, but they are all empty now. We keep only a few prisoners these days and they are all on this level."

"What have they done?" Imroz asked through the muffling of his handkerchief.

"There are two murderers, a thief who was caught stealing horses—a grave offence as you may know, Dolmina. A violator of women, one who tried to kill Prince Achad many years ago, and three who are mad beyond reason. Not many to watch over these days."

"Only eight. That is hardly worth bothering over," the physick observed.

The Ponos captain stopped and turned back to look at him and Imroz.

"There are few in Daeamon Keep who are foolish enough to break the prince's law; his justice is swift. When these few live out their sentences, there may be a day when all the levels will be closed up forever."

"A day when I shall rejoice," Imroz said softly.

At the turn in the passageway, the captain stopped at the first cell and handed the torch to the physick.

"This one's been here for thirty turns of the sun, they tell me."

The key in the cell door made a cold, eerie sound, a hollow rattle like the final breath of one dying. The heavy iron door scraped against the stone floor, its ancient hinges screeching in protest.

The captain took the torch from the nearby bracket and handed it to the physick.

"Here, you may see him for yourself."

The physick merely nodded to the guard then ducked into the black hole that was the opening to the cell. The amber, flickering light of the torch cast grotesquely-shaped shadows across the cell walls and out into the corridor. For long, silent moments, Imroz waited for the physick to emerge, growing more and more anxious.

Alarmed, the dolmina finally snatched the torch from the captain's hand and thrust it into the cell so he could see for himself.

"What is it?" Imroz asked, his panic rising upon seeing the physick's pale face.

"You must attend me, Dolmina," Lael called from the interior of the cell.

Hesitantly, Imroz bent down to enter the black, little cell. It took a moment for his eyes to adjust to the darkness and to the flaring brightness of the torches.

He looked at the floor of the cell and barely stifled a scream.

The dead, open eyes of Physick Nadir stared directly back at him. Behind him, Imroz made out the filthy, crumpled form of his cell mate huddled into the corner, mindlessly rocking back and forth, babbling to himself.

"Blessed Verlian!" Imroz gasped.

"It appears he has not been dead for long," the physick observed.

Imroz turned from the grisly sight, away from the hideous, gaping gash in Nadir's throat and the pool of blood spreading over the floor. He leaned against the entrance to the cell, suddenly sick. Who could have done such a thing? How did they get by the guards? And how, by Verlian's blade, did Nadir get into this cell?

The physick Lael appeared utterly devoid of fear or emotion, as if Nadir's mutilated corpse was no more unsettling than that of a dead rat. Lael grasped Imroz's arm and pulled him closer to the light of his own torch. His dead-black eyes seemed to have taken on a light of their own, like a cold-fire, searing into his soul. Imroz shuddered.

"Tell the guard it appears Physick Nadir was attacked by his cell mate," he said in a low, threatening whisper. "Tell him we need to get his body to the surgery for examination."

"But Physick Lael, how could he have done it? The man's an idiot, he has no weapons."

The physick took a harder, almost painful grip on his arm. "Do it," he ordered, "or do you wish every warrior in this keep down upon us?"

Imroz nodded and, after taking one last glance at the dead physick, stepped out into the corridor to relay Lael's orders.

The princess and Prince Achad would have to be informed. Dread crept through his bones like a penetrating chill from the sea. And when Assur returned from his journey north, Imroz would have to tell the Ter-Rey. He felt his bowels turn to water. Panic and dead-cold fear clutched at his belly.

He would also have to tell Swordmaster Rame.

THE BODY OF the dead physick lay on the surgery table, covered in a death shroud that was rapidly becoming soaked with blood.

Dolmina Imroz paced the confines of the surgery, wringing his hands, petrified with fear.

"When the captain makes his report to Prince Achad, I know I shall be made responsible for this. Verlian protect me!" he said despairingly. *And when the Swordmaster finds out, I shall be ripped limb from limb.*

"Calm yourself, Imroz," Physick Lael said soothingly. "The cells are under Captain Rykal's direct supervision. You are only required to make sure all is running smoothly in the Keep. It is the captain who must explain how the physick got into the cell. He must also explain how a complete imbecile would have been capable of killing a relatively robust and healthy man."

"*You* do not know the Swordmaster," Imroz said heatedly. "After the Ter-Rey has my head, the Swordmaster will have my body. By the Goddess's sword, how I hate them! They are still savages, Physick Lael. Three hundred sunturns has done nothing to change them. Do not be fooled by their so-called new civilized ways. It is all a sham, a mockery of the word. They will always be barbarians. They are born with a sword in their hand and will die with one in it!"

The physick drew back the bloody sheet from Nadir's body, exposing the severed throat.

"I shall make my report to the prince and tell him I suspect suicide as the cause for the physick's death, as I am certain the cell mate could not have done it. He will interrogate the captain, of course. Perhaps he has some clues...?" the physick's voice trailed off.

Imroz stopped pacing to look at Lael.

"Perhaps you are right. After all, it is not like I had a hand in this; I was never even near the cells. But still, the Swordmaster will question me..." His voice began to rise in panic.

"Do not jump to the conclusion of your imagined guilt, Imroz. There is, of course, no proof that you had anything to do with this."

"I have been seen arguing with the physick many times! We did not agree on several things. That of itself could be misconstrued as a possible motive."

"You are hysterical, Dolmina."

Imroz pointed a warning finger at the physick. "You do not know these barbarians. Especially Lord Rame. He will use this incident as an excuse to see me dead." Imroz turned from the table and passed a hand over his tidy hair. "If only I were in Volt...never to deal with these people again!"

"Not if I can convince him that the physick took his own life." Lael paused delicately. "There may be another way to detract attention from yourself?

"How so?" Imroz asked anxiously.

The physick slowly stroked the small patch of beard on his chin, studying the bloodied body before him.

"Tell me, Dolmina Imroz, are you acquainted with every part of the keep, every room and chamber, every corridor, hall and storeroom?"

The dolmina blinked rapidly, confused. "Yes, but..."

"And you know the whereabouts of the Ter-Rey's private quarters and those of the princess?"

"Yes, of course, but..." His eyes widened. "You do not mean to implicate Princess Kitarisa! That is more than madness, it is certain death."

"Your reasoning leaps beyond the point, Dolmina. Allow me to finish. I have no intention of implicating our sovereign lord or his lady, or anyone else of his family." Lael smiled slowly. "However, I may have a way to solve all our problems."

"*Our* problems, Physick?" Imroz asked skeptically.

"Exactly so," the physick said, returning his greedy smile. "You hate these barbarians, do you not? Their arrogance and their cruelties. You would do anything to be free of your obligations in this dreaded Keep and return to the warmth of Volt."

"Perhaps. I am not sure I understand you, Physick."

"Things can change, Dolmina, if you are cooperative," Lael said so softly that Imroz was uncertain if he had heard him correctly.

The physick moved closer to Imroz and the dolmina found himself taking a hesitant step backward, away from those cold eyes and the fathomless expression.

"We can defeat them, Dolmina," Physick Lael whispered, sending a dark chill up Imroz's spine. "But first, you must tell me a few of your secrets. Exactly where are the most sacred chambers in the Keep?"

Chapter Seven

A COLD DREAD PERMEATED Assur and all his warriors as they galloped back to Daeamon. Both Saar and Exbrel decided to accompany him and many warriors from both their tribes followed.

Assur drove both horses and men to their limits in a desperate race across the frozen plains and rivers. Rest was minimal; meals were mere handfuls of food. No fires were lit nor were any tents erected to offer sanctuary from the cold and snow. Warriors hastily dug through the snowy drifts to find scant forage for their horses.

As they approached Daeamon, Assur's throat went dry and his heart sank. Black, greasy smoke spewed from several of the rooftops inside the great wall. He spurred Adzra into a gallop toward the northern wall and gate. The gate itself still held firm, but he knew without having to see it that Daeamon had fallen from within. The side opening, the smaller gate designed to accommodate one horse and rider at a time, opened when the lone guard at the watch saw them approaching.

Adzra clattered through the narrow gate, across the false inner bridge that had been lowered and down the cobbled passageway to the innermost courtyard.

It was worse than Assur had feared.

The bodies of warriors lay littered across the courtyard, some still holding their swords in clenched fists. Many were alive, but immobilized on the very spot where they had fallen. The most chilling of all was that some appeared to be completely untouched, only dazed, as if they had not fully realized what had occurred.

He dismounted and ran to the nearest warrior, still struggling to shake the unknown effects of the attack.

"You! What happened?" he demanded, clutching the warrior by his jerkin.

The man shook his head and tried to focus on Assur's face. "They came so fast," he gasped.

"Who?"

The warrior shook his head again. "Don't know. From the sea...boats. There was cold...so old you couldn't fight or think." The warrior sagged in Assur's grasp, too drained to go on. Assur eased him back onto the cobbled yard.

He turned and ran up the stairs with Rame right behind him, taking three steps at a time. Inside the keep, both stared, appalled at the sight. So many dead, their throats slit, but the majority of the warriors appeared as if they were just awakening from a mind-numbing sleep. A few, more alert than the others, recognized Assur and stumbled up to him.

"My lord! Praise to the Goddess you have returned."

"Who has done this! Who has breached Daeamon Keep?"

The nearest warrior spoke first. "They were not warriors, not like we know them, my lord. Strange men with tattoos on their throats—and silent. They came at dawn."

"How did they get in? Who let the great bridge down over the chasm?"

"They did not get in that way, lord," the second warrior said.

Rame appeared to recognize the young warrior with a bandage still bound around his chest and nodded toward him.

"Then how did they get in, Cai?" Rame asked.

"Through the dungeons from below the keep, a passageway from the sea."

Assur nodded grimly. Only a handful of people in the Keep knew about the secret tunnel connecting the lower-most dungeons and chambers to the rocky shore just outside: he and Rame, Achad, Sethra, Kuurus and the fearless Nattuck. And one other. One who would need to know in case of a true siege and would be obliged to lead the women and children and the other citizens of Daeamon to safety while the warriors fought above. One who would know every corner of the Keep.

Assur looked at Rame's darkening expression and knew what he was thinking. Even Rame's sternest resolve could not hide the seething fury in those black-marked eyes. They had been betrayed by one who had been given their highest trust.

"Where is Dolmina Imroz?" Rame snapped at the warrior.

"I am not sure, Lord Rame. I believe he is gone." The young warrior passed an exhausted hand over his bound hair. "My lord, there is more bad news, much more." He looked hesitantly at both the princes before him, clearly unwilling to tell them what he knew.

"Tell us!" Assur demanded.

"It is Prince Achad. He...he did not survive the battle. He was slain, defending Her Highness and Princess Sethra. I am sorry, my lord."

Assur lunged for the warrior and grabbed him by the edge of his jerkin. "Where is Princess Kitarisa!"

Tears started to form in Cai's eyes. "Taken, my lord. They took her and Princess Sethra...and Lady Davieta. They are gone and they have taken the Spear!"

PRINCE D'ACHADEK FELL as he had fought, with both swords in his hands and a sneer of defiance on his lips. He died, not as the others with his throat slit, but of multiple sword wounds and a final deep thrust to his chest. He had fallen before the altar stone in the holy chamber of the Keep, defending Talesia's most sacred object with the last beat of his brave heart. It had been a fierce struggle.

Near him lay the third neck collar, the final mockery to Talesian invincibility. And the Sacred Spear was indeed gone.

In quick order, Talesian discipline ruled once more and the dead were quickly removed to be placed on their own funeral pyres. Their swords were given to their families and the Holy Chanter was summoned to perform the last rituals.

Assur watched in grim silence while the fires consumed the warriors, sending them to Verlian where they would dine at Her side, assured of Her grace and eternal glory.

When it came time for D'Achadek's pyre, both Assur and Rame knelt before it, their swords set on the ground in front of them, tips crossed. With their palms placed flat beside them, they bowed their heads to offer their own private words to the Goddess.

Assur knew Rame was nursing his own personal hate and grief. His own grief for his father was eclipsed only by his fears and anger over Kitarisa's abduction and the theft of the Spear. The kind of hatred now burning in his heart far outstripped his hatred for the witch Malgora, or for her vile minions, the Wrathmen. It even surpassed his rage for Prince Kazan and his traitorous plotting. The treachery against him and his people, the abductions of Kitarisa, Sethra and Davieta, filled Assur's belly with a sick loathing. Vengeance seemed too soft a word, too easy an answer. So did death.

Tribal grief knew no such restrained thoughts. Siarsi warriors re-slashed their own faces, adding more terrible scars to their already frightening countenances, and several Chaliset warriors cut their inner-arms, a short stroke above their fire marks making an Oath of Honor to their dead prince.

When the last ember died out, Rame and the assembled warriors rose to their feet and waited respectfully.

Slowly, with deliberate steps, the Holy Chanter approached Assur.

He carried Achad's swords before him, tips crossed and stopped in front of Assur. In a rite so ancient, its origins long lost to memory, he began to chant the ceremony bequeathing swords from father to son.

The Chanter bowed over Achad's crossed swords and waited while Assur picked up his own and pressed the crossed tips to his brow then passed them to Rame. Assur's swords would be set aside and held in safekeeping to be given to his own son one day. Now he would accept Achad's.

Assur sheathed his father's gold-hilted swords on his back and turned to the assembled warriors behind him.

"Prince Achad has been Summoned to the Goddess and many more of our brothers will journey with him to Her great hall. They will enjoy Her grace, but now we have much work to do. The Narusuba have defiled all our holy places and the Caverns; they have taken our most sacred relics and they have murdered too many to mention. Both the princesses Kitarisa and Sethra have been abducted, as well as the Riehlian, Lady Davieta." He glanced at the two tribe princes standing near him. "Lords Saar and Exbrel have joined us in this fight. We begin by finding where the Narusuba have gone with the relics. *E Teya sa Verlian*. Verlian calls us."

He nodded curtly to the attending warriors then spun on his heel and strode back into the keep.

THE DOLMINA PROVED difficult to find. A painstaking chamber by chamber, inch by inch search of the keep had begun with Rame in the lead. His lean features hardened into a grim scowl. When he found the dolmina, he would tear the man's heart out with his bare hands.

In a narrow corridor, in the deepest, blackest dungeon, they finally found him leaning against the wall and barely alive. His head lolled against the damp wall as he tried to turn away from the bright glare of the torch.

Rame knelt down and jerked the wretched man into a more upright position. "Where are they?" he snarled.

Dolmina Imroz struggled to focus on Rame's angry face. His own eyes were nearly swollen shut from a blow to his head and blood oozed from his throat.

"He took them. The Physick Lael took all of them," he whispered hoarsely.

"Where?" Rame demanded. He shook the man's shoulders, desperately trying to keep life in him long enough to reveal his secret.

The dolmina smiled thinly through bloody lips. "The relics belong to the Beast and the physick has your women," he croaked.

"Where did they take Sethra and Kitarisa!"

The dolmina struggled to stay upright. Death was near. "I will tell you nothing, savage." He last breath came out in a long hiss as he slumped back against the wall, dead.

"What now, lord?" Cai asked anxiously, shifting the torch to his other hand.

Rame let the body fall against the wall. "I don't know." He struggled a moment to organize his thoughts. "Search his clothes."

Both he, Cai, and one other warrior began rifling through Imroz's clothes, hoping to find a clue, anything that might lead them to the relics or the women, or both.

"There is nothing, my lord," Cai said despairingly.

"Then we search his body. Get him into one of the chambers," Rame ordered.

The dolmina was a tall man and it took four of the them to wrestle him into the nearest chamber and place him on the scarred table that had served long ago as a place for the most hideous Talesian tortures.

With efficient strokes, Rame and Cai cut the dolmina's clothing from his body. Rame spotted the fresh, bleeding tattoo just above the gash in his throat.

"It is just as I feared. He has become Narusuba. The Shygul Islands of the Narusuba...where the Shades live," Rame said grimly. "And the princesses have been taken there along with the relics."

"But why?" Cai asked, his young face a mask of anger and disbelief. "The dolmina was from Volt. This mark is fresh; he could have been recently pressed into their service, my lord."

"I do not know. Don't know!" Rame pounded his fist on the table, the concussion itself causing the dead man's left hand to fall away from his body and dangle over the side of the table. Something clattered to the stones of the chamber and immediately, Rame knelt down to find it.

Blood still clung to the back of it, attesting to the fact that she had struggled against her captor, only to lose it when he tore it from her ear.

Rame clutched the tiny object in his fist and felt his belly contract as if a knife had been driven into it.

It was one of Davieta's ear jewels.

Rame's men were thorough. Each of the five lower tiers of the dungeons were inspected cell by cell, until they came to the last secret cell with its false back wall that had been forced open, revealing the long dark tunnel to the shoreline. It was through here the Narusuba had gained entrance and taken the entire keep. Rame and the others could even smell the sea from the entrance of the cell.

With angry strides, Rame strode down the length of the underground tunnel until he reached the opening to the rocky shoreline. A scrap of beach rising above the pounding waves was all that was needed to allow for one or two small launches to land.

Rame squatted down, examining the still visible keel marks and numerous footprints left in the sand. The attack must have happened shortly before they arrived, as the tide had not turned in yet to wash the marks away.

He squinted out to sea as if hoping to catch the last of the marauders' ships sailing away.

"They caught the outgoing tide," he muttered. "They should be half-way to Port Eeas by now."

"What are you looking for, my lord?" Cai asked respectfully.

"Something doesn't make sense. The Narusuba do not build longships for traveling great distances—they sail only in the safer inland waters of the Volten Sea. Narusuba ships cannot be beached, only anchored offshore."

"And this means what?" Cai questioned anxiously, looking from Rame's scowling face to the marks in the sand.

"It means the Narusuba had help. These are not the keel marks of any Narusuba vessel. These marks were made by Volten longships, possibly war vessels, designed to be run aground."

"Like the Ponos's longships?" Cai asked.

"Yes."

"My Lord Rame!" Nattuck called from the tunnel entrance. "Come quickly!"

Rame sprang to his feet and ran back toward the entrance with Cai close at his heels.

Nattuck's scarred face was drawn.

"More grave news, my lord. We found the body of Physick Nadir in the surgery, with his throat slit like the dolmina's."

"Again, Physick Lael. It would appear he is the one who planned the attack and allowed the Narusuba into the keep."

"He is Volten; he must be," Nattuck said firmly.

Rame nodded in agreement.

"Then the ships are Volten," Cai concluded, nodding toward the keel marks in the sand.

Rame followed the direction of Cai's gaze then looked up, squinting into the overcast skies. "He took them to Volt, or maybe to Shygul." He shook his head. "But which one?"

THE NOISE IN THE great hall was deafening as angry warriors shouted above the rest, each trying to be heard. Assur, Rame, Exbrel, and Saar stood behind the massive table at the head of the room pouring over a tattered ancient map, the only remaining document to be found showing the southern islands and continents. It had taken the Wordkeeper hours to find the dusty, old map stacked with other ancient documents on a back shelf in his private chambers.

"We shall destroy the Narusuba and the Qualani for this outrage!" one red-faced Siarsi shouted.

"Are we to stand for this, like whipped dogs?" another roared.

"Silence!" Assur brought his fist down on the table with a loud crack. "You will be silent, or I'll have you all removed from my presence."

The shouting simmered to a low rumbling as the warriors reluctantly obeyed.

"No decision can be made until all the facts can be assessed," Assur said.

"I say we take as many ships as we can from Saar's tribe and sail to the Narusuba, to their islands. Let them face us like men instead of the cowardly dogs they are!" Exbrel said heatedly.

Loud voices rose in agreement, and again, Assur had to raise his hand threateningly to regain their silence.

"Even Saar doesn't have enough warships," Rame said calmly.

"Rame is correct," Saar interjected. "The Ponos keep only enough for our purposes. There are not enough longships to completely take Volt."

"Then it is time the Ponos learned what it means to be Talesian again! Are you afraid to fight, Saar?" Exbrel said angrily, leaning over his meaty fists that were planted firmly on the table. "Or has your tribe gotten too soft?"

Saar visibly bristled at the insult and every Ponos warrior in the room reached for his sword.

"Enough!" Assur roared at them. "You will cut our own throats before we begin. You shame me with your lack of discipline. Our brothers are scarcely with Verlian and you disgrace their names with your bickering." He cast a hard gaze about the hall, silencing everyone. "We must think clearly, before we are all dead. Remember, our enemies still have the relics and the princesses. We restore nothing while we argue."

Saar let his sword slip back into its sheath and nodded.

"You are right, of course, Prince Assur. But what do we know for certain? We know the Narusuba have take our most sacred relics and the women of the Ter-Rey's family. They have left by boat, presumably for the Shygul Islands, or for Volt, where they will use them for their purpose. They have attempted to make the Qualani appear as having done these deeds, but this has become only a poor attempt to confuse us."

"And to create dissension among us. They knew we would be quick to anger and eager to annihilate the Qualani," Rame interjected grimly.

"*And* distract us from pursuing them," Assur said. He touched the old map spread before him. "How far is it to Volt by sea, Saar?"

The Ponos tribe prince leaned over the table to scrutinize the map. "It is on the southern coast of this continent at the mouth of the West Sherehn. Ten days, maybe eight if the winds are with us."

"How many war ships can you sail?"

Saar shook his head, almost sorrowfully. "Only nine great longships remain."

Exbrel made a loud noise of disgust. "You disgrace us all, Saar!"

"That is enough!" Assur shouted at the Siarsi prince.

"The question remains, where can we find more ships and enough to carry warriors and supplies so we can fight the Narusuba?" Saar asked.

Assur ran his finger down the long line of the great river Sherehn on the eastern side of the Adrex Mountains, tracing its path past the symbol of a black Keep representing Gorendt, on down to where the river spilled into the great Sea of the Volt. He then tapped the great tower symbol of the splendid city that lay across the Volten sea: Maretstan.

"The Maretstanis ply their trade up and down the Sherehn and throughout the Volten Sea. They have many great ships and I know Prince Dahka has many fitted for battle. Dahka owes me his oaths and bonds after nearly betraying me to Kazan and that woman-fiend Malgora."

"You mean for the Maretstani prince to give you ships?" Saar asked, somewhat astounded.

"Dahka will crawl on his belly and beg my mercy if he does not!" Assur snapped. "He narrowly escaped his Summons for high treason. No, it will be Dahka's pleasure to give me his ships."

He glanced at Saar. "How many days to Maretstan?"

"With good winds, ten to fifteen."

"We will need more men than we can assemble now and besides, we need those to stay behind and guard Daeamon," Rame said.

"I will stay and protect Daeamon and all of Talesia if necessary," Exbrel rumbled.

Assur nodded. He motioned to Rame and Saar. "Come, attend me. We have many plans." He looked up and over their heads to the awaiting, expectant warriors in the great hall. "Sharpen your blades and pray to Verlian for your Summons!"

Assur rolled the map into a tight cylinder and nodded curtly for his most favored officers to follow him. There wasn't a moment to waste. He turned on his heel and swept out of the hall trying to push Kitarisa from his thoughts. Warships and battle plans seemed to elude him. The image of that strange dream kept recurring—the creature, so like the image the Reverend 'Fa had become to fight his beloved Kitarisa.

He had nearly lost her for good.

Assur felt a rising, smothering sense of dread. For all he knew, she and the others might be dead already.

THE LAST OF the great Ponos longships heeled into the wind fighting the rough, swelling seas. Red triangular-shaped sails bellied full, straining to take in the last breath of wind in order to achieve more speed.

Assur braced one foot against the narrow stern of the lead longship and glanced upward at the two towering masts creaking and groaning in the wind.

After three days of feeling like one step ahead of his own Summons, and two days to regain his appetite, it was a relief to have his legs under him and his stomach back where it belonged. No one had paid any attention to him, even if he was the High Prince. Well, he could not care now. He was a horseman, not a sailor and if any of these Ponos thought less of him for consigning all his meals into the sea, he took consolation in the fact that few, if any of them could handle a horse. Besides, he could not worry about that—the sacred relics and the three women were his main concern.

Assur sensed Lord Saar move next to him and shifted his weight to both feet, grasping at a steadying line near his head. He was glad Saar was with him. The Ponos tribe prince knew well these waters and had the uncanny ability to get more speed out of the lean ships he commanded.

The sleek longships were the last of their kind—the majority of the Ponos ships having been refitted into fishing vessels, or broken up for other purposes. But Saar's command ship, the Scourge of the Sea, as well as eight others remained as they were originally intended: swift, terrible ships of war.

"Three more days, my lord," Saar said quietly, "and we should have calmer seas and better weather." He nodded toward the skies. "The Daughter Ponosel will bless us and lead us to the safe waters of Maretstan."

"Are you so certain she will lead us, knowing her Bow has been stolen?"

"All the more reason for her to guide us."

Assur gave a soft grunt of approval. "Be sure you include the Goddess in your prayers."

"It is done, my lord. The Daughter will intercede for us to the Holy Goddess. I know we shall have Her blessing."

Assur glanced at Saar. The blood-red markings around his eyes could not hide the firm conviction he saw in them. He liked Saar—liked his calm and balanced opinion of things. Unlike the hot-headed Exbrel, Saar was a quietly determined man, with a sensible, orderly mind.

"I am thankful for your confidence, Saar. We need all of it for this undertaking." Assur tugged at the folds of his fur cloak, trying to prevent any more of the sharp wind from penetrating his bones.

"I am certain the Narusuba have them, my lord. All the facts point in their direction. The dolmina confirmed it. However, it is most disturbing as to *why* they would steal them. The relics have no useful value and they cannot be sold. Who would want them? They have no meaning except to us."

"Unless they are for some other purpose, involving my sister and the princess."

"We will not know until have those Maretstani ships, my lord, and reach Shygul."

Assur nodded absently. They would have no answers until they reached the Shygul. He hoped Rame would have more luck than he and maybe end these terrible events before it escalated into a full-blown war.

Chapter Eight

RAME SWUNG DOWN from his boldly-marked horse and knelt next to the hoof prints imbedded in the soft earth. He touched the nearest print and ran a tentative finger around the deep groove where the horseshoe had left its mark.

"How many, my lord?" Cai called to him.

"Six, maybe seven and one heavily packed horse. They will be slowed up when they cross the Adrex." Rame squinted up at the sun making a quick assessment of the time they had remaining in the day. "They will stop soon."

"Then we were right; they are heading north," Cai said.

Rame stood up and brushed the dirt from his fingers. "Yes, it is the longer route, but it is easier. And they will have to cross Riehlian lands."

He mounted the horse again and sidled next to Cai. "We will find them, I have no doubt of it." He nodded to Nattuck. "Wait here until Cai and I return." He nudged the Trigian about and headed up the fading trail with Cai close behind him.

Three days ago Rame had ridden out from Daeamon with a company of ten warriors heading through the mountains, when they had come upon the strange tracks. The trail left by their quarry had begun to fade as they climbed higher into the Adrex Mountains, but none of the men doubted his tracking skills. They never questioned his decision to divert from the main trail to try and locate the small band of roadwilds Rame was determined to find.

Even though they were well ahead of their original schedule, not even Rame would dare to jeopardize their mission, except that the Qualani tracks were too fresh and too intriguing to overlook.

"What if they are the particular Qualani you seek, my lord?" Cai asked.

"Then they will die," Rame said curtly. "They have been outcast by the Qualani tribe and by their Shalman. They know their days are numbered."

Rame had not told anyone of Lady Davieta's attack and the loss of her family, save the brave Nattuck. The fierce Siarsi was fanatically loyal to House dar Daeamon. Assur once commented that Nattuck was more Siarsi than all of the tribes put together. Nattuck would take Rame's secret to Verlian Herself before telling anyone.

As for Cai, the young warrior had firmly attached himself to Rame since the day of his mishap in the practice arena. Cai would die for Rame. He had also taken his Oath of Duty for Princess Kitarisa and for Lady Davieta. There was nothing he would not do for either of them and if it meant tracking down Qualani renegades, he would follow Rame beyond the Barren to do it.

For now, it was just as well. The long arduous journey to Riehl would cool their tempers. Deep within Rame's saddle pack, he carried Assur's orders for him to take command of a legion from Riehl Province and for the Prime Governor, Raldan Mar'Kess, to take them down the Sherehn River to Gorendt where they would secure another legion. After Assur had acquired the Maretstani ships, he would meet Rame, Mar'Kess, and the legions in Volt.

Although Rame had never met Mar'Kess, he had heard much from Assur. Mar'Kess had originally been one of Prince Kazan's trusted captains in Gorendt, until he learned of the plot against Assur from the hated Reverend 'Fa, Malgora. Mar'Kess had fought hard and served well fighting for the Ter-Rey. He had taken complete control of the frightened Riehlians, marshaled their forces, reinforced their garrisons and staunchly held the city against an impending siege.

Assur had the highest regard for Mar'Kess and made him Prime Governor of both Riehl and Gorendt provinces until the proper succession to their thrones could be resolved. He had advised Rame to treat Mar'Kess with great honor—he was an ally of the Ter-Rey and had taken personal Oaths and Bonds.

Rame allowed for only a half day to search for the makers of the mysterious tracks before resuming their journey east. As the sun began to lower in the western skies, he became more determined. If Davieta's attackers were this close, he would not miss the opportunity to avenge her.

The hardy Mountain Trigian horse clambered over the rough trail, head down like a hound as if knowing it was stalking something. At the crest of the hill, Rame halted and looked down into the shallow ravine. He frowned.

There were no roadwilds, only a handful of Qualani women, two or three small children, and one horse that appeared to have been packed with all of their possessions. The six women were gathered around a low campfire, rubbing their arms and stamping to keep warm. Occasionally, one of the children would whimper, but was quickly silenced. Rame studied them for a moment then backed his horse away to speak to Cai without being overheard.

"They are not outcasts, but I think they are running from something. There are only women and children."

"My lord, you cannot mean to slay these women...for whatever reason," Cai protested in quiet tones.

"I have no intention of slaying them—they are not the ones I seek," Rame answered shortly.

"Then, what is your will, my lord?"

The Swordmaster turned his head away from Cai, pondering the situation. They were clearly not the outcasts he sought, but it was strange that these women, Qualani women at that, were here in the woods, alone, and without protection. He detected no weapons among them, but he could see that they were afraid and were running from something.

"We will approach cautiously and show them we mean no harm. Perhaps they have information we need."

Cai shifted uneasily in his saddle. "I have no desire for a Qualani knife in my ribs. I am told their women know how to handle a knife. What if their men are hiding and wait to ambush us?"

Rame snorted in disgust. "Have you forgotten everything you have learned? The Qualani do not permit their women outside their circle of lodges unless they are under escort. If their men are nearby, or even their horses, ours would hear them and show it. We would have seen their tracks. Have you not been watching the signs? Pay attention!"

Cai immediately bowed his head. "I forget myself, lord. Your forgiveness."

Rame only grunted his answer and nudged his horse over the ravine. Only Cai would be permitted to ride alongside him. The others would remain at the main trail, alert and wary.

The two horses shuffled and scuffed through the underbrush, immediately signaling the Qualani women. All six of them jumped away from the fire, knives drawn and fearless before the two Talesian warriors.

"If you're looking for sport, Talesians, you have six knives to fight before you reach any of us," the tallest woman said, stepping forward. She was dressed like the rest of the women in dirty hides and ragged skins. One of her fur leggings did not match the other and in her rough hands she held a rude knife, much worn and chipped from hard use.

Rame held up both hands, as did Cai, signaling their desire for peace. The women did not lower their knives but eyed them all the more warily.

"We will not harm you. It is only by chance that our paths have crossed, but we would ask only for some information," Rame said in Qualani.

The woman's brows shot up in surprise. For a Talesian to speak the Qualani tongue was rare enough, but that he spoke it so perfectly was remarkable. Most all conversations between Talesians and Qualani were done through an awkward blend of both tongues, and with signs and gestures. Many times it was the Qualani tribesman who was forced to learn halting Talesian in order to communicate with their haughty overlords.

"You speak as us, Talesian. How is this possible?"

"It was learned long ago," Rame responded shortly, offering no other information. "We travel under the Will of the Ter-Rey and will leave you soon. I am Lord Ramelek and this is the warrior Cai. We need only some information from you."

"And if we do not give it?" the dark-faced woman replied, as if testing him.

"Then we leave you to continue your journey...with the mothersun's blessings."

The woman wavered momentarily. She did not lower her knife, but some of her caution seemed to lessen.

"What is it you wish to know?" she asked skeptically.

Rame shifted in his saddle and lowered his hands to the reins. "Not long ago, the Ter-Rey and I rode north to speak with the Holy Shalman. We learned there are outcasts, renegade Qualani riding these woods. The Shalman gave us his permission to track down these outcasts and slay them. The Riehlians seek them, too. Perhaps you know of them?"

The woman hesitated and glanced back at the others. An older woman, gray-haired and stooped, nodded slightly to her.

"I might. What do I get in return?" she demanded.

"What do you need?" Rame answered.

Again, the leader of the women turned to the others as if seeking their advice. The older woman nodded to her a second time.

"Food," she said quickly.

Rame turned to Cai and gave his orders in brusque tones.

"Ride back to the others. Get whatever spare provisions you can find: cheese and some dried meat. Bring teki... We will hunt game tomorrow."

Cai nodded and spurred his horse back up the ravine where the others waited.

Rame looked down at the tall woman, who was still unafraid, but maintaining her caution.

"My officer rides to bring you provisions." He rose in the stirrups a little to look over her head at the others. "Are you all well? Any of you injured?"

"We are well enough, warrior-lord. Why should you care? Talesians have no dealings with us."

"The information I require is vital for both our tribes. These marauders have attacked Qualani and Talesian; they have attacked Riehlians without provocation. They have committed murder and they must be punished," Rame said firmly.

Before the woman could answer, Cai's horse broke through the underbrush and trotted up next to Rame's. Cai nudged the horse nearer to the woman and leaned down to hand her the leather satchel full of food and provisions.

She eagerly snatched the bag from Cai's hands and turned to the others. Two rushed forward to take it from her, momentarily forgetting their caution. Hunger forced away the last of their fear. Eager hands passed the food from one to the other. Some of them began cramming the food into their mouths, heedless of the barbarians watching them.

"You see that?" the lead woman asked bitterly. "They are starving. We've had no fresh food for a week and the children have no milk. Soon, we will have to eat the horse."

Rame studied her for moment, not missing the concealed anguish in her voice.

"Did *they* force you to this?"

She swallowed and nodded. "Yes."

"Where are they? We will find them and bring them to justice."

The woman's head snapped up. Tears rimmed her tired dark eyes. "When they were driven out of our lodge circle and made nameless, they took us with them, forcing us to serve them and cook for them. We had to follow as we had no one to defend us. For a time we were content, but then they began the beatings. We could take no more. Eight days ago we ran away at night while they were on one of their raids. We killed the guard and stole his horse. We will journey back to our lodge circle and beg to be accepted by the Shalman."

"And if he does not?"

"Then we will die, starve. No one may return to the circle without the Shalman's acceptance." She looked away for a moment to brush away her tears.

Rame glanced at Cai who had been watching the whole proceedings and understanding little of it. "My lord, have they told you of these renegades?"

"Yes. We will have our answer soon."

Swiftly, Rame pulled off one of his long fur-lined gauntlets and reached behind his neck to unclasp the gleaming silver collar. He gestured sharply for the woman to approach him and before either she or Cai could say anything, he dropped it into her hand. The silver plates, each embossed with black-enameled owls, caught the waning light of the sun and glittered in her palm like a cold fire.

"Take this to the Shalman. Tell him it is the collar of Rame, the One-Who-Speaks-As-Us. He will know. Tell him I will find the Outcasts and bring them to justice. They will shame the Qualani no more."

The woman clutched the collar for a moment, scarcely believing his words.

"If you sell it, you will surely die," he said severely. "Now, where are they?"

"You would do this for us?" she whispered, astonished.

"Yes. Now, tell me."

"They are south, near the headwaters of the Tamis. They are changed, my lord. They are servants of the Others."

"How many?" Rame asked sharply.

"Twelve. The leader is a man who has taken the Outcast name of Chu'Nahk, but he has become a servant of the Others." She carefully placed the neck collar within the folds of her hide mantle.

"And how will I know this "Chu'Nahk"," Rame asked, already knowing her answer.

"He has only one eye." The woman touched her right eye with a dirty forefinger.

"Who are the 'others?'"

The woman looked confused for a moment, trying to find an explanation. "They are the Servants of the Beast. They bear the mark on their throat." She touched her own throat then stooped down and drew in a small patch of snow: a diamond-shape with a crude sign of a dagger running through it.

He studied the all-too-familiar mark and nodded to her. "What is their purpose?"

"I am not sure, my lord. We were not told, but they are

determined to ride south, to Volt. I heard Chu'Nahk say that the work of the Beast would begin in Volt." She shrugged. "I do not understand this."

Rame nodded again and gathered up his horse's reins. "My thanks. We will leave you now and wish the mothersun's blessings upon you."

The woman bowed her head in acknowledgment. "May you be twice-blessed by Verlian."

RAME NUDGED HIS horse up the slope of the ravine, heading back to the awaiting warriors. As the horses labored through the brush and snow, he swiftly explained to Cai what had happened.

"Qualani outcasts are heading for Volt? What is in Volt, my lord? Volt fell long ago to infighting."

"For whatever the "work of the Beast" means. It may mean the Narusuba have again taken a foothold in Volt. Perhaps they are determined to try to regain what land they attempted to take during the Volten Wars."

Cai looked startled. "They cannot do that! They have no claim. Prince Aettilek crushed them during the time of Emperor Shadressian. I know this to be true. My clan's Wordkeeper nearly beat the lesson into me."

"The Narusuba *have* no claim," Rame agreed, "but they may have decided to begin their foul work in Volt. The relics may be there, too, or on their way."

On firmer ground, Rame nudged the Trigian into a swift canter. When they rejoined the company, they all followed Rame's lead and quickly urged their own horses to pick up a faster pace.

"But my lord, why did you not ask if those women needed our help, our escort?" Cai called to Rame.

"Because they would have refused."

"But there are any number of dangers: roadwilds and marglims. The outcasts may catch them again. They may never reach Qualani lands."

A light smile touched Rame's firm mouth. "They will, Cai. Believe me, they will."

The eastern side of the Adrex proved easier going once they crested the summit of the northern pass. The trail was well traveled attesting to the great numbers of Talesian warriors who had crossed and re-crossed the mountains during the battles against Kazan and the 'Fa.

The thinning snow turned the trail to a muddy beaten pathway traversing all the way down the eastern slope, gradually widening into the main road leading directly to Riehl. Riehlian travelers, merchants, and the odd free-warrior passed them with respectful nods, but no one stopped them or asked their business.

When Rame saw the great towers of Riehl Keep from afar, gleaming in the bright afternoon sun, he wondered about Mar'Kess. Assur's admiring opinion of him and Kuurus's glowing reports were reassuring, but it worried Rame that the Prime Governor might be unable to muster enough Riehlian warriors, or enough boats to carry them down the Sherehn River to Gorendt and then on to Volt. The war against Kazan left many Riehlian dead and perhaps a growing reluctance to support the Ter-Rey in any new ventures, regardless of their duty and oaths to him.

Cai rose in his stirrups and pointed to an oncoming band of horsemen, riding hard across a grassy field just beyond the road and the scattering of trees.

"We have been noticed, my lord."

Blue and white surcoats amidst dark riding leathers were a certain indication of Riehlian warriors and Rame noted with tight approval that they all rode exceedingly well.

Their leader, a tall man with hair as gold and brilliant as the sun, skidded his gleaming bay horse to a stop before Rame and raised a hand in salute.

"We welcome you, Talesians. Permit us to—"

The man stopped suddenly, his jaw dropped in surprise as recognition lit his entire face. Without warning, he immediately swung down from the bay and motioned frantically for the others to do the same. Reins in his left hand, he sank to one knee and beat his right palm to his left shoulder. There was a hurried shuffling of men and horses as each of the remaining warriors also dismounted and knelt, offering their own salute to Rame.

"Great Lord, this is an unexpected pleasure. I had no idea we would see you again so soon. Forgive my manners. Riehl is at your disposal." He looked up and smiled warmly at Rame. "It is good to see you, my Lord Assur."

Rame cast an uncomfortable glance at Cai. He dismounted the black horse and motioned for the man to rise.

"Please rise...warrior. There has been a misunderstanding. I am not the High Prince, D'Assuriel, but I am kin to him. I am Prince Ramelek dar sa Sabiann, his uncle and Swordmaster to Daeamon Keep. Verlian plays Her little joke by having made us nearly alike and confusing those around us." He offered the man a tight smile as a kind of apology.

"Ah, Lord Rame! His Highness made mention of you on many occasions. An honor, my lord." He bowed his head again. "I am Raldan Mar'Kess, Prime Governor of Riehl. Although today, you catch me away from my duties."

He gestured to his men around him to rise then turned back to signal another cluster of riders waiting quietly near a thick stand of trees. To Rame's surprise, they were women, elegantly attired in dark-colored riding dresses, long gloves and veiled hats. For a fleeting instant he thought of Davieta and how perfectly suited she would have been with those women.

The women approached cautiously. Once seeing Rame, they began to tug at their skirts, preparing to dismount so they might offer him their own respectful curtsies.

Rame held up his hand for them to stop.

"It is unnecessary, ladies."

The five of them nodded, still uncertain and then bowed politely from the waist.

"As you can see, we were attempting a hunt, but there is little game in these woods today." Mar'Kess nodded, then acknowledged Rame's serious look by gathering up his horse's reins in preparation to mount. "Perhaps it is just as well. What news, my lord?"

Rame looked at him frankly. "The news is grave. We are on the verge of another war. There will be no time for hunts, my Lord Mar'Kess," he said a little brusquely.

Mar'Kess swung onto his horse as did Rame and the others, at once serious and duty-bound. "Then follow me."

RIEHL WAS JUST as Rame had hoped, from the superb food and sumptuous rooms in the Keep, down to the simple barracks for the humblest stableboy. He at once liked the city's neatness, an orderliness that appeared to be both a Rielian trait and a dominant factor in Mar'Kess's character.

In the armory and barracks, no detail had been overlooked. Weapons hung in tight precision, well-oiled, sharp, and in perfect condition. Horse harness and saddlery all gleamed with proper care. The horses themselves were in solid flesh, fit and keen; the warriors, prepared.

Every inch of Mar'Kess's domain revealed the kind of order that appealed to Rame's innate sense of discipline, but for all Riehl's harmony, the city and keep were a marvel of beauty and style.

The proud Riehlians cherished their artistry in architecture and craftsmanship as well as in their art and music. Graceful arches and columns soared through the stone fabric of Riehl, supporting the city and its great walls. Laid out in ever larger concentric circles, it boasted the three successive walls that surrounded the city: the first, the low outermost wall used primarily to hold the grazing flocks and herds. A second inner wall with four staunch towers at the compass points, along with stout gates and watchful guards, held Riehl secure. The final innermost wall surrounded the great Keep itself—the city lay between these two great walls and since the arrival of Mar'Kess, remained armed, manned, and well-stocked with provisions. Any enemy considering attacking Riehl would think carefully before taking on such a foolish venture.

The city's only blemish was Prince Kazan's headless, rotting corpse still left hanging from the southern rampart—a grim reminder of Assur's wrath. No one dared touch it since the day Kazan had been publically flogged by Assur, beheaded, then dragged up to the highest battlements and hung by the wrists for all to see. There was little left, save for the twisted bones and dried sinews holding it together. Soon, they too would fall into a bleaching, brittle heap at the base of the wall. Even then, the bones would be left there until they turned to dust.

Rame allowed himself a moment to contemplate his nephew's justice and decided it was appropriate, if not severe enough. If it had been him, he would have drawn and quartered the traitorous prince, then hung him there alive, exposing him to the cold, the sun, and whatever else came by to devour him.

Mar'Kess responded promptly, almost eagerly to Assur's commands. The long barges were quickly brought out and provisioned. General orders for an entire legion were sent out and almost overnight, the great fields surrounding Riehl were filled with camping warriors and restless horses.

"You are well-prepared, Mar'Kess," Rame complimented him crisply.

"I thank you, my lord, but fifteen turns of service to Kazan taught me never to be caught unguarded or unprepared. And, the battle with His Highness has taught the lesson well to the Riehlians. We have been too vulnerable and too complacent. The prince's peace may be his will throughout the Eastern Lands, but it is wise to keep your blade sharp."

Rame nodded in agreement, his estimation of Mar'Kess rising another notch. "Your preparations will make this task all the easier.

Your Field Commander tells me we may sail for Gorendtin two days."

"There will be enough?" Mar'Kess asked.

"It had better be, or all is lost. If a legion is not enough to hold Volt or take Shygul, I will shear my hair and die shamed," Rame vowed.

Mar'Kess nodded, knowing Rame's vow was not in jest. The cutting of a warrior's hair was a touchy subject. Shorn hair was a mark of shame, barring any Talesian entrance into Verlian's Hall when Summoned.

Once underway on the Sherehn River, the going became easy, almost leisurely. The hundreds upon hundreds of horses stood shoulder to shoulder in the deep-bellied barges, protected by tarps overhead, while both Talesian and Riehlian warriors alike had little more to do than line the railings of their own transports and watch the scenery as they sailed down river.

They sailed past the ruin of Sherehn Keep, now reduced to rubble having been burned and gutted when Assur and his men rescued the Lady Kitarisa and her half-sister Alea from its confines. Rame shook his head in disbelief at the sight of the blackened wreck. It was a great pity it could not have been saved, as the keep was so strategically placed between Riehl and Gorendt. As an outpost to the outlying tribal lands farther to the east, it would have well-served their purposes.

Long before they arrived at Gorendt, the remaining Siarsi warriors that had been ordered to stay and keep Assur's peace, galloped their horses up and down the river shoreline, shouting their welcome.

"So much for discipline," Rame muttered irritably. He would make certain to reprimand their Lead Captain. High spirits he could forgive; wasted purpose he would not.

At the docks, row upon row of warriors both Gorentdian and Talesian awaited them. As there was no prince to rule Gorendt, except for the First Commander and the members of the Council Circle, Mar'Kess and Rame were greeted by a large, stern man in leathers and a surcoat of dark green and black—the old Gorendtian colors. Next to him, a nearly jubilant Siarsi captain went down on one knee, his wide smiles fairly splitting the black scars on his cheeks.

The big Gorendtian dropped beside him and beat a cautious palm to his left shoulder. "Gorendt welcomes you, my lords," he said in a deep, rumbling voice.

"Rise, Commander Vidun and you, Captain," Mar'Kess ordered.

"I shout praises to Verlian in Her Sacred Hall that you have arrived safely," the Siarsi exclaimed.

"And to everyone else in the Eastern Lands, as well," Rame said ominously.

The Siarsi captain turned white and again went down on one knee. "Your pardon, my lord. I gave the men permission to ride out...I take full responsibility."

Rame held up his hand for him to stop and scowled. "See that it does not happen again." He turned to Mar'Kess and raised one sweeping brow. "You will show me Gorendt."

Within the time it took for the horses to be led off the barges and saddled and for Governor Mar'Kess to escort him to the four towers of Gorendt Keep, Rame now knew why Assur risked so much to free Kitarisa and to defeat Kazan. Even the hardened warrior in him recognized a rule made too harsh, a control grown beyond the limits of good sense. The people of Gorendt cringed at the mere sight of him.

The soaring dark walls of the Keep, bristling with its triple rows of defensive spikes lining the topmost battlements, met with his grim approval, but the groveling terror of its people living within its walls did not.

Governor Mar'Kess noted his fixed frown and nodded. "They are whipped dogs, my lord. Even after Kazan's death, they still fear reprisal from the High Prince. And, you will pardon me, but your resemblance is more than striking, it is...uncanny. They think you are Prince Assur come back to punish them."

"Then, no one knows our true purpose?" Rame asked.

Mar'Kess shook his head. "Most believe the legions are here to punish Gorendt or to impose a harsher rule."

Rame frowned again, saying nothing.

"Their spirits are nearly broken, my lord. They are too afraid. I have tried to establish a new order by reinstating the Council, but they are weak and fearful. Kazan was a cruel master. They still await the lash."

Rame nudged his black mount closer to Mar'Kess's bay horse. "Are they still loyal?" he asked in a low voice.

"They have no choice. Disobedience brought punishment, but I tell you this my lord, if you can restore their trust, they will die for you. I know these men; they are good warriors."

Rows of stern-faced officers in green and black surcoats lined the inner courtyard as Rame and his escort rode through the last great gate.

Commander Vidun barked one sharp order and the entire assemblage snapped to attention. Rame dismounted slowly and handed the reins to Nattuck. He strode down the rows of warriors, scrutinizing each face and the details of their uniforms. Stockier men than the long-limbed Talesians, but solid-looking and fit, they stared straight ahead, not daring to challenge the severe examination from Rame's black-patterned eyes. He took in the well-worn scabbards and the slightly shabby-looking but neat surcoats worn over plain mail hauberks.

He heard Mar'Kess, standing at his elbow, clear his throat.

"These are the remaining Field Commanders, First and Lead Captains of Gorendt. Will you want them to swear Oaths and Bonds to you now?"

"No," Rame said firmly as he passed the last man.

Mounting the low tier of stairs leading to the Keep's entrance, Rame turned to the assembled officers before him.

"I am not the High Prince," he said brusquely. "I am Prince Ramelek dar sa Sabiann, blood-uncle to D'Assuriel and the Swordmaster of Daeamon Keep."

Rame began to slowly unbuckle one of his armguards then the other, handing them to Mar'Kess. He held up his bared lower arms so all could clearly see the owls and scythes burned into his flesh.

"However, I *have* been sent by the Ter-Rey to carry out his orders." He lowered his arms. "I am not here to punish. I am here with Lord Mar'Kess to assemble a legion, but this time to fight for your *own* lands. Kazan is dead for his treason and Gorendt has paid enough in blood." He took the armguards from Mar'Kess's hands. "Commander Vidun?"

"My Lord Ramelek?" the commander responded promptly.

"I will see all Field Commanders within the hour and then I will inspect the arsenals and barracks." He again scanned the respectful rows before him.

"The remainder of you will take your ease until that time," he said in a less harsh tone. He turned on his heel and gestured to the Prime Governor.

"You will show me my quarters, Mar'Kess. Please."

HE HELD A BOW in his hands, a bow of such exquisite workmanship he found himself reluctant to use it. Gold beaten over breok horn and silver inlays gleamed in his hands—Ponosel's Bow. How did he...?

And then the cold so bitter it chilled his lungs and heart and gripped his belly. He shook his head, forcing the numbing sensation from his mind.

After the cold, he heard it, smelled it. A guttural snarl and the stink of sulphur. He turned and heard himself choke.

"Rame?" A soft whisper, racked with pain, called to him.

"Davieta?" Almost a sob. He could barely look at her. She was hanging from some kind of frame, tortured by ropes biting into the frail columns of her wrists stretched above her head. She looked down on him, eyes dulled by her interminable suffering.

"Rame," she whispered through cracked lips. "Kill me, before it does."

"No!" he heard himself shout. With hands that had never trembled before, he fitted one of the gleaming arrows into the bowstring, nocking it tight against his cheek.

He saw it now. Monstrous, hideous. The creature Kitarisa had fought—the same beast Assur told him she had become in the great battle. The elongated head reached toward the black sky and roared its loathsome breath. Fire spumed through sharp, yellowed teeth, roiling above Davieta's head.

There is no such thing...it cannot exist. Gone, long ago.

The head snaked down, crouching low, covering the diamond tattoo at its throat and took a step toward Davieta.

Her eyes, dark with pain, filled with tears as she tried to jerk feebly against her bonds. Another sob, unknown to him, as the fear caught in his throat.

"Hold still, A'lara," he said through clenched teeth. His aim was true, dead on the rope that bound her left wrist.

The beast lunged for Davieta, snapping at her bare feet dangling just above its jaws.

"Kill IT!" his mind screamed. He did not know why, but he ignored the warning. He took a firmer stance and aimed at the rope. The arrow flew straight, a shimmering thread of light into its mark, severing the rope. Davieta wrenched downward against the remaining bonds holding her right wrist. She moaned softly.

He found the second arrow, nocked it, and again drew the gleaming feathers tight against his jaw.

"Hold, A'lara, hold!"

The beast leaped again, bellowing fire and a cloud of stinking vapors obliterating Davieta from his view. He heard her scream and the sound of tearing cloth. The arrow flew.

<u>*"Before I leave the sky, Ramelek!"*</u>

Rame jerked upright, gulping for air. He never had nightmares; rarely did he dream. He kicked off the fur coverlet and sat up on the edge of the bed. He looked down at himself, covered in sweat, his whole body shaking uncontrollably.

"By Verlian, what is happening to me?" He wiped his hand across his brow and down his damp face.

Davieta. His lovely Davieta. In pain? A prisoner?

He clutched futilely at the threads of the dream until it slipped forever beyond his memory. But Davieta's pain remained. He could still see it in her eyes and hear the agony in her voice.

Rame sank back onto the bed, his hand to his eyes. The trembling stopped. He forced himself to conjure her in his mind: the pale heart-shaped face, the sable-silk of her hair and those haunted, soft eyes. His A'lara, his Davieta, was in terrible danger and he had to help her. Find her.

Hours later, he stopped in startled mid-stride on his way to the stables, realizing he was now referring to Davieta as...his.

Chapter Nine

KITARISA AWOKE TO the sound of rushing water. Musty straw scratched her cheek. She smelled the sea and the heavy odor of damp wood. A dingy yellow light from a battered lantern cast deep shadows through the low-ceilinged space, a small airless compartment in a ship.

She propped herself on one elbow, her head only inches from the beam above her. Davieta lay next to her curled in a tight ball, asleep. Dried blood crusted her left earlobe where the ear jewel had been torn away during her struggles with Dolmina Imroz.

Traitor, Kitarisa thought contemptuously. He was the one who had betrayed them to that fiend, Lael, and revealed the secret passageway from the dungeons to the sea wall. Whoever, *Lael* was....

Physick Lael was no physick. Using guile and false smiles, he had convinced her, Sethra, and Davieta to come to the surgery on the pretext of showing them its newly restored condition and to demonstrate a new procedure. Kitarisa should have heeded Davieta's warning looks, but she went anyway, eager to see how the new physick had improved conditions in the surgery.

A cruel surprise awaited the three of them. All the Ponos guards had been slain as had the remaining prisoners. No one heard their cries for help as Lael, Imroz, and another man they did not recognize forced them down to the lowest level of the dungeon to a cell with a secret door that opened to a tunnel leading out to the sea shore.

Once the door had been opened, strange men with tattoos on their throats rushed in and filled the keep. The three women were forced into one of the ancient torture chambers, guarded by Imroz, while Daeamon Keep fell to the silent intruders. With Assur, Rame, and the others gone to the north, there were few warriors left to fight against them.

Kitarisa held back bitter tears of remorse. The Keep had fallen because of her. If only she had listened to Davieta....

The dark animal presence within her began to stir, demanding to be released. Kitarisa forced the creature back into the deepest recesses of her mind. *Now* was not the time, but she knew she would not be able to silence it for long.

She watched Davieta slowly uncurl, then turn over, facing her. "My lady...Kitarisa? Where are we?"

"We are in the hold of a ship. How do you feel?"

"Hungry. Ill." Davieta tried to sit up, but bumped her head against the beam. She rubbed her head while rearranging herself into a more comfortable position. "How long have we been in here?"

"I do not know." Kitarisa peered into the dark corners of the compartment. "I do not see Princess Sethra, either."

Davieta looked at her, alarmed. Her voice dropped to a frightened whisper. "What if they killed her?"

Kitarisa clutched Davieta's outstretched hands. "I cannot believe they would do that. She, of all us would be more valuable to them. She is the Ter-Rey's sister."

The ship creaked and groaned, shifting with each swell of the sea. The two women clung tightly to one another to keep their balance until the ship settled.

Davieta shook violently unable to conceal her terror. Tears choked her voice. "Forgive me, my lady. I am so frightened. What are they going to do to us?"

Kitarisa held her close, hoping to dispel some of Davieta's fear as well as her own. "I do not know. Try to be calm. We must think."

"Yes," Davieta said, nodding and looking more determined. "You are right." She settled onto the straw and pressed the backs of her hands to her eyes, blotting her tears. "I will try, my lady."

"Good."

Gathering strength from Davieta, Kitarisa struggled to make sense of their situation. Physick Lael had kidnapped the three of them for an unknown purpose, but she sensed it had something to do with the Sacred Weapons. The wild-eyed men who had conquered Daeamon Keep were not merely looking for her or the other two women, but the Sacred Spear, the soul, the *a'kenns,* of the Talesian tribe.

Intuitively she knew the ship was sailing south along the coast toward the Sea of the Volt—perhaps they were heading for great Volt itself. She had never seen the ancient capital, but had heard of its majestic towers and magnificent palaces. It had once been the city of the emperors until Cael III was overthrown 300 sunturns ago, just at the time of Ka'Tiya the Beloved, the First Ter-Reya.

Kitarisa forced ancient history from her mind and tried to think of a logical reason why they would be sailing toward

Volt—if that truly was where they were going.

Volt was at the crossroads, the center of all the known provinces. The cosmopolitan Voltens had long ago forsworn their allegiance to Verlian in favor of the god of commerce and trade. From the northernmost province of Riehl at the headwaters of the Sherehn, down the river and across the Volten Sea to Maretstan, ships from all over Talesia came to Volt to trade their goods. Merchants traveling from the far eastern provinces of Asserlia and from beyond the Barrier Wall came to the great city to mingle and to bargain. Even the Talesian tribes often traded with Volt.

What if they *were* being taken to Volt, Kitarisa wondered. Why? For what purpose? Another dreadful thought jolted her. What if they were to be sold along with all three of the Sacred Weapons—a profane bargain instigated by that vile physick, Lael?

Sickened by such thoughts, Kitarisa could not bring herself to tell Davieta. She knew her lady's maid lived with the constant terror of her past—the loss of her entire family and of her own violation at the hands of ravaging roadwilds. Their abduction from Daeamon had only heightened Davieta's fears.

Too weary to struggle with their dilemma any longer, Kitarisa sank back into the straw. She had time. The voyage to Volt would take several days and during that time she would piece together this foul mystery.

After three more days of suffering in the cramped hold of the ship—food and small jugs of water occasionally tossed down to them—Kitarisa and Davieta were at last permitted to stand and be led out onto the deck. There was no sign of Sethra.

They clung to each other, trying to maintain their balance with aching, stiffened legs on the shifting deck. To Kitarisa's surprise it was night and the ship was moored to creaking pilings next to a wide dock.

From the shadows Lael stepped forward and bowed slightly, his mocking insolent bow. "Ah, princess. At last! Your discomfort is at an end."

Kitarisa felt herself bristle at the sight of the lean man. "How dare you, whoever you are! How dare you do this to us! I demand you release us and return us to Daeamon Keep."

He laughed softly and took a step closer toward her and Davieta. "That is not possible. You are too valuable for our purposes. But do not fear, the unpleasantness is over. You will be treated well, as a woman of your rank deserves," he said, his smile a curve of contempt on his sallow face.

"And what of Princess Sethra? She is ill...she—"

"She is unharmed, lady. Merely an induced sleep until the proper time for her to awaken. She has already been taken to a safe place." He spread his hands apologetically. "All of this was necessary, I assure you."

"What is this 'purpose'?"

The self-named physick frowned, now clearly irritated by Kitarisa's demands. "You will know in time," he snapped. He abruptly gestured to the nearby sailors. "Bind and gag them!"

Rough hands bound Kitarisa's and Davieta's hands behind their backs. A dirty rag was tied tightly around their mouths and they were blindfolded. The same rough hands shoved them across the gangway to the dock and into a small wagon. A whip cracked and the wagon lurched forward, throwing both of them onto their stomachs, face down in the straw.

Kitarisa could barely breathe. She kicked at the straw, struggling to roll on her side. She heard Davieta moan and wondered if she was hurt. The jarring ride over the heavy cobbles felt like she was being beaten to death.

Gratefully the ride did not last long. When they came to a stop she again felt hard hands drag her from the wagon. Her shoes were gone. Sharp, cold stones gouged painfully into her unprotected feet.

Kitarisa shuddered as she took a ragged breath. She knew that smell all too well—the smell of pain and death—the way her father's dungeons smelled in Gorendt Keep. She heard the faint, far-away screams of the wretched souls that were dying from their terrible punishments and heard the heavy, grinding clank of metal gears raising a gate.

Kitarisa caught a sob in her throat. If this place was anything like Kazan's dungeons, there would be no way out. Except one. As a corpse.

THERE WAS LITTLE else to do except try and comfort one another. In spite of the warmth outside, the cell in which they had been imprisoned was as cold and dank as any cell in Daeamon Keep.

The two women huddled together, clutching at the one ragged blanket they had been given, trying to ward off the damp and their terror. The ship's hold had been terrible, but the confinement in the cell was far more horrifying than they could have imagined. As soon as their eyes adjusted to the dark, they discovered they had been placed in a cell barely high enough for them to stand up and the floor was covered in more ancient, filthy straw. How many generations of miserable prisoners had died within these walls, never again seeing the light of day, or hearing the sound of a compassionate voice?

Fear had overcome Davieta to the point where she turned away from Kitarisa and began to vomit quietly into the straw.

When finished, she turned and clutched at Kitarisa's arms, sobbing. "I am sorry, my lady, I cannot seem to stop shaking."

Kitarisa nodded, trying to hold back her own sick fear. "I know." Desperately, she tried to think of something to calm the two of them, something to keep them from going mad.

"Listen, what did the physick, or whatever he is, tell us, in the ship. Think, Davieta! Think of something, anything that might help us."

Davieta pushed at her tears with the heels of her hands and drew in a ragged breath. "Well, he said we were needed for something... 'our purposes' is how I think he put it."

"Yes, I think so, too. Davieta, I do not think they are going to kill us because I think we are too valuable, especially Sethra."

Davieta nodded. "Three women, three weapons."

"Exactly. We are hostages for some kind of bargain, so it would serve them well to keep us alive."

"What if their demands are not met?" Davieta asked, shivering.

Kitarisa had no immediate answer. She clutched the blanket to her shoulders; it gave little warmth to ward off the damp chill that settled through her. They had been given no other clothing since their arrival in the dungeons, save for the clothes they wore when abducted from Daeamon.

Food consisted of a rough wooden bowl filled with stale bread, moldy cheese and a handful of dried meat. Neither Kitarisa or Davieta could stomach the poor fare, but instead took hesitant sips from the water bucket near the door of the cell.

Eventually, they could not fight their utter exhaustion and sank into the straw, asleep.

It must have been dawn as a faint thread of light slipped through a crack in the cell door. It wasn't the light that awoke Kitarisa, but the loud, rasping sound of the bolt across the door being pulled back and the screech of metal on metal as it was pulled opened. Kitarisa sat up and rubbed at the ache in her wrists. Davieta jumped to an upright position, clutching the ragged blanket to her chest.

A tall guard thrust a torch into the cell ahead of him then bent low to clear the ceiling. He wore crossed bands of crimson enamel across his chest and a short, kilt-like garment of red and yellow to mid-thigh. Heavy sandals laced to the knee covered his lower legs, and bright gold and red-enameled armguards encased his arms from wrist to the elbow.

He gestured for Kitarisa to get up. "You! Follow me!"

Kitarisa glanced at Davieta and hesitantly got to her feet.

"Where are you taking me?" she asked in a shaky voice.

"You will find out soon enough. Get moving!"

The big guard reached for her arm and roughly jerked her to the door.

"Kitarisa!" she heard Davieta gasp.

Having no patience with her reluctance, the guard shoved her through the cell door into the dim corridor of the dungeon. Another attending guard braced his shoulder against the heavy cell door and pushed it back. The door banged shut and the bolt screeched into place, but it was not loud enough to drown out the sound of Davieta's terrified sobs.

The guard did not lead her to another cell, but up the darkened, grim stairways and corridors to the upper levels. Once beyond the massive iron gates, she passed into open, bright courtyards and long sweeping porches supported by graceful columns and arched ceilings. Another flight of stairs led to another corridor, ending at a pair of doors of beaten brass and inlaid copper.

Two more of the scarlet and yellow-clad guards stood unmoving before the doors, each armed with a stout spear and a wicked-looking sword at his side.

Her escort stopped before the guards and nodded curtly.

"Inform the Lady Ghalmara that the prisoner has arrived."

Kitarisa bridled at the word "prisoner." She drew herself up, her anger overshadowing her fear.

"*Princess* Kitarisa dar Baen, soldier, *and* the betrothed to the Ter-Rey!"

The soldier said nothing, but simply glared at her as if he were contemplating a mere insect. The great door swung open behind the guards and Kitarisa was shoved into the room.

From somewhere the soft melodies of the dalcet floated above the sunlight as it streamed through the exquisitely etched glass in the high-domed ceiling, filling the round chamber with radiant light. At the center, the sound of water pattering from a pink-hued marble fountain adding to the cheery warmth of the chamber.

The guard's hard hand pushed at her shoulder, forcing her to kneel on the brightly patterned carpet.

"You will kneel, slave!"

Angrily, Kitarisa jerked her arm away from him. Long-buried indignant pride surfaced in her—didn't any of these people realize who she was?

"How dare you speak to me in that manner! I am no one's slave."

The guard bristled and took a threatening step toward her.

"You may leave, soldier," a high feminine voice ordered from the back of the chamber.

Kitarisa squinted into the bright light that blocked her from seeing the owner of that voice. A fragile laceleaf tree at the right hid the woman who had spoken, until she stepped away from the brilliant sunshine.

Palest lavender silk, threaded with fine gold veiled a slender form, barely concealing her seductive charms. Honey-gold hair fell to her waist, held back at the brow by a finely wrought band also of gold and tiny gold bells encircled her slim ankles sending off their delicate sound with each step. In one hand, she held a fan of ivory, crested with fluttering white plumes.

"You *are* a slave here, Kitarisa," the voice went on.

Kitarisa felt her stomach tighten into a cold knot at the sound of that selfish, proud voice—a voice she knew all-too well.

The blonde girl stepped out of the streaming light into Kitarisa's full view. Nothing could have prepared her for the utter shock at seeing the person standing before her.

"Alea!"

"No, Kitarisa, I am the Lady Ghalmara now, wife to the Counselor, Lord Jadoor of Volt. You will address me as such."

"How can you be here? The High Prince banished you in Riehl. You—"

"A pointless question, Kitarisa, since I *am* here."

Ghalmara signaled to the discreet servants standing to the side of the room, who brought in a cushioned couch and set it near the fountain. Ghalmara reclined gracefully onto the couch then signaled again for two slim girls in diaphanous gowns to stand over her with their enormous feather fans.

"I am a princess by birth, Kita. I see no reason for me to deny my own birthright."

"*Were*, Alea. You were. The High Prince banished you before the court in Riehl. You have no ranks and titles. Nothing!"

Ghalmara's eyes narrowed. "I will remind you once, Kita, of how I am to be addressed. It is Lady Ghalmara. Do not forget it."

Kitarisa's chin lifted a little. "Then you will not call me Kita," she said coldly.

A contemptuous smile curved Ghalmara's pink mouth. "Very well; agreed. But, you are mistaken. I do have ranks and titles since my marriage to my lord husband. He is a sweet little man, but quite unambitious. He is content with his scrolls and books, his papers and discussions with his learned friends. You would like him, Kitarisa. You could share discourses on tonics and distilling weeds." Ghalmara laughed cruelly at her.

"You are mad, just like father," Kitarisa said angrily. She shifted on uncomfortable knees. Even the rich carpet could not cushion the unrelenting hardness of the floor beneath it.

"I am not mad at all. Father was merely careless Kitarisa, and I do not intend to be careless. There is a great deal I want and I *will* have it."

"What is it you want, *Lady* Ghalmara?" Kitarisa asked sarcastically.

"Do you know what place this is?"

"Volt, I presume," Kitarisa said.

"Yes, but this particular place? It is the palace that once belonged to a Ter-Rey!" Ghalmara's bright laugh was as brittle as shards of broken glass. "Long ago, the Emperor Shadressian had this palace built for his favored warlord, Prince Aettilek—your barbarian's great, great..." She waved her hand airily. "His long past grandfather. It is too amusing...a banished princess now living in the residence of a Ter-Rey." She leveled her gaze at Kitarisa. "How *is* your ugly savage, Kitarisa?"

Kitarisa clenched her jaw and looked down, refusing to answer Ghalmara's insult to Assur.

"Very well," Ghalmara said, unruffled by her choice of words. "How is our illustrious High Prince?"

"He is well and will not rest until he finds us."

Again, a hard, cheerless laugh. "He will have a difficult time finding you Kitarisa. When he does, he will have to bargain for you."

Kitarisa's head snapped up. "Bargain for what? My life? Or for Princess Sethra's, or Davieta's? He will not bargain with someone he has disgraced. Banished!"

Ghalmara stood up and flung her little fan to the floor. "You will not talk to me in that manner Kitarisa." Arms folded across her chest, Ghalmara began pacing like a caged animal.

"You have not seen it, Kitarisa. The Keep. Moggadure Keep. House of the Emperors. And do you know what? It is empty. The great citadel to Volt's glory lies empty—a rotting hulk fit for only vermin and the worms. It lies wasting away, while the Council of this city argues over shipping tariffs and the price of fish!" She stopped and faced her. "I will have it," she whispered fiercely.

Kitarisa looked up at her in horror and saw the same look as she had seen in father's eyes: a madness beyond redemption.

"Alea...Ghalmara, you cannot be serious."

"I am very serious. There will be a new Empress to rule Volt and more. The lands that lie beyond these walls are vast. I will restore Volt's ancient splendor and rule it from Moggadure Keep." She looked down triumphantly at her. "You will help me achieve this Kitarisa. You will beg the Ter-Rey and he will concede."

"I will do nothing of the kind. My life will not be held in forfeit for your mad ambitions. You invite war, Alea. Destruction!"

Kitarisa rose on her knees and pointed a warning finger at her half-sister. "The Ter-Rey is no one to trifle with—you have seen his wrath. Father is dead because he underestimated the High Prince's power. If I am harmed, he will punish all who he thinks are responsible. He will level Volt. He will burn it to the ground and sow every inch of its soil in salt!"

"Not unless he knows he will destroy the very thing he seeks," Ghalmara said triumphantly. She lifted her chin proudly. "He will not destroy Volt, because I have them. I have your holy relics!"

Kitarisa sank back to her heels, silent and stunned. How could *she* have them? They were carried off the ship that night. Unless she truly had them...?

"You have them?" she whispered. "Where are they?"

"They are safe." Ghalmara turned, not looking at her.

"You are more insane than Father," Kitarisa said heatedly. "I am worthless next to the Sacred Weapons. You know that. If you harm them, you will bring ruin to the tribes."

"Exactly." Ghalmara's hand clenched into a small tight fist. "The world wearies of the barbarian's rule, Kitarisa. I have the means to destroy that ugly freak of a man and all of his filthy tribes! The Reverend 'Fa was right, but she went about it the wrong way. She only wanted her sanctuaries back and to worship her precious Medruth. But my allies have helped ravage the barbarians' most sacred places, causing chaos. Destruction from within, that is the only way. The tribes are in disarray, Kitarisa, and soon they will fall, broken and helpless. They will kneel before the Beast and pay homage. They will beg for mercy!"

"Alea, no. You cannot do this!"

Ghalmara's hand came down on Kitarisa's cheek in a stinging blow. She reeled to the floor; blood oozed from the corner of her mouth. Just like Kazan, only Alea was beyond madness. The girl was demented.

"I have warned you once, Kitarisa. You will call me by my right title."

Kitarisa struggled to her knees and then to her feet. Every fiber in her being raged at her vicious half-sister. The sinister fury within her began to stir again. The last of the intimidated princess who grew up under Kazan's harsh hand had vanished. She faced Alea. Her chin went up defiantly. She was the promised of the Ter-Rey and no one could intimidate her now.

"I warn you *Alea*. You will not do this. I will defy you and stop you in any way I can even if it means my own Summons. Father is dead and his foolish ambitions died with him. I killed the 'Fa and I will kill you, if necessary. You will die for your treason. If I do not, then the Ter-Rey will crush you and everything in his path to restore those Weapons."

An ugly sneer twisted Lady Ghalmara's pretty features.

"I think not, dear *sister*! He will bargain, or the weapons will be his ruin!" Ghalmara took a threatening step toward her. "How long do you think your precious barbarian will rule once those weapons are destroyed? The tribes will rip him to pieces!" She turned to the great doors. "Guards!"

Almost immediately, the heavy door swung open and the yellow and crimson-clad guards strode into the chamber.

"Take her away. Collar her. She will learn her place in this house." Lady Ghalmara, the former Princess Alea, spun on her heel, away from Kitarisa.

She had no strength to fight the burly guards, but only managed to muster enough courage to call out one last time, "He will destroy you. Alea...don't..." She never finished. One of the guards cuffed her soundly in the jaw. Kitarisa sagged between them, her head lolled to one side.

If Alea's guards knew who she was, they did not appear to show it or care. They dragged her down the corridors and stairways of the magnificent palace. Her bare feet were now cut and bleeding from the rough stones of the courtyards and dungeon steps.

When she did at last recover, she was not with Davieta. Nor Sethra. She was alone and as she tried to stand she felt something jerk painfully around her neck.

Her hands fumbled in the dark to find the source of the pain. Kitarisa gave a little cry of despair as she touched the cold steel around her neck, tracing the chain running from it through the dirty straw that was her bed to the heavy ring in the wall.

Alea had chained her like an animal.

THE TALL, SLIM form slipped from behind the laceleaf tree and bowed slightly.

"She was reluctant, my lady?" Shakiris asked smoothly. "I fear there will be no cooperation from the Princess Kitarisa. She is a strong woman; I noticed this during my stay in Daeamon Keep."

"She is a stubborn fool!" Ghalmara said hotly, pacing back and forth across the gleaming floor. "Father tried his entire life to beat some sense into her."

"It is apparent your father was unsuccessful, however, your objective and that of the Narusuba may still be achieved."

Ghalmara stopped pacing to cast a scrutinizing look at the dolmina. "How so? You heard her, she will not bargain for us. We will have to fight the Ter-Rey for Volt."

"Quite true, but he has not met with the Narusuba face to face. He must learn obedience first hand."

Ghalmara folded her arms across her chest. "You do not know this prince, Shakiris. Assur broke the back of the East's finest armies and destroyed the Wrathmen. My father's rotting corpse still hangs on the gates of Riehl and you prattle about obedience?" She held up a warning finger. "Kitarisa was right. We must not trifle with this barbarian. He will do exactly as she said. He will burn Volt to the ground if anything happens to those relics, or to her."

"But he will not, once he is in *our* control."

Ghalmara looked up at Shakiris and frowned.

"You are so confident he will bow to your master? The Reverend 'Fa thought the same and look what happened to her?"

"You sound uncertain, my lady," Shakiris observed coolly. "You cannot be losing your resolve now, I trust?"

Ghalmara turned away from him and sat down on the edge of the couch. "No," she said soberly. "Only I have learned to be cautious. Father was not cautious and the 'Fa was not patient enough. I must be careful; Kitarisa is intelligent and she has more power than she realizes."

Shakiris leaned over her. "Volt is within your grasp, my lady. Do not falter now. The Talesians are in disarray. The Ter-Rey will take his legions north to the Qualani and spend the winter crushing them."

Ghalmara shot him a warning glance. "But not for long. They are not fools. Your little trickery is only a temporary diversion. Once they realize they have been deceived by their so-called physick, they will come to Volt."

"Agreed, but by the time they arrive, it will be too late. They *will* bargain, my lady, and they *will* submit."

Chapter Ten

THE DIAPHANOUS GOWN clung to her newly bathed skin like a soothing caress, but could not quell the terrified hammering of her heart. The sheerest of rose-hued silk hung in graceful folds from her shoulders down to the little gold sandals on her feet. Even now, Davieta could scarcely believe the sudden change in her surroundings.

She had been taken from the cell and brought to these sumptuous chambers where she had been bathed, perfumed and dressed in the finest of silk then left alone, to wait.

Davieta shuddered and clutched her arms to herself. The air was warm, even languid, but she only felt the chill of her fear. She wished she could think more clearly and fight these feelings of desperation. She knew intuitively why she was here, and wished it were not true— she had been brought here for Physick Lael.

In Daeamon Keep, she had noticed his sly, ardent glances, similar to those of Dolmina Imroz, except the physick's attentions had roused within her only feelings of disgust as if having been touched by something vile. The dolmina was easily ignored, but Physick Lael filled her with loathing.

There was no other reason for the delicate clothes and sensual surroundings. He would use her and when his lust had been satisfied, discard her like an unwanted garment.

She clutched at the enameled collar locked around her throat. The attending slave girls begged her to wear the collar since they would have been severely punished if she had not allowed them to lock it around her neck.

The food on the brass tray had been left untouched even though she was nearly faint with hunger. Davieta knew the food would not stay down even if she did try to eat it. She pressed her palm to her churning stomach and sat cautiously on the edge of one of the brocaded cushions scattered about the room.

She forced herself to be calm and try to think rationally. She would not submit to him. Never would she allow herself to be victimized again like she had been before—she would rather die.

Davieta stood and began to pace the confines of the room. She must escape, if not to get away from that hideous man, but maybe to find help.

She had not seen Kitarisa since they had dragged her away two days ago and left her to await her own fate. What if Kitarisa were dead? Or Sethra? What if she was the only one left, far from her home and beyond any possible chance of rescue?

Davieta did not dare think of that possibility. Instead she focused her mind on trying to get away. She looked frantically around the room, hoping to find something of value, something she could sell or use to bribe her way out of Volt. The airy draperies enshrouding the low bed were beautiful but entirely worthless and the small decorations were equally of no value.

Davieta started at the sound of the door opening. She backed away, stumbling over the heavy cushions. The door burst open with a gush of cool air from the corridor.

Physick Lael...or whoever he really was, entered the room. The dignified robes of the physick were gone. A dark tunic over leather riding trousers and the enameled bands that crossed over his shoulders fastened in a wide band around his waist, now revealed the muscled body of a warrior. He did not wear a sword, but it was clear he had not come into the room for swordplay. His usually bland, almost unreadable expression had been replaced with the hungry look of a predator.

"Lady Davieta, you are lovely, as always," he said in a voice as silky as the gown she wore. He stepped closer and traced cool fingertips along the line of her jaw. "Lord Rame's infatuation with you is quite understandable. But such a waste. It is my good fortune you are beyond his reach."

Davieta shuddered and pulled away from his touch.

"Lord Rame will find us and you will be punished," she said heatedly.

Lael threw back his head revealing the black tattoo on his throat and laughed a mirthless, cold laugh. "I very much doubt that. By now, he is on his way to gather an army—an expected move on his part. I would do the same myself, if I were him. However, his efforts will be too late. You have another journey to make, beautiful lady, and it will be soon."

Dread knifed through her belly as she took another step away from him. "What do you mean, another journey?"

"You are quite valuable, Lady Davieta, as are the other two. We have waited a long time for the signs to be right—the Measure and Balance must be perfect for our purpose."

"I will be no part of your filthy purposes, physick!" Davieta backed away from him again, brushing against the table bearing the tray of food. Her fingers skimmed against something hard on the tray and instinctively, her hand closed around it. It was only a small fruit knife, carelessly forgotten by one of the slaves. She prayed Lael did not see her hide her hand within the folds of her gown.

His smile was a thin, cruel line. "I am not the estimable physick you would think, dear lady. I have dispensed with that title. You must call me by my true name, Shakiris." He stepped closer to her and placed one hand lightly about her throat. "So sweet," he murmured. "There is more to you than outward appearances would reveal."

His other hand also closed slowly around her throat, just over the collar. In a heartbeat she would be dead, her neck snapped like a dry twig.

"Princess Sethra is a little fool, isn't she? And Princess Kitarisa...?" He shrugged slightly. "She does not suit me. She is the barbarian's whore and will soon serve the Beast. But you, Davieta, are Riehlian, well-bred and refined. A lady. You are not worthy of that bad-tempered savage, but you are exactly suited to me."

His hands tightened ever so slightly and tugged her toward him, his face inches from hers. Davieta's heart hammered so painfully in her chest she could scarcely breathe.

Never again! Never again! She closed her eyes and felt his hands, *their hands*—filthy, greedy hands—and the laughter, the sound of tearing fabric and the pain.

"Take your hands off me!" she said through gritted teeth.

Abruptly, he did, lifting his hands high to the side, a look of mock contrition sketched his sharp features. "I would not harm you Davieta, but would have you come to me willingly."

"I would rather die than submit to you, any more than I would submit to that traitorous dolmina, Imroz."

"The dolmina suited our purposes and was no longer needed," Shakiris said coldly.

His gaze flicked slowly over her until he noticed her hand hidden at her side. "What are you hiding, Davieta?" He took another menacing step toward her and held out his hand to her. "Give it to me."

Davieta gripped the knife even more tightly, determined not to obey him. She backed away toward the open doors that led to the high terrace just outside the room. He would certainly take the knife from her by force if she did not think of something quickly. Slowly, purposefully, Davieta backed out to the terrace, holding the tiny knife in front of her—her only defense against him.

"Davieta, you are foolish to think you can hurt me with that." He gestured to the knife.

"If I cannot stop you, then I will die, physick...whatever you are," she said grimly.

Her heel touched the parapet and she stopped. She drew one leg over its edge, never taking her eyes from Shakiris, then her other leg until she was in position, poised to jump. She glanced down to the hard stones of the inner courtyard. They seemed so far away and yet somehow welcoming.

"Davieta!" he said sharply, seeing that she was quite serious in her intent.

He took another step and she raised the knife even higher. She glared at him defiantly. "One more step and I will do it."

Believing her, Shakiris reluctantly lowered his hands, palms upward and backed a step.

"Very well. We cannot have you destroying yourself now that we are so close to the completion of our plans."

"What are your plans? I demand to know this. What else can you do? You have taken the most sacred relics of the Talesians, you have killed Prince Achad and you have abducted us. You have done all this," she said angrily.

The tall man pressed his lips in a tight smile. "We are Narusuba; we will do what the Master bids us do."

"I *know* what you are; my father told me about you. You are a Shadow, a soul-stealer and assassin, you—"

"For the good of the world, Davieta. You will be part of it. You will help restore the power of the world to its rightful Master. You and the others will be a part of it—a ritual of the highest purpose, the purest of sacrifices. Taking the relics had no real meaning other than to disrupt the barbarians. Their rule must end, Davieta. You will help us defeat them." He took a cautious step forward.

"Never," Davieta snapped, edging back a few more inches.

Shakiris stopped, now wary. "Ah, lady. I concede. If I leave the room will you come down?"

"It will not matter. You will come another time, and another, until you get what you want."

He paused, clearly weighing her words and his own. He raised an apologetic hand.

"I will leave you, Davieta, and I will not come again until it is time for our journey. You and the Princesses Sethra and Kitarisa will be escorted with all honors. Now, please come down."

Davieta's gaze never left his. She still did not trust him, but it suddenly occurred to her that alive she might be able to help Kitarisa and Sethra. Slowly, she slid from the edge of the parapet until she was again standing on the terrace only a few feet from him. She held the knife firmly, never wavering.

"Go, now. Leave me."

"You must first give me the knife," he said with unusual gentleness, taking a hesitant step toward her.

She almost did, almost gave the knife to him, until she saw it in his eyes: his lust and the madness. With a swiftness she did not know she possessed, Davieta struck. Fleetingly, she recalled the terrible ruthlessness with which Rame had struck that drunken Physick Nadir in the surgery room and hoped she could wield even a fraction of that strength.

Gathering all her resolve, she drove the knife at Shakiris's chest. Like the fang of a viper, the tiny blade found its mark, cutting through the leather of his tunic and burrowing deep into the flesh just above his belly.

Surprised and reeling with pain, Shakiris staggered back from her and sank to his knees, clutching at the blood pouring through his fingers.

"Filthy little bitch!"

Davieta stared horrified at her handiwork. She had never even struck her sons, much less attempted to murder someone. The man coughed, horribly, and leaned over his knees. The action galvanized her. She turned and ran.

Like the proud man he was, Shakiris had confidently entered Davieta's room without bothering to post a guard outside the door. She breathed a tiny prayer of thanks to Verlian and ran down the corridor in the general direction of what she hoped was the back of the palace, toward the stables. She had no idea how she would find her way, except she knew to go north. Riehl was north and so was Raldan Mar'Kess. Safety. Home.

It was late and most of the guards were now beginning to feel the effects of late-night guard duty. Several were dozing at their posts. One had even slid down the supporting wall he had been standing against, fallen into a deep sleep.

Even in the warm night air, Davieta felt the cold horror of what she had done. Her hands shook and her teeth rattled so loudly she was convinced she would be heard at any moment.

In the dark stables she heard the reassuring sounds of horses snuffling through their hay or thumping at their feed tubs. The nearest horse shoved his head out over the stall door and nickered at her.

"Hush," she whispered, placing a hand over the horse's soft muzzle.

Davieta was no expert with horses, but she had ridden many times in Riehl, usually on safe old horses that had been set aside for the timid or elderly. She wasn't even sure how to saddle a horse. Saddling and bridling had been relegated to stableboys and grooms. Davieta fumbled with the unfamiliar straps and buckles of the bridle she found hanging on the wall just across from the friendly horse.

"Hold still," she whispered again.

The little horse seemed amused by her attempts to bridle him and tossed his head up and down, curling his upper lip as if laughing at her efforts.

Whether through luck or Verlian's kindness, she did not know, but finally the bridle slipped on correctly and she led the horse from the stall. She glanced up at the crescent that was Verlian's light.

"Thank you, Goddess."

She led him up to the nearby water trough and after managing to balance precariously on its edge, she flung herself onto his back, scrambling and struggling to find her seat.

The back gate was open, facing north. She put heels to her horse's flanks and urged him out of the cobbled yard. Above the clattering of his hooves, she distinctly heard Shakiris's voice, a long howl of rage and pain.

"Fiiiiind heeeeerrrrr!"

With the moon over her right shoulder, Davieta headed north. The faithful horse moved tirelessly, almost eagerly as if glad to be free of the confining stall.

Too afraid to be seen by day, she hid within the dense underbrush, resting and allowing the horse to eat. At night, she pressed on, unsure of her exact destination. She wished fervently she had paid closer attention to her husband's endless lectures on tracking and finding one's way in the wild. Coll would have known; so would Rame.

She hung her head over the horse's neck and caught a sob in her throat. Dearest, handsome, fierce Rame. How shocked he would be if he could see her now and angry like Coll. Yet, Rame was not like him at all. Coll had bellowed and roared like a breok bull, demanding everyone's attention. Rame's temper was the controlled fury of a warrior. And how she had teased him. A silly court flirt toying with a leashed tiger.

Davieta bit her lip, shamed at the memory.

On and on she rode with the moon at her right by night, and the sun at her left by day. In two days she lost both sandals and the silk gown was in shreds forcing her to steal a rough tunic left hanging to dry outside a small village.

She ate what she could find and when she didn't eat, she lay exhausted at the horse's feet while he grazed greedily of the sparse spring grass. At least the animal would survive, she mused bitterly.

Davieta lost track of the days. Her legs became raw and chafed from the constant rubbing against the sweaty sides of the horse. The sturdy animal plodded on, heading north. Somewhere within the depths of her mind, she realized she had not seen anyone during her journey, including the flesheaters—an uncanny accomplishment and entirely without design or planning.

The farther north she traveled, the colder it became until she thought she would certainly die. Davieta shivered violently, clutching the horse's neck, trying to absorb some of the animal's body warmth.

Still he plodded on as if knowing where to go. He clambered up a hill, through the trees and stopped at the crest. Davieta stared down at what lay before her: tents and wagons, hundreds of horses and men encamped alongside the Sherehn River. In the waning light she could just make out their surcoats—some black and green, while others were gleaming white and blue, Riehlian colors.

It could not be true. What were Riehlian warriors doing this far south from home? She passed a weary hand across her eyes.

I must be dreaming. I am so tired.

Besides, what if they were not Riehlians? What if they were like the others?

Never again. I will never allow any man.....

But her horse would have none of her reluctance. Recognizing his own kind, he whinnied to the hundreds of horses tied up about the encampment. They responded, eagerly welcoming the newcomer.

The horse crested the ridge and half-slid, half-trotted down the hill. Davieta hung on grimly to his mane, but her strength was gone. At the bottom of the hill, she looked up to see dozens of men running toward her, some of them shouting, some trying to corner her mount.

Past caring, she could no longer cling to the excited horse and slid from his back to the hard-packed earth.

If the warriors were not Riehlian, she prayed they would at least kill her mercifully and spare her what happened before....

"BY VERLIAN'S BLADE, it looks like a woman," Mar'Kess exclaimed.

Rame watched Mar'Kess rise from his camp stool, pointing in the direction where his men were racing toward one lone horse, running loose into the encampment. Someone small, like a child or a woman, clung to its back, apparently lost or perhaps fleeing from something.

He tossed the remains of his wine into the fire and stood, too, mystified by the unknown visitor who had managed to enter their encampment unseen by any of the guards posted around the area. Rame made a mental note to speak to the First Captain in the morning.

He stood by Mar'Kess watching a small horse, a lady's riding horse by the looks of him, trot into the camp, dodging the outstretched hands of the guards trying to capture him. Rame at once recognized the slender curve of a woman's leg clinging to the horse's side. Whoever she was, it was obvious she was trying to outrun someone or something.

One of Rame's own men managed to grab the bridle and brought the frantic horse to a halt. The woman never looked up. Her small hands, clutching the mane, trembled with exhaustion. Before anyone could catch her, she lost her grip and slid from the horse, falling heavily to the ground.

Rame knelt down next to Mar'Kess and gently reached to turn her over. Long, dark hair clung about her pale face in ragged strands; her lips were dry and cracked from lack of water. Glancing down, he noticed the caked blood on her bare feet. Whoever she was, she had been running for a long time, without apparent direction and with nothing but the clothes on her back.

He brushed away a lock of hair and started, almost jumping up from the shock. Her lids fluttered open and Rame found himself looking into soft, liquid-dark eyes, filled with pain and terror.

She ran a swollen tongue over her cracked lips and tried to speak, but all she could manage was a weak, sobbing whisper.

"Please don't...! Don't! *Don't!*"

His hands shook, his heart pounded in his chest. "By Verlian's sacred blood! Davieta!" He looked up into Mar'Kess's stern face. "Mar'Kess, it is Lady Davieta!"

Rame gathered her into his arms, holding her tightly, at once trying to hide the sudden unfamiliar tears of relief and shock welling in his eyes and the mounting rage against whoever had done this to her. He rocked her back and forth, comforting her, reassuring her, while hiding his grief and horror within the thick softness of her hair.

"Davieta. A'lara, it is me, Rame. Do not be afraid. You are safe! Safe!"

He felt Mar'Kess's hand on his shoulder. "My lord, let us take her into a tent where she can be tended to..."

Unable to look at him, Rame nodded. He slipped his right arm under her knees and lifted her up. She weighed next to nothing. Her frail body, starved from lack of food and wracked with cold, shook against him.

He would kill the man who had done this. He would tear out his heart with his bare hands and feed it to the marglims. He would—Rame struggled to think of a punishment severe enough to match this despicable crime against Davieta.

Once inside his tent, he placed her on the low bed. In the lamp light he could see the dark hollows under eyes in sharp contrast against the alarming whiteness of her skin. He took her hands in his, rubbing them, trying to generate warmth.

"Davieta, A'lara, do not be afraid. Nothing will happen to you."

Once the physick arrived, Rame watched as the coarse tunic was removed from her slight form and saw the blood on the ragged silk gown underneath. He couldn't take any more. He left the tent, his own blood burning through his veins like a fire out of control. Never in his entire life had he felt so furious, so consumed with hatred.

Mar'Kess caught up with him. "My lord, as difficult as it seems you *must* control your anger. I do not believe she will die. You must remain calm in order to find out what happened."

He nodded. "Of course, you are right. I am allowing my emotions to control me. But, it is difficult. I have never had such feelings for—"

"I understand. She is a lovely lady. It is painful to see her in such distress, but I believe she was being followed. Someone is after her. Shall I send out a patrol? Whoever it is cannot be far."

Rame looked at Mar'Kess, startled. "Yes, of course. At once. And, if you find him I want him brought to...me," he said grimly.

He watched Mar'Kess shudder, and suddenly realized he had just given the order like Assur.

AT DAWN, DAVIETA awoke. The canvas above her head moved slightly. A tent.

She felt the warm blanket over her chest, sensed the bandages wrapped around her feet and the fabric of the shift-like garment she wore. Although still weak, she knew she would be all right...she knew *nothing* had been done to her.

A noise caused her to look to her right. Slumped in a camp chair set next to the bed, a gray-haired physick slept quietly. Davieta must have made a noise, because immediately he awoke and noticed her.

"Ah, you are awake." He pressed gentle fingers to her brow. "No fever...a good sign. How do you feel?"

"Tired."

"Are you hungry?"

"Yes, very."

The physick rose and headed for the tent opening. "Excellent. I will send for something right away. However, I want you to know, there is a prince just outside, frantic with worry. He is desperate to see you."

"Who?"

The physick smiled. "Why, Prince Ramelek dar sa Sabiann, himself!"

Color warmed her cheeks. Rame! She hadn't been dreaming after all. It *was* Rame who had held her and tried to calm her fears. By what extraordinary magic had he found her?

After the good physick had ladled a small amount of soup down her throat, he allowed Rame to enter the tent along with a worried-looking Mar'Kess and one other officer.

Seeing Rame so reassuring and fearless brought fresh tears. She turned away, sobbing.

He knelt down next to her and placed a gentle hand to her hair. "Davieta, you are safe. Nothing will happen to you."

She heard the concern in his voice and knew her presence was causing him incalculable anguish. "I know. But, I thought you were...him."

"No one will hurt you. Please, do not weep."

Davieta turned back to him and nodded. His face, so dear to her, so fierce and handsome, was etched with a mixture of worry and raw anger. She saw the deep tenderness in his eyes, but also the ruthless, unforgiving line of his mouth.

"I know."

Rame found a small campstool, placed it next to her bed and sat down. "My lady, can you tell us what happened?"

"You must not tire her, my lord," the physick cautioned. "She will recover, but she is very weak and needs rest."

The prince nodded. "I will try to be brief. Who...who did this to you?"

Davieta swallowed, determined not to cry. "It was that physick, Lael, my lord, except his name is not Lael, but Shakiris. He is a Volten and a Narusuba. Dolmina Imroz helped him."

Rame glanced up at Mar'Kess, who merely nodded, then turned back to her. "Go on."

"Not long after you and the others left for the Qualani, Physick Lael came to the princess and insisted she visit the surgery to see all the improvements he had made. I did not want her to go; I never trusted the physick. I did not like him. He was always...looking at me like Imroz."

She watched Rame's jaw tighten, but he said nothing.

"Kitarisa decided to see for herself. We all went down, the princess, Sethra and me. But they tricked us. They had killed all the guards, all the prisoners. The dolmina put a knife to Sethra's throat and forced her to show them where the secret passage was, then they shoved us into a chamber."

Tears thickened her throat, but she swallowed them and forced herself to go on. "They let those men in...so many. They killed the old Ter-Rey and took the Spear."

Fresh tears came unbidden down her cheeks. She felt Rame's hand on her arm.

"Do you want to stop?"

She shook her head. "No. Let me finish." Davieta drew a ragged breath and continued. "They pushed us down the tunnel and into a ship. They did something to Sethra, made her sleep, but so still and deathlike. After days in the ship, we landed in Volt. They took Kitarisa and me to a dungeon cell. Later, someone came for her. I do not know what they did to her...I just do not know.

"Then the physick, or whatever he is, sent for me. There were other slaves. They made me wear a silk gown and I was forced to wait for him. He...he..." She stopped and again looked away from Rame.

He caught her hand in his, squeezing it. "Did he harm you? Did he force himself...?"

"No," she said in a small voice. "But, he is evil, my lord. He is Narusuba and they want us, Sethra, Kitarisa, and me, for something. A beast. Then, I stabbed him."

Surprise and something close to pride registered on his face. "You *stabbed* him?"

"It was only a little fruit knife, but I know I hurt him. He screamed and I ran to the stables. I found the horse and I just kept going. I did not know where except I knew if I kept going north, I would be home." She stopped, tears again welling in her eyes.

"Did you kill him, this Shakiris?"

"I do not know," she whispered. "Rame, you must stop him. They are evil and they want to control everyone. And, I think they have all the Sacred Weapons. They are using them to start a war among us, to divide us."

"I knew it," Rame muttered.

"I think she has had enough, my lord prince," the physick said. "Let us leave her so she can sleep."

"Of course." His eyes, so predatory, like Assur's, were gentle. "Davieta, you have done well. You have given us the information we have needed. We will find them and destroy them." He brushed back a strand of hair from her forehead. "Sleep now."

Before she realized what he was doing, Rame bent down and brushed a light kiss on her cheek. He rose and left the tent, leaving her breathless, her heart pounding and wondering if she should believe what had just happened.

Outside the tent, Rame turned to confer with Mar'Kess and his other officer. "It is as I suspected—I told this to Assur. Taking the weapons was only a ruse to divide us. What they really wanted was the women."

"But, why?" Mar'Kess asked.

"The Narusuba have always been secretive. We will not know until we find this Shakiris and question him." Rame stared stonily across the encampment, jaw set. "Before I kill him and the Qualani roadwilds."

Mar'Kess looked at him questioningly. "Qualani roadwilds, my lord?"

"Lady Davieta's family was murdered by Qualani roadwilds. They will die for this."

Mar'Kess shrugged and attempted a wry smile. "You leave no one else for the rest of us, my lord."

Rame made a derisive noise in his throat. "The Qualani are dead men. And this Narusuba dog, Shakiris, will beg me to die before I am finished with him."

"I thank and praise Verlian I am not your enemy, my lord. You sound much like your esteemed nephew and I do not doubt you will carry out your promises as does the Ter-Rey."

"You forget, Mar'Kess, I am the Swordmaster. I taught Assur how to fight and how to kill."

"His skills are formidable," Mar'Kess said approvingly.

"Yes, he knows almost as much as I..." Rame folded his arms

across his chest. A cruel hard look crossed his lean features. "But not everything."

Chapter Eleven

AS LORD SAAR HAD promised, after eight days the waters changed abruptly from choppy gray to a serene azure. Saar's warriors now plied the long oars and trimmed the great sails to gain more speed from the warm, southern winds.

Assur and the others discarded the heavy winter furs and leather jerkins, favoring a wide band worn over the right shoulder with their swords strapped across their backs. Assur was glad for the constant flowing breeze. Without it, the air became humid and oppressive.

He glanced over his left shoulder at the far shoreline, still content to see the reassuring signs of land. They would soon break away from the long western coastline of Talesia and head across the equatorial waters toward Maretstan.

He sensed Kuurus near him and turned.

"We should see the outermost reefs in a day, two at the most," Kuurus said wearily.

Like Assur, the scar-faced Siarsi had not enjoyed their voyage. Kuurus had complained loudly and often to anyone who would listen, that he longed for real earth beneath his feet and the reassuring familiarity of a horse.

"You are not the sailor you thought, eh, Kuurus?"

"No, lord. Saar can have his ships and the great seas. I will stay with the open land and solid ground." He sighed heavily. "Would that I could change places with Lord Rame."

"And leave me to suffer with his temper and foul moods? No, Kuurus, I am heartily glad Rame is *not* here."

Kuurus shrugged. "Still, my lord, I am eager for dry land."

Assur agreed with Kuurus; he'd had enough of the violent pitching of the ship and the unpleasantness of seasickness. He would be only too glad to arrive at Maretstan and put sailing behind him. But even then, it would not be for long.

Assur knew Prince Dahka was deeply in his debt, owing him for not only sparing one of Maretstan's most distinguished field commanders, but for the life of his daughter Princess Dahsmahl as well. Dahka had foolishly sent warriors to Gorendt to join with the armies of the now-dead Kazan in the doomed war at the Rift Cut. Although

Dahka did not personally participate in the battle, his daughter had been sent to Gorendt as a bride-offering to Kazan's son, Alor. When Kazan had been defeated, the Maretstani field commander, Borosa, had hastily surrendered his sword and re-established his oaths and bonds to Assur. He spared Borosa and the beautiful Dahsmahl, but sent a clear warning to Dahka: cease all traitorous activities or suffer a fate worse than Kazan. Maretstan's prince quickly came to heel—he would do anything for Assur to keep his crown and his head.

Assur needed his ships and he knew Dahka would supply them, while Rame would bring warriors from Riehl and Gorendt to help find Kitarisa, the Lady Davieta, and his sister. Then the Narusuba would be crushed and the Sacred Weapons would be brought back to Talesia.

At the thought of Kitarisa, Assur felt his belly tighten. What had happened to her? Who had taken her? And Sethra? The enormity of what had occurred in Daeamon Keep sickened him—the abduction of the women and the theft of the holy weapons. Achad's murder. Mere vows of vengeance seemed weak and unworthy of such despicable crimes. Assur wanted more than vengeance, he wanted the punishment of those who had committed this abomination against him and all of Talesia. Only blood would satisfy his need for revenge.

The next morning one of the crewman spotted the distant shore of Maretstan. Prince Saar ordered Assur's colors run up the foremast—the banner of the Ter-Rey—a field of red bearing his black crest of a rose and sword encircled by a crown. Soon, they spotted escort boats sailing toward them with Dahka's slim banners of violet and black fluttering in the freshening breeze. Assur hastily prepared by donning more appropriate attire and pressing the simple gold circlet across his brow.

The entire convoy turned and swept into the crescent-shaped harbor as hundreds of surprised Maretstanis lined the shoreline to gape at the nine Ponos warships and the fiercesome warriors from the north.

Too large to be tied to the piers, all the warships remained anchored in the middle of the harbor, while smaller boats transported Assur, Saar, and a handful of officers to shore. Once standing on the wide dock, a cluster of anxious-looking officials hurried forward and bowed.

One man with black hair and a beard, robed in maroon and gold and having recognized Assur as the Ter-Rey, stepped away from the others.

"Great Lord, you pay us an unexpected honor, an extraordinary honor. We are completely surprised by your arrival." He bowed deeply. "Allow me to introduce myself: I am Her Highness's Court Dolmina,

Liaden."

"*Her* Highness? What has happened to Dahka?"

The Dolmina Liaden looked slightly aghast. "Did you not know, Great Lord? Prince Dahka is gravely ill and has been so for several moonturns. The princess has been named his regent and heir; she now rules in his stead."

Assur shook his head. "No, I did not know this. Why was I not informed?"

Deep furrows lined the dolmina's brow. "Messages were sent by courier. Did you not receive them?"

Glancing at Saar, who looked equally as puzzled, Assur turned to the dolmina. "No messages were ever received. But, no matter. I will discuss this with Princess Dahsmahl when I see her." He gestured to Saar. "You will pay homage, Dolmina Liaden, to tribe prince Saar of the Ponos."

Liaden bowed as did the men behind him. "A great honor. Please allow us to escort you to the palace." He gestured to a nearby coach drawn by four finely-bred grays—horses that reminded Assur of Adzra who was still stabled in the belly of one of the Ponos's warships.

He climbed into the coach, along with Saar, Kuurus, and the dolmina. The others, the Maretstani officials and the handful of officers accompanying Assur, followed in the other coaches that had been provided.

Unlike the grim austerity of Gorendt Keep or the stark magnificence of Daeamon, Maretstan was a wonder of towering spires and turrets of pink and cream marble. Built long before Volt was even a cluster of huts along the Sherehn, Maretstan distinguished itself from other Talesian cities as the gateway to the far eastern provinces and beyond to the Barren. As a city of artisans and craftsman, Maretstan boasted the finest wares in all Talesia: exquisite silks, handwoven carpets, goblets of rare glass and magnificent weaponry, particularly the famous and deadly double-crossbows.

Assur refrained from revealing his admiration. His fears for Kitarisa and the stolen weapons rose with each passing moment. Later, he would allow himself to enjoy the glories of Maretstan and its fabled riches.

The coach stopped before a square and a stairway that led up to the palace. Trees lined the square, along with sculpted beds of exotic flowers bursting in full bloom. Once they arrived at the base of the stairway, Assur looked up and noticed no ranks of warriors protecting the glass and gold entrance to the palace. Only two guards stood on either side of the great doors.

"No one guards the princess?" he asked.

"Indeed, no," Liaden said. "Maretstan is a free and civilized city—there is no threat to Her Highness."

Assur said nothing, but did not like the dolmina's response. There ought to be guards, particularly now with danger so near.

However, once inside the palace, six tall warriors wearing the Maretstani colors immediately flanked Assur and his officers.

Liaden smiled apologetically. "These are Her Highness's personal guards. It is only a courtesy, my lord."

Again, Assur said nothing, but allowed the guards to escort them down the long, high-ceilinged corridor that opened into a great, airy hall of golden-hued marble and gleaming arched windows. No one sat on the simple black throne on the raised dais—only a few courtiers hovered nearby in small clusters of twos and threes.

"Where is the princess?" Assur demanded.

All talk ceased. Liaden began making discreet hand gestures indicating everyone should kneel. It took a few moments for the astonished courtiers to realize who had entered the hall unannounced.

"By Verlian's blade, it *is* the Ter-Rey," one exclaimed.

The courtiers and attending guards all dropped to one knee, right palms pressed to their left shoulders.

"Rise," Assur ordered.

"Great Lord, Her Highness awaits you in her private official chamber," Liaden said, gesturing to a door at the side of the hall.

Assur nodded and followed the dolmina, leaving Saar and the others with the anxious-looking courtiers. A single guard stood at the ornate door and hastily opened it, allowing only Assur to enter.

A small, regal figure, attired in a gown of black velvet with slashes of violet on the sleeves, stood before a tall narrow window overlooking the fabled city and harbor. Upon hearing the door close, she turned to face him.

"So, it is true, Great Lord. I thought my dolmina and the counselors were jesting when they said *nine* Ponos warships had just entered the harbor." She approached him slowly, then sank into a curtsey. "We are surprised and honored by your presence."

Assur returned a polite bow. "I apologize for the sudden intrusion and trust you and Prince Dahka have not been too inconvenienced."

She turned away from him, clasping her hands together, and looked down. "My father is not well, my lord. In fact, he is not expected to live much longer."

"My condolences...I did not know."

"He has never recovered from his shame—his betrayal and disloyalty to you. And the war...for sending me away to marry Kazan's son, Alor. It has all been too much for him. He has lived in torment since the day Commander Borosa and I returned from Gorendt."

"But, he *did* send his forces against me—"

Dahsmahl shook her head. "Against his better judgment; Kazan tricked him into thinking that you—all of Talesia—had joined forces with Riehl to reconquer the Eastern provinces. Kazan convinced him that you would take Volt, defeat Maretstan and destroy our trade agreements."

Dahsmahl turned back to him, her serene lovely face pale with grief. "My father is old. Sometimes he is not wise and is easily swayed by those who are stronger and more forceful in their opinions. He meant no betrayal. He was misled, deceived and now he is paying for his weakness. He is dying, my lord, and I *beg* you to spare him your wrath and let him die in peace."

Assur studied Dahsmahl, at once recognizing the full measure of her anguish. Maretstan was an enormous city-province and the complex Maretstani laws, while allowing female heirs to rule, forbade them to marry once they were crowned. When Dahka died, she would be left to reign, alone, bearing the full weight of her father's responsibilities and his shame.

"I am grieved to learn this, princess," he said softly. "But, I acted as was to be expected under the circumstances. Your father committed treason; he sent an army against me. However, I am not above reconsidering my decisions. Will you allow me to see him?"

Dahsmahl nodded, not looking at him. "Forgive me, my lord." She touched a fingertip to her eyes, pressing away the threatening tears. "Please, follow me."

At the back of the room, a door opened to a dimly-lit hallway that led to wider corridor. Silent-footed servants bowed to her and to him, as they glided by on their various duties. Dahsmahl stopped before an ornately carved door guarded by two large, fully armed warriors—both eyed Assur warily until they realized who he was, then hastily stood aside.

She opened the door and led him into a shadowy, quiet room with a massive bed bearing the frail form of Prince Dahka. Long white hair framed a face of ashen skin as brittle as parchment, and deep set eyes, sunken with illness and despair.

The princess knelt by the bed and took one of Dahka's hands into hers. The old prince turned to her. A trace of a smile touched his pale mouth.

"Father, I have brought someone to see you. He is very important and he has come a long, long way."

"Who, my child?" Dahka asked in a whispery-dry voice.

"You must promise not to distress yourself, Father. He is here as a friend and has come to forgive you."

"Who is here?"

"It is the Ter-Rey, Father," Dahsmahl said gently. "The High Prince, D'Assuriel."

Dahka turned his gaze toward Assur. Tears brimmed his eyes. "The Ter-Rey is here? Verlian have mercy! By Her blade, I—!"

"Hush, Father," Dahsmahl soothed. "All is well. He is not here to punish you."

Dahka clutched at his daughter's hand, his eyes were filled with confusion. "I do not understand. Why has he come?"

"Calm yourself. Hush, now." Dahsmahl brushed an errant silvery strand from her father's cheek, smoothing it into the rest of his hair. "He will not hurt you."

Assur bent down, taking hold of Dahsmahl's shoulders and gently moved her aside. He knelt by the great bed so Dahka could see him clearly.

"My lord Dahka, I have come to Maretstan not to punish you but to ask for your help."

The old prince looked up at Assur, searching his face. "You are the High Prince? Yes, yes, I believe you are. I remember seeing your father crowned Ter-Rey...long ago." Dahka smiled wistfully. "It took me nearly a full turn of the moon to travel all the way to Daeamon Keep. You do have the look of your father, D'Achadek, but I recall you were just a lad then—such a solemn, serious young prince."

"I never acquired my father's high sense of humor."

Dahka eyes again filled with tears. He struggled to lift himself up. "Forgive me, Great Lord. I never meant to betray you. Kazan convinced me with falsehoods. Had I known... Allow me to swear again my Oaths and Bonds to you!"

Assur nodded. "Be at peace, my lord. The past is behind us. You are forgiven."

"May Verlian bless you. She will take me into Her hall—"

Too overcome with emotion, Dahka lay back, exhausted.

Assur glanced up at Dahsmahl. He desperately needed to ask her father about the ships, but her look warned him to let the old man rest.

He rose and touched Dahka's shoulder. "Sleep now, my lord. We will speak later."

A manservant who had been hovering nearby re-assumed his duties and began smoothing the blankets to make Dahka more comfortable.

Dahsmahl hurried out of the room with Assur close behind her.

"I thank you, Great Lord, for your kindness. You have removed a heavy burden from his heart and mind. He will go to the Goddess in peace."

"My only regret is that I did not know sooner."

"I begged him to petition you, but he would not listen."

They hurried back through the somber hallways to her private chamber, where Assur immediately spoke to her about the ships.

"You must know why I am here—message birds were sent. Daeamon Keep was taken by Narusuba and the Weapons have been stolen. My sister, Princess Sethra, and Princess Kitarisa who will soon be my lady wife, and her own lady, Davieta, have been abducted by these fiends. My father D'Achadek was murdered in cold blood defending the Sacred Spear. I need ships, Princess—at least six to take Shygul and bring these criminals to justice!"

Caution shadowed Dahsmahl's eyes. "You must be cautious, Great Lord. There is danger in Maretstan."

Assur frowned. "What danger?"

Emboldened, Dahsmahl placed a light hand on his arm. "They are here, too, my lord. Narusuba. They have infiltrated the city; their spies are everywhere. When they find out you are here and learn your purpose, they will do everything they can to stop you. Even I am in some danger. I trust only a handful of my counselors."

"Liaden?" he asked.

Dahsmahl shook her head. "I am not sure. He seems loyal."

"And the servants?"

"My personal house servants have always been irreproachable. Even Borosa..."

"Commander Borosa? I demoted him in Riehl for leading his warriors against me."

"Borosa is ever loyal, my lord. He has faithfully obeyed your commands. He would never betray me or you. When we returned from Riehl, he found his wife and children, dead. They say they had been murdered by Qualani roadwilds." Dahsmahl choked on fresh tears. "Since then, he has re-devoted his life to my service and chose to stay here in Maretstan."

142   C. L. Scheel

"You trust him?"

"With my life."

He studied her serious lovely face for a long moment, assessing her honor and her sincerity.

"Only with Maretstani ships can I defeat the Narusuba."

She returned his earnest stare, her gaze never wavering. "You shall have all the ships you need, Great Lord."

THE BUTT END of a spear prodded Kitarisa awake. She looked up through the dim, dusty light at a grim-faced guard glaring down at her.

"Get up."

She struggled to her knees until the chain stopped her. The guard muttered angrily as he leaned his spear against the cell wall. He fumbled for a key attached to the ring on his belt then reached for the collar around her neck. She heard a hard click as the metal opened and the collar fell to the straw.

"Now, get up."

Her knees hurt and her feet were ice cold, but she did not allow the guard to see her discomfort. She felt his hand on her shoulder, rudely pushing her toward the entrance of the cell. Once in the corridor, she was met by three other guards, who said nothing, but indicated she should follow them.

She climbed the scarred stone stairway to the upper levels of the dungeon and as before, stepped out into the warm Volten sunshine. All four guards flanked her as they moved across the courtyard to an entrance at the back of the palace. Another series of stairways led them to a large bare room with one tall window, the ancient glass cracked and barred over with iron.

At the back of the room she saw two low beds. A plain, threadbare blanket had been left at the foot of one; the other bed held the sleeping form of a woman: Sethra.

With a cry, Kitarisa sped across the room to kneel before Assur's unconscious sister. "Sethra? Can you hear me?" She gently shook the princess's shoulder.

"She can't hear you," said one of the guards. "She will sleep until the mistress gives the orders for her to be awakened."

The guard stepped back and slammed the door shut, leaving Kitarisa once again feeling alone and desolate. At least the room was warmer, she mused. And the bed, although not more than a cot, was softer and cleaner than the filthy straw in that damp cell.

Kitarisa tried patting Sethra's cheeks and calling to her, but

Assur's sister would not awaken. She studied the girl's still form, her red-gold hair spreading over the thin mattress like a coppery web. She was truly lovely and probably favored her mother, since she looked nothing like her father, the now deceased Prince Achad.

Kitarisa smoothed the shabby blanket, tucking it high under Sethra's chin to keep her warm. Realizing Sethra would not soon awaken, she rose and began a thorough inspection of the room.

At one time it had probably been a magnificent bedchamber. Hints of past grandeur clung to it. The floor made of exotic inlaid woods, now scuffed and stained from neglect, still revealed an exquisite artistry and design.

To the side of the room, she spotted what remained of a black granite fireplace. It was chipped and broken in several places; the hearth was bare and showed no remains of a fire, not even the thinnest coating of ash.

As she moved about the room, she tried to imagine how it might have looked during the time of the long-ago Ter-Rey, Aettilek, and somehow sensed that he had been in this very room, a room where a High Prince would have slept. It then occurred to her that even though she and Sethra were confined to a long-forgotten room in a long-neglected wing of the palace, it was where they *ought* to be.

Weary but still restless, she had nothing to do but gaze out the window at an old inner courtyard below. Birds and small animals nested in the crumbling barracks where horses and warriors had once been housed.

As the light faded and the room grew cooler, she curled up on the bed, growing increasingly drowsy. Sethra's breathing was soft and steady and soon Kitarisa found herself drifting in and out of sleep.

Later, she awoke to the sound of the door being unbolted and opened. Instead of surly guards, a plainly-dressed servant woman, her gray hair plaited into two thin braids, entered the chamber bearing a tray of food and a single burning taper. A manservant followed her carrying a small table. He set it between the two beds then hurried out of the room.

"There now, you'll be hungry," the woman said, placing the tray on the table.

Kitarisa studied her hoping to find some semblance of compassion in her coarse features, but after the appalling confrontation with Alea— *Lady Ghalmara* she reminded herself—she decided to speak to the woman cautiously.

"Thank you...?" she said, gesturing to the food.

"Zenna," the woman replied.

"...Zenna. I have not had this much to eat for several days. It was kind of my sister to think of us."

Zenna smiled. "Your *sister*? You mean the Lady Ghalmara? No, my lady, she did not instruct me to bring the food. The dolmina, Master Shakiris, instructed me to see to your needs. He has been quite concerned about you and the young princess." She nodded at the sleeping Sethra.

"And, has he said anything about what will happen to us...?" Kitarisa paused delicately, hoping the servant woman would give her some much-needed information about Sethra's condition as well as the whereabouts of Davieta.

Zenna removed the lid from a chipped bowl containing a pale broth, then broke a small loaf of bread in two. "Do not worry yourself about the princess. She only sleeps." From her pocket Zenna produced a brown glass vial and handed to her. "Here. My master says you may awaken her now. When you hold this under her nose, she will revive in an instant."

Kitarisa uncorked the vial and passed it swiftly under her own nose. She did not know what the concoction was, but it reminded her of strongspice—a powerful remedy that when waved under the nose of those who had passed out, jolted them back to consciousness, particularly swooning, love-struck young ladies.

"You are certain this will awaken Princess Sethra?" she asked suspiciously.

Zenna smiled and nodded. "Oh, yes. Master Shakiris said it would work perfectly."

Kitarisa recorked the vial, reluctant to awaken Sethra while the servant was still in the room. There was something about Zenna she did not trust—perhaps it was her manner or her too-generous smiles.

"Master Shakiris is very thoughtful to all who serve him well."

Suspicions roused, Kitarisa pocketed the vial. "You serve Master Shakiris, too?"

"In the humblest ways, but I owe my life to him. Five moonturns ago, I was a beggar on the streets of Volt. My man had died and I have no children. I was near to starving when my master found me."

"He took care of you? Restored you?"

"Oh, yes. Saved me, he did. I would do anything he asked of me."

There was no doubt in Kitarisa's mind that Shakiris was really Physick Lael. She watched as Zenna bent over the bowl on the tray, the neckline of her simple tunic gaping open to reveal the toughened dark skin of her throat.

"I will leave you now, my lady. If you need more food, tell the guard. He will inform my master, who will tell me."

Kitarisa felt a low chill shoot up her spine. Her instincts had been right: Zenna could not be trusted. Still fresh-marked in her skin was the tattoo, the mark she had seen on the men who had invaded Daeamon, a diamond shape, pierced through by a dagger.

The cautious interview came to an abrupt end. Kitarisa did not respond to her extravagant praise of Shakiris.

Too unwitting to realize what she had said or done, Zenna dipped her head politely, turned, and left the room.

KITARISA ATE THE soup hastily, too hungry to care if it was watery and weak-tasting or that the bread was somewhat stale. Anything was better than the vile food that had been left for her and Davieta while they were confined in the cell. And, she needed her strength before she attempted to revive Sethra. Explaining what had occurred during their long, tortuous journey to Volt would be daunting enough—Kitarisa could not be sure of how the princess would accept what had happened, particularly the death of her father, Achad.

What would they do to her and to Sethra? And where was Davieta?

It had been several days since she had last seen Davieta and Kitarisa sensed she was no longer within the palace...or Volt.

The violent animal rage began to build inside her again. Soon, it would be unstoppable. She would be changed, not knowing what she was, or who she would harm.

A rising, sickening sensation almost prevented Kitarisa from finishing the food. She shoved the bowl aside unable to eat. Despair filled her. She lowered her face to her hands to silence the oncoming tears.

Assur, forgive me. Find me before it is too late.

SHAKIRIS STRODE DOWN the cool corridors of the palace toward Lady Ghalmara's chambers, still burning with indignation and rage. She had gotten away. That stupid girl had not only cut him with a knife, but had also managed to flee the palace and get out of Volt without a single guard or warrior noticing her. *No one* had seen her and that particular detail made him more enraged than the fact that Lady Davieta had actually escaped.

The cut had been painful but not life-threatening. After the initial shock, Shakiris had awakened Lord Jadoor's own personal physick and ordered him to stitch up the wound. A tight bandage about his belly and large doses of a pain-killing tonic kept him on his feet. Anger gave him strength.

He would find her. Oh, yes, he would find her. His sweet, guileless, *cruel* Davieta. And, she would be punished....

At Ghalmara's door, he stopped and reflected on the forthcoming interview with her. Another tantrum, no doubt. Her impatience and greed were beginning to fray her resolve, but she was young and ambitious—so like her father. It mattered little to Ghalmara as to how she achieved her ultimate objective, to rule all of Talesia as empress. If it meant every tribe must submit to the will of the Beast as minions of the Narusuba, so be it. Like Kazan, all Ghalmara wanted was power.

Shakiris had to admit grudging respect for the determined young woman. If she had been a man, she would have been a formidable warrior. She was no one to slight or disregard. As Lord Jadoor's wife, she wielded considerable influence over him and the Council of Volt. Those who defied her were either chained up in the dungeons below, or dead.

The guards allowed him to enter her chamber. Ghalmara stood at the back of the sumptuous room, on the terrace overlooking the harbor below. Her servant women had been dismissed, as she was alone, garbed in a somber-hued tunic and simple gold bracelets on her wrists. She did not turn to face him when he bowed and murmured a polite greeting.

"My lady has called me?"

"Yes, I did." Her voice was cold as winter ice.

"You are disturbed, my lady?" he asked cautiously.

Ghalmara turned around, her lovely face a hard emotionless mask. "I am displeased." She waved a piece of paper in his direction. "Do you know what this is?"

"It appears to be a note, perhaps a message."

"It is. It is from one of your Narusuba spies. From Maretstan."

Shakiris felt the blood leave his face. "Indeed," he said with forced calm. "A pity, my lady, that I have not had the opportunity to read it. What does it say?"

"He says that we must act quickly or we shall be discovered."

"Discovered?" Shakiris sensed the menace in her voice and knew he was on dangerous ground. Except for Davieta's escape, events were proceeding as planned. He could not fathom what the spy meant.

"Here read it. Or, perhaps I shall simply tell you myself." She held up the letter to the soft light streaming into the room.

"It says: *...I beg to inform you that if certain actions are not taken quickly, you will be discovered and all plans will be compromised. It is my duty to inform you that the Ter-Rey and High Prince, D'Assuriel, has arrived in Maretstan with a convoy of Ponos warships. He has met with Her Highness, Princess Dahsmahl—for what purpose, I cannot say at this time, however it is possible he may attempt an attack...*" She glanced at Shakiris. "Shall I go on?"

Shakiris pondered the message and the depth of Ghalmara's anger. "We must assume that His Highness has reasoned out what has become of the Sacred Weapons as well as the women. He is not a fool, my lady, but he has acted much faster than we anticipated."

"You told me he would be occupied for the rest of the winter in a war with the Qualani! Now we find he is under our very noses, in secret communication with that whore, Dahsmahl. She will do anything for Assur; her father is dying and she does not have the full support of her council."

Shakiris tried to sound calm. "I believe we should examine what the Ter-Rey actually knows."

"He knows that you abducted his sister and his pretty new bride." Ghalmara sneered as she began her all too-familiar pacing, her anger rising with each step. "He also knows the Qualani did not steal the weapons."

"But he does *not* know exactly where the weapons have been taken. He can only guess."

Ghalmara whirled on him. "You think he will not find out? You underestimate this barbarian, dolmina. My father did, and his bones yet dangle from Riehl's highest battlement."

"I would never underestimate him, my lady. I observed him closely at Daeamon Keep." Shakiris took a step toward her. "He is not invincible. He can be brought down yet."

"How?"

"By accelerating our plans. All Narusuba warriors are in place throughout Volt and Shygul, awaiting my orders. Once the Ritual has been completed, we can strike."

"What do you suggest we do?" she asked skeptically.

"I will take the women to Shygul. Then, we bait the trap."

Ghalmara resumed her pacing; her small hands clenching and unclenching at her sides. "You make it sound so easy. What about the weapons?"

Fear had begun to creep into her voice. Ghalmara was a strong-willed young woman, but she did not possess her father's cold-blooded ruthlessness. Caution tempered her. Shakiris smiled to himself. Fear would be her downfall and he would take full advantage of it.

"It *is* simple, my lady," he said softly. He took a step closer to her. "Prince Assur has gone to Dahsmahl to obtain reinforcements—perhaps for warriors or ships. He will use them to find the weapons and his bride-to-be." Shakiris leaned toward Ghalmara to emphasize his next words. "*But he cannot be in more than one place at one time.* By the time he finds the weapons, it will too late."

"And what am I to do?"

"You must trust me. All you need do is to wait."

"What if the Ter-Rey comes here, demanding the weapons and the women?"

Shakiris smiled openly at Lady Ghalmara, relishing the triumph of his plan. "Tell him. Give him his precious weapons and tell him the women are in Shygul."

Some of the defiance returned to Ghalmara's cold blue eyes. She glared at him. "The High Prince is no fool; he will know it is a trap!"

"Of course he will, but he will have no choice. And when he and his men arrive, they will be defeated. The Ritual will be completed and the Beast's power will begin. When I return, you will have all of Volt. All of Talesia will be yours within a single moonturn and the barbarian will be defeated." He did not dare touch her, but allowed his gaze to travel slowly over her lovely body, lingering for a fraction of a moment on the curve of her breasts. He heard the tiniest intake of breath; a hushed gasp.

She said nothing for a moment, then, "Very well. Prepare to leave Volt. I will arrange for a ship. Bring the women as soon as Princess Sethra is strong enough to travel."

Shakiris bowed, smiling. "By your Will, my lady."

He hastened out of the chamber, pleased with the way the conversation had turned. Ghalmara was afraid and she would begin to make mistakes—mistakes he would be able to use for his own purposes. And, he would have her yet.

Beautiful, stupid little spider. You will be crushed as the others.

But he had one task yet before him. Another foolish woman. She had not gone far, he knew it. Davieta was a lady's maid, soft and easily intimidated, having no knowledge or experience in the wild. There were those who could find her. Easily.

He stopped, pondering his next move. He had many obedient minions to call upon, particularly one. His lip curled in disgust. That filthy, one-eyed Qualani had served him well in the past. He would do so now, or lose the other eye.

Chapter Twelve

IT WAS HEAVIER than he imagined—the silver hammer he held in his fists. It gleamed in the dull light of the torches with its own kind of ominous fire.

The Hammer of Siarsia—the Weapon of Verlian's last daughter. How, by all that was blessed of the Goddess, did he *happen to hold the most sacred object of the Siarsi tribe? He wasn't Siarsi; he wasn't even Talesian. He had no right to hold this holy weapon.*

He heard the guttural roar and whirled on his heel to find himself facing the creature again. Raldan shuddered. Just like the 'Fa, maggot-white, stinking of its own sulphurous breath and the blood from its victims.

It turned on awkward leathern wings. Yellowed talons scrabbled against the loose rocks as it scuttled toward him. It reared its elongated head and roared fire into the night sky, obliterating the last vestige of Verlian's light.

Raldan took a step back. His heel brushed against something solid like a rock. He looked down at the pale round object and gave it a cautious tap with the toe of his boot. It was as large as a great melon—a green-gray mottling covered its hard surface. He nudged it again. An egg.

The creature suddenly hissed and Raldan looked up in time to see it rush forward a few steps, only to stop.

"You want this, don't you maggot?" Raldan raised the Hammer and the beast roared in frustration. It backed up, writhing and snaking its head back and forth, never taking its eyes from the egg at his feet.

Raldan smiled and hefted the Hammer. "Get back, you stinking worm."

The beast hissed again, black tongue slavering over ragged teeth, as a long stream of fiery breath cooled to a vile yellow cloud, gushing from its great mouth. It backed away from him, slowly, awkwardly, its bag-like belly scraping against the ground with each clumsy step. It stopped and waited, eyes roiling.

Raldan looked beyond the beast and saw her—a woman hanging by her wrists from a great frame. Startled, he looked again, momentarily forgetting the beast and the egg. He had never seen such a woman: hair like streaming fire and skin as pale and shimmering as the sky at dawn. Her head hung back, eyes closed, but there was something remarkably familiar about her face. Her eyes fluttered open and for a moment she looked at him, her mouth working soundlessly as she tried to speak.

"Help...me," she whispered weakly. "Please." Her eyes closed and she sagged against the ropes binding her wrists.

Raldan looked at the great Hammer in his hands and knew what he had to do. He swung the ancient weapon over his head and brought it down with all his strength onto the orb at his feet. Green-black ooze squeezed from the jagged cracks in the shell, stinking of the foul creature within. A red eye and the edge of a small tooth glinted from the dark birth fluid. He brought the Hammer down again and again, until there was nothing left but shards and vile scum.

The beast screamed its fury and desperate loss. The pale head writhed in the night sky, alternately bellowing charred smoke and white-hot fire. Raldan stepped back, clutching the Hammer, astounded by what he saw and what he had done.

Enraged the beast reared up, exposing its belly and the emblazoned mark on its throat. Raldan raised the Hammer over his head, now wishing fervently he held his sword. The Hammer was useless against such a creature as it writhed uncontrollably, lashing back and forth, tormented by the loss of the egg. More of the hot fire boiled from its mouth, so much that Raldan could not see beyond it.

The beast stopped and for the last time lifted its enormous head to the skies and drew a great breath into its lungs, swelling itself to monstrous proportions. In one rush of breath it bellowed forth white fire, an engulfing wall of heat that obliterated the woman and the impenetrable blackness of the night.

Raldan heard her scream, shrill, horrible and wracked with pain. When he looked again, only two charred fragments of rope dangled from the frame.

He dropped the Hammer and sank to his knees, covering his face in shame.

Before I leave the sky, Raldan!

AS THE SUN HOVERED over the western sky, turning the slopes of the distant Adrex to deepening shades of violet and indigo, Mar'Kess stood next to Rame on a high hilltop overlooking far-off Volt. Behind them, the warrior Cai and Commander Vidun waited patiently. Below the ravine, the long columns of mounted warriors awaited their orders.

Mar'Kess snapped open the glasseye and peered down at the ancient city. As the light of day slowly melded into dusk, he saw a hundred thousand pinpricks of light—lamplight, torches, and fires coming to life, flickering and gleaming, reminding him of jewels in a lady's crown. The Sherehn flowed like a languid blue ribbon around Volt into the wide, curving harbor. All looked peaceful, but he knew it was only an illusion. Beneath her tranquil disguise, Volt teemed with deceit and black secrets.

Rame opened his own glasseye and scanned the city. "I can make out the palace and the Keep. How many guards?"

Mar'Kess turned his glass on the magnificent old palace. "I doubt the Keep is being guarded. The palace may have fifty men. I worry about the Narusuba. They could be anywhere. Their powers are limited, but deadly."

Rame snapped the glass shut. "Inform the First Captains of their attack positions. When we are within striking distance, we will take the city before dawn. Select two men for a sortie; we need to get into that palace."

Mar'Kess nodded—an easy task. He would secure Cai, of course, and the stalwart Commander Vidun. Most of the First Captains already knew their positions—they only needed to form their companies and be advised of the time to attack.

He hurried to his horse, anxious to fulfill Lord Rame's orders. While the responsibilities of Prime Governor were challenging and agreeable enough, he had missed the excitement of battle. He looked forward to capturing Volt and finding the lost Sacred Weapons as well as finding the red-headed woman who haunted his dreams.

DAVIETA HAD TRIED to make herself as unobtrusive as possible, knowing Rame and the others were intending to invade Volt, but found herself the object of several tense interrogations. Not only by Rame, but Raldan Mar'Kess and a war-hardened Gorendtian, Commander Vidun, had questioned her repeatedly about Volt and where she had been held. She wished she could have recalled more of the palace and the dungeons, but the night she had fled from Shakiris, she took scant note of her surroundings.

After gaining what little information she had to offer, Rame ordered her to stay near the camp physick, Kett. He was a quiet, kindly man, who tried to make sure she was comfortable and appeared to appreciate her assistance with simple tasks—rolling bandages and taking stock of the surgical supplies.

She soon discovered that living amidst hundreds of tense, edgy warriors forced her to remain in the background as much as possible. She ate alone and slept in the tiny tent provided for her.

With her strength restored, Rame had arranged for her to ride the lady's horse she had ridden into the camp, but well to the back of the column. And although Cai had offered himself for the duty, Rame chose two Riehlian warriors to guard her.

She knew they were not entirely content with their orders. Watching over a single woman instead of riding with their comrades was considered an unimportant duty, not worthy of a warrior's skills, but they dared not disobey Lord Rame. They scarcely spoke to her but remained polite as well as protective.

By Rame's order, the barges had been abandoned, moored in the shallow shoals along the Sherehn's riverbank, hidden within the dense trees and vegetation. The great barges filled with noisy horses and men would not allow them to enter the city undetected. The wagons were also abandoned and horses packed with the provisions for easier transport.

The pace toward Volt quickened. By spreading out and moving in smaller companies, they were harder to recognize as every warrior had been commanded to replace their identifying surcoats for plain, drab-colored ones. No emblem or mark of rank distinguished them from common free-warriors, or a band of hunters looking for game.

Rame permitted several brief stops along the way to keep the horses fresh and allow Davieta to rest. She watched as Rame trotted his horse back along the long column to find her.

"You are unwell?" he asked bluntly.

"No. Oh, no. I am quite well. Please, do not worry yourself about me."

He nodded. "You must inform me the moment you need rest."

Reaching across the space between them, he took her hand in his and placed a light kiss to her fingertips. "I will not lose you again."

"I promise. You will never lose me, my lord," she said, smiling at him.

An embarrassed flush tinged his cheeks. She watched as he glanced sharply at the two nearby warriors, a dangerous, warning glare. Rame said nothing more but nodded curtly to her, then put heels to the Trigian.

FOR TWO MORE days, they headed south toward Volt, ever watchful for Narusuba, Volten spies, or the dreaded marglims. They saw no one which surprised even Mar'Kess: no travelers, no villagers or even the occasional free-warrior. No bands of roadwilds prowled the roads or forests. Even wild game was scarce, which clearly troubled Rame and the others.

As the sun settled behind the Adrex, Davieta sat quietly on her patient horse awaiting the order to proceed. No one near her spoke, but she heard the soft murmuring of a few men riding ahead and the occasional snorting and stomping of a restless horse.

Cool evening air brushed her cheek. Night birds fluttered in the trees above her head and insects began their insistent chirping. Strange to hear such comforting sounds, since only a short while ago she had been sitting within Daeamon Keep, watching the snow fall and hearing the sharp winter winds blast against its walls. It was not yet near summer, but the warmer climate near Volt felt reassuring after the harsh cold of the north.

She stifled the urge to sigh, hoping Rame or Mar'Kess would soon give the order and allow the men to set up camp. She was tired after a long day, unaccustomed to riding for so many hours.

Her husband Coll had ridiculed her for being too soft and utterly useless for anything but stitchery and dancing. A part of her rebelled against such accusations. Even though Coll was dead, murdered, he still had been wrong.

She had survived a brutal attack and had been forced to watch her entire family put to the sword. She had assisted Princess Kitarisa in saving Cai, who now followed her around doing anything she asked in order to fulfill his personal Oaths and Bonds to her. She had managed to wound Shakiris before escaping. That in itself was a remarkable feat and one which Rame had commented upon repeatedly since she had arrived in the encampment.

Davieta allowed a true sigh to escape her lips.

And, Rame... He unnerved everyone with his threatening looks and sharp words. No one dared question his authority but not one man in the entire legion spoke ill of him. He was exacting in his orders, but never unfair, nor was he unjust in meting out discipline. Rame was feared, but respected.

Somehow Davieta knew this was what he expected of his men, but around her, he became a completely different man. The hardness in those black-patterned eyes softened. The line of his mouth became less grim. She did not fear him like she had feared Coll—Rame would never harm her. She was, however, watchful of his jealousy. Having lived with a hot-tempered husband and raising two head-strong little

boys, Davieta knew how to contend with jealousy. Rame was not filled
with jealousy toward her, alone, but for another, a man who held more
power than he, and in Rame's eyes, perhaps did not deserve it. Rame's
jealously of Assur was apparent to everyone, except him.

Regardless of his temper and his surly manner, she could not help
her own feelings. Rame had her heart, if only he knew it.

The wind shifted and suddenly the birds ceased flying—the
insects grew silent. Davieta felt her horse grow tense. His head went up
and his ears pricked forward. The Riehlian guard at her right glanced
her way. He, too, had noticed the change in the night air.

The cool breeze shifted again, then stopped. For a moment, she
could not see anything, as if an impenetrable white cloud had fallen
over her eyes. A hard, bitter cold crept around her feet, up her legs to
her knees. The little horse snorted and tossed his head but did not
move.

Davieta felt the cold rise to her hands, threading through her arms
to her shoulders. A terrified scream gathered at the back of her throat
but was silenced by a large hand clamped firmly over her mouth.

The guard to her right groaned and sank forward over his horse's
neck, unable to speak or cry out. Davieta did not know what had
happened to the other warrior as she was pulled down from her horse
and dragged across the soft, damp earth, her legs numb and useless.

Groping, greedy hands lifted her to the saddlebow of another
horse. She felt a hard arm encircle her waist, pulling her against the
lean body of the man riding behind her. Nothing, in all her dreaded
nightmares, could compare with the terror gripping her heart. Unable to
resist her captor, she could not even cry out.

No! Never again!

Between the pale flickering light of Verlian and the dark sinister
shadows, Davieta saw several horsemen nearby wearing ragged furs
and stinking hides. She knew who they were and what they wanted.

She felt the man behind her take a firmer hold of her waist as he
spun the horse around and headed into the forest. His rough bearded
mouth brushed against her ear; his words chilled her heart.

"Say nothing, or you die."

One of the renegades reined away from the others, nudging his
horse close to her. A broken-toothed grin split the man's hideous face
as he silently laughed; the single eye mocked her.

An uncontrollable shudder wracked through Davieta's limbs. Not
him. Not again.

"I have message from my master," the one-eyed Qualani leader

said in clumsy Talesian. "He say, he now holds the knife..." He
chuckled. "After he done with you..." He grinned again, then pointed to
himself. "Me."

RAME RODE THE black Trigian through the dense forest as fast as he
dared, with Mar'Kess, Commander Vidun and Cai hard at his heels.
Hatred thrummed through every nerve, revenge consumed him like a
deadly venom. One of the Riehlian guards who had survived the attack
had also seen Davieta's abductors: a band of Qualani outcasts, led by a
filthy, one-eyed roadwild.

That Narusuba fiend would die first, then the Qualani dog.

He reined in his exhausted horse, allowing the others to catch up
and rest their own animals.

"How much farther?" he asked Mar'Kess.

"Less than a day, I should think."

"You have seen Volt before?"

"Yes, twice. It is a great city, my lord. Temples, palaces and
Moggadure Keep."

"Who rules the city, now?"

Mar'Kess shrugged. "I am not sure. Since the Rift Cut War, the
Eastern provinces have been unsettled. I, myself, have been too busy
seeing to Riehl as well as Gorendt. I have heard rumor that a woman
governs Volt. However, it is only a rumor."

"Where does she live?" Rame asked.

"Most likely in Aettilek's palace."

Rame cast a skeptical glance at him. "The first Ter-Rey's palace?
How is this possible?"

"The last emperor, Shadressian, built the palace for Prince
Aettilek who had led the Voltens to victory against the Narusuba. An
interesting irony, my lord. This time we fight the Narusuba and Volt. If
this woman truly rules the city, she would choose the palace as the
Keep has not been used for many hundredturns and is nearly a ruin."

"And, the Sacred Weapons? Where would they be hidden?"

Mar'Kess shrugged. "I have no idea. They could be anywhere."
He glanced at him; a smile quirked at the corners of his mouth. "I
suppose, we will simply have to ask."

Rame took Mar'Kess's light attempt at humor with good graces.
He liked the Riehlian governor; they worked well together.

"Tell me, my lord, what does Princess Sethra look like?"

The tenuous high regard Rame held for Mar'Kess faltered
slightly. "Why should you be interested in my niece?" he asked

suspiciously.

"Because, I do not know what she looks like. I know Princess Kitarisa and Lady Davieta, but I do not know the other lady. How will I recognize her if we are separated?"

Mollified, Rame's estimation of Mar'Kess resumed its high marking. "She has her father's high spirits and her mother's beauty. She is fair, with eyes as blue as the sea and hair like fire."

Mar'Kess remained quiet for a moment before saying softly, "I find red hair most beautiful."

And for once, Rame did not get angry.

RAME HAD GIVEN the order for the warriors to take Volt at first light. He had little sympathy for Voltens. They had allowed those Narusuba-fiends to take control of their city. If they could not defend themselves from being overpowered by such a treacherous faction as the Narusuba, then he, himself, would see it done. He would take back Volt and restore order. Rame knew Assur would have done the same.

Volt would be surrounded from all sides. The only escape would be by sea, but Rame had also sent aloft five message birds to Maretstan, advising Assur to set sail for Volt with all speed. A few Voltens or Narusuba might escape, but when the long ships arrived, no one would be able to slip through the Ter-Rey's grasp.

Night had settled over Volt by the time the four slipped into the silent, dark streets. Captain Vidun found a secluded place near the outskirts of the city to leave the horses. Even though there were only four, the horses would make too much noise, clattering over Volt's cobbled streets.

All of them wore helmets—Mar'Kess providing Rame with a Riehlian field commander's helmet, crested in stiff black horsehair and a single black feather springing up from the brow.

Rame tugged the visor down over his eyes. The Narusuba's power affected the eyes first, then took control of the limbs, rendering their victims paralyzed by a mind-numbing cold.

A handful of Voltens wandered the streets: a drunken old sailor with a jug of sour summer ale and a pair of anxious-looking servants hurrying through the city on an errand for their master. But there were no warriors and no Narusuba.

As they passed the great crumbling hulk of Moggadure Keep, Rame wondered if there were any Narusuba at all in Volt and if the entire scheme—stealing the weapons and abducting the three women—had been a hoax. Or, that Kitarisa and Sethra were elsewhere. He dismissed that idea. Shakiris had abducted Davieta, twice. Instinct told Rame that she and the other two were needed for more a sinister purpose, not just to satisfy one man's lust.

Only a few torches fluttered outside the main entrance to the old palace. Smaller than Moggadure, the palace still retained some of its grandeur from a bygone era—the time of the emperors and of the First Ter-Rey, Aettilek.

"The main gate is open, my lord," Captain Vidun whispered, nodding to the massive front gates that stood open, but guarded by only six warriors wearing scarlet and yellow armor.

"They do not appear to be Narusuba," Mar'Kess said in a low voice. "These are just palace guards and there are none standing watch at the walls, either."

Rame nodded. "They are too confident or they do not anticipate an attack."

"If we kill these guards, we may awaken the entire palace. The game will be up, my lord, and we will have lost the element of surprise," Mar'Kess continued.

"Vidun, Cai, wait here and keep watch," Rame said tersely. "Mar'Kess and I will get inside. We may have to take this palace in another way."

The two officers nodded and slipped into the shadows while Rame and Mar'Kess crept closer to the gate. Distracting six bored guards was easier than they imagined—a pebble tossed in the opposite direction of the open gate sent them off hunting for an imaginary intruder.

Both swords drawn, Mar'Kess and Rame slipped inside and melted against the inner walls, keeping well away from the flickering torches and hidden from Verlian's silver gleam.

Another surprise awaited. No other warriors were keeping guard of the inner courtyard.

"I do not understand any of this," Rame murmured beneath his breath. "Where are they?"

Mar'Kess did not answer, but nodded in the direction of the lights glowing from rooms in an upper story at the back of the palace. "Someone is here."

"I do not like this, it is too easy and it stinks of a trap." Rame eased around a stone pillar, one of dozens that supported a long colonnade leading to another entrance into the palace.

"If we are trapped," Mar'Kess said softly, "we will have no way of informing Cai or Vidun."

"I will give you the signal as soon as it becomes too dangerous. Get out and return to the legions. Wait for Assur."

They continued their silent exploration of the palace, passing dozens of darkened, uninhabited rooms—some sumptuously appointed, others appearing to have been abandoned.

At the juncture of three corridors, they heard a door open and close, then the footsteps of two people approaching them—a man and a woman.

Rame and Mar'Kess slipped into the shadows and watched as Shakiris and a beautiful young woman with hair the color of honey and amber strode past them.

"My ship leaves with the tide; I do not have long, sweet lady."

"And the weapons?"

"I leave them with you. Keep them safe. You will use them to negotiate with the barbarian prince, once he arrives. Make no mistake, my lady, Prince Assur will be here," Shakiris answered. "When I return, we shall have all of Talesia."

The two stopped not more than ten paces from where Rame and Mar'Kess were hiding. Rame felt his heart beat in huge, thundering beats. He held his breath and drew back deeper into the shadows, drawing on all of his training to remain silent.

"When do you leave with the women?" the girl asked. "I will be glad when they are gone, particularly Kitarisa. She has been nothing but an annoyance to me, as she was to my father. She has always stood in my way, cheating me of what has been rightfully mine."

Rame saw Shakiris nod slightly. "Once the sacrifice has been made to my Master, we shall be free to achieve our purpose—Volt and its riches shall be yours and I will have the Beast's blessing to make all of Talesia submit to his will. The barbarians' days are numbered."

"How long will it take for you to reach Shygul?" she asked, sounding a bit plaintive.

"Four days at sea, my dear, then another to reach the sanctuary. The ritual takes place as soon as Verlian wanes. When Her light is gone, we begin..."

Rame heard the young women laugh softly. "It is a great pity that Malgora could not have been more cunning or my father more patient. They were fools."

"Fools that have paid the highest price." He took the her hand and placed a slight kiss to her palm. "A price, we two, will benefit by...immeasurably."

She responded by smiling at him—a knowing, secret smile.

"Immeasurably."

The two continued down the corridor until they disappeared into the darkness.

"I cannot believe it is true," Mar'Kess breathed softly.

"What cannot you believe?" Rame asked.

"That woman...that girl, the High Prince banished her, along with her brother."

"Who is she?"

"She is Alea, Kazan's daughter and Princess Kitarisa's half-sister. Assur took all her titles and lands, then had her banished to the Catacombs."

"It must be she who now rules Volt. How is this possible?"

"I do not know, my lord. But it is certain she intends to see Kitarisa die by this "beast." I would assume that man, her lover, is Shakiris?"

Rame nodded. "He is. It is also clear they intend for all three to be sacrificed. We must find them, before the tide turns and they are taken away."

They continued their silent search, moving stealthily through the palace until they entered a dilapidated wing, smelling of age and decay. At the end of the corridor, they found a door secured with a simple bolt and lock. Both of them sensed this was the place where the women were being kept.

Mar'Kess drew back his sword and looked at Rame, who nodded. In one deft stroke, Mar'Kess struck the lock, shattering it. Deftly, Rame snatched the broken lock from mid air before it landed on the floor.

Mar'Kess grinned at him. "You are fast, my lord. No wonder you are the Swordmaster."

Rame answered with a soft grunt and pocketed the lock. "It was you who wielded the sword, Mar'Kess. Of course, it is a Talesian sword," he added with a touch of wry humor.

The great door creaked open and the two men slipped inside. Both of them raised their visors, astonished by what they saw.

At the far end of the room, all three of the captive women were gathered around a tall window, struggling to push it open, trying to escape.

Davieta whirled about when she heard them enter the room. It took a moment for her and the other two to recognize them.

"Rame!" she gasped. Davieta dropped the odd-looking tool she was holding and sped across the room, throwing herself into his arms.

Rame embraced her awkwardly, still clutching his swords.

"Verlian's mercy. You are safe," he breathed. "They did not harm you?"

He felt her nod against his shoulder.

"Yes, we are unharmed, for now," he heard Kitarisa say from behind Davieta. "It is good to see you, Lord Rame. We had nearly given up hope."

He released Davieta, reluctantly, then bowed to Kitarisa. "I, too, thought we would never see you alive again." He noticed Sethra, who approached him slowly. Although much paler and thin-looking, his niece still had the fire of defiance in her eyes, as fiery as her brilliant tresses.

She embraced him lightly. "Lord Rame, Uncle." She noticed Mar'Kess and nodded to him. "Who is this?"

"This is Raldan Mar'Kess, Sethra. The Prime Governor of Riehl."

"And an old friend—one who helped find Assur in the Catacombs and won the war at the Rift Cut," Kitarisa said warmly. "I am most glad to see you, Mar'Kess."

Still holding his swords, Mar'Kess bowed slightly. "It pleases me that you and the other ladies are unharmed. But, we have little time. The one called Shakiris will return for you soon. He intends to sail with the tide, straight for Shygul."

Rame noticed the shattered glass in the window and the broken bed where the legs had been removed to use as tools. "You were trying to escape?"

Davieta took his arm and propelled him toward the window. "Yes. The iron bars are rusted and weak, but we have not yet been able to break them."

Both Rame and Mar'Kess re-sheathed their swords, then began examining the window, testing the strength of the decaying iron bars.

"You almost succeeded, my lady," Mar'Kess said to Sethra. "I commend your resourcefulness." He hefted one of the metal legs taken from the small bed nearby.

Rame peered down at the neglected courtyard below, noticing the broken brickwork and crumbling mortar. "Where were you headed, once you made your escape?"

"We had hoped to make it back to the encampment," Davieta explained.

"It was her idea," Kitarisa said. "She said she knew where you were."

Although there was a strained look about her, Rame also saw the flare of determination in Davieta's eyes. She had not been crushed—

her spirit was unbroken and it pleased him. For a moment, he allowed his hard warrior-exterior to drop. He touched Davieta's cheek and smiled. "You did well."

"My lord, we must hurry," Mar'Kess said. "If we are to get out in time..."

Rame turned toward the window and began knocking out more of the broken glass. He tested the iron bars Davieta and the others had tried to break. The old iron had been weakened, but it still held. He motioned for Mar'Kess to help him. Both of them leaned against the bars, pushing with all their strength. The ancient metal groaned as if in pain, until the bars gave away and crashed to the courtyard below.

Mar'Kess nodded toward Sethra. "I'll go down first; it is not that far to the ground."

Sethra hurried to the window, gathering up the ragged hem of her gown. Kitarisa followed her, then turned suddenly to Rame.

"Where is Lord Assur?" she asked.

"Maretstan. He is acquiring ships to attack Volt from the sea. Do not worry, my lady, he should be here within a day, not more than two."

"Does he know about the weapons?"

"He does. After Volt falls, he intends to sail for Shygul. The Narusuba have caused all this and he will see them destroyed."

"And the physick, this...Shakiris?"

"I will kill him myself, my lady," he said grimly.

A noise startled them—heavy footsteps coming from the corridor.

"We have been found out," Kitarisa said softly.

With one leg over the edge of the window, Mar'Kess motioned frantically for Sethra and the others to hurry. "We can just get away..."

"No, there is no time," Rame said. "Get out, Mar'Kess. Find Cai and Vidun. Get back to the legions. Assur will be here soon."

"My lord..."

"Go. That is an order, Mar'Kess," Rame snapped.

The Riehlian slipped silently over the side of the window and disappeared just as the door latch rattled.

Rame turned slowly and drew the two swords from his back. Davieta, Sethra, and Kitarisa gathered behind him. They said nothing, but he could sense their fear.

He raised the swords and took a defiant stance. Whoever was behind that door would have to kill him first. Hatred and vengeance settled around his heart like an icy hand. He hoped the intruder was Shakiris as he would enjoy cutting him to pieces.

Hard boots scuffled outside the door; a shrill voice gave a command and the door swung open.

Chapter Thirteen

"DID YOU REALLY think you would get away?" the golden-haired beauty asked coldly.

She stepped into the room with Shakiris at her side. Several warriors, clad in crimson and yellow, stood just outside the room, swords drawn. Rame knew he had almost no chance of defeating them and would certainly die, but he also knew they would not dare to harm the three women standing behind him.

"Alea!" he heard Kitarisa gasp.

"Silence. I have nothing to say to you!"

Rame watched warily as Shakiris motioned for several of the Volten warriors to enter the room—a smirk twisting his lips. "Well, well, we meet again noble Prince." He bowed mockingly. "I should be honored. To capture the great Ter-Rey of all Talesia, so far from Daemon Keep, is an extraordinary stroke of good luck. Wouldn't you say so, Lady Ghalmara?"

Rame noticed Ghalmara's surprised expression and suddenly realized that the helmet he wore completely covered his hair and hid most of his face. To them, he did look like the Ter-Rey.

The fools think I'm Assur.

He did not respond at first, hoping Kitarisa and the others would not say anything either. The words of the Qualani Shalman flashed through his mind: *Two, who are one, to fulfill the same purpose.*

"Good fortune or maybe your fate. Either way, *Physick* Lael, you will die by my hand," Rame retorted.

"Interesting. This, I should like to see, since you are quite surrounded. The odds are against you, Lord Assur. I must confess, I marvel at how you were able to enter Volt completely undetected and I have no doubt you will fight bravely, but in the end..." He spread his hands apologetically.

"Alea, stop this," Kitarisa snapped. "What do you think you are doing? Aiding this...monster?"

Alea drew herself up. "I am not Alea, I am Ghalmara. Do not forget that! I am taking back what is mine, *dear sister*...what this barbarian took from me." She pointed to Rame. "He was the one who banished me. He destroyed Father and humiliated Alor; he took away my rank, my title, and my land; he sentenced me to the Catacombs."

"You deserved your punishment," Kitarisa retorted angrily. "As did all of you!"

"Take them!" Ghalmara shrieked.

The warriors tightened their circle around Rame, while more entered the chamber and seized the women.

Rame raised his swords. The first Volten stepped forward and struck. The blow was easily blocked and Rame took advantage of the warrior's inexperience. With deadly precision, he sliced the right-hand sword downward, diagonally across the Volten's face, cutting him from brow to cheekbone. The warrior howled, dropped his sword and grabbed his face. Rame's second blow with the left sword slashed him across his unprotected upper legs. The Volten fell to the floor, writhing in his own blood.

Shakiris raised his gauntleted hands and began to applaud. "Excellent, my lord! You are a credit to your Swordmaster. It is a pity he is not here to see your skills."

"He will be disappointed. I have not killed you. Yet."

"I doubt you will have that opportunity," Shakiris warned ominously. "The game is over, High Prince. Surrender your swords."

Rame faced Shakiris. The swords flicked into position. "My Swordmaster taught me that I must never surrender my swords," he said in a low chilling voice. "You will have to take them from me."

"So be it!" Shakiris motioned for the remaining five warriors in the room to attack.

Even though he was outnumbered, Rame flew at them, killing two instantly. The remaining three circled cautiously, clearly reevaluating the level of his fighting skills. Rame blocked another feint from the warrior to his right—a high backstroke cut across the warrior's upper arm. The man hissed in pain and dropped his sword, clutching his bleeding arm.

"Enough!" Shakiris shouted. "You have caused enough damage for one day, Lord Prince. Surrender and let us be done with it."

"Find your sword," Rame growled, raising his in challenge.

Shakiris frowned and before Rame could strike, the Narusuba stretched out his right hand, palm flattened directly toward him.

"I don't need a sword, barbarian."

Instantly, Rame felt the cold consume him, rising rapidly from his legs, through his chest to his arms. He cursed himself for forgetting to lower the visor as his mind slowly stopped functioning. He could not move, but stood frozen on the very spot he was standing. He fought the cold and the paralyzing numbness taking over his mind, but the strength of his hatred was not enough. Rame sank to his knees; the swords slipped from his hands, clattering loudly as they struck the floor.

"Take him below," Lady Ghalmara commanded. "Chain him."

Two Volten warriors grabbed him by the arms, forcing him to stand. Rame struggled to maintain his balance, but the warriors showed no mercy. He stumbled on useless feet as they dragged him from the room, down the dim corridor to the dungeons below.

Rame felt nothing. His mind went blank, almost dead. But he heard her—clearly—Davieta's desperate sobbing rising above Ghalmara's mocking laughter.

ONCE AGAIN, ASSUR found himself clutching a shroud line to steady himself against the heaving deck beneath him. This time, however, he did not suffer the dreaded nausea, but made certain he drank some of the foul-tasting concoction the Maretstani sea captain had given him.

It was called bellyleaf—a black brew made from a bitter powder mixed with wine, used to remedy seasickness. Assur soon found out it wasn't a leaf at all, but the dried, ground-up parts of some crawling sea creature. He shuddered. At least he felt better—he had none of the roiling sickness that had kept him on his back for three days during the first voyage.

Kuurus was again at his side, but had remained remarkably quiet about the voyage to Volt.

"The captain says we should see Volt tomorrow, my lord."

"At least this trip is shorter, eh, Kuurus?"

"Yes, but it does not make it any easier. One day or ten days—even one moment aboard this wooden monster is one moment too many."

Assur nodded in agreement. They were horsemen. Lord Saar and all the Ponos could have their ships, as could the stalwart Maretstani seamen.

He gazed across the water at the convoy of war ships Princess Dahsmahl have given him, each filled with warriors, weapons and horses. She had been generous—ten ships combined with the nine Ponos long ships would be a formidable force. Volt, he knew, would fall easily, but Shygul... Assur had no knowledge of the mysterious archipelago far to the south and east of Volt. He knew of no one who had been there and fewer who actually knew how to find it.

Captain Jarrash, however, appeared confident. He reminded Assur of Lord Saar, quiet and serious, having a steadying influence over his crew. His ship, *Ironfist,* led the way across the brilliant blue waters of the Volten Sea—a fresh wind pushing them along at a swift pace. They would be in Volt by morning and Assur hoped they would quickly find Kitarisa and the others, as well as the weapons. He was tired of war and death. He wanted only to return to Daeamon Keep so that he and Kitarisa might marry.

For the first time, Assur was afraid for her, for his sister and for Lady Davieta. The specter of betrayal and destruction sharpened his resolve. Somehow, he would find that traitorous physick, the Qualani renegades and the Narusuba killers who had murdered his father. They would die, all of them, by his own hand if necessary.

But if Kitarisa were to die...?

Assur could not think of that possibility—dared not think of it.

Before giving in to such disturbing thoughts, he turned his attention to the horizon and Volt. Kitarisa *had* to be there; she *must* be there and alive.

Why else would he still be seeing her in his dreams?

RAME STOOD IN THE center of the cell, arms outstretched, hanging by his wrists from chains bolted into the walls. The last of the numbing cold had dissipated, leaving him exhausted and aching from standing so long. Every muscle in his arms burned; the iron manacles cut bloody gouges into his wrists. He had not been given any food or water for...hours. Days maybe. He did not know. All that kept him alive was hate and the memory of Davieta's frightened tears as he was dragged away.

As long as he remained alive he would find away to kill Shakiris. For Davieta he would remain patient. He would endure the starvation and the pain in silence. He would not be here forever.

Shakiris's warriors had taken his swords and helmet, stripped him to the waist, then beaten him with a redreed—a sharp, tough river reed suited admirably for the occasional stroke across the backside of a disobedient pupil. A beating on bare flesh was excruciating.

Fortunately, the beating had not lasted long as the Volten warriors soon grew bored, realizing that Rame would neither scream nor would he beg for mercy. They left him alone to suffer and to nurse his growing hatred.

He suddenly heard the lock rattle and the bolt being thrown back. The door opened slowly. He expected Shakiris or the crimson and yellow-clad warriors returning to beat him again, but was surprised when the slim form of Lady Ghalmara entered the cell. She stood before him, cool and arrogant, her wine-red gown concealing her from neck to ankles, but emphasizing every seductive curve.

She studied him for a long moment before speaking.

"You look like him but you are not Assur. Who are you?"

Rame returned the frank stare. "Who do you think I am?"

"You are an imposter sent by that barbarian to deceive us."

"No more an imposter than your Narusuba *physick*, princess." He grinned at her sardonically. "Or, maybe he is simply your lover?"

Ghalmara glared at him furiously. She drew back her small hand and struck him hard across the face. The numerous rings adorning her fingers cut sharply into the flesh of his mouth and cheek.

His gaze never left hers. "Then he must be your master." He spat blood at her feet, daring her to strike him again.

"You vile creature, filthy barbarian! I should have you whipped to death. Who are you? I demand to know."

He leaned toward her, straining against the chains and grinned. "Am I not the man who banished you? Look at me, my lady, and tell me I am not Assur."

"Talesians do not cut their hair," she said scornfully.

"But I have cut mine. A Ter-Rey may do whatever he wishes."

Uncertainty crossed Ghalmara's delicate features. She stepped back to look at him, taking in his shorter hair and his outstretched arms.

"You are not Assur," she said decidedly. "You are someone else, someone I do not know, but I believe you are close to the Ter-Rey."

"Am I?"

"I could have you killed. You are worthless to me."

Rame struggled to stay on his feet, but managed to pull himself upright.

"Then do it, *Princess Alea*, and find out what happens when you murder the High Prince and Ter-Rey of all Talesia."

"How dare you...! I will not listen to your threats." Ghalmara spun on her heel, heading out the cell door.

"Enjoy ruling Volt while you can, but be warned. There are others following me. Are you willing to risk your life for taking mine?"

He watched her stop; her slim back became rigid, but she did not speak.

"If I die, my lady, so will you. And Volt will be burned to ashes."

GHALMARA HURRIED THROUGH the dark back streets of Volt

clutching the hood of her cloak closer to her face. She dared not be seen or recognized. She had not taken an escort guard or even one of her maids—she could not risk it. No one must know where she was going or who she was seeing.

Few people roamed the streets of Volt this late at night. By her own order, Shakiris enforced a strict curfew on the citizens—they were not allowed on the streets after the mid of the night, unless it was a dire emergency. Those who disobeyed her order were caught and punished. She liked it that way, ruling Volt with a tight rein and an iron fist.

It had all been done so easily: bribing the guards before she entered the Catacombs; fleeing to Volt, where she hastened to ingratiate herself to Jadoor, the most senior council member in the city. In less than a week, the old fool had fallen for her charms and false smiles. He readily married her and quickly relented when she insisted on taking over the administrative duties of Volt. Jadoor returned to his books and papers, leaving her with an entire city to rule as she pleased.

Then came Shakiris with his cool manner and intriguing ideas. He both frightened and fascinated her, and although the idea of taking him as a lover had been tempting, something stopped her. Maybe it was the way he looked at her, hiding his contempt beneath the thinnest veneer of respect.

But he was ambitious, like her. She cared nothing about his "beast," nor did she care about the Narusuba—she had seen very few of them. Shakiris kept his shadowy minions well out of sight. Most of them resided on the Shygul Islands, far from Volt. But, Shakiris was powerful as well as dangerous. Although she had learned to conceal her fear, Ghalmara acted cautiously when she was around him.

The shadows along the streets deepened as she turned a corner into an unlit alley. She spotted the single torch fluttering outside the inconspicuous door—the sign on it had only one word: Redsilk. It was enough. The silkrooms were only permitted one word to declare their business.

She knocked and waited impatiently until an old man with greasy gray hair and two missing teeth opened the door.

"Good evening, my pretty. I am Old Zek. Have you come for business or do you seek employment?"

Ghalmara almost slapped the man, but forced herself to remain calm. "No, good sir. I am here to find someone, an old acquaintance of mine."

"Ah, indeed." He winked and motioned for her to come in. "Have you been in Volt long?"

"No," she lied. "I am trying to locate...he is a distant relation of mine. It is important I find him."

Old Zek chuckled. "There have been many like you, hunting for their errant husbands, or sometimes a wayward son."

"He is not my husband!"

Ghalmara almost regretted her decision in coming here. The place reeked of perfume, sweating bodies and the strong odor of rapturewine. She had never indulged in the bad-tasting opiate that smelled like sour ale and made one behave like a slow-witted breok. She wrinkled her nose and pressed a handkerchief to her face.

"Who is it you seek, my lady?"

"A young man, about my age. His name is Aloreth, a Gorendtian."

"Ah, young Aloreth. One of our best customers. I believe he is in the back."

The old man led her through dimly-lit passageways, lined with heavy draperies that muffled the sounds coming from the various rooms. Zek stopped at one and rapped lightly on the narrow door. No one answered, but he opened the door anyway and stepped inside.

Ghalmara nearly gagged at the sight. Her brother lay sprawled on several large cushions, embracing two scantily clad woman who were both kissing and fondling him passionately. The small chamber stank of rapturewine.

"Leave us!" she ordered.

The girls jumped at the sound of her voice and hastily grabbed their garments. They said nothing to her but fled the room in a flutter of silk and jangling ankle bells.

Her brother eyed her mockingly, not bothering to get up or indicate where she should make herself comfortable.

"Ah, Alea, dear sister." Alor reached for a large goblet and sipped from its contents. "Or should I say, Ghalmara. I never know which name to call you."

"Don't drink that!"

"Why not? I like it and besides, why do you care, *Lady Ghalmara?*" Alor smirked at her and took another swallow. "I think I will call you Alea for the moment. Ghalmara is too grand a name for a silkroom, don't you think?"

"I think you are stupid from too much of that so-called wine. For once, act like what you are, a prince."

Alor's laugh was bitter. "I, a prince? You forget Alea, I have been banished, just like you. Our lands and titles were taken from us. Now I must use the name of "Aloreth" to hide my ignoble identity." He set the goblet back on the small table near his elbow. "Or, have you forgotten all this so soon?"

"I will never forget, but I will never become what you are: a depraved—"

"You will never become like me, Alea, because you are ambitious and mad...like our father."

Alea said nothing, but continued to glare at him.

Alor passed a weary hand across his brow and touched a knuckle to his pale, wispy moustache. "What do you want with me?" he asked in a tired voice.

"I have come for some advice," she said, controlling her anger.

Her brother made a disgusted noise in his throat. "My advice? I'm honored."

Alea sat precariously on the edge of a large cushion. "Listen to me, I am in great danger. Everything I have worked to achieve may be ruined. Someone of extreme importance is here in Volt."

Alor raised a brow. "Oh? I can't imagine who."

Swiftly, she explained what had happened concerning Kitarisa and the other captive women, then the mysterious intruder she had captured who looked and acted astoundingly like the Ter-Rey.

"The High Prince is here?" Alor asked, astonished. "How can that be? Are you sure?"

Alea rose and began her agitated pacing. "I don't know. He *seems* to be exactly like Assur, but there is something different about him."

Interest piqued, Alor sat up. "How so?"

"He is...harsher, more menacing."

"Where is he now?"

"I have him chained up in the dungeon." She stopped to face her brother. "He said something that frightens me. He warned me that there were others who would follow him and avenge his death if I had him killed."

Alor stood up, all traces of intoxication and debauchery vanishing from his face. He took hold of Alea's shoulders, forcing her to look at him.

"If he is the Ter-Rey, then you had better act quickly. Release him now, Alea, or you *will* die. If his armies are on the way here and once he finds out Kitarisa and the others are gone, he will burn the city to rubble. You know that."

"I have his precious weapons."

"Do you? Where is your so-called dolmina, Shakiris?"

Alea hesitated. "Gone. He left two nights ago with the tide. He has the women."

"But, he left the weapons with you?"

She looked down and nodded. "Shakiris said they would be used as the instruments to guarantee my claim to Volt."

Alor turned away and flung up his hands. "What have you done, woman? We are all dead. If Assur finds out you have them—"

"What if he isn't the Ter-Rey?"

Her twin whirled around to face her. "Then who do you think is following him? If not his own armies, then quite possibly it is D'Assuriel himself coming with all his legions. Either way, you are dead, Alea, and so is Volt."

Frightened by what Alor had just said, she struggled to control her shaking hands and the sick knot in her stomach. She tried one last tactic. "What if he's bluffing? What if he is no one, but an uncanny look-alike?"

Alor looked at her for a moment. "You are a stupid little fool, but you may be right. There is a way to find out. Go back to the dungeons and look at his arms."

She blinked, not comprehending. "Look at his arms?"

"Look at the firemark on his lower arms. If it is a rose and a sword encircled by a crown, then dear sister, you have indeed chained up the High Prince of all Talesia. If there is no mark, then he is an imposter or...it is all some kind of ruse."

"And then what do I do?"

"Get rid of him, as fast as you can."

Alea nodded, grateful for the thread of hope Alor had given her. The man in her dungeon could not be the Ter-Rey—he had to be an imposter.

She left the silkroom after briefly embracing her brother. He was not without some use. Once outside, she filled her lungs with the cool night air. She had to hurry. Lavender light just touched the eastern skies.

Alea raced through Volt's empty streets, back to the palace. Instead of going to her own apartments, she ran down the ancient stone steps to the dungeon below. A sleepy guard acknowledged her with a respectful nod.

"I want to see the prisoner."

The guard hastened to find the keys then led her down into the black passageways of the dungeon. At the prisoner's cell door, he stopped.

"You want me to awaken him?"

"He is asleep?"

"Passed out, my lady. I unchained him and let him lie on the floor. You needn't worry. He's not going anywhere."

She nodded and allowed him to unlock the door. Once inside, it took her a moment for her eyes to adjust to the dark. The prisoner lay on his back in an exhausted sleep, one arm bent across his eyes; the other at his side, palm turned up, the inner flesh of his lower arm plainly visible.

"Give me that," she said, indicating the torch. The guard handed it to her.

Alea thrust it down close to the man on the floor, holding it directly over his arm. With her heart in her throat, she slowly examined the bare skin. There *was* a firemark, but it wasn't anything like Alor had described. No rose, sword, or crown.

She could just make out the design burned into his arm: a great owl in flight with a scythe clutched in its talons. *What did that mean?*

Now more frightened than ever, Alea handed the torch back to the guard and fled the cell. She raced to her apartments and hastily changed into warmer garments to ward off the growing chill permeating her body.

She was truly alone. Shakiris had not only deceived her with his sly reassurance, but had at last persuaded her to submit to his caresses. She had allowed herself to succumb to him, nearly shattering her resolve. He had no intention of coming back as he had the three women. She had been abandoned with that pack of filthy Qualani roadwilds and a garrison filled with warriors whose loyalties were bought only with gold. Even her husband, Jadoor, could not help her. Too old and frail, he would never begin to grasp the enormity of what she had done.

Her future loomed before her ominously. What would happen to her? Failure filled her with dread as she tried to think of a way to extricate herself from the hopeless snarl she had made.

Fool!

As she paced the confines of her chamber, she happened to glance out the window and stopped. Fear changed to panic. For an instant she felt as if her heart had ceased to beat.

The pre-dawn light touched the still, night-black waters of the harbor below, casting cool shimmers over the gentle waves. The harbor was filled with them; she stopped counting at ten. Alea had never seen so many ships in one place—Maretstani war ships and the dreaded longships of the Ponos tribe—all anchored in the harbor.

The largest ship had been moored closest to Volt and a banner run up the tallest mast. It was the royal banner of the Ter-Rey: the rose and sword encircled by a crown, emblazoned on a field of black.

Assur was here.

Alea fought the unaccustomed feeling of genuine terror. She had to get away.

Who was that man chained in the dungeon?

Chapter Fourteen

ASSUR SAT ASTRIDE his fretting horse grateful to be on land again. Even though the voyage from Maretstan had been of short duration, he had eagerly disembarked from the longship and helped his men unload a few of the horses. After several days of being confined in the cramped hold of a ship, all the animals were high-spirited and unruly. Adzra had been unusually fractious and Assur had to curb the big gray several times before the horse settled down.

Bigger, dirtier, with too many buildings crammed together along the surrounding hillsides, Volt was not the splendid ancient city Assur had always imagined. Great buildings, now mere fragments of their past grandeur, lay in crumbled ruins. Some had been awkwardly restored—a clumsy patchwork of repairs to once magnificent temples and palaces. Only the Ter-Rey's palace, smaller than the dead-hulk of Moggadure Keep, hinted of Volt's imperial past. Assur knew there would be little or no resistance in securing the city. Still, he took no chances. He sent several outriders ahead to look for a possible ambush by the Narusuba; he wanted no one succumbing to their insidious powers.

He heard Kuurus trot his horse alongside.

"All is in readiness, my lord. We await your order."

"Any sign of the Narusuba?"

"None. They seem to have fled. The palace, however, is still guarded by a few loyal retainers. They may put up a fight, but we can easily defeat them."

Assur looked up at the bright blue sky. A cheerful, pleasant day for conquering, he mused to himself. In the old days, the tribes would have simply descended upon the city without warning, crushing it—ransacking and burning everything in their path. On this cool serene morning, regaining control of ancient Volt would be a relatively easy task.

He tugged on his helmet, crested in stiff red horsehair and a black feather. "Give the signal," he said quietly. "And, Kuurus, no innocents are to be harmed; the women untouched. Am I clear?"

Kuurus beat his right palm to his left shoulder. "Yes, Great Lord."

Row upon row of mounted Talesian tribesmen and Maretstani

foot soldiers began their march into Volt. The chilling clatter of hooves and the ominous sound of hundreds of boots pounding the cobblestones sent Voltens scurrying to their homes like terrified mice. Those who stubbornly refused to get out of the way would suffer for their foolishness. Old men cursed, shaking their fists as the long columns of warriors demolished the marketplace, trampling melons and fish along the way. Dogs cringed in doorways; mothers snatched unsuspecting children from the streets, just missing the oncoming hooves.

Assur soon realized there were no Narusuba or Volten warriors to stop them. At the front of the palace, they halted. Through the tall iron gates, he noticed a group of warriors, clad in crimson and yellow armor, standing guard before the inner door—several were positioned along the battlements. He nodded to Kuurus.

"Open the gates by order of the Ter-Rey!" Kuurus shouted.

The order was met with silence. Assur growled an oath under his breath. "The fools." He pulled his sword and pointed to the gates. "Pull them down."

A dozen ropes were looped over and through the iron bars and stretched taut. At his signal, the warriors backed their horses until the bars were torn away from the walls and came crashing to the ground.

With the pommel end of his sword, Assur cracked his visor down over his eyes then heeled Adzra toward the palace. The big horse jumped easily over the tangle of rope and iron in his path.

The brightly armored guards surrounding the doors crouched in a ready stance, swords and spears drawn. Assur shook his head, amazed by their defiance and their loyalty to a leader or leaders who had no regard for their well-being or their fate. Their brave attempt to guard the palace was futile; they had no chance.

He nodded to Kuurus, who signaled the men to attack. It was all over in a matter of minutes. Maretstani bowmen brought down the few guards on the battlements in one volley. Assur and twenty Talesian horsemen clattered up the stairs easily subduing all the Volten guards, forcing them to surrender before they could return a single blow. Several of Lord Saar's men entered the side entrance that led down to the dungeon, easily subduing the remaining guards.

In less time than it took to march through the city, Volt fell, with only a handful killed.

Assur did not like any of it—it had all been too quick and too brutal. He sensed a trap, like the time he had been ambushed at Broken Oak by Malgora. Only this time, he sensed something different, more treacherous and cunning.

Through the wide gilt and copper doors, across the black and red tiles, Adzra's hooves rang a cadenced battle march. Few torches lit the interior of the palace as Assur rode toward a simple raised dais at the back of the hall. Seated upon a throne of black granite was a beautiful girl-woman clothed in white silk and gold, with hair the color of honey and amber. Around her stood more of the Volten guards and a ragged band of men wearing filthy hides and furs. Assur's lip curled in disgust. Qualani. More importantly, their one-eye leader stood next to the dais holding a length of chain in his hands.

Assur looked at the other end of the chain and was stunned by what he saw. Except for the defiant glare, Rame knelt like a whipped animal before the dais, his hands chained together before him, his back beaten raw and bleeding. A fresh wound bled freely from under the iron collar fastened around his neck. Assur felt rage mount within him. He could just make out the symbol of the Narusuba, the diamond with a dagger thrust through it. They had marked Rame as their own, but there was no way of telling if he had succumbed to their control.

"So, you have finally come for him. I wondered how long it would take you, *Great Prince*," the woman-child on the dais said haughtily.

Assur looked at her. It took a moment for him to realize who she was...the willful, spoiled daughter of his last enemy, Princess Alea.

"My mistake was to allow you to go free. This time, I will not make that mistake," Assur said in an ominous voice. "Let him go or you will die, Alea."

She rose, a look of triumph marring her pretty features. She lifted her chin. "No."

Assur signaled Kuurus and the other warrior at his side. Immediately, they reached for their bows, fitted arrows, and aimed them directly at her.

"I will give you one moment to reconsider. Release him, or you *will* die."

Alea smiled triumphantly. "I do not believe you will do that, barbarian lord." She nodded to the Qualani, who pulled a knife from his belt and pressed it to Rame's throat. "If I die, *he* dies and you will not get what you came for... I have your precious weapons."

A palpable tension filled the dimly-lit hall. Adzra nervously pawed the tiles as Assur glanced at Kuurus, whose arm began to waver as he strained to hold the arrow steady.

Even though he was in terrible pain, the rage glittering in Rame's black-patterned eyes told Assur everything. He motioned for Kuurus and the warrior to lower their bows.

"So, it is you who has the Sacred Weapons. Did that physick, Lael, sell them to you?" He folded his arms across this chest. "Where is he and where is Princess Kitarisa?"

Alea smiled again. "His true name is Shakiris and he is not here, neither are the others. I know exactly where they have been taken, but I will only tell you on my terms."

"And, for him?" Assur gestured to Rame.

"He stays as my guarantee you will honor your part of the bargain. He is obviously your relative. Perhaps your brother? The resemblance is extraordinary—for a time I was fooled. But he is too valuable to simply return to you."

"I do not make terms with traitors," Assur said sharply.

"You will, High Prince. Withdraw your men or he dies."

Had it been anyone other than Rame, Assur would have simply killed the girl and the Qualani, but he also knew that Rame would willingly sacrifice himself for the tribes as well as for the Sacred Weapons. He was a Chaliset and knew the price of honor. But Rame was Assur's uncle and the finest Swordmaster in all Talesia. He would not leave him or risk letting him die if he could help it.

Marshaling all his self-control Assur nodded. "Very well. I will withdraw my men to the ships, for now. But I shall return at dawn."

"Then you will leave Volt to me?"

"I will consider it, but only if the Weapons are returned and I know where I will find Princes Kitarisa and the others."

"You are not quite so foolish or arrogant as you seem, Lord Assur, but how can I trust you?"

"Because my word is my bond and you hold my uncle as your captive."

A fair brow quirked over her eye. "Your uncle, indeed? I did not realize I had such an esteemed prisoner. Perhaps we should not have been so...rough with him." She smiled cruelly, indicating the open wounds on Rame's back. "But does it not cause you some anguish simply leaving him here?"

"The Sacred Weapons are more important than his life. He knows that."

"Unfeeling, savage animals," Alea sneered.

Assur raised his visor, knowing there was no danger from Narusuba and glared at her. "It was *you* who had him beaten," he said icily.

Her jaw hardened. "Leave now, barbarian, or I will have his throat slit now, before you."

He heard Kuurus angrily mutter something under his breath and sensed the rising fury from the mounted warriors behind him.

"Indeed. Before you do, you will allow me to say farewell to my kinsman. He may yet die and I would offer him the Supplication to Verlian." He kept his anger in tight control. "However, know this: I do not readily bargain with traitors or negotiate with liars. You have until dawn, Alea. You will bring me the Weapons and tell me exactly where Shakiris has taken the princesses, or I will burn this palace to the ground with you in it."

Alea appeared to consider his request then thrust out her chin. "You are bluffing."

"Am I?" He saw her waver. Uncertainty flickered through her eyes and he knew she was afraid.

Assur looked at Rame kneeling on the floor, the Qualani leader still holding the knife fast against his throat.

Blood seethed in Assur's veins, seeing his uncle humiliated and scarred, but he also knew Rame harbored no self-pity, nor would he ask for mercy. Too proud and too honorable, Rame would rather die than allow anyone to see him beaten or defeated.

"You will be Summoned by the Goddess for your bravery, Ramelek—may She keep you." Assur quoted the ancient Supplication in a firm voice. "May you dine in Her hall and feast upon lamb and honey. May the Ancients honor you as will we...the warriors of all the tribes, who you leave behind."

At Alea's nod, the one-eyed Qualani eased his hold on Rame, allowing him to respond.

Rame struggled to answer, but managed to speak in a fierce whisper. "May the Goddess allow me to remember you, my brothers. The Ponos of the Sea, the Siarsi of the Plains and the Chaliset of the Keep. From the legions of Riehl, to the warriors of Gorendt and Sherehn, I pray Verlian to be remembered and avenged!"

"Verlian keep you," Assur uttered. He looked at Alea. "Tomorrow, at dawn. Do not disappoint me. You will do as I command or I level this place over your head."

He spun Adzra around and headed out of Prince Aettilek's ancient palace, Kuurus and the others close behind. The horses clattered down the wide steps to the ruined courtyard littered with the bodies of Volten warriors.

Kuurus sidled his horse abreast of Assur's.

"My lord, forgive me, I know Lord Rame will fulfill his duty and die with honor, but his response to you...that is not how the Supplication goes," he said, looking bewildered.

"No, but that fool girl does not know the Supplication, does she?" Assur afforded his old comrade a grim, knowing smile. "Rame just told me that all his men are here."

At dawn, Assur sat astride Adzra in the courtyard of the palace awaiting the arrival of Alea and the Sacred Weapons with eight mounted warriors at his side each carrying a flaming torch. All the other horses and warriors had returned to the ships waiting for the order to set sail for the Shygul.

Kuurus's horse shuffled and pawed nervously at the cobblestones. "She is late, my lord. Maybe she has escaped?"

"She cannot escape," Assur responded shortly. "Alea is not as reckless as her father was, but neither is she as clever."

"Do you think she will bring the Weapons?"

"She knows what will happen if she does not bring them. However, whatever she does, I *will* get Rame."

Their conversation was interrupted by the sound of the palace doors opening. Six burly warriors led the procession carrying on their shoulders a large, elaborately-carved chest supported by two long poles running through rings along each side of it.

"Where is she?" Assur muttered angrily. "What has she done with Rame?"

Only her personal guard in crimson and yellow armor descended to the courtyard. They halted a few paces in front of Assur's horse and set the massive box on the ground.

"As you can see, *Great Lord*," the nearest warrior said insolently, "we have honored your command."

Assur looked at him coldly. "Open the box."

The warrior shrugged and opened the lid. Assur rose in his stirrups to see better what was inside. Nestled in layers of fine, clean straw were, indeed, all three of the Talesian tribes' most sacred objects.

"Where is your mistress and the Qualani outcasts?"

"We do not know; we were not told. We are only hired palace guards. You have conquered Volt, ground it under your heel and now you have your weapons. There is no one left to capture or punish."

Assur's eyes narrowed. "Tell me where she went."

"Our duty, here, is done. We answer to no one, not even barbarians."

"Do not provoke me, warrior," Assur warned ominously. "I will ask you one last time...where did she go?"

The warrior again shrugged. "You tell me, Talesian."

Before anyone could respond, Assur reached for one of the five knives sheathed in the saddle cloth behind his right leg. In one smooth motion, Assur stepped down from Adzra and seized the warrior by the throat, backing him into the courtyard wall—the point of the knife pressed upward, deep under the man's jaw, just short of cutting him.

"I will take no more of your insolence. You tell me where Alea and her Qualani dogs went or I ram this behind your eyes."

The creaking-sound of dozens of bowstrings being drawn tight filled the quiet courtyard, the arrows aimed directly at the remaining Volten warriors.

The guard began to shake uncontrollably, his former arrogance evaporating like smoke. "In truth, we don't know, b-b-but perhaps north."

"Where, north?"

"Uncertain. Maybe Gorendt. She gave us her final orders for the weapons, then left."

"And the Qualani?" Assur demanded, almost growling his words.

"They went with her."

Assur let the man go with a swift jerk. He pointed the knife at him. "If I discover you have been lying, you lose your tongue."

The guard rubbed his throat and nodded.

"What shall be done with these ill-mannered swine?" Kuurus asked, who had again taken his place by Assur's side. He gestured to the remaining Voltens still standing in the courtyard. At Assur's nod, the Riehlians hidden along the battlements hurried down and swiftly took all the warriors prisoner.

"Chain them and take them below," Kuurus commanded.

Assur gathered Adzra's reins and swung up into the saddle. "We must find Rame and see that he is tended to."

Kuurus signaled to two Gorendtians standing nearby, who hurried away to find the Swordmaster.

In a short time, the entire palace was under control, every room searched and guards posted at strategic locations. All Alea's prisoners were released, later to be brought before the Volten council to discover if they indeed deserved their punishment, or to be let go.

From the midst of the prisoners, Rame approached Assur slowly. Someone had freed him from the chains and iron collar. Beneath the blood and grime, revenge and gratitude warred across his face. He stopped and inclined his head.

"My thanks. Another moment—"

"And you would have been Summoned. I thank the Goddess you have been spared."

Rame hesitated. "If the Goddess spared me, then I thank Her. If not, then I owe my life to you."

"It does not matter if you believe Verlian spared you or not. It is enough that you are alive. We have much to do and we need every warrior who can carry a sword."

Assur noted the Swordmaster's questioning look and knew what he wanted to know. "Alea and the Qualani have fled, possibly to the north."

In spite of his wounds, Rame looked as if he were ready to start a battle by himself. "They violated Lady Davieta, murdered her family and have continued to murder others. They helped the Narusuba steal the Weapons, kill our tribesmen and bring down Daeamon. To all this, they helped murder your own father, my half-brother!" Rame's anger made his voice shake. "If you do not go after them and punish them, now, then I will!"

Assur studied his near look-alike and saw in him the same intense desire for justice as he craved. Blood caked Rame's throat and his back was riddled with the bleeding cuts left by the redreed. Unless he was helped by one of the Daughters of Verlian, an empathic healer, he would bear the scars for the rest of his life.

"I understand your anger, but we do not have the time, Rame. We have the Weapons and we must sail for Shygul at the next tide. But I promise you, we will find them and they will be punished."

"Very well, but I demand this, Assur. You *will* let me kill the Qualani leader. You have Shakiris and the Narusuba, but leave the others to me!"

"Agreed." Assur nodded toward Alea's remaining warriors being led away in chains. "What would you have me do to these?"

"They are bought dogs. They are loyal only to those with the most gold. Do with them as you will."

"As you wish. They will remain imprisoned here. Will you be well enough to fight by the time we reach Shygul?"

"Ready enough," Rame answered curtly. He started to turn, but stopped. Some of his anger seemed to cool. He shrugged slightly. "Forgive me, Assur...my temper. Again, I thank you for my life."

The Ter-Rey drew himself up taller and bowed slightly from the waist. "It has been my honor, Swordmaster."

Rame returned the bow, then spun about and headed back into the palace, apparently to gather what remained of his clothes and to find his swords. Assur watched him for several moments. It was evident that Rame was in a great deal of pain, but in true Talesian tradition, did not allow it to bother him.

Later that day, Assur noticed Rame had finally given into the ministrations of a camp physick. A glimpse of a white bandage swathed about his chest just showed from beneath his leather jerkin. Another bandage encircled his neck, hiding the Narusuba mark. Rame sat tall and unmoving on his ardent Trigian horse as he rode out of the palace courtyard. It was then Assur again recognized something in his uncle that he, himself, had sought during the long, dark days of the Rift Cut War and when he had entered Daeamon Keep after it had fallen.

Vengeance.

RAME RECOVERED FROM his ordeal. The scar on his throat scabbed over and healed quickly, but he hid it by fastening a wide leather band around his neck. Seething and silent he rarely spoke during the voyage to Shygul, which troubled Assur. He knew Rame was filled with pent-up rage and bent on revenge. Daily he sharpened his swords and spent hours before a simple wooden target nailed to the bow rail of the ship where he practiced throwing his saddle knives. He never missed hitting it dead-center. Not once.

As the fleet sailed farther south and east, the air grew stifling and humid. Tunics and jerkins were discarded; only swords remained strapped on. The horses grew hot and restive in their cramped stalls. Several times a day, sea water had to be sponged over them to keep them cool. An occasional freshening breeze helped relieve all of them, as well as filling the sails, but as the days dragged on, both Ponos and Maretstani seamen spent more hours bending their backs over the great oars.

By the tenth day, Assur noticed that Captain Jarrash could not conceal his worried look. He consulted his charts, took readings from mysterious-looking instruments and scanned the horizon with his glass.

"How much farther, do you think?" Assur asked quietly.

Jarrash closed his glass and frowned. "According to my charts, we should be seeing Shygul any time. However, we must make a decision soon, my lord. We cannot go much on longer. As it is, we have just enough water and provisions to return to Maretstan...if we turn back now."

"How many days can we risk going on?"

"Two, but no more than three," Jarrash said slowly. "After that, even if we ration the water, we'll start losing the horses."

Assur nodded. "Very well, we'll continue for another two days, then turn back. Signal the fleet."

Rame, however, was not pleased with his decision. Assur saw the murderous look in his uncle's black-patterned eyes and knew that if he had been in command, the fleet would have gone on until everyone died of thirst or starvation.

Another day passed with no sign of the Shygul Archipelago. Assur sensed the rising despair and resignation among the Talesian warriors. Avenging the theft of the Weapons, the fall of Daeamon Keep and the abduction of the three women was slipping away with each stroke of the oars.

As the sun began to slip beneath the horizon, turning the western skies to brilliant hues of pink and orange, one of the Maretstani crewman spotted land and called out to the captain.

"Way land!"

Peering through the glasseye, Assur made out the looming hulk of a dark island, thrusting above the choppy gray sea. Clouds had gathered, threatening a rain storm. Captain Jarrash came alongside him and pointed to the island.

"I make out a cove near that cliff. We will anchor there for the night and send men ashore to see if they can find fresh water." He looked up. "We can catch some of this rain, too."

Night settled over the longships as they anchored inside the deep-water cove. A narrow strip of sand ran along the shoreline and massive cliffs rose high above it offering no easy access to the island. Four men were sent out in a small boat to search for water and to see if the island was inhabited.

Assur watched through his glass as the men ran the boat onto the shore, then began their slow, arduous climb up the steep rock incline to the rim of the cliff. After what seemed like hours, they finally reached the top and disappeared over the edge.

"How long do we wait to see if they come back?" Rame asked.

Assur turned around, surprised by Rame's sudden willingness to speak.

"We will wait until dawn. If there's no sign of them, I will send another four to climb that cliff. But only the cliff. I will decide then what we are to do."

"What if they don't come back? The first four, that is..."

"Then we can assume this is the island where the Narusuba are hiding." He studied the island for a moment. "But we do have the cover of darkness."

Long, wearisome hours passed with nothing to do but stand in the light drizzle and wait. Rame gave up his vigilant watch and went below to rest. Mar'Kess, who had been staying near the men and keeping an eye on the horses, approached Assur. A worried frown creased his brow.

"If we do not get these horses on land soon, my lord, they will become too weak to eat or drink."

"I am aware of this, Mar'Kess. By dawn I will know what should be done."

To everyone's relief, the four advance warriors returned just as the sun began to rise on the third day. They climbed aboard the longship eager to tell their news."

"There is water, my lord, plenty of it," one of them exclaimed breathlessly. "We have discovered a stream and a waterfall in the interior of the island."

"Praise Verlian," Mar'Kess murmured.

"Any indication of Narusuba?" Assur asked.

The warrior shook his head. "No, lord. The island is quite small, however, at the far end, on the eastern shore, one can easily see the next island only a short distance away. When the tide is low, you can cross on land—a narrow causeway, a dry pathway, connecting the two islands."

"Excellent," Assur said.

"Did you see anyone on the other island?" Rame had come up from the lower deck when the four warriors arrived, keenly attentive to their report.

"No, Lord Rame, but last night, we did see a few flickering torches. There *is* someone over there."

Assur pressed the men for more details and finally came to the decision that the ships would sail at night around to the eastern side of the island where the horses and men would go ashore. Under the cover of darkness and with the tide low they would be able to find out if indeed the Narusuba inhabited the second island.

As dusk gathered, the great longships slipped around the tiny island and were run aground onto the soft sand. Men and horses plunged through the shallow surf to the shore. Silently, the warriors hurried for cover under the nearby trees and underbrush. Assur was at first pleased with the swiftness of their landing, but soon became worried about moving so many men and animals across the narrow strip of dry sand connecting the two islands.

He looked up at the clear sky. Verlian was waning—a thin white crescent illumined the blue-black night. In another day, perhaps two, the Goddess's light would be gone. They would be able to cross the causeway undetected.

Too easy, his mind whispered. Taking Volt had also been too easy, almost as if they had been encouraged...invited. *Another trap?* He had to take that risk. They had come too far to stop now. The Sacred Weapons must be returned and Kitarisa must be found along with his sister and Lady Davieta. If he returned to Talesia without the weapons, or if the women were found dead, he would incur the wrath of all the tribes; he would die disgraced and dishonored—there would be no place for him in Verlian's Hall. He and all his line would be shamed, forever.

But, somehow he did not believe Kitarisa was dead—the dreams were stronger now and came to him every night. That hideous creature, a scaled loathsome beast just as Kitarisa had become in the Catacombs....

A beast.

A light chill danced up Assur's spine.

Before I leave the sky, D'Assuriel!

Chapter Fifteen

AT DAWN, ASSUR had his first glimpse of the far Shygul island across the narrow channel. The eastern island thrust upward from a narrow sandy shoreline, a massive crater enshrouded in deep green foliage. Exotic birds, feathered in jewel-like plumage called from the branches of strange-looking trees. The thick fragrance from the numerous flowers entwining the trees settled over the island like a seductive perfume.

"I don't like it," Kuurus commented. "Too hidden, too dense with trees. Any number of Narusuba could be hiding within those forests."

"And, nearly impossible to attack without being seen," Mar'Kess added.

The four of them—Assur, Rame, Mar'Kess and Kuurus—stood at the bow of Saar's great longship, studying the island, making evaluations and comparing them with Captain Jarrash's numerous nautical charts. Lord Saar stood nearby, looking at the island through his long glass.

"I do not like the fact that we can be seen by whatever is on that island and that we must wait for the tide to free our ships," Kuurus added. "The Narusuba must know of our presence by now."

"Agreed," Assur said. "But they don't know our numbers."

"Neither do we know theirs," Rame interjected.

The reality of their situation settled upon them like an unwanted burden—there seemed to be no other way to approach the island than through the forest, leaving them exposed to the Narusuba and their ships vulnerable to attack.

Assur squinted up at the early morning sky. "Tomorrow night, Verlian will wane. There will be no moon. It is then we must assume the sacrifice will take place."

"As I have dreamed it, my lord," Mar'Kess said suddenly.

"You have dreamed of this, too?" Assur asked, astonished.

"As have I," Rame said.

"Then, it is true." Assur turned away from them, unable to speak. That creature. The fire. They had seen it, too. All three of them had seen the beast and they knew they had to kill it before it killed....

Suddenly, Assur knew what to do. His orders came decisively.

"Saar, take half the fleet around to the north side of the island. The Narusuba are probably waiting there. Take only the best archers and prepare the catapults for launching fire. Stay out of range. Tomorrow night, when the moon is gone and at my signal, engage the Narusuba. Draw their attention away from the center of the island."

"Your Will, Great Lord," Saar responded briskly and bowed.

"And the rest of the fleet?" Rame asked.

"They stay here with the warriors. If we time this right, we will be on these ships and out to sea before the Narusuba can stop us.

Later, as dusk settled, the tide began to turn back. Just after the mid of the night, a narrow, sandy bar of land began to appear between the two islands, just wide enough for a horse to cross.

Assur made his preparations along with Rame and Mar'Kess. They saddled their horses in silence, each man knowing what the other was thinking. An unspoken bond sealed their purpose. They had this night and the next day to find Kitarisa and the others. The following night, Verlian would be gone from the skies and Shakiris would begin his ritual.

Dread filled Assur as he fastened the last buckle of his armguards, then pulled on his helmet. What if they were too late? He remembered his promise to Kitarisa. Could he fulfill what she had asked of him?

The urgency of what was before them forced Assur to attend to the matters at hand. "Bring the Sacred Weapons," he commanded, nodding to a handful of nearby warriors, who were eagerly waiting to assist him. They sketched a hasty salute and hurried aboard the ship, returning quickly with the long, ornate box. They set it before him and stepped back respectfully.

Assur knelt down and unfastened the catch. The heavy lid opened easily. Inside, the three Weapons gleamed softly in Verlian's dying light.

He reached for the Spear. It felt strange to hold it, here in this remote place, so far from Daeamon Keep.

"Take the Bow, Rame."

The Swordmaster stepped forward. "Should not Mar'Kess take it?"

Assur shook his head. "You have seen the same visions. You must take the Bow. Mar'Kess has great skill, but you are the better archer."

Rame reverently lifted up the sacred Bow of Ponosel and the quiver that held only seven gold-tipped arrows. He bowed to Lord Saar, who in return nodded solemnly.

"Mar'Kess...the Hammer," Assur ordered.

The Riehlian Governor looked askance at him then at Kuurus who was watching the proceedings with keen attentiveness.

"Are you sure, Great Lord? I am not Siarsi; I am not even Talesian."

"Like Rame, you have had the same vision. You must take the Hammer."

When all three Weapons had been packed onto their horses, Assur signaled them to mount. Only three of them would climb to the top of the crater-island. Kuurus would accompany them only half-way then wait in hiding with the horses.

Astride Adzra, Assur looked down on Lord Saar, Captain Jarrash and the others.

"If we do not return by dawn after tomorrow night, then you must assume we are dead. Return to Maretstan for reinforcements if you need them. Saar, you *must* find and retrieve the Weapons. That is my final Will."

Lord Saar beat his right palm to his left shoulder. "It shall be done, Great Lord. May Verlian protect you and guide your sword."

Assur nodded and reined the gray around. The horse jumped at the touch of his heels and headed swiftly across the connecting bar of land, the others following single file. The horses snorted and tossed their heads, eager to be off, while their hooves churned the warm, shallow water into the sand.

KITARISA AWOKE TO the sound of dripping water, the rank smell of blood and ancient death. She lay face down on cold, unyielding rock and as she slowly turned over on her back, she realized she was lying at the bottom of a gigantic pit. The opening far above her had been barred in thick iron, allowing only faint threads of light to filter down from the stars in the night sky.

She sat up, shivering. Rough-hewn walls surrounded her, too steep to climb and too high for her to be heard if she called out for help.

Instinct told her she was on Shygul. From that terrible moment when she, Davieta, and Sethra were dragged from that ancient palace in Volt, she knew they would be brought here. All three of them had been forced to drink a foul-tasting liquid that made them sleep. There was no other explanation; they had to be on the island where Shakiris intended to complete the ritual he had spoken of to her and to Alea.

For a moment, Kitarisa almost felt sorry for her half-sister. Too greedy and vain, Alea had never seen through Shakiris's far-reaching plan to bring the Narusuba to power. She had only been a pawn, a tool in his end game. Kitarisa wondered if Alea were already dead.

She glanced down at the garment she wore. Her own clothes, as ragged as they were, had been replaced with a long-sleeved, flowing gown of white silk that covered her from her neck to her heels. She wore no shoes and the damp rocks made her feet cold and clammy to the touch.

Sacrifice. She knew the garment meant she was part of some ritual sacrifice and strangely enough, she also knew she was not the one to be sacrificed. *She*, however, was the one Shakiris had wanted all along, not Sethra.

That frightening realization made her understand the purpose of her rock prison. It was a cage for something monstrous...a beast.

Anguish shot through her. *Now it will happen.*

Her hand went to her neck and she felt the drying sticky blood still clinging to a small wound cut into her throat. Sometime during their voyage to Shygul, either Shakiris or one of his shadowy minions had cut the diamond-shaped Narusuba symbol into her—made her like them.

Kitarisa stood on trembling legs and attempted an exploration of her black prison, the long silk gown trailing behind her. Her eyes adjusted quickly to the darkness. She looked up again and noticed certain strategically carved rocks jutting out at measured intervals up the full height of the cave walls...like handholds. Clawholds.

Where was Assur? Surely he had followed them? Did he know...?

Her brave, fearless Assur. She knew he would not want her now and there would be no joining ceremony, once she had made the change—just like before. The transformation would come, soon. The animal heat, the killing rage within her was already growing.

Assur *must* have followed after them—to find the Weapons and for Davieta and Sethra. Would he even try to find her? She, who had allowed Daeamon Keep to fall? How could she *not* expect Assur to fulfill his promise to her? He was bound by it. He would kill her to save the others.

Kitarisa did not want to die, not here in this cold forbidding place. She wanted to return to Daeamon Keep and start anew with him. The last fragments of her long-held misgivings dissolved with the sudden realization that it was Assur she loved more than her craving to be alone and safe from surrendering her heart to anyone.

Restless, she began pacing the confines of her cage. The bones in her hands began to ache and harden. She felt her eyes start to burn. The smell of fire was in her nostrils, tasting bitter at the back of her throat.

Kitarisa snaked her neck upward and saw the moon, Verlian's sliver of light—the presence of the Goddess—and prayed she would be allowed to remember her humanity.

Goddess, let me remember; do not let me kill him!

For the last time she tried to silence the savage, animal call within her...and failed.

AT LOW TIDE, the shoreline around East Shygul widened, making their dash across the open expanse of gleaming white sand even more dangerous. They found a trail—narrow and winding—leading up through the dense forest to the very top of the crater. Even though the air was much cooler at night, it was a long and laborious climb. All four horses were soon exhausted and lathered with sweat. Assur stopped several times to allow everyone to rest.

Although they saw no wild animals, not even the brilliantly-colored birds, Kuurus remained wary, keeping one sword at the ready. He was convinced every twisted branch or coiling black vine was a poisonous snake ready to strike. Twice, he clawed and tore furiously at a dangling flower tendril that had become entwined around his face and hair.

"Don't like snakes," he muttered during one of their rests.

"They are terrified of you, Kuurus...fleeing for their lives," Rame observed wryly. "I know, I would. You frighten even me."

Mar'Kess stifled a soft laugh. "A rare moment of humor, my lord. You choose a curious occasion to be amused."

"I have been reminded from time to time that I am an ill-tempered savage with the manners of a wounded boar. But occasionally, I do find some things amusing. Like...Kuurus's imaginary snakes."

"Imaginary!" Kuurus exploded in a fierce whisper. "I imagine nothing, my lord!"

Assur, who had been listening to the entire conversation, chirruped to Adzra and begin heading up the trail. "One should always listen to the Swordmaster, old friend," he said, trying to hide the amusement in his voice. "Besides, Kuurus, how do you think the snakes managed to get to this rock, way out in the middle of the ocean? Fly?"

Kuurus remained silent for the remainder of the climb, but stubbornly kept his sword resting across his saddlebow...just in case.

All humor vanished when they reached top edge of the crater. They dismounted and tied the horses well out of sight, then crept to the rim, bellies flat to the underbrush as they peered down at the horror they saw below.

THE HARSH RAYS of the early morning sun cast a pitiless glare on what they saw deep inside the crater. Assur tried to suppress the growing sense of dread building within him. The others, too, were silent as they absorbed the grim sight. They all knew what would happen in this forbidding place and who would suffer.

Flint and cinder, crushed into sharp, black gravel covered the entire expanse of the crater floor. Only two large objects marred the bleak surface. A large fire pit smoldered at the very center. Behind it, a low platform had been raised, with a scaffold-like crossbeam built over it. From the beam dangled four short ropes where two victims might be hung by their wrists.

"It will take place here," Mar'Kess murmured. "The ritual. They will be sacrificed."

"Not if I can help it," Assur muttered. "We must find them before night comes."

"And how do you propose to find them without being seen?" Rame asked. He nodded to the far eastern edge of the crater. "We don't know what lies beyond that rim."

"Well, I do not intend staying here all day to find out," Assur said. He nodded to Kuurus. "Keep your sword sharp. Remain here and watch in case we don't return. You are our last contact to Saar and the others. If something should go wrong, you must inform them."

"Done, Great Lord."

Rame drew his sword then cuffed Kuurus on the shoulder with his free hand. "And keep an eye out for those snakes."

Kuurus said nothing, but Assur could see by his wry grin that he was clearly amused by Rame's little joke.

They left Kuurus and crept along the rim of the crater, staying low and hidden in the thick underbrush. As they approached the southern end, the breeze freshened, giving them much needed relief from the heat, but the wind also brought a pungent animal smell rising from the crater floor. Assur looked over the edge and saw the source of the odor.

"We missed seeing that earlier," he said, pointing to the massive iron grating just behind the scaffold covering a large round pit. It had been bolted shut, keeping whatever was inside from climbing out. Assur fought the growing despair in his heart. He knew—or at least he thought he knew—who was down in that pit. He dared not tell the others, but suspected that Mar'Kess had already guessed. The Riehlian had fought with him at the Rift Cut and had seen those two creatures flying above the battling armies, roaring their hatred and spewing streams of fire from their enormous jaws. No one had ever seen such strange beasts before, but later, the body of that fiend, Malgora, had been found at the base of the Cut where one of those creatures had fallen.

The other....

Assur pushed back the horrifying image and attempted to concentrate on finding her before it was too late. The meaning of the dream was now clear. Before Verlian waned he had to find Kitarisa.

Rame touched his shoulder and pointed northward over the edge of the crater to the shoreline below. From their high vantage point, they could make out a great mass of armed men, milling about the beach and low slopes of the northern side of the island. Fire catapults had been strategically placed to strike any vessel that happened to venture into the harbor.

Saar had guessed correctly—there *was* a crescent-shaped cove, ideal for anchoring several ships and offering easy access to the shore. Assur also noticed by its clear, light-blue color that the water was not very deep. With their shallow drafts and wide beams, the Ponos warships could easily sail close to shore without touching bottom, but in doing so, they became easy marks for the Narusuba.

Beyond, Assur could make out the rising rock cliffs at the far side of the cove. With any luck, Saar and the fleet were behind those cliffs, awaiting the signal to attack.

"We have had a rare piece of luck," Mar'Kess commented. "Look there."

Not far from where they stood, a narrow trailhead broke over the edge of the crater, leading down to the floor below.

"Praise Verlian," Assur muttered.

"I do not think Verlian had anything to do with it," Rame said in an annoyed tone. "The trail was built for lookouts to climb up here and scan the harbor. Although I do not understand why they have not posted guards or any kind of sentry."

"Perhaps they do not believe guards are needed," Mar'Kess suggested.

"Or, they are so afraid of us, they need every man if we should attack by ship," Assur said.

The Swordmaster shook his head, clearly not pleased with either reason.

"No matter. We wait here until nightfall." Assur settled himself into the shade of a large nearby bush, sword across his knees. He closed his eyes against the bright glare of the sun. "At least there are no marglims."

Mar'Kess sat next to Assur, allowing the Swordmaster to take the first watch. He grinned up at Rame. "And no snakes, either."

Rame responded with a sardonic smile.

No snakes, no marglims, Assur silently agreed. But there was something else...something far more terrible than either he or the others dared to contemplate.

"YOU HAVE DONE well, Shakiris," the deep, melodic voice said quietly. "Three women of noble blood. And this one...a royal, who has already felt the power of the Beast within her. She will serve admirably for our purposes."

Shakiris bowed to the tall, regal man with snow-white hair, majestic in his pale robes. "I am gratified, Master."

"It is a shame she will eventually have to die. Such a magnificent creature."

"But she will serve a greater cause, Master," Shakiris observed.

"True, but it is still a great pity."

The two men moved cautiously across the floor of the cavern, keeping a wary distance from the enormous creature. Its eyes, gleaming and roiling red, watched them as if examining its prey. The raw smell of sulphur and burnt cinder exuded from its black-scaled body; faint white threads of acrid smoke streamed from its nostrils with each guttural breath. A long heavy chain had been bolted into the wall and fastened to a wide collar of iron encircling the creature's throat.

Massive jaws gaped, revealing rows of razor-sharp teeth, and a black, forked-tongue slid in and out, as if testing the air or anticipating the taste of the two men watching her.

"Can she harm us?" Shakiris asked.

"Yes, but for now we are safe. We must remain on our guard, especially after I complete her transformation."

"Tonight?"

"Yes, Shakiris. When the eye of the moon dies and the black night, alone, fills the heavens, you will bring her to me. We begin what must be done."

"What must be done," Shakiris repeated.

Both men bowed respectfully to the creature, turned and headed for an iron-barred door hidden behind a large boulder, well away from the dangerous beast they left chained to the wall.

They did not hear the throaty rumble filling the dark pit, a heavy forlorn sound that might have been mistaken for a sob.

Chapter Sixteen

A PROFOUNDLY BLACK night settled over the island and the surrounding sea like a death shroud. Unable to move, the three warriors looked down from their high hiding place at the grim spectacle.

At the back of the crater, from the depths of a cave entrance, dozens of figures swathed in gray robes emerged each carrying a torch. They moved silently toward the center and surrounded the low-burning fire. At some unseen signal, they lowered their torches to the pit until the smoldering wood burst into flames, rising higher and higher, until the entire crater was lit in an eerie orange light. Macabre shadows stretched and danced across the high, sloping walls as each figure raised their torches to the sky.

"They must be the Narusuba," Mar'Kess whispered.

"Finally, we see them," Rame muttered. "I was beginning to think they were only creatures of someone's imagination...until I was stopped by that...Shakiris."

"I am certain he will be part of the ritual, but you are not to kill him yet, Rame. Wait until we get the women out."

Rame nodded.

Another flurry of movement caused them to look again at the cave entrance. More Narusuba appeared; one led a single horse pulling a small cart. The horse had been blindfolded so it would not panic at the sight of the roaring fire. The harsh sound of the wheels and the horse's hooves crushing the brittle cinder stones sent chills down Assur's spine. This was no dream. It was going to happen.

Two women sat in the cart. Even in the poor light of the torches, they knew who they were. There was no mistaking Sethra's tumble of flame-red hair and the gleaming black mass of Davieta's dark tresses.

Kitarisa—Assur knew—would not be in that cart.

The horse was stopped. Rough hands dragged the women from the cart and shoved them onto the platform. Both were clothed in long white gowns, completely covering them from neck to ankles. Neither appeared to comprehend what was happening, as if they had been drugged.

Their arms were pulled over their heads; their wrists tied by the cords. Then, they were slowly pulled up until they hung, suspended over the platform, facing the fire, their backs to the locked pit.

"This is very difficult for me," Rame muttered thickly, as he rolled onto his back and slid down next to Assur and Mar'Kess.

Mar'Kess peered cautiously over the ledge. "How accurate is your archery?" he asked Rame.

"Excellent," the Swordmaster answered bluntly.

Raldan tugged at his sleeve, pulling him alongside. He pointed to the ropes. "Can you cut them down at this range?"

Rame studied the ropes, not looking at Davieta or Sethra. He shook his head. "I am not sure. Possibly. At this distance and in this poor light I might hit them, or sever an arm."

Assur nodded. "Too risky, Raldan. We need to get closer." He looked about anxiously then pointed to the great open maw of the beast's lair. "There *must* be another way in..."

"There's no better way than the direct route," Mar'Kess muttered as he slipped over the rim and headed down the narrow pathway.

Both Assur and Rame followed him, keeping low and moving as silently as possible. The rough path led back and forth through a series of switchbacks, until it ended at the floor of the crater, deep under the shadows of the rock wall. No one had seen them.

"This reminds me of the Catacombs," Mar'Kess whispered.

Assur held up his hand to silence him.

"Now what?" Rame asked in a low voice.

"I need to get below and see what is in this pit," Assur said, gesturing to the grate.

"When do we signal the fleet to attack?" Mar'Kess asked.

"When we see what is below," Assur answered.

It must have been the heat, or the latent effects of the Narusuba, but Assur found himself struggling to make decisions—to give orders. He had never fought such an obscure enemy, one that had powers he could not defeat. He did not know what the Narusuba truly wanted or why Kitarisa and the others were to be sacrificed.

He glanced at the expectant faces of Rame and Mar'Kess. They knew he had little time to make long, involved plans or give complicated orders. They must act quickly, or both Sethra and Davieta would die. Assur also knew he must find Kitarisa before she, herself, became a victim of Shakiris's ritual.

"It seems Verlian is with us this night," Mar'Kess said, nodding toward the cave entrance.

It appeared that all the gray-clad devotees were now outside on the crater floor, waiting for the ritual to begin. The fire roared higher and hotter into the night, illuminating the two women hanging from the scaffold beam.

Rame ground his teeth and Assur heard Mar'Kess's draw in a ragged breath. Both Davieta and Sethra would not last much longer. Although they could not see their faces, the sleeves of their gowns had slid down revealing their bare blood-streaked arms.

"We need to get into that cave," Assur said.

Progress was slow. At any moment, one of the gray-clad Narusuba standing around the fire might notice them and stop them with the paralyzing cold. Besides their swords, Assur and the others each carried one of the Sacred Weapons. Of the three, the Sacred Spear was the most awkward. Its great length, thrusting up behind Assur's back, made him an easy target.

Stone steps spiraled down into the black recesses of the crater. A single flame from each of the tiny lamps set into small carved-out niches in the rock wall was their only light as they crept through the narrow tunnels. A cloying, musty stench, along with the smell of sulphur, filled the stagnant air.

"We must be near the base of that pit," Assur uttered in a barely audible whisper to Rame.

Rame nodded and pointed to a juncture in the tunnel just ahead of them. The three flattened to the walls as they heard the screeching sound of metal upon metal—the hinge of a heavy door, then the clash of that unseen door slamming shut.

Two male voices filtered through the gloom.

"She is ready, Master," the first man said and Assur knew it was Shakiris.

"Yes, and now she is hungry. You will proceed above. You have only moments before it is to begin."

From the shadowy cave walls, Assur watched the two men cross the juncture then stopped. The first man, dressed in a gray and maroon robe, Assur recognized as the one-time physick, Lael, who now called himself Shakiris. The other man was older, white-haired and dignified, but extraordinarily tall in his stark white robe that flowed from his shoulders to the ground. A gold diadem at his brow glinted in the weak light. At least he would make an easier target, Assur thought fleetingly as he watched Shakiris hurry down the down the far tunnel; the other man turned and walked right past them, heading into the tunnel in the opposite direction.

Once they had vanished completely from sight, Assur heard Mar'Kess say, "I suggest we look behind that door, my lord."

"Agreed."

Without making a sound, they eased into the juncture and discovered a heavy iron-barred door directly across the tunnel. To the right of the door, a single blazing torch had been bracketed into the rock wall.

Rame examined the door as Mar'Kess held the torch over their heads. "It is not locked."

"Too easy." Assur glanced down the tunnels branching off from the nearby juncture, half expecting one of the maroon-robed priests to appear from the gloom.

"Whatever is in here, obviously cannot open a door," Mar'Kess said.

"Or, cannot fit through it," Assur added grimly.

Rame pulled the door open just wide enough for the three of them to slip through. Inside, they were immediately stopped by a large rock protrusion. There was only one way around it, a narrow chiseled passageway to their right.

Assur drew his sword and moved around the rock.

Only the flickering light from the fire above cast enough light through the barred grate down into the enormous rock-hewn pit and the single creature held within it. Assur's heart sank.

It was her.

The creature, cinder-black scales glittering, its great leathern wings folded against its body, looked up with gleaming red eyes to the bolted grate above its head. Threads of smoke streamed from the flared nostrils and slipped through the blade-like teeth lining its jaws.

A loose pebble broke free as Rame brushed against the rock wall, sending it rattling to the cave floor.

The huge head swung around. Eyes, swirling like crimson oil, spotted them. The spined crest behind its head flared an ominous warning.

"Shakiris's beast," Rame murmured, "as I have seen it in a dream."

"As have I, but..." Mar'Kess said, shaking his head. "The creature I saw was white."

Sick at heart, Assur gazed up at the creature. He saw the mark of the Narusuba cut into its throat and knew what he must do.

"We must kill it before it is allowed to kill Davieta and Sethra," Rame said.

The beast lowered its head, enough so they could make out the bony ridges over the eyes. Intelligence gleamed in those roiling orbs as it appeared to study them. A loud snuffling noise escaped its nostrils along with more of the thin, white smoke as it found their scent.

"We must kill it now, my lord," Mar'Kess admonished, "while we have the chance."

Assur lowered his sword and shook his head. He stepped back to the protective rock. "We cannot kill her," he said sorrowfully.

Rame looked at him, incredulous. "By Verlian's blood, why not? It is the creature from our visions, the one we must destroy!"

"She is not the beast we seek. She is Kitarisa."

Even in the dim light of the cave, Assur saw both Rame's and Mar'Kess's astonishment. He edged behind the protective rock, motioning them to follow him.

Rame's annoyance was apparent. "My lord, what do we do now? If we cannot kill this...whatever it is, how can we save Davieta and your sister?" He jerked his head in the direction of the beast. "You know the priests will release it soon. It will devour the women before we can get out of this cave."

Assur shook his head. "How much time do we have until Verlian wanes?" he asked Mar'Kess.

"Uncertain. Maybe hours, maybe only a few moments. But, I do know this, we must find that creature's eggs."

Assur scowled, not understanding.

"In my vision, I destroy an egg...with the Hammer," Mar'Kess said.

"As long as Verlian lights the sky, we still have time."

Rame made a disparaging noise. "*If* we still have time..."

A sudden loud noise from above made them shrink deeper into the shadows. The beast swung around, chain rattling, having lost interest in its human intruders. It looked up again, stretching its long scaled neck toward the grate covering the opening.

Assur peered around the rock and watched as the monstrous creature reared onto its hind legs and began to claw for the stones protruding from the rock walls. With alarming speed, it scrabbled upward until its head was just below the grating.

The beast drew a breath, swelling it like a bloated leather sack. Then, a roar, thunderous and deafening. Brilliant white fire flared from deep within the creature's mouth, streaming upward through the grate into the sky. The air around them felt as if it had been boiled to raw smoke. It stank of sulphur and the bitter smell of burned rock and ash. The walls began to shake, sending rivulets of stone crashing to the cave floor.

"Pray Verlian, it does not see us," Mar'Kess said.

"She will." Assur nodded toward the door. "We need to get out of here, before she turns on us."

They hurried out, slamming the heavy iron door into place and making sure the latch and bolt were secure.

"Any ideas where we go next?" Rame asked.

Mar'Kess pointed down the dark tunnel ahead of them—a different tunnel—one Shakiris and the tall priest had not entered. "There."

Torch in hand, Mar'Kess led the way. "We need to separate. We will never be able to signal Saar in time."

Assur ran behind him. "First, we find that egg."

The tunnel grew longer and narrower, taking several turns, but they saw no other adjacent tunnels. Finally, Assur made out the faint glow of light ahead of them. Unlike the Catacombs, they were not forced to find their way through an endless, twisting labyrinth.

As they approached the glowing light, the tunnel widened, until it opened into a large, circular cavern. Minerals and natural crystalline rock formations glittered in the fluttering light from dozens of torches.

It took a moment for them to comprehend what they saw.

"By Verlian's blood and blade," Mar'Kess whispered, "I do not believe my eyes."

Not one, but hundreds of green-gray eggs the size of large melons littered the cavern floor. The time for their hatching was near as several of the eggs undulated and throbbed with the new life within them.

"It is a nursery," Rame breathed. "An entire nursery of those...things." He turned accusing eyes on Assur. "And, you think that *creature* should live?"

Assur stared at the sea of pulsating eggs. He had not been prepared for this. Instinct told him that this was the true reason for the ritual—Sethra and Davieta would be sacrificed for these abominations. And Kita? Was she destined to be some kind of caretaker for these creatures?

Rame's outrage shattered the last fragment of Assur's misgivings. He knew what to do; the dreams had told him—had told all three of them what to do.

"Enough, Rame. Burn them," he ordered. "Destroy and burn them."

Mar'Kess swung Siarsia's great Hammer from his back and hefted it in his hands. He raised it, preparing to smash the nearest egg at his feet, when a low rumble made them look up.

At the back of the cavern, hiding in an alcove carved into the rock, crouched another creature smaller than the one in the great pit, but equally as malevolent. Age had turned its dusky scales to dirty white; an ancient creature with eyes the color of blackened blood.

Mar'Kess raised the Hammer. "You want these, don't you maggot?" he spoke directly to the aged beast.

It rose on trembling legs, trying to muster fury from its long-ago youth. It roared, filling the cavern with its foul breath and flickers of acrid fire.

Mar'Kess smiled. "Get back you stinking worm." He raised the Hammer and brought it down on the nearest egg, shattering it into green shards and oozing yellow scum.

The beast's roar was more like a scream of loss and desperation. It tried to rise on shriveled back legs, but could only writhe from side to side in helpless frustration.

Again and again, Mar'Kess brought the Hammer down, destroying every egg in his path.

Assur did not have to give Rame his next order. The Swordmaster pulled the Bow from his shoulder and nocked one of the arrows into the string, then drew the feathers to his cheek. He took dead aim on the tattoo mark in the beast's neck.

"Now," Assur commanded as he reached for one of the torches on the cave wall.

The arrow flew just as Assur dropped the torch into the seething mass of dying creatures and vile birth fluid. The flames sizzled and popped as they began to consume the shattered eggs.

Rame's arrow shot straight into the diamond mark. Howling in pain, the beast writhed, shaking its head back and forth trying to dislodge the deadly arrow. Blood gushed from the wound, spilling onto the burning dead eggs as the foul smoke began to thicken the air of the cavern.

"Go, my lord!" Mar'Kess shouted. "I will finish these and meet with you later."

Assur nodded. Both he and Rame turned and fled the cavern, while the beast's bellowing death cries grew fainter and fainter.

"Keep your sword sharp, there may be more of those things," Rame said as he ran alongside Assur.

Avoiding the great pit where the other creature was kept, they raced for the stairway leading up to the crater floor. They were too late. Angry gray-robed Narusuba descended the curving stairs, swords drawn.

"Visors," Rame called over his shoulder.

Outrage did little to aid the maddened priests. Untrained in weapons, they fell swiftly to two skilled swordsmen.

Gray-clad bodies littered the stairway as Rame and Assur emerged onto the crater floor. Many of the priests were still standing around the fire pit, some in disarray as they noticed the smoke escaping through weak areas in the rock walls or from natural vents. The last of them had surrounded the grating, frantically trying to open it.

At the center of the crater, Sethra and Davieta still hung by their wrists, alive, but unaware of what was happening behind them. Above, Verlian was now a fragment of white, a mere strand of light in the sky.

"Go above, Rame," Assur's order came sharply. "Signal Saar's ships."

When Rame did not move, Assur whirled on him. With his visor down, it was impossible for Assur to see his uncle's eyes or read his expression. "What is the matter with you? Go!"

Rame raised his sword in a warning gesture. "If you let that *thing* kill Davieta and Sethra, I will kill you myself!"

Chaos and madness filled the crater. More of the distraught priests had fled, heading down into the caverns to try and save the last of the beast's eggs. They had all but forgotten their ritual.

"This is no time to argue. Get to that ridge and warn Saar!" Assur roared.

"I warn you, Assur—"

In two strides, Assur was before Rame, grasping his shoulder straps in one fist. "You dare threaten me? This is my Will and your duty. Defy me, Swordmaster and I'll see you punished for treason."

"Would *Kitarisa* want this? Would she want them to die?" He jerked his head in the direction of Davieta and Sethra. "You *know* how they will die."

"Would you have me *kill* her?" Assur snapped.

Through the oblique slits in his visor, Assur could see the rage glittering in Rame's eyes—a rage as violent as his own.

"You have no choice, *nephew*."

Assur released him and stepped back. Rame was right. He could not forget his promise to Kitarisa. He would do what he must, for her sake. He lowered his sword and nodded. He turned on his heel and headed back into the cave.

Rame grabbed a torch and raced up the pathway to the rim.

ARGUING WITH ASSUR had always been pointless, Rame bitterly

reminded himself as he climbed the trail. Once again, he was allowing his emotions to cloud his judgement, disrupting his effectiveness as a warrior. This was no place for his feelings to overcome him. But, the dreams had been frightening. He knew what that creature would do— devour both Sethra and Davieta. He had seen the empty, dangling cords charred black.

At the rim of the crater, he stopped, panting for breath. He didn't bother to rest, but took a second gold-tipped arrow and wrapped it in a scrap of cloth, then lit it with the torch he had brought with him. Dropping the torch, he fitted the arrow into the Bow then pulled the string back with all his strength. He aimed high, over the far northernmost rim of the crater. It didn't matter where the arrow landed as long as Saar saw it.

He took a deep breath and let go. The flame streaked upward like a tiny thread of lightning, soaring high into the nearly moonless sky. Rame waited, still holding his breath. Then it came—the answering signal. Saar would attack.

Rame turned and headed back down the trail. He had five arrows left and one was for that creature, if Assur did not stop it in time.

Once back on the crater floor, Rame hid in the deep shadows and watched as the last of the maddened Narusuba priests fled for the lower caves of the crater. He glanced about, noticing no one else near him except for the two women still hanging from the crossbeam. He crept toward them, both swords drawn. The fire in the pit had died down and he found himself struggling to see either Setha or Davieta in the fading light. They were still alive. Neither uttered a sound and Rame could scarcely bring himself look at them.

"Come no closer."

Rame raised his visor and spun around, searching the gloom to find the owner of that voice.

"You need not bother trying to save them; they are lost to you."

"Who are you?"

"In due time, barbarian lord."

Rame began backing toward the platform, ready to turn and cut through the ropes binding the women. With any luck, both Assur and Mar'Kess would soon return to help him.

"Whoever you are, I demand you release these women!"

The voice chuckled. "You think because you are the great Swordmaster you can make demands and expect to be obeyed? You have no authority here, and no power."

"Release them, now!"

A tall form emerged from the smoke. "I can no more release *them* than I can our new mother."

Assur stared at the arrogant black-haired man. "You!"

Shakiris bowed mockingly. "Am I addressing the true Ter-Rey, or your imposter?"

"You know who I am, *physick!* Tell your master to release the women."

"I fear I cannot do such a thing. They are needed to complete our ritual. They are all necessary—three women of noble blood and one who has felt the Beast within her. She knows her purpose. She will be the mother to us all."

"There is nothing left," Rame said angrily. "The eggs have been destroyed and the old one who guarded them."

"A *few* have been destroyed, my lord," Shakiris said smoothly. "But surely you do not think they were the only ones? We have been preparing for over three hundred turns of the sun, since the time of your ancestor, Prince Aettilek. We have awaited her for a long time. She will care for her young and raise them to rule this world, as they did so long ago. *They* are our true masters."

"We will burn all her eggs!"

Shakiris smiled. "Even so, she is still the vessel for future generations. The Master will ensure she has more, so her line is continued. When the Master completes the change, he will—"

"That is impossible!" Rame had heard enough. He lifted his swords and stared straight at his enemy, hatred settling around his heart like a winter frost. "You're dead."

Shakiris raised his right palm toward him. "Don't be a fool, Ramelek. I have been with the Master for longer than you can imagine. Kitarisa is his now and their children *will* rule this world once again, as is the right of all Narusuba."

Too late to protect his eyes, the fierce cold hit him like a solid wall. Rame fell to his knees unable to move. Instinctively, he clutched his arms close to his chest but clung grimly to his swords, determined not to drop them. In a dim corner of his mind, he recalled his own vow. If the creature was not destroyed, it would kill Sethra and Davieta—it would eventually kill them all. He suddenly realized what the Bow was for. He had one chance to stop this madness.

While his limbs did not function, he could still hear and see.

A loud crashing noise filled the interior of the crater. Rame managed to look up, past Shakiris's bowing form. The grate was gone. Something began to emerge from the black depths of the pit. First, claws...five enormous talons clutching the edge, then another five. Slowly a head began to rise, a sinister dark shape with eyes that glowed like hot embers. Rame's gaze followed upward as the monstrous creature kept rising, until it crawled out of its lair to stand on four taloned feet, wings spread to the fouled air and its head raised high above the insignificant beings before it.

Rame stared at it in horror; the first time he had ever felt fear. "Verlian, Summon me. Let it be quick."

Shakiris turned away from him to face the beast, his arms outstretched. "Praise to the Mother-of-the-Skies. At last we welcome you and give you these offerings..."

With Shakiris's attention diverted, the cold began to drain from Rame's body and limbs. Feeling returned to his numb fingers and hands. He slowly straightened and took a firmer grip on his swords.

"Honor us by accepting this sacrifice," Shakiris intoned.

Rame stood and raised his swords, ready to strike, when the beast suddenly spotted the two women dangling above the wooden platform. Eyes swirling, it moved closer to Davieta and Sethra, then stopped. It lowered its great head to examine them. Its blade-like teeth hovered inches from their feet. Even though it was still bound by the iron collar and chain, in one breath it would incinerate both women; one snap of its jaws and they would be devoured.

Slowly, Rame re-sheathed his swords then slipped the Bow from his back. One chance.

The full meaning of what he was doing finally took hold. Why Kitarisa had been made to suffer this terrible fate, he could not understand. When had it happened to her in the Catacombs during the War? Some final, lingering curse from Malgora, the dead 'Fa?

He raised the Bow, drawing the arrow tight along his jaw and took aim for the Narusuba tattoo carved into the beast's throat.

"Take the women down first," Mar'Kess's warning whisper came from just behind his right shoulder. "Then, him. We'll take the beast last."

Rame froze, still holding the arrow poised. He drew the bowstring tight and heard the taut searing sound of the arrow flying toward Davieta, severing the cord binding her left wrist. She jerked down and moaned softly as her entire weight hung by a slender right wrist. Her head lolled back and both Assur and Rame could see the glaze of pain dulling her luminous eyes.

"Hold, A'lara, hold!" Rame called to her.

A second arrow sang from Ponosel's Bow, severing the second

cord. Davieta fell to the wooden platform, not moving.

Shakiris whirled on them. "What are you doing?" he roared at them. "She will kill us all!"

In rapid succession, Rame sent two more arrows, cutting the cords that bound Sethra. She, too, fell to the platform.

"You cannot do this!" Shakiris faced him, anger riddling his pale face.

"Stand aside," Rame warned.

He drew his arm back and again trained the gleaming arrow at the beast's throat. Kitarisa would have wanted it this way, he thought fleetingly, and he knew Assur would not want her to live as the creature she had become.

Kill only when your heart is cold and without feeling.

Rame felt his heart tighten into a knot of white-hot pain.

My lady, forgive me.

The arrow flew from his hand, lancing through the rank smoke.

"No!"

Faster than anyone could have thought possible, Shakiris lunged in front of him, arms flailing. His lean body arched high, like a dark blade, taking the arrow straight into his chest.

A monstrous roar filled the crater as the beast lifted its head high as the chain would allow and spewed flames into the night sky. The ground shook and the walls of the crater seemed to come alive with falling rock.

Rame stood unmoving, aghast by what he had done. Shakiris lay in front of him, eyes still wide open, his mouth working frantically as he tried to speak his last words.

"Don't...kill her!" Blood trickled through his lips and he coughed. "She...must live...for us." He coughed again, a horrible choking sound, and fell dead—his long pale hands clutching at the arrow piercing his body.

"We must get the women." Rame heard Mar'Kess's sharp reminder, jolting him into action.

Rame stepped over the fallen body of Shakiris and slung the Bow across his back. He felt no pity for the dead man. Vengeance had been satisfied. He had done what he had promised Davieta. Her tormentor was dead. Rame reached for the arrow and yanked it free from Shakiris's chest, then turned and hurried to the platform with Mar'Kess close behind him.

Both Sethra and Davieta moaned as they tried to revive them and get them to their feet. Davieta would not open her eyes, but Sethra looked up at him.

"Leave us," she whispered hoarsely.

"Don't be a fool, Sethra," Rame said. "Can you stand?"

She nodded weakly. "I think so."

"Help her to her feet, Mar'Kess."

There was no time to be gentle. Mar'Kess tugged Sethra to her feet, wrapping an arm around her waist and half-dragged, half-carried her to the far wall of the crater.

To his despair, Rame could not revive Davieta. He touched the soft hollow of her throat, seeking the beat of life. It was still there, but very weak. Time was running out. He had no time to comfort her. She hung lifelessly in his arms as picked her up and hurried to catch up with Mar'Kess.

Under a shallow ledge of rock, they knelt and gently laid the two women close to one another.

Mar'Kess nodded at something moving not far from them. "There's how we'll get them out."

The horse, harnessed to the small cart that had brought Sethra and Davieta into the crater, stood not far away, still blindfolded and trembling with terror. The poor animal could smell the fire and the creature, but could do nothing to save itself. Glancing at its forelegs, Rame noticed that the priests had cruelly hobbled the horse so it could not run.

Mar'Kess pulled a knife from his belt. "I will get it," he muttered and ran, bent low, toward the horse.

Rame looked up at the monstrous form swaying above them. In the few moments it had taken to free Davieta and Sethra, the beast had not moved, but continued to watch them as if observing mere insects. A low, warning rumble escaped its throat.

Rame heard Mar'Kess approach leading the horse. While he had unharnessed it from the cart, the blindfold still covered the horse's eyes.

"Get them out of here," he ordered while not taking his eyes from the beast towering over them.

Mar'Kess did not argue with him. Out of the corner of his eye, Rame watched as he first lifted Sethra onto the horse's back. Weakened by her ordeal, Davieta was barely conscious as Mar'Kess lifted her up behind Sethra. Using a cut strap from the harness, he looped it around Davieta, then tied her to Sethra so she would not fall off.

Rame slung the Bow from his shoulder. With the last arrow, he nocked it and aimed directly at the beast. "Go Mar'Kess! Save them!

Leave this to me!"

Mar'Kess tugged at the horse's bridle and began leading the frightened animal to the trail. The beast roared its frustration, seeing its prey being taken away. Even blindfolded, the terrified horse screamed and reared, almost throwing Sethra and Davieta to the ground.

The creature lowered menacing jaws to Rame. A guttural sound came from its throat, as it waited for him and the panicky horse to move.

Rame steadied the arrow, aiming for the throat.

"Rame," he heard Mar'Kess call out softly. "Try to speak to her. Say her name."

He hesitated, unsure if he had heard Mar'Kess correctly. Cold sweat ran down his cheeks into the edge of his beard; his arm shook. Could he truly bring himself to kill her...?

"Call to her, Rame! Call her by name!"

"Kitarisa?" he said softly, feeling foolish and frightened at calling such a huge creature by name. Rame raised the Bow a fraction. "Kitarisa! No! Don't kill them!"

The beast seemed to hesitate a moment, then turned its head toward him. The liquid-red eyes roiled. Did she remember him? Would she remember Assur?

"Go while you have the chance, Mar'Kess. Take my niece and Davieta and leave."

"Lord Rame?"

"Go!"

"She will kill you, my lord."

"So be it," Rame said quietly. *Res Teya Sa Verlian.* "Verlian calls me. It will buy you time; Sethra and Davieta will be alive." Rame steadied the arrow aimed at the tattoo mark. "I know what I am doing, Mar'Kess. Leave while you can."

Rame glanced up into the night sky and suddenly realized that the moon had at last, waned. Verlian's light was gone.

Chapter Seventeen

THE GUARDIAN BEAST was dying and Assur heard its final death throes echoing through the tunnels before he reached the base of the coiling stairway. Mar'Kess had left the ancient creature writhing in its own blood and the eggs burning to putrefied ash. He knew there had to be more eggs. A creature that old did not jealously guard only one clutch of eggs, but must have more hidden. The sulphurous smoke now burned in Assur's lungs, clotted at the back of his throat and in his nostrils.

Where the tunnels met, he stopped, coughing and panting for breath. Bodies of Narusuba priests littered the floor, having fallen where he and Rame had slain them.

Assur heard no sounds coming from the locked pit. The Narusuba had already freed her and he had to hurry. He turned toward the corridor that had not yet been explored. The torch he carried had long gone out. He seized another from the bracket in the wall. Feeble light filtered down from the crater floor above. He hoped it would be enough for him to find his way back; he had no desire for getting lost in this underground inferno.

With the torch in his left hand, sword in his right, Assur hurried down the dark tunnel, mindful of the added burden of the Spear as well as his swords strapped to his back. He had vowed on the blood of his father that Talesia's most sacred weapon would be returned, intact. If he didn't, Kuurus would undoubtedly have his liver on a platter. Assur smiled at the thought of the tough Siarsi warrior. It was a shame he was not here to help him; the creatures would not stand a chance.

The tunnel went on endlessly, burrowing deeper into the earth. Every fifty paces, he found another small chamber filled with the greenish-gray eggs, ready to hatch. He soon discovered that by using his sword to destroy a few, then setting fire to them, he obliterated the entire clutch.

In chamber after chamber, Assur continued to wield his sword until every egg he found was crushed and burning. He sensed there might be more, but he could not look for all of them. Duty and the fear that some of these vile creatures might have somehow escaped forced him on. He had to find the secret of freeing Kitarisa.

Smoke from the numerous chambers had begun to seep into the tunnels. If he did not get out soon, he would either suffocate or burn.

The tunnel began to narrow and dropped sharply—the rock walls seemed to close in as the smoke slowly dissipated. Assur began to smell something different—something foul and old. Water trickled and dripped from black shale walls that had been clearly cut and shaped by human hands. The tunnel opened into another cavern, enormous and vaulted, reaching high and deep into the belly of the mountain-crater. He raised his torch. Like the smaller cave, a million pinpoints of light from natural minerals sparkled from the ceiling, casting an eerie glow throughout the great chamber.

An ancient evil permeated the place and Assur sensed he had entered the domain of something more terrible than he had ever encountered. Even the Catacombs had not roused such instinctive fear. Dread nettled his spine like white-hot needles. He took a firmer grip on his sword and stepped into the cavern.

It took a few moments for his eyes to adjust to the dark, but what he saw filled him with new horror. The torchlight illuminated the looming walls that had been gouged out into hundreds upon hundreds of niches—narrow, black cavities filled with bones. Assur almost dropped the torch.

A dank pool of brackish water separated him from the back of the cave. It reeked like a noxious poison and clung to his boots in a slick black scum as he waded through it to the wall. The lowest row of hollowed-out crevices was only inches from the cavern floor. Assur dropped to one knee to examine the bones in the nearest niche. He touched the frail white skull. A few brittle threads of hair remained—hair that had once been the color of Sethra's, brilliant red-gold, but now faded to dull yellow. Her little hands—the fine-boned hands of a lady—were still clasped together over her breast. The gold of her rings, fused to charred bones, winked in the dim light.

Despair filled him as he thrust the torch into the next niche. Fragments of a gown clung in decaying webs of gilt thread to what remained of the skeleton. In the next were the remains of a girl even smaller than the others. Her pitiful form curled tightly, knees to her jawbone, revealed her last moments huddled in terror.

Assur stood and looked up at the hundreds of filled crevices. They were all women. Some of the small skulls still wore a glittering diadem or crown proclaiming the wearer as a royal woman or one of noble blood. A sickening fear sliced through his belly. So were Sethra and

Lady Davieta. And, Kitarisa? He now understood the reason why she was here. A mother....

He thrust the torch before him and spotted the last rock-hewn crypt. Only one remained. It was empty. This was where they would bring her...when they were done with her, when she had served her purpose.

"How do you like my brides?" a deep, silky voice asked, stopping Assur in his tracks. "I have over four hundred. Does that surprise you?"

He heard the rasp of scales on stone and the hollow, huge breaths of something monstrous.

"They are with me for all time," the voice whispered, "as will my next lady. She is mine, a woman of royal blood who has felt my presence within her and knows my strength. I have waited for over three hundred turns of the sun for her."

"Kitarisa will never be yours!"

"As she will never again be yours, High Prince of all Talesia. She has been changed...as I have..."

"Show yourself!" Assur roared, taking a firmer grip on his sword and raising the torch higher.

"Brave words, Noble One. Are you certain of your request? As it shall be your last."

"Come out, worm!"

A hiss of a sigh. "You dare to challenge me, even in my own lair? You are a fool, barbarian."

"Then, it is a fool who will kill you."

"Ssssoooo be it, prince. My kind ruled long before yours and shall do so again, as it was in the beforetimes."

From the back of the cave, Assur detected movement—a black shape moving within deepest black—the blink of a gold eye shimmered through that darkness, the scrape of talons on broken shale. Assur tossed the utterly useless sword at the edge of the pool and reached for the Spear on his back.

Almost twice the size of Kitarisa, the Beast stepped from the inner cave and reared its gigantic head above him. Streams of gray-white smoke streamed from its nostrils and its leathern wings filled the cavern as it swayed above him.

Assur heard it speak again—slithered words through a forked tongue and yellowed teeth the length of his forearm lining massive jaws.

It cocked a swirling amber eye at him. "You think to defeat me with that? A mere stick? You are a greater fool than I thought,

Talesian."

Assur felt the rush of the oily black water at his feet as he backed a step. "Come out, or are you afraid, you stinking maggot?"

"I have never been afraid...I am Master here."

One step, then another. The fore talons were now wet with the brackish ooze.

"I do not miss this close, Beast," Assur warned.

Two more steps, you bag of filth.

"Neither do I. My question is, barbarian lord: do you think you can survive being burned to ash before you take your next breath?"

Another step; a hind foot in the oil-water.

Assur raised the Spear to his shoulder, sighting along its gleaming length to the throbbing mark in the Beast's neck. "I think the question becomes..."

The creature hissed ominously; its spined tail lashed from side to side. One last step and all four taloned feet were in the stinking sludge. In one swift motion, Assur flung the torch into the water at the base of the Beast's belly. Instantly, flames shot upward, surrounding the creature, burning it where it stood.

"....can you?"

Chalisetra's Spear flew from his hand, directly into the tattooed mark in the Beast's throat. A deafening roar filled the cavern as the huge creature reared its head and spewed a stream of blinding white flame into the rock above. Enormous wings beat the befouled air, fanning more flames. The Beast screamed in helpless fury as it thrashed and struggled to free itself of the Spear that had completely pierced through its neck. Blood ran from the terrible wound, into the black water, mixing with it, joining with it, as the flames rose even higher.

The entire cave was on fire as the Beast lay writhing in an agonized death dance.

Assur took one last look at the pitiful remains of the long-dead princesses. At least this would be their funeral pyre. They would be cleansed and welcomed by Verlian, not left to rot in this obscene crypt.

"May Verlian Summon you," he called and bowed his head to the rows and rows of niches, now consumed with flames.

The vision had been fulfilled. He had lost the Sacred Spear, but somehow he knew Kuurus would understand. So would Achad.

The heat was too much even for him. Assur took up the sword he had dropped, un-sheathed the other and fled the cavern.

By the time he climbed up to the crater floor, fire had already begun to consume everything below—a sharp reminder of his final moments within the Catacombs where fire had destroyed the last of the hated White Sisters. Assur knew there were more of those aged white creatures trapped in long-forgotten caves and caverns, left to die while trying to protect what remained of their precious horde of eggs. All that really mattered was the Beast was dead. There would be no more of his kind to torment the world.

The fire found more pockets of the oily black water and like succumbing to a vile plague that destroys from within, the entire island began to collapse.

Assur raced up the curving stone steps, stumbling over the bodies of the slain Narusuba, dodging the cracking and heaving rock walls. Once on the surface, he stopped. It was worse than he had feared.

From the swirling smoke, Mar'Kess ran toward him, leading the blindfolded horse. "My lord, we have freed both women. We can get them out if we hurry." He nodded in the direction of the narrow trail.

"And Rame?"

"He is still..."

Even in the darkness, Assur could see Mar'Kess's distress.

He said nothing, but looked over him and saw Sethra on the horse's back clinging to its mane. She lifted her head and attempted a weak smile.

"So, my lord brother, you found us."

Assur reached for Sethra's arm and steadied her. "Yes, at last. Are you well enough to ride from this place?"

"Well, enough. But I fear for Davieta."

Lady Davieta had survived the ordeal, but clearly was not as well as Sethra. Smaller and not as strong, Davieta leaned against Sethra, exhaustion and pain marring her luminous dark eyes. But, she was alert and aware of her surroundings.

Assur also touched her arm. "My lady, we will have you away from here, soon."

"My lord Rame?" she asked weakly through dry, cracked lips.

"Rame...will follow us." He nodded to Mar'Kess. "Get out of the crater. Find Kuurus!"

Mar'Kess tugged at the horse's bridle and hurriedly led the animal away.

Through the blinding smoke, Assur was able to just make out Rame standing before the cinder-black creature, aiming the last arrow of Ponosel's Bow directly at its throat. Assur edged around the open pit, hoping to somehow reach Rame's side before he was noticed.

"Do not kill her, Rame," he warned in a low voice.

"Why not? We will never get out of here alive. She will burn us the moment we turn and run."

"Maybe she cannot...she is still chained."

"Oh, she will burn us, even though she cannot fly." Rame's arms began to tremble slightly.

Assur glanced upward at the massive swaying head. The iron collar was still fastened about the beast's neck, the long heavy chain trailing along its spine, across the crater floor and down into the pit.

"Rame, you cannot kill her. It was not in the visions... You have freed Sethra and Davieta; Mar'Kess has destroyed the eggs and I have killed the Beast."

The Swordmaster hesitated. "I do not wish to die here, Assur," he said grimly.

"Neither do I. Put up your weapon. If anyone is do it, it should be me."

Rame slowly eased the arrow from the bowstring, but never took his eyes from his target. "You must hurry. I believe we have played out the last of our luck."

Assur turned to face the creature, a being that had once been human, now a deadly animal. How could he kill her with mere swords? Kitarisa did not deserve this, to die as some unnatural beast with no memory of her true self.

He raised his swords. "Take her down if I miss," he ordered grimly.

She hissed a final warning and shook her great head back and forth, rattling the chain.

...do what is right, even if it means my life. Promise me, Assur....

Assur looked straight into those menacing red eyes, finding nothing human, only malevolence. "I promise, Kita," he whispered and hurled his right-hand sword at the tattoo, just below the iron band around the creature's throat. The blade arced true and struck its mark, but did not penetrate the black scales. The sword clattered harmlessly to the ground.

She glared down at him and took another threatening step.

Assur hastily switched the other sword to his right hand, took closer aim and threw it. Again, the sword struck the mark but did not pierce the hardened hide.

This time, the blow was not ignored. Enraged, the creature hissed and roared, snaking its head down, seeking him and Rame like stalking fresh prey. It scuttled toward them, talons raking the charred cinder rock. She reared up, straining, fighting against the chain and iron collar, then filled her lungs with an enormous breath.

"Now, Rame!"

The Swordmaster swiftly refitted the arrow into the Bow and took aim. The arrow streaked through the choking black smoke straight toward the beast.

And missed.

Assur saw the shock and disbelief on Rame's face; Rame never missed. Defenseless now, they both began to back away. Assur dropped to one knee behind a nearby boulder, trying to remain as calm as possible and think of a way to escape.

"Any ideas?" Rame asked, crouching next to him. "I'm not throwing *my* swords." He sounded disgusted and faintly ashamed.

"If we can get to the rocks near the wall..."

The fire came suddenly, a searing blue-white stream pouring from the beast's open jaws—a fire so hot the cinder-rock crisped to blackened ash before it melted beneath their feet. They turned and ran for the crater wall.

Behind them, they both heard a hard cracking noise and a deafening roar. Assur glanced over his shoulder; the crater wall behind the pit grating was aflame in a massive inferno. Fire, fed by more underground pockets of the black water, shot into the night sky. The earth shuddered, then heaved violently, opening cracks like dozens of rivulets that zig-zagged from a larger, widening chasm, shooting across the crater floor faster than Rame or Assur could run.

"The crater is breaking up," Rame panted.

They made it to the wall and slid behind a huge boulder, just as another torrent of the beast's fire burned across their path.

The ground bucked and split again; more fire shot upward from the depths of the crater. The beast roared its frustration, then fear. The earth beneath its taloned claws began to split into a gaping fissure that spread backward toward the pit. Assur watched, helpless, as the creature bellowed and fought the collar and chain that kept it from saving itself. Each beat of the great wings only added to the inferno. It scrabbled at the collapsing earth, desperately trying to keep from falling back into the pit. In one final effort, head and wings straining for the sky, the creature lost its fight.

Assur watched as she slipped slowly, majestically, over the edge and fell. Rocks and dirt poured through clutching claws. A last stream of white fire and the horrible, desperate bellowing suddenly became the high, piercing scream of a dying woman.

For a long moment Assur stood, unable to move, listening to the roar of the fires and shattering sounds of the crater breaking up beneath their feet.

Rame, too, seemed rooted to the spot where he was standing, transfixed by what had just happened. "She did not suffer, Assur. I am sure of it."

Again, Assur felt the rage and unutterable pain——just like the first time when she had fallen from the Rift Cut and died. Only this time, there would be no Holy Daughters to bring her back.

Exhausted and past caring, Assur ran toward the pit. By some extraordinary fate, the whim of Verlian, his father's swords lay near the edge of the fissure, undamaged. He re-sheathed them, but suddenly realized it did not matter if he still had Achad's swords or not. He had lost everything. His father was dead and the Sacred Spear was gone. And Kitarisa... He stood at the edge of the crumbling pit and gazed down into its smoke and ash-filled depths. She was down there.

He felt Rame's hand on his shoulder. "We must go. Now, Assur."

"Leave me."

"Don't be a fool! This island will be gone before the sun rises."

Assur shrugged off Rame's hand. "I need to find her. I will not leave her down there."

"You will never get out. You will be trapped. You'll die down there——!"

"What does it matter? Here..." Before he could be stopped, Assur swiftly un-looped his father's swords from his back and shoved them into Rame's hands. "You hold the tribes. Take Achad's swords and return to the Keep. You will have Davieta at your side...take the dar Daeamon firemarks, Rame. It is what you have always wanted. Rule Talesia as the rightful Ter-Rey!"

The Swordmaster stared at him, too overcome to say anything at first. Sweat and grime creased his face, emphasizing the black patterns around his eyes and the naked rage Assur saw within them.

"You are mad, Assur!"

"Am I? What if it were Davieta? Would you leave her down there?"

Loyalty and right judgement warred across Rame's taut, tired features.

"Well?" Assur pressed.

Rame made a disgusted noise in his throat and thrust the swords back at Assur. "You are still mad, my lord nephew, but you are right." He held up a warning hand. "But we only go as far as we can...until we know we cannot find her."

"Agreed."

By another extraordinary stroke of fate, the holding pit itself was not on fire. As the smoke and dust cleared, they could see that some of the collapsed rock had formed a relatively easy way down. The huge clawholds, hewn from the rock along the inside wall of the pit, still remained. Assur and Rame dropped from level to level, until they were nearly to the pit floor.

The beast was gone, as Assur knew it would be, but he could not find Kitarisa. In spite of the light from the fires above, it was too dark to see anything, until Rame stumbled over a section of chain half buried in the dirt.

"Here, follow this."

Frantically, they both dug through the loose rocks, pulling the remaining length of chain free until Assur's hand brushed against something covered in cloth.

"Kita, Kita!"

She lay awkwardly on her side—the huge neck collar, too large for a human, encircled her entire body. Rame helped him slip it over her shoulders and flung it away.

Assur pushed her gently onto her back and brushed away the dirt from her face and hair. He touched her cheek. "Kita?"

For the second time, Assur felt the knifing pain of loss. Not again. He could not lose her again. Rame's fingers caught his shoulder.

"She's gone."

"No." He gathered her close, pressing his face into her neck and rocked back and forth, fighting against the long-disdained urge to weep.

Until he felt something in her body spasm. A shuddering breath and her back arched sharply between his hands. Kitarisa gasped; her right arm thrust against his shoulder. She began to cough violently, struggling to breathe.

Assur looked up at Rame. The Swordmaster nodded. "Praise Verlian," he said softly.

Kitarisa tried to sit up, but Assur wouldn't let her. "Wait, Kita. Save your strength."

Her eyes fluttered open, unfathomable dark pools in a moonless night. "Assur?" She fumbled to touch his face.

"Yes, A'lara, it is me."

"That thing...inside me...?

"It is gone. You are free."

Her fingers found the edge of his sword strap—grasping it tightly.

"Assur, I cannot see!"

"It is night and there is no moon..."

A sob caught her throat. "No, Assur, I cannot see anything!"

Rame's expression told him they had little time left. Glancing below, Assur noticed more of the brackish, oily water seeping across the floor of the cavern; the fires were getting closer. "Kitarisa, we will help you later. We must go. Can you walk?"

She shook her head. "I do not know."

Assur quickly felt the length of her legs and arms for broken bones. Finding none he helped her to her feet. As she sagged against him too weak to stand, he bent forward and lifted her over his shoulder.

It was slow going, slipping and stumbling up the rough-hewn stones, but between the two of them, Assur and Rame managed to carry her to the surface.

The crater floor was almost entirely consumed by fire and twisted into rubble. Flames shot up through the numerous fissures and cracks in the earth. Showers of glowing rocks exploded into the sky, and fell back, scorching the surface of the island.

They hurried to the trail at the far side of the crater wall, hoping it hadn't been obliterated. To their surprise, a man holding the reins of a wild-eyed gray horse stood at the opening to the trail, a huge grin splitting his scarred cheeks.

"Kuurus!" Assur was never so glad to see the faithful Siarsi.

"My lord, we had nearly given up on you. And, Lord Rame. Alive, I see."

"Barely," Rame managed to say.

"Here, I have brought you Adzra—the only horse I could coax down this trail."

Assur nodded to the handsome gray. "He'll serve." With Kuurus's help he eased Kitarisa onto Adzra's back and guided her hands to the long, thick strands of the horse's mane. "Hold on, Kita."

She nodded mutely as Assur turned the horse and led him up the trail, Kuurus and Rame at his heels. Once at the top of the crater's edge, they were met by Mar'Kess, holding the reins of the other horses. To Assur's relief, Sethra appeared unharmed, but deeply tired from her ordeal. She faced him, the light from the fires below lighting her fair face and brilliant hair.

"You are well, brother," she said, smiling. "And, Kitarisa?"

"Is alive."

Sethra looked at her but said nothing. No time would be wasted with idle talk. Assur spotted Davieta, entwined in Rame's arms, sobbing against him. For the first time, he noticed his uncle did not look like the Swordmaster, hard and unforgiving, but like any other man, holding the woman he loved close to his heart.

Now Rame would understand why he had to go back for Kitarisa.

No orders were needed to mount their horses. Mar'Kess easily pulled Sethra up behind him, while Kuurus lifted Davieta behind Rame. She wrapped her small arms tightly around him, pressing her cheek to his back.

Assur swung onto Adzra's back. Too weak to ride behind him, Kitarisa sat before him, across the saddlebow. He took a firm hold of her waist, pulling her against him and heeled Adzra to the rim trail.

With Kuurus riding at the rear, leading the cart horse, they urged their mounts down the winding trail to the shoreline below. The first threads of dawn touched the eastern sky as they reached the narrow causeway.

The crater island was dying a wrenching, burning death. The earth still writhed and heaved beneath their horses" hooves as they approached the long strip of sand separating them from the western island. The tide had turned back, the water reached the horses' knees.

Assur urged the big gray into a faster gallop. He could hear Rame's black pounding behind him at his right and Mar'Kess's bay at his left, all racing to keep from being swallowed up by the fire and the sea.

The pale silk of Kitarisa's sacrificial gown whipped across his left knee like a banner leading them on to dry land. As the first light of the morning sun broke over the looming cliffs, Assur saw the horizon fill with billowing sails and knew they would reach the safety of Saar's great longships.

Chapter Eighteen

FOR THREE DAYS, Davieta kept to herself. She would not see Rame or let him see her tears. She wept bitterly for what had happened to him—his pain, the scars riddling his back, the tattoo carved into his throat and his utter exhaustion.

She saw him briefly, once—a stolen moment, caught in his fierce embrace. They spoke only a few words, hurried avowals of love and a desperate kiss goodbye.

The city had fallen into chaos. Renegade Narusuba, looters and thieves still roamed the streets causing havoc, burning and pillaging what was left of the ancient city. Both Rame and Mar'Kess had been commanded to restore order by leading patrols throughout Volt and into the outlying areas.

For Assur, Davieta grieved as she would grieve for any man who had almost lost the one he loved above all else. As the Ter-Rey, he was expected to show nothing, to let no one see his anguish for Kitarisa. And, he didn't. For hours, she watched him pace the room next to Kitarisa's, waiting for her to revive and ask for him, and all the while, said nothing of the deep hurt in his heart. Only his eyes revealed his suffering.

Davieta wept the longest for Kitarisa. During their voyage back to Volt, as she lay on a cramped cot drifting in and out of sleep, she sensed Kitarisa lying next to her. At times Davieta was aware of the kindly ship's physick trying to ease the princess's suffering, but Kitarisa would not sleep. She lay unmoving in the darkened cabin, staring sightlessly at the beams above her head.

Assur brought all of them back to Prince Aettilek's ancient palace where Kitarisa was given the finest rooms—Alea's former apartments. Davieta stayed near Kitarisa's side offering her water or soothing cups of shen tea, hoping she would respond. Even the Volten physicks could find nothing seriously wrong with her—she had not suffered any broken bones, or wounds. She had not been burned. Surely, they said, nourishing meals would bring her strength back, as would some exercise and fresh air. They puzzled over her stillness and her refusal to speak. Nothing was the matter with her....

Except for her eyes.

Strong light caused Kitarisa incalculable anguish. Davieta kept the draperies drawn, blocking out Volt's brilliant sunshine. Only at night did she allow the soft radiance of Verlian's returning light to enter the bedchamber. In spite of this special attention, Kitarisa still could not see.

At first, only Davieta had the courage to look at her. Kitarisa's eyes had not changed back—entirely red, no whites, no pupils, save for the black vertical slits—the malevolent eyes of a loathsome animal.

Davieta wept for Kitarisa; wept the tears Assur could not....

When she was spent, weary of her grief, Davieta resolved to regain some semblance of normalcy by resuming her role as Kitarisa's lady's maid. There was no use in forever lamenting what had happened. She was determined to set things right as best she could and in doing so, kept her mind from thinking about Rame.

After several days of restoring order to Volt, Assur, at last, requested to see Kitarisa. Davieta dressed with care; her gown, found amongst Alea's vast, abandoned wardrobe, had been refitted to her slight form. Full-length sleeves with deep lace at the wrists covered the scars made by the ropes.

When Assur finally entered the bedchamber, Davieta retreated to a shadowed corner, uncertain what would be expected of her. He said nothing, but knelt by Kitarisa's side. In sorrow, Davieta watched him gaze at her, taking in her pale, deathlike appearance and the red, sightless eyes. He touched her brow lightly.

"Kita'lara," he murmured. "Please, speak to me."

Silence.

"Kitarisa, please," he pleaded more urgently. She did not respond. In despair, Assur pressed his brow into his hand, the long fingers covering his eyes. "Has she eaten anything, Lady Davieta?"

Davieta emerged from the dim corner of the room. "Yes, my lord—a bit of broth and some tea."

"Does she sleep?"

"I do not know, but I think when I leave the room she closes her eyes for a short time." She came to stand next to him, desperate to find some way to ease is suffering. "I am sure she does not feel any pain, my lord."

"Of that, I, too, am certain, but what I fear is that she will never return to us. That her eyes..." He shook his head. "It is twice now that Kitarisa has faced her Summons, but only once has she been restored to me. It will not happen again." He spoke so forlornly that Davieta thought her own heart would break. She had no words, nothing to say to him to offer any real comfort.

"Perhaps if you asked for a Holy Daughter...from the Catacombs to come and help her?"

"I do not think there is time. It is so far to the Catacombs, even if I sent a message bird now, by the time they arrived..." He buried his face in both his hands, too bereft to continue.

Davieta turned from him, clasping her hands before her. There must be a way! Some answer, some hope.

"I do not know what to do, Lady Davieta," he said finally. "I am the High Prince of all Talesia; I have seen the armies of those who have defied me, slain, cut down like ripe wheat; I have laid waste and destroyed everything in my path; I have killed and I have punished, yet I can do nothing to save her. Why is that, good lady? Why has Verlian given me the power to rule a world—the authority to destroy anything and anyone I choose, but not the power to save her, the only one who means anything to me? Tell me why this is so?" he asked bitterly.

"Perhaps, because it is not your place; a power that strong is not for..." She was about to say *men*, but Assur cut across her words.

"...mere princes?" His voice was raw with anger. "Or, maybe it is only *barbarians* who are denied this ability."

"My lord, I only meant—"

He stood wearily and made a dismissive gesture with his hand. "I know what you meant. Forgive me, Lady Davieta, but I am tired of this cruel game."

How alike he was to Rame, she thought. So dark and intense. Right and wrong were quite clear to him. He suffered no misgivings about the *rightness* of his own purpose and the ability to control it. But, saving Kitarisa was beyond his power and the simple acknowledgment of this fact clearly angered him beyond his inability to help her.

"Someone must know this secret," Davieta said, anxiously clutching her hands before her. "There must be some of the Narusuba left who know how to reverse this terrible curse...someone who knew Shakiris."

Assur grew quiet. He stared beyond her to the heavy draperies. "Yes, someone who was close to Shakiris, who knew his plans and what he was." He turned back to Kitarisa and again, knelt next to her. "There is only one who might know and she has fled."

Davieta nodded, knowing who he meant. "If we could find Alea..."

"Yes, *if* we can find her and *if* she knows Shakiris's secrets...which I doubt." He glanced back at Kitarisa's still form. "In the morning, I shall send a message bird to the Catacombs."

LIKE HER FATHER, Alea had fled for her life. She barely managed to escape Volt disguised as a Qualani woman, just slipping past the ever-vigilant Riehlians who had surrounded and began patrolling the outskirts of the city. Her Qualani guides had cautioned her that there was a good chance they would be caught, but Alea refused to accept their warning.

For days, she and the outcasts rode north, hoping to outrun the Ter-Rey and his warriors. There was no doubt in her mind that Assur would succeed in defeating Shakiris and his so-called "master." Assur had what he needed. The Sacred Weapons were his and once he had reached Shygul and completed his task, he would return to Volt to begin looking for her. She knew he would pursue her, relentlessly. He would hunt her down like an animal, never tiring, never giving up. And when he found her, he would have his vengeance. So would his ruthless uncle, Rame.

Panic almost made her careless. She had few choices left and there were even fewer places where she could hide. Since the Rift Cut War, Assur had regained absolute control of the Eastern Lands. Once the word had been sent out to all the provinces and to the great Keeps in Riehl and Gorendt, Alea would have even fewer chances for escape.

After several days of running, she and the Qualani came upon the one place where they could hide, at least until their horses had rested and she could devise a new plan. She cared nothing for her filthy companions. They were bought dogs anyway, like the warriors she had hired to guard the palace. The Qualani outcasts were only interested in thievery and gold. Their one-eyed leader had agreed to lead her out of Volt for a hundred gold talins. Once they reached a safe destination, she would give him another hundred. But, Alea had no intention of parting with any more gold. Once she had worked out her escape, her so-called escorts could fend for themselves. And, if Assur found them? She shrugged to herself. It was not her concern.

Alea did not miss the irony of hiding within the burned-out ruins of Sherehn Keep, the very place where Assur and his men had first found her and Kitarisa. The common roadwilds who abducted them had been destroyed and the Keep burned to rubble. Still, there was enough left standing where she and the Qualani could hide for several weeks, unnoticed. The ancient underground chambers were still intact.

The Qualani gathered around a low fire, muttering between themselves, or perhaps to wonder how much more gold they were going to get, while Alea kept to herself pacing and thinking. She didn't like their secretive ways, or their sly glances in her direction, but she couldn't worry about them now. Her immediate future pressed upon her, forcing her to make an annoying decision.

There was only one place left where she could hide and the other irony was that it was the same place Assur had intended for her all along—a place of seclusion where women hid themselves from the world. It was vast and almost impenetrable. Safe. Only soft, stupid women lived there. Alea smiled to herself. If that's where Assur wanted her to be, then she would oblige him.

The Catacombs would be hers.

THERE WAS NO need to send the message bird. At dawn, as the first threads of light touched the eastern skies, an alert guard manning the northern battlement spotted the somber ship emerge from the mists of the Sherehn River. It was like no other ship anyone had ever seen— sleek, dusky-colored—without gleaming brasses or copper and crowned by great black sails. It swept majestically into the harbor and anchored near Prince Saar's longship.

After commending the guard for his vigilance, Assur went to the battlements to discover who would emerge from the mysterious ship.

One woman, cloaked in dark red, was rowed to shore in a small boat by four lean-limbed men, wearing tunics of the same dark red. Each man wore his hair long, tied back with three strands of white cording. They helped the woman to the dock, then bowed and stood back respectively as she made her way to the city. Assur knew who she was and immediately sent an escort to bring her to the palace.

Once she entered through the gilded doors, silence pervaded the hall. Those who were standing near him, including Rame, bowed deeply as the small, robed figure approached the black granite throne where Assur sat waiting for her. He remained wary as to why she had come to Volt, without being summoned or by his request.

"The Goddess's blessings, Great Lord." She bowed to him and pushed back the hood of her cloak.

"You have survived a great ordeal and I thank Verlian you are not injured."

"Yes, the Goddess be praised." He inclined his head politely. "You honor us, Daughter Jizrella, but we are uncertain as to why you have come all the way from the Catacombs to Volt."

"But, you sent for me..."

Assur frowned, not understanding. "I sent no message...at least, not yet."

"The message came to us in a way unknown to you...perhaps somewhat unconventional, but we have heeded your call and I was told to come as quickly as possible."

"Then, I am indeed, grateful to you. We have need of your healing abilities."

"I know," she said kindly. "The princess has not recovered. I have come to apologize and to offer a way that will restore her to us."

Assur leaned forward. "You know how to reverse what has happened to her?"

"Yes, but it will take the efforts of many; the price will be high for some."

"And what price is that?"

"One life must be given to correct the Balance, then all will be as it was. The world will be aright, again."

"Whose?" Assur asked sharply.

The Holy Daughter lowered her gaze and bowed slightly. "I do not know, Great Lord. It is the Will of Verlian. She will decide."

Unease filtered through those standing within the somber hall. A few muttered softly between themselves. Rame cast a questioning look at Assur.

"What if the price is too high? What if that one individual does not wish to surrender their life for Kitarisa?"

"My lord, the Narusuba have done great harm by upsetting the Measure and Balance. The world will not be right until this is corrected. You, Prince Ramelek, and Lord Raldan Mar'Kess have reversed much of the damage by destroying Shygul. However, within Kitarisa lies the greatest wrong, both to her and to all that we know. A single life surrendered to the Goddess may be a great price for some, but for the Balance of our world, it is indeed, small."

"What is it you request?" Assur finally asked.

"You must bring Kitarisa to the Catacombs. You and the others," she nodded to Rame and Mar'Kess, "must come, too. You must bring the Weapons, even though there are only two remaining. And, you must bring one of Kitarisa's blood. You must find and bring her sister, Alea."

Assur studied the serene-faced Daughter. He owed much to her. She had saved his life when he had been taken prisoner, crippled and maimed by the corrupt White Sister, Malgora. He was bound in chains and near death from his internal wounds and broken bones when the Daughter Jizrella, one of the last empathic healers living within the

Catacombs, had found him in time and restored him. She had called the Affliction from him, given back his life so that he could defeat Malgora and her minions. Later, Jizrella and the other remaining Holy Daughters had brought Kitarisa back from the brink of her own Summons.

"She has fled, Holy Daughter. We do not know where she is."

"Alea must be found, Great Lord. If she is not, Kitarisa will die, the world will not be restored to the Balance and this time, we will not be able to bring her back. The Goddess will Summon her, forever."

THE DAUGHTER WAS permitted to see Kitarisa and stood over her, fingertips lightly pressed to her brow.

Assur leaned against the window, arms folded across his chest; Davieta stood nearby, trying to appear calm.

"There is time," Jizrella said. "Kitarisa is strong and has fought the corruption within her. But, she is beginning to weaken. We must depart soon."

"I have begun the preparations," Assur said. "We can leave at first light." He watched the Daughter for a moment. "Can you do nothing for her?"

"I have eased her discomfort and removed the Narusuba mark from her throat. She will rest easily until we reach the Catacombs."

"And her eyes...?"

Jizrella shook her head. "Only Daughter Thespa can do that, for she is the strongest among us. She knows what must be done."

Davieta took a hesitant step forward. "Holy Daughter, I would ask...can you also help Lord Ramelek? He was cruelly beaten. He bears fearsome scars upon his back—the mark of the Narusuba is still on his throat."

The Daughter smiled at her compassionately. "This will be done, but he must wait until we reach the Catacombs. You need not fear, Lady Davieta. The Affliction will be called from Lord Rame."

Davieta inclined her head. "I thank you Holy Daughter."

"And, the Affliction must be called from you, as well as Princess Sethra."

"I...?" Davieta looked startled. "I do not understand."

Jizrella nodded, indicating her hands. "Do you not still bear the scars of your own ordeal? This, too, shall be corrected."

Davieta rubbed nervously at her wrists, as if trying to hide the ugly scars left by the ropes.

"You have suffered more than the scars upon your wrists, Lady

Davieta. You have endured impossible pain and loss. You have survived humiliation and great shame. I pray Verlian that some of this anguish may be alleviated."

"If it pleases you, Holy Daughter," Davieta murmured.

Jizrella returned her attention to Kitarisa. Her fingers brushed lightly against her eyelids, closing them over the alarming red stare. "She will rest now and truly sleep, but I would ask you, my lord, if you know the whereabouts of Kitarisa's brother, Alor?"

"No. I have not seen him since I banished him...in Riehl, after the war. I banished both him and Alea."

The Daughter looked puzzled for a moment. "The strangest thing... I sense Kitarisa believes he is near, very near." She glanced up at him. "Would Alor know the whereabouts of Alea?"

At once alert, Assur straightened. "Perhaps. What else do you sense, Holy Daughter?"

"Something...red. Not her eyes, but what she sees. "Red.... something?"

"Here, in Volt?" he asked.

"I believe so."

"I shall begin a search at once. Perhaps Verlian has chosen the life She demands."

IT TOOK ALMOST the entire night, but they finally found him in Redsilk, sprawled upon the floor in a back room, sodden with rapturewine. Assur had no patience with those who succumbed to the foul drink and ordered Alor dragged into the street then thrown into a horse trough to clear is head. The one-time Prince Alor, son of Kazan dar Baen, came up spluttering, hurling curses at Assur and those who had tossed him into the water.

Assur observed the outraged young man while still sitting astride Adzra. "Enough? Perhaps you need another soaking?"

Two hard-eyed Gorendtian warriors dragged Alor from the trough and shoved him dripping and shivering to his knees before Assur.

"So, my sister was right. You have come to Volt, to find the Weapons and seek some kind of vengeance, I presume?"

"You have been too long drowned in your drink, Alor. I have already been here once and have had my vengeance. The Narusuba are gone, destroyed. It appears your sister, Alea, is also gone with her pack of Qualani dogs, but to whereabouts unknown. Tell me where."

Alor pawed the water from his eyes. "How would I know? I am not advised of her activities nor acquainted with the company she keeps."

Assur looked aside, fighting anger. *Another* defiant fool.

"I have no time for this." He nodded to the warriors who were keeping a close eye on the young man. "Bring him with us. A few days in irons, chained in the belly of a ship ought to encourage his memory. Take him."

Alor was forced to his feet and dragged away, but remained silent. Assur would waste no more time with threats and knives. Alor would talk. He was smarter than Alea and had no loyalties. His need to survive was stronger than his pride. Being chained up in the hold of a ship without women or rapturewine would make him reveal Alea's whereabouts faster than any promise of punishment.

Chapter Nineteen

AS THE SHIP SAILED northward up the Sherehn River, once again Assur and his men donned their heavy leather jerkins and thick fur cloaks. A thin coating of snow still clung to the ground and the nights were sharp and cold. It seemed strange to be traveling where winter still clung fiercely to the land, when only days before he and the others had been sweltering in the moist heat of the southern seas.

Sethra and Davieta remained below, keeping a vigilant watch over Kitarisa. As Jizrella promised, the princess slept peacefully, unaware of where she was, or where she was going.

After another three days of steady progress, the river split around the small island where Sherehn Keep lay in ruins. Bridges, that at one time spanned the riverbanks to the island, had been withdrawn. As they approached what was left of Sherehn, Jizrella ordered the ship to stop and drop anchor. A scattering of snow crusted the mass of charred timbers and blackened stones. A fragment of a wall remained and clinging to it, the tattered, faded remnants of a clan banner.

Assur stood at the ship's rail alongside Rame and the Holy Daughter. "Is there something wrong?" he asked her.

Jizrella studied the blackened hulk of the Keep. "I sense something. Someone is hiding in there. I am not sure who it is."

"Allow me to take a few men and investigate the island," Rame said.

Assur nodded. "Agreed. Summon Mar'Kess, young Cai, and ten well-armed men...and we wear helmets, Rame. Daughter Jizrella, do you wish to accompany us?"

"Yes," she said slowly. "And perhaps...?" She shook her head. "No, we will be enough, for now."

Swords drawn, Assur and the others approached the keep with caution. Only a few of the high walls still stood and there were no lookouts posted along the crumbling battlements. The rest of the keep had been reduced to scorched rubble. However, the stairway to the underground caverns was intact. Having been down this passageway before, Assur took extra precautions. He did not like descending into a place where there was no light and no way of knowing who or what lay ahead, waiting to ambush them.

The stairway widened as they stealthily worked their way down to the lowest level—an enormous vaulted chamber, supported by massive pillars the size of great trees. Instead of bare stone, the entire floor of the cavern had been covered in fine red sand—soft footing for horses. To their left, deep into the cavern, were hundreds of stone stalls that had once been the stabling for the war horses of some long-forgotten military commander, or a visiting prince.

At the back of the immense chamber, the huge, drawn up ramp, sealing off the last opening to the outside of the keep, rose ominously, disappearing into the shadowy recesses of the ceiling.

Assur and his men moved silently across the floor. A few torches flickered. As they descended into the depths of the cavern, the hollow sound of river water leaking through the weakened walls grew louder.

Both Assur and Rame stopped suddenly, startled by what they saw—a band of Qualani warriors, no more than eight in number, crouched before a small fire warming their hands over the low flames.

Rame took a step forward and raised his visor then spoke in Qualani. His words, cracking with authority, needed no translation. "Drop your swords!"

Trapped, the Qualani outcasts rose, tossing their weapons aside as the Talesians quickly surrounded them. Hands above their heads, they stepped away from the fire.

"So, you find us, eh?" their one-eyed leader said, grinning, as he moved away from the others. He nodded at Rame. "I know enough of your words, Talesian lord."

"Then you will speak to me," Assur interrupted sharply.

The Qualani first looked at Rame, then back to Assur. Confusion riddled his scarred face. "You are also the great Talesian lord?"

"I am the *only* Great Lord, Outcast. You will show proper respect."

The leader spread his hands apologetically. "But, I only see you, Great Lord, one time, eh? You and your warriors cover yourselves." He gestured to their helmets.

Assur raised his own visor. "Where is she?" he asked bluntly. "Where is the woman you brought from Volt?"

Chu'Nahk shrugged. "Maybe I tell you, maybe no."

"Do not annoy me, Outcast," Assur warned. "You helped her escape Volt. Now, where is she?"

Assur felt his uncle's searing rage and knew if the Qualani leader did not produce Alea quickly, he would die in a matter of moments. Rame raised his sword and took another threatening step forward.

Chu'Nahk was Lady Davieta's attacker and was probably the one who had killed her two sons. He was also the man who had bound Rame in chains and held a knife to his throat. Assur knew the Swordmaster would never let the Qualani leader out of the cavern alive.

Again, the filthy Qualani shrugged, almost indifferently, then motioned to his men. From their midst, they shoved a bedraggled-looking woman in front of them.

The change was startling. From a once haughty beauty, to this unkempt, wild-eyed creature, Assur almost didn't recognize her. Alea glared at him through a tangled mass of dirty blonde hair. Hatred filled her wide blue eyes. Her elegant attire had been exchanged for the rough clothes of a Qualani woman—a stained tunic, filthy hides and scraps of fur. Assur knew at once what Chu'Nahk and the others had probably done to her. No longer respected as their benefactress, Alea had undoubtedly suffered the same fate as Lady Davieta.

Chu'Nahk took her arm and thrust her before him. "You want her, she is yours. But, you let us go, eh? We make bargain."

Assur grimly assessed the situation. No bargains, not even for a scheming traitor like Alea.

"The Holy Shalman of the People gave me the authority to punish you, Outcast," Assur said. "Not only have you shamed your tribe, but you have murdered children and violated women. There will be no bargain."

The Qualani's single eye widened. "You speak of the Holy Shalman? You lie, Talesian!" He beat his fist to his chest. "The Qualani do not kill children. We serve the Mothersun..."

"Now it is you who is lying," Assur said. He looked at Alea. "What have they done to you?"

"I will tell you nothing, barbarian!" she said angrily.

Assur nodded toward his men. "Cai?"

"My lord?" the young warrior responded promptly.

"Bring Lady Davieta here. Let us see if she recognizes the one who murdered her sons."

Cai sprinted out of the cavern and up the wide stairway leading to the ruined keep above.

A long, tense silence ensued, until the Daughter Jizrella stepped forward. "Alea," she said quietly. "You must come with me now."

Alea lifted her chin. "Why should I?"

"Because, you have disrupted the Balance and it must be restored—the way the world should be. Besides," she added gently, "do you want to remain here with them?" Jizrella gestured to the gathered

Qualani.

"Do you think I care for the Balance of this world, *Holy Daughter?*" Alea said coldly. "The world has given me nothing. Everything I have ever wanted has been taken from me!"

"Everything you have ever wanted, was never yours for the asking, Alea," Jizrella admonished quietly.

"Even if I came with you, do you think *he* will let me live?" Alea jerked her head in the direction of Assur. "He wants my blood; I must pay for what I have done."

"That may be true, but first you must come with us to the Catacombs. Regardless of Lord Assur's punishment, the Balance must be restored, the Measure secured."

Alea folded her arms across her chest. "Suppose I choose not to go with you?"

Assur had heard enough. "It is not for you to decide. You *will* go with the Daughter to the Catacombs. It was where you should have gone in the first place."

Seeing she had no real choice in the matter, Alea surrendered with a brief nod of her head and an icy glare—she was no fool and Assur knew she would do anything to ensure her chances for revenge.

He nodded to have her taken her away. Two warriors stepped forward—two highly disciplined Ponos, who would tolerate no foolishness from the one-time princess.

Alea readily yielded to the warriors, until they all heard a sound coming from the top of the stairway and looked up. Cai had returned, escorting Davieta and Sethra down the wide steps. Both women looked shocked by Alea's appearance, but genuine fear flickered through Davieta's dark eyes when she saw the Qualani tribesmen. She and Sethra sketched a curtsey to Assur and to Rame, but remained standing near Cai.

Assur nodded to her and his sister. "Lady Davieta, I have brought you here to identify these Qualani. Do any of them look familiar; do you recognize them?"

Davieta stepped forward, nervously clutching and wringing her small hands. "Yes, my lord. I do recognize them," she said softly.

"Who are they?" Assur asked.

She hesitated. It was clear that seeing this particular band of men terrified her, forcing her to relive a terrible tragedy. Tears filled her eyes; she began to visibly tremble.

Rame, who had moved to her side, placed a protective arm around her.

"My lady?" Assur again asked of her.

"They...they are the ones who killed my husband and my..." She looked down. "My sons." Tears streamed down her pale cheeks.

"And?" He was loathe to keep forcing her to remember what had happened, but Assur had to hear from Davieta's own lips who had attacked her.

"It was h-h-he who forced me..."

Assur pointed to Chu'Nahk. "This one?"

She looked up. "Yes! It was him. He killed my husband and my sons, then took me...!" She did not finish. Davieta's sobs rang through the hollow cavern and Sethra rushed to her side trying to help Rame comfort her.

Worry replaced the arrogant look in Chu'Nahk's one eye.

"You take the word of a woman over a warrior of the People?"

"I would take the word of *anyone* over the word of an Outcast," Assur retorted.

Chu'Nahk glared at Davieta, then leaned over and spat into the sand at Assur's feet. "You are a bought dog, Talesian, and she is a liar!"

Assur saw Rame look up; his fury was so palpable, even the Talesians guarding the Outcasts grew tense and wary. He stepped away from Davieta and raised his sword, beckoning the leader with his free hand. In the deep shadows of cavern, Rame's black-patterned eyes narrowed to menacing slivers filled with hate. "You're dead."

The circle of watching warriors widened around them as Rame handed both his swords to Assur, then stripped off his leather jerkin. He pulled a sheathed knife from the top of his boot and faced the one-eyed Chu'Nahk, who did the same, circling around Rame, grinning.

Assur would not interfere. He had heard what he needed to hear. He did not doubt Davieta's word, nor did he question Rame's right to defend her honor or seek vengeance on her behalf. The Qualani Outcasts had proven their own treachery and guilt. Besides their crimes against Lady Davieta, they had allied themselves with both Shakiris and Alea; they had abducted and forced their women to aid them; and finally, they had bound and tortured his own uncle.

Assur folded his arms across his chest. Let it be so. Barbaric or not, Rame would see justice done to this particular criminal.

Even with one eye, Chu'Nahk was clearly not inexperienced nor afraid to fight. He crouched, wielding a large, wicked-looking knife, undoubtedly the same knife he had held at Rame's throat.

Rame settled into a taut fighting stance, holding the saddle knife lightly, ready for the first strike. The torches cast their fluttering light across the red sand, glinted from the knife blades and revealed the raw scars still riddling the Swordmaster's back. Assur pressed his mouth into a grim line. Unless Chu'Nahk was exceptionally skilled, he did not stand a real chance.

The Qualani struck swiftly, the blade missing Rame's belly by several inches as he easily sidestepped the blow. Undaunted, Chu'Nahk stepped forward again and swung at the Swordmaster. This time, their blades met and locked. The big man leaned his entire bulk into him, hoping to force Rame off balance, but the Talesian had other plans. He ducked out from under the knife-lock and struck, cleanly driving the blade deep in the Qualani's side. The man's eyes flew open, more from astonishment than pain, and he slowly let the knife slip from his fingers.

The Outcast hadn't given up yet, but fell forward heavily on his hands and scrambled through the sand, trying to find his knife. Rame never gave him the chance. He swiftly stepped over the stricken man, pulling him up by the hair, back into a kneeling position. The knife had finally found its mark as Rame jerked the blade from Chu'Nahk's side. The Qualani leader howled in pain, but Rame remained unmoved by any of it.

Reversing his grip on the saddle knife, he made a double-fist around its hilt and viciously drove upward until it slammed into the unsuspecting man's face. There was a sickening, cracking noise as Chu'Nahk's jaw shattered from the blow. He fell heavily to his side, gabbling and screaming through the hideous ruin that was his face.

"*That* is for your disrespect to me. This..."

Again, the Swordmaster grabbed the man by the hair and pulled his head back. Blood oozed from the wreck that once was the man's mouth. As easily as cutting open the belly of a fish Rame slit the Qualani's throat. Blood gushed in a torrent of red as he let the Outcast's body fall into the dust.

"...is for the violation of Lady Davieta and the murder of her family." Rame looked up at the panic-stricken Qualani tribesmen, then turned his gaze to Davieta, who tearfully bowed her head to him, acknowledging what he had done.

It was over so quickly, no one could speak. Even Assur, who had seen Rame use a knife many times, was astonished at the brutal swiftness in which he had ended the Qualani's life.

From the shadows, the ever-vigilant Mar'Kess stepped forward and bowed. "My Lord Assur, allow me to have the remainder of these

Outcasts taken to Riehl for punishment. Lord Rame's work here, is done. Lady Davieta has been avenged."

Assur nodded. "Agreed." He signaled Cai. "You will take all of these tribesmen to Riehl where they are to be imprisoned and later punished."

The ardent young Cai assumed command of the Talesian warriors, who wasted no time disarming and binding the remaining Qualani tribesmen. "And...this, my lord?" Cai gestured to Chu'Nahk's body lying face down in the red sand.

"Leave it," Assur ordered sharply. "He is meat for the worms. It is all he deserves."

THE VOYAGE UPRIVER continued for another three days until the ship dropped anchor in a quiet inlet at a bend in the river. They were near the mountains of the Catacombs, rising above the east side of the Sherehn. Assur wasted no time ordering the horses to be herded to swim the short distance to the shoreline.

The Daughter Jizrella permitted Kitarisa to be awakened. Although still unable to see, she readily submitted to being helped into a small boat and rowed to shore with the other women.

Alea remained silent and wary, while Davieta and Sethra kept their distance from her, occupying their time by assisting Kitarisa.

Once everyone was on shore, Assur swung onto Adzra's back and ordered the long column of warriors and the women to proceed into the winding passage through the Soldrat Mountains to the Catacombs. He glanced back at Kitarisa riding a quiet horse led by an attentive Mar'Kess. She clutched the horse's mane, appearing determined not to fall off or cause herself to be an additional burden, but it disturbed Assur greatly that she was so fragile and unable to see. She seemed to know that the sight of her red eyes alarmed everyone and kept her gaze lowered.

The cool, indigo shadows deepened along the pathway and the looming black granite walls seemed draw in, closer and closer, until the trail opened abruptly at the entrance to the Catacombs. Carved into the towering red sandstone, the facade of the great temple rose high above them from the bedrock into the dusky evening sky. Massive pillars supported an intricately carved opening, with stairs wide enough for three horses abreast to enter into it.

Assur gave terse orders for the warriors to remain outside keeping watch, while he, Rame, and Mar'Kess followed Jizrella and the women up the steps into the gloom of the temple. Under the menacing watch of two burly Siarsi, both Alor and Alea were also escorted inside.

It seemed like an eternity since he had last stepped—ridden Adzra—inside the Catacombs bearing Kitarisa, battered and broken after her battle with the 'Fa. He had come to the Holy Daughters with the faint hope that they might be able to restore her. They did, but now he was even more unsure if they could help her. There were limits to the Daughters' empathic powers to heal and this time, what tormented Kitarisa might be too difficult even for them.

Across the wide floor, a high dais rose at the far end of the temple and upon it, a simple altar. A low fire burned and flickered in the circular depression cut into the center of the temple floor, casting soft shadows across the walls and the strange creatures carved into the red stone.

Before the dais stood a small, motherly-looking woman, dignified and serene in dark red robes. At her side stood four other women, similarly attired. They bowed in unison to Assur.

"Welcome, High Prince," she said warmly. "We are honored to see you again. And, Daughter Jizrella, I am pleased you are returned to us safely."

Assur returned a slight bow. "Daughter Thespa. It is unfortunate we are here on so grave a matter."

Thespa noticed Kitarisa. "We have been expecting you. My dear, you have suffered greatly."

Kitarisa performed an awkward bow. "I am sorry I must burden you again," she said in a soft melancholy voice.

"You will not be a burden. The world must be restored and the Affliction of the Beast within you must be called out, Kitarisa. I am only sorry that this has happened to you."

"Can you do this, Daughter," Assur asked. "Call the Affliction from her?"

"I can. Kitarisa will be free of the dark presence within her but at a great price, my lord. Calling the Affliction from her will take all of my abilities; this will be my last. But I do this willingly, to amend for my terrible error."

Assur frowned. "What error is that?"

"It was I who caused Kitarisa to transform for the first time. It was my responsibility to call back the transformation. I neglected to do so, now I must pay the full penalty for my mistake."

Kitarisa tried to look at the Holy Daughter with her sightless red eyes. "Daughter Thespa, it was not your fault. That old man...in the caves...he was the one who caused me to change into that beast."

"That is not entirely correct, my dear. He would not have been able to cause the transformation unless someone knew the beast was within you. That would not have been done without Shakiris. Shakiris brought you to the island, because he knew the creature was still within you. And, the only way Shakiris knew, was because Alea told him."

Chapter Twenty

NO ONE SPOKE. ASSUR stared at the Holy Daughter, not sure if he had heard her correctly. Alea had betrayed Kitarisa to that fiend, Shakiris? It was unthinkable.

"That is a lie!" Alea said angrily. She jerked free from the guards' firm hold on her arms and stepped toward the Daughter. "How dare you? How dare you accuse me of such a thing?"

Thespa turned to Alea, her gaze cool. "I do not dare anything. You cannot hide from the truth, my child. It was you who told Shakiris of Kitarisa's transformation at the Rift Cut. With this knowledge, so began his conspiracy. And yours. You joined with him, did you not? A malicious bargain, made as a retaliation against the Ter-Rey for banishing you and consigning you to the Catacombs." Thespa's voice dropped to a threatening whisper. "And, for vengeance, to destroy your sister. For this, Alea, the Balance has been unsettled. You are here to restore it."

"No!" Alea suddenly raised her hands and lunged at the Holy Daughter, but Assur stopped her in time. Clasping her wrists in a vice-like grip, he shoved her to her knees. Alea's anger gave way to sobs. "No! I didn't mean to... Only... Kita, please! Do something!"

Kitarisa reached out blindly, fumbling for Davieta's supporting hands. Her chin went up; her sightless red gaze turned hard with contempt. "Why, Alea? Why should I? You have hated me since you were a child. You *and* Alor. You turned Father against me; you did everything to bring misery into my life. And, you have conspired, twice, against the Ter-Rey."

Alea managed to writhe free of Assur's grasp and reached for the hem of Kitarisa's gown. "Please, Kita, I'm sorry. Do not let them do this. I am your sister...!"

Assur did not stop her, but watched closely to see that she did not harm Kitarisa.

"Please Kita! Do not let them kill me!"

Agonized tears ran down Kitarisa's cheeks. Assur watched her struggle with her conscience. The bonds of family were just as strong as her sense of justice. She did not respond to her half-sister's pleading, but stood taller, resolute, even though her trembling hands revealed her inner anguish.

Keeping a firm hold on his own rising temper, Assur asked, "What do you intend to do with her, Daughter?"

Thespa smiled sadly. "Before anything else, my lord, I must show you something. You must know the true meaning of this place. But, only you may know this. Please come with me."

Assur did not want to leave Kitarisa, but had no other choice. She, along with the others, would have to wait until he returned. He motioned for the two Siarsi to take Alea into custody once more, but was surprised when Alor came forward, stopping them.

"Allow me, my lord," he said, taking a firm hold of Alea's shoulders, lifting her to her feet. "I will watch her." Alor nodded respectfully to him and to Thespa. There was no mockery in his eyes. The perpetual, contemptuous sneer was gone. He drew Alea back, holding her against him while she continued to sob.

Assur said nothing. It was clear that Alea was too over-wrought to be a threat to Kitarisa, or to anyone else. He acknowledged Alor with a warning look, then followed Thespa out of the hall, down the dimly-lit tunnels—the same tunnels he had recently fought in to overthrow the 'Fa, Malgora, and free the warriors she had gathered and enslaved for her own vile purposes.

The Catacombs extended deep into the Soldrat Mountains, an astonishing maze of tunnels, chambers, corridors and enormous caves—great temples and shrines carved in stone to honor some ancient, unknown gods. Assur marveled at how Thespa managed to find her way through the endless labyrinth, until she opened a door, old as the world and black with age. Once inside, he stopped and gazed upward, overwhelmed by what he saw.

"We have counted over ten thousand books in this room alone." Thespa moved to the nearest shelf built into the granite wall, filled with books from the floor, almost to the ceiling. Softly-lit lamps illumined the chamber, revealing its remarkable collection. "It is a treasure trove of knowledge; its mysteries we have only begun to unlock."

"What, by Verlian's blade, is this place?"

"It is the library of an ancient people, long gone from our world. All the books are written in a strange, foreign tongue: texts on sciences we do not yet understand, manuals on medicine we cannot begin to read. It is all here: art, histories, mathematics, philosophies...the entire knowledge and wisdom of a race that has been destroyed, lost to us forever."

"How long have you known of this place?" Assur moved slowly

about the room, taking in the endless rows of volumes lining the shelves.

"For many sunturns. Malgora knew of it, but forbade anyone to enter this room. She feared it. She understood very little of what was in these volumes, but what she did know, she guarded jealously. Only after you came here and freed the warriors and after Kitarisa destroyed the 'Fa, have we been able to begin to unravel its secrets."

"And what have you discovered?"

Thespa moved to the center of the room and touched a large open book placed upon a carved, blackwood stand. She ran a light fingertip down the edge of the yellowed pages. "This is the only volume we found that was written in the Talesian old tongue, Asserlian, and translates some of the unknown language into a few recognizable words. From this, we have been able to piece together what happened here."

"Why must I be the only one to hear this?"

She looked up and studied him for a moment. "Because what I tell you will affect how you rule Talesia from now on. There will be difficult choices..."

Assur folded his arms across his chest. "I have been making difficult decisions all my life, Daughter. My most pressing concerns are for Kitarisa and the return of the remaining two Sacred Weapons."

"I know, my lord, but the secret of the Catacombs is of equal importance."

"Very well, Daughter Thespa. Tell me this secret."

She slowly turned from him, as if gathering her thoughts before speaking. "What I am to tell you must not leave this room. Will you agree with this, my lord?"

"Shall I take an oath upon my knife?" he asked, sarcasm just touching the edge of his words.

Thespa whirled around to face him. "This is not the time for mockery, my lord! Kitarisa's life and the lives of all you know hang in the balance. Do you wish to hear this or not?"

Assur bowed his head slightly, acknowledging his offense. "Forgive me, Holy Daughter. I misspoke. Please continue."

She paused again, then placed her hand gently on the ancient book. "We have concluded that at one time the great beasts, those creatures, into which Kitarisa and Malgora were transformed, lived in the world; that there were no people and all life was in the Balance. These creatures were intelligent and lived here, within these caves and caverns. This was their home. Some time in our past, an unknown race of humans arrived. They were either fleeing from something or hid within the Catacombs; perhaps they sought the beasts for protection. They appeared to have lived together, peacefully, for a time.

"We believe the ancients then learned how to transform, to become as the beasts themselves, to hide and confound their enemies. In doing so, they corrupted the knowledge from the texts, twisted this ability into something malevolent. Malgora used it for her evil purposes, but Kitarisa is the last to experience this ability to transform. It is an unnatural change, my lord. When I called this transformation upon her the first time, it was done under the most dire circumstances. Now it must be undone." She touched the book again. "We believe the ancients killed the last of the beasts, stole their secrets, then fled south to the Shygul. The word "narusuba" is a corruption of the ancient Asserlian word for what is not natural...not measured or balanced. Those in the Shygul had become unnatural and corrupt."

Deep distress riddled Thespa's gentle features. "We must remove this unnatural evil within Kitarisa." She placed an admonishing hand upon his arm. "But the price to do this is another life. The Affliction must be called from her; her a'kenns returned."

"What do you mean?" Assur demanded.

A new ring of urgency caught in Thespa's voice. "Another must take her place."

Assur nodded, suddenly realizing who Thespa meant. "Then, Alea betrayed her?"

"Yes, my lord. Alea was the one who betrayed Kitarisa to Shakiris. Alea was there, at the Rift Cut War. She knew, because her father was her mentor and Malgora was her mistress."

Assur bowed to the Daughter, too stunned to answer.

Thespa raised her hand, a gesture both of supplication and blessing. "Go, D'Assuriel. Bring them to the Great Chamber."

THEY ALL GATHERED in the enormous chamber, deep within the Catacombs. The light from hundreds of torches bracketed to the three tiers of balconies encircling the chamber cast dancing shadows across the red granite walls and cobbled stone floor.

At the very center, Assur helped Kitarisa kneel before the Holy Daughter, Thespa. Positioned at four points around Kitarisa, stood Mar'Kess with the gleaming Hammer of the Siarsi and Rame, holding the Bow of the Ponos. Assur stood directly across from the Daughter, facing Kitarisa with both swords held crossed over his chest.

The other women and the Daughters formed a larger circle around them, watching Thespa's final empathic intercession. Alea, still guarded by two stern warriors, remained wary-looking and tense. And Alor, for once attentive and solemn, stood by her side observing the ceremony with keen interest.

Thespa raised her arms and spoke in a hushed voice. "Verlian, Goddess of all, the Mother who watches us from the skies, who gave us Her Daughters, Chalisetra, Ponosel and Siarsia, give us strength and wisdom and right will."

A soft white light began to swirl around Kitarisa's body and engulfed her.

Thespa closed her eyes and began to chant the ancient, unknown words—words that had been lost for hundreds, maybe thousands of sunturns, but now rang through the cavern, calling upon the forces to transform Kitarisa.

Assur had only seen Kitarisa go through the transformation once; he knew what to expect, but it did not ease his mounting dread.

It started with her hands. Pale, slender fingers began to stretch and elongate turning into powerful, sharp claws. Cinder-black scales lapped and overlapped, rippling and rushing over the entire surface of her body. With an aching groan, Kitarisa arched her back, turning her now fierce-red gaze upward.

Assur fought the sickening feeling in his belly as the sound of rending, tortured flesh, turning itself from one being into another, obliterated Thespa's soft chanting.

In moments it was over. Before them stood the towering figure of a monstrous creature where Kitarisa had once knelt.

Thespa raised her hands toward the great beast. "Child of the Catacombs, we have called for you to speak for your kind."

Assur heard it speak—they all did—in a resonant voice, a sibilant, silky whisper.

"You have called me again, Daughter of Verlian. What is your will?"

Every nerve in Assur's body sang with warning. This creature was not Kitarisa; it was the incarnation of death. He took an involuntary step backward and clutched his swords all the tighter.

"I have called you to return what you hold within you," Thespa answered. "The a'kenns of the woman must be given up. I must ask you to surrender it, to return it to her so the Measure of life is in order; the Balance may be restored."

"And, why should I?" the beast asked, sorrow touching its voice. "I am the last. Know this, Holy Daughter, if her a'kenns is returned, I

244 C. L. Scheel

shall be no more. I shall be forgotten as all of my kind has been forgotten."

"You shall not be forgotten, Great One," Thespa continued. "You are the last who can tell us the secrets of the Catacombs; you are the last who holds the knowledge of the ancients; you are the last who controls the power within you to change. We will not let you leave us."

The beast cast a gleaming red eye upon the Daughter. "You would do thisss?"

"Yes."

The Daughter's simple answer seemed to confound the creature. Assur watched it turn slowly, swinging toward him, then lowering its great head to study him eye to eye. There was only curiosity within those swirling red orbs and a wary watchfulness.

"We have been betrayed by man before," the creature said softly; its breath, smelling of flint and fire, spilled from a black tongue and slipped through menacing teeth. "Why should I trusssst you?"

"Because I am bound to do so." Thespa took a step closer. "I ask you to surrender the a'kenns of Kitarisa."

Great leathern wings beat upward. The beast reared its head. "How will I exist if I sssurrender her a'kenns? I will have no form..."

"I will offer you mine," Thespa said firmly.

The gathered Daughters gasped as did Sethra and Davieta. Even Assur stared at her, too astonished to speak.

"It was I who called this unwanted transformation upon Kitarisa; it is I who must correct the imbalance."

"But, Daughter, you told me Alea would be offered—"

"My lord, I told you that she was the one who betrayed Kitarisa, but Alea need not make this sacrifice. It will be enough for her to remain here and learn our ways. Was this not your Will, in the first place?"

"It was, but Alea's treason against me is almost as great as her father's. This," he gestured to the massive creature looming above them, "is the result of her greatest treachery, against me and Kitarisa. Alea cannot go unpunished!"

"Remaining here for the rest of her life will be—"

"No!" Before anyone could stop her, Alea broke free of her guard and snatched the knife from his belt. In two strides she was behind the Daughter, a slim arm wrapped tightly around her neck, the edge of the knife pressed into her throat.

"You all speak as if I were not here, as if I were some kind of object to be bartered," Alea said angrily. "I have no intention of staying in these wretched caves, for anyone." She jerked her chin in Assur's direction. "You will let me go or I slit the old woman's throat."

Alarm filtered through the gathered Daughters, many of them now too frightened to speak. Rame and Mar'Kess cautiously set down the Sacred Weapons they had been holding and drew their swords.

Assur slowly lowered his own swords. "You cannot get away. There is no place where you can run; no one will protect you."

Alea's grip on Thespa tightened. "I will take my chances, barbarian." She took a step back, dragging the helpless Daughter with her. "Did you really think I would willingly stay here and become a part of that *thing?* Kitarisa is gone, High Prince. Whatever is left of her has been consumed by that creature."

Both Rame and Mar'Kess began to inch toward Alea, never taking their eyes from her hand clutching the knife.

"This is madness, Alea, you cannot do this," Assur said, trying to keep his voice calm.

"Why not? Why should I accept this punishment? I have done nothing wrong except to be obedient to my father, and take back what was rightfully mine!"

"What was rightfully yours, Alea? To take Volt? Betray Kitarisa or start a war?"

"Kitarisa," she sneered. "A spineless, mewling creature just like her mother! She never understood father's ambition nor his great plans."

"That is enough," Assur warned in low voice. "With each traitorous word, you only make this worse for yourself."

Alea laughed sharply and pressed the knife edge deeper into Thespa's throat. "You cannot threaten me, barbarian. One step closer and I kill her, then you will never get your precious Kitarisa back!" Alea took another step backward, holding the Daughter firmly in her grasp. Her eyes never left Assur's.

"Alea, don't," Alor's quiet voice came from behind her. Surprised, Alea let her grip slacken for a moment.

"Let her go," he continued. "The High Prince is right; this is madness and you know it..."

The girl never had a chance to respond. The beast, who had been watching the entire scene, suddenly crouched low, head down level with Alea. The red eyes gleamed and the massive jaws dropped open revealing the rows of vicious teeth. Black claws rasped the cobbled stones as it crept forward—muscles bunched and tense like a predator stalking prey.

A new kind of terror gripped Assur's heart. They were all vulnerable before this creature. Swords were ineffective. Siarsia's Hammer, useless, and Rame had no more arrows to shoot from Ponosel's Bow. The Sacred Spear was gone.

If the creature chose to turn on them, one breath of flame from those terrible jaws and they would be incinerated to ash. If they all died, his beloved Kita would remain imprisoned, as one with that monstrous animal. And, the world would fall into chaos.

The black tongue again slipped over cruel-looking teeth. "Let her go, princcccessss...or die."

Assur watched Alea falter, as she stared in horror at the enormous beast, poised to strike. Almost reflexively, her arm dropped and Thespa hurried free of her grasp. In that moment, both Mar'Kess and Rame scooped up the Weapons from the cavern floor and slipped around to stand next to Assur.

Held transfixed by those terrible eyes, Alea raised her free hand beseechingly. "Kitarisa...you can't kill me," she whispered.

"I am not Kitarisssssa," the creature hissed softly. "I only hold her a'kenns within me—the force of her life." It took another menacing step toward Alea, jaws gaping only a few feet in front of her.

Alor spoke again, this time in a more determined voice. "Alea, no! Come away. Come back."

The girl did not hear him. She raised the knife—a foolish threat to a creature of such immense size. "I'm not going to stay here, Kita. Not for you, or this loathsome beast."

"Alea, no!" Alor repeated, but his protest again went unheeded.

"She's mad, just like her father," Thespa exclaimed. "I must call the Affliction quickly, my lord. The transformation must be reversed now, if we are to save Kitarisa. If Alea provokes the creature, it will retaliate and we all will die in this cavern."

Assur nodded grimly. There was little they could do to stop the beast; their weapons were useless. Their only hope was for Thespa's intervention.

"Alea must stay where she is so I may finish the ritual. Once she receives the transformation, then she can be managed, controlled."

"How do we achieve that?" Assur asked, keeping one eye on Alea.

"Distract the creature; keep it occupied until I am finished."

Through swift hand signals, Assur ordered all of the women out of the Cavern; the men who remained, including Alor began to fan out behind Alea, swords drawn.

Assur cracked his swords together sharply. "Here, beast! Look here!"

The red gaze turned abruptly from Alea to him. An annoyed, guttural sound escaped the creature's throat.

"No, here, beast," Rame called in a loud voice as he, too, beat his swords together. "Come and fight me!"

Together, all the warriors began taunting the creature as it moved wildly from side to side, trying single out which warrior it would destroy first. Lost in the confusion, Alea stood still, arms raised—her bright hair a shimmering, fluttering aura around her head.

Thespa's voice rose frantically and the pounding beat of the swords became louder. The beast grew increasingly agitated, roaring its frustration. Assur began to fear that soon it would strike at one of them. Still defiant, Alea raised her knife even higher.

The great creature reared up, drawing an enormous breath, poised to incinerate her in one terrible stream of fire.

Suddenly, from their midst, Alor broke away and ran toward his sister. Unlike the other men, he was unarmed, but did not appear frightened. Assur had no time to stop him.

"Alea!"

Distracted, she whirled around to face her brother, just as he caught her in his arms and pulled her back. Assur heard her gasp, then a strangled, choking sound. He was not sure what had happened, but it scarcely mattered. Thespa's workings had at last taken effect. A blinding light engulfed the entire cavern, whirling about the black creature and the two figures before it. With a final roar, fire blasted from the creature's jaws, upward into the high ceiling in a long, white-hot stream that charred the rock to cinder.

Assur raised his arm against his eyes to block the intense white light. Even the other warriors were forced to bend low, covering their eyes and stepping back from the bright glare and fiery heat.

In an instant it was over. A tense silence filled the cavern as they realized what had occurred. Huddled on the red cobbles lay Alor, arm draped protectively over Alea's body. Blood spilled and pooled from a narrow wound in her chest. Her wide blue eyes were open, fixed and staring. Next to her, lay the knife. Assur closed his eyes and shook his head slowly. Alea was dead.

Next to Alor lay an even smaller figure, clothed in white. Assur re-sheathed his swords and hurried to Kitarisa's side. Gently he turned her over, then pulled her into his arms. He held her for a long moment, willing her to be alive, when he heard Thespa's voice above him.

"She lives, my lord, and the transformation was completed in time."

He looked up. "But Alea is dead."

"Yes, but not her brother." She gestured to the Daughters returning to the cavern, who were now helping Alor to stand on trembling legs. He groped sightlessly for their steadying hands as they led him away.

"He will be well-care for, Great Lord. And, we will give him the ability to see again."

"And, the creature...?"

"Alor will live as Kitarisa was; he will have the beast within his a'kenns. But, it is not such a bad thing. From him, we will learn the secrets of the Ancients and translate the old texts."

Assur looked down at Alea's lifeless body. "Did he kill her?"

"No, my lord. He tried to save her, but the knife turned on her. In a way, I think she wanted it this way. Alea liked nothing of this world and I pray Verlian, she is at peace."

The two Siarsi who had been ordered to guard her stepped forward and lifted Alea's lifeless body from the stones and carried her away.

"We will see to her funeral pyre. I fear it would be too much for Kitarisa to bear." Thespa bowed. "You have endured enough suffering and sorrow, Prince D'Assuriel. Take your lady and return home with my apologies and Verlian's blessing." The Holy Daughter bowed again, turned and silently hurried out of the cavern.

Rame, Mar'Kess, and the others had also left the great chamber, leaving Assur alone, with Kitarisa in his arms. He stood, still holding her close, when she stirred and opened her eyes—now returned to their natural, lustrous-brown color.

He tilted his back to gaze upward at the high dark ceiling of the great chamber. His voice, raw with emotion, echoed from the stone walls, "I thank you, Goddess."

Chapter Twenty-One

ONCE AGAIN, KITARISA stood in her chamber before a high window that overlooked the sea. But on this radiant summer morning, the waves were calm, the sky a bright, shimmering blue—a day for joy and laughter. She had come full circle; tomorrow she would be crowned Ter-Reya. Everything had been prepared. A new Spear, crafted even finer the old one, would be finished in time and blessed by the Wordkeeper and the Chanter for the ceremony. And, this time there would be nothing to stop the impending ritual from taking place. No wars, no plots, no frightening, sinister presence within her.

In her hands she held her mother's crown. She gazed at its delicate beauty, astonished that she would now be permitted to wear it. It was only last autumn that she was still under the control of a cruel father. Now, she was about to be joined with the most powerful man in all Talesia. A remarkable outcome after a sequence of equally remarkable circumstances.

Kitarisa placed the crown on her head and caught her reflection in the window glass. She looked strangely serene for someone who had endured a war, an abduction, and an unnatural transformation. Lady Davieta said she looked content, but Kitarisa was still uncertain. She tried to dismiss the uneasiness within her heart; it would not look well for a new Ter-Reya to appear distressed or unhappy.

She turned from the window. At least Davieta would enjoy the forthcoming festivities. Her former lady's maid now glowed with new-found happiness. All physical traces of her ordeal had vanished, as had Rame's. Soon, they were to be joined, but Assur had added another reason for their happiness: Rame would rule over both Gorendt and Volt, with Davieta at his side.

Kitarisa smiled as she thought of Rame—a much changed man. He would always be the fierce-tempered Swordmaster, but Davieta's gentle influence had made him calmer, less inclined to anger.

And something else....

Four days earlier, a courier, clothed entirely in hides and skins, galloped through the gates of Daeamon Keep seeking Prince Ramelek. He carried a small package in his saddle pack—something he alone must give to the Swordmaster. No one was certain what the package contained, until Rame appeared the next day wearing a link-plated collar about his neck, made of heavy silver and embossed with black owls. He appeared pleased, almost light-hearted.

Later, Kitarisa took Davieta aside and queried her about the curious incident.

Davieta shook her head. "I am not sure what it all means. There was a letter that came with the collar. Rame would not read it out loud but I did overhear him say to young Cai, something about, 'they returned safely and were accepted into the circle.' I do not know who he was referring to..."

The little mystery would remain a mystery, but for now it did not matter.

A soft knock made her turn around. "Come in."

To her surprise, it was Assur. He entered her chamber carrying a small box. Seeing him, alone, always made her heart beat a little faster. She never quite knew how she should conduct herself when she was near him: reserved and respectful, or warm and loving. She did love him, she knew that now, but his very presence—who he was—made her cautious. Proud, yet restrained, Assur had the uncanny ability of appearing both intimidating and accessible at the same time.

He bowed to her. "I have brought you something for tomorrow's ceremony. It was my mother's."

Kitarisa took the small box and opened it. A small gasp of surprise escaped her lips. A single ruby diadem, set in gold and attached with two fine chains lay within a wrapping of white silk.

"It was designed to match Verlian's Tear," he said, touching the red stone dangling from his ear. "It should be fastened to your crown, worn across your brow."

"My lord, it is exquisite. Thank you. I will wear it with great honor."

He took her free hand in his and pressed it to his lips. "I believe my mother would have been equally as honored. I am only sorry your own mother did not live to see this day."

"I am sorry, too. But she died so long ago. I can only hope she is at peace."

"I am sure they both are." Uncertainly shadowed his black-patterned eyes, darkened their unfathomable blue color. "Can you forgive me?"

"For what?"

"For what happened to Alea?"

Kitarisa looked down. "Alea chose her own path. You did not kill her, neither did Alor. She destroyed herself and somehow, I think that is what she wanted all along. I think she has found her own sort of peace."

"And Alor?" he asked softly, his gaze anxious.

"Alor will be well-taken care of and he will be invaluable to the Holy Daughters. I do not grieve or worry for him. Besides," she added with a small smile, "he shall be surrounded by dozens of attentive women. I do not think he will suffer."

Amused, Assur raised a sweeping black brow. "And, with Mar'Kess only a few days ride in Riehl, Alor would not get far if he decided to escape."

"I am glad you have made Mar'Kess Lord of Riehl. He is a fine, worthy man and deserves such a noble rank."

"He will make an excellent prince and rule well. I have no doubt of it."

"Perhaps, an even happier prince if he had someone by his side...?" she added mischievously.

He nodded knowingly. "Ah, Sethra. She is a match for any man. But, let Mar'Kess settle; let him find his way first, before he decides to pursue Sethra. She can cool her heels for a time—learn to control some of her headstrong ways."

"I think she will wait, quite happily, my lord."

"And you? Will you be happy here, with me?" Assur bent to her, black brows drawn over his earnest, questioning gaze. "I will not see us joined if you still hold any regrets."

The last of her fears slipped away like mist before a warm, morning sun. She did not answer him because there was no need. No sound except the sea echoed through the chamber as her silent kiss welcomed him to her heart.

~*~

C.L. Scheel

"My sixth grade teacher encouraged me to write, but an opera star inspires me to persist, to stay with it."

Like most authors, writing has been a part of Christine's life for as long as she can remember. "If it is in your heart, there is no way you can ignore it or stop it."

Under A Warrior's Moon is her first published work in the science fiction/fantasy genre, and she has plans for two sequels. Having penned several works in other genres, Christine also intends to expand into the paranormal and eventually mainstream.

Born in Portland, Oregon, but raised and educated in the Pacific Northwest, Christine finally settled in Reno, Nevada and resides there with her family, a fluffy red chow-chow, and recently, an elegant, stuck-up black cat. Her interests range from horses to ballet; mountain hiking to opera. However, books and writing are closest to her heart.